# Alligator Creek

## By

### June McNaughton

*To my dearest friend of long standing. Don't sell your lemonade too cheap.*

*Love from June to Duke*

This book is a work of fiction. Places, events, and situations in this story are purely fictional. Any resemblance to actual persons, living or dead, is coincidental.

© 2002, 2003 by June McNaughton. All rights reserved.

No part of this book may be reproduced, stored in a retrieval system, or transmitted by any means, electronic, mechanical, photocopying, recording, or otherwise, without written permission from the author.

ISBN: 1-4107-1547-7 (e-book)
ISBN: 1-4107-1545-0 (Paperback)
ISBN: 1-4107-1546-9 (Dust Jacket)

This book is printed on acid free paper.

1stBooks – rev. 02/20/03

For RLG, of course…

## *Acknowledgments*

Special thanks to:

DR. SARA PUTZELL, next door neighbor, mentor, critic, without whose encouragement this book would never have been finished.

THE ATLANTA VILLAGE WRITERS GROUP, and especially the VWG Novel Critique Group: Dudley Hinds, host and founder of the novel group, and hard-working members: Jay Clark, John Cunningham, Sarabenne Evesong, Karl Foelsche, Bob Hamilton, Jim Harmon, Ken Haskins, Kip Kimbrough, Alice Parsons, Barbara Lucas, Tony Miller, Larry Smith

CAROL LEE LORENZO, fiction writing teacher extraordinaire.

DR. NEIL KAHN, who kept me going with understanding and samples of Paxil.

The knowledgeable and generous Okefenokee Swamp Park Director and the Waycross Hilton Hotel Manager.

My supportive family and friends, as well as the few skeptics among them.

And most of all, to the world's nicest tough guy, CHRIS CRAMER, who spiritually and financially launched "Alligator."

## *Prologue*

*Leading into the vast mystery of the great Okefenokee Swamp is a serene little stream called "Alligator Creek." It approaches the darkness of the swamp quietly through forests of South Georgia pines, the tall, fast-growing fodder for the commercial interest of lumber barons and pulp-mill masters. It offers sanctuary to the isolated remnants of tough, anti-social families of "swampers", who still defend their fierce independence of modern society, living close to nature, making whiskey in their hidden stills.*

*Alligator Creek harbors a wealth of water-creatures: fish, amphibians, water-birds, reptiles. Its ancient aristocrat is the mighty, fearless alligator, resting in arrogant authority right below the surface of the black water.*

*The riches of the Okefenokee have lured adventurer, fisherman, hunter, capitalist, refugee, entrepreneur down the lush pathway of Alligator Creek, beneath the stately, bearded cypress trees into the fecund variety of the swamp. Twisted rails and rusted locomotives, overgrown man-made channels, crumbling homesteads and abandoned stills attest to its temporary welcome and ultimate rejection. The swamp prevails.*

*The beauty and mystery of the Okefenokee have called along Alligator Creek to philosopher, artist, poet, photographer, hopeless romantic. On the gentle stream they have floated into wisdom, peace, a glimpse of the cosmic life force. They have gone away forever enriched. The swamp bestows.*

*The voyager is repaid in kind. The swamp endures.*

## *Chapter 1*

Christine looked out the kitchen window through the waves of heat, out toward where she knew the wild stretches of the Okefenokee Swamp lay steaming. She rinsed the last breakfast dish, set it in the drainer and pulled the plug, letting the soapy dishwater suck down the drain. As she wiped the dishtowel over her cereal bowl, her eyes were unfocused with boredom, and she forced her imagination past her small backyard, out into the unknown mystery of the swamp just ten miles away. She'd heard about it, but she'd never seen it. Could she really be so close to miles of impenetrable forests, black waterways inhabited by strange and dangerous animals, a labyrinth of secret passageways for alligators, bobcats and bears, a stop-over for exotic migrating birds, a hideout for carnivorous plants? She shuddered. It both intrigued and repelled her. She could feel it out there behind the tall pines in her little yard.

She snapped back into reality as Danny turned off the irritating put-put of the lawn mower and the silence rang in her ears for a minute. Danny was her teen-aged next-door neighbor. Sweat gleamed on his broad shoulders, and his blond hair stuck to his face in ringlets. Her arms prickled as she watched the muscles moving under his skin. How would it feel to have that easy strength flowing through her own body? He lifted the mower into the storage shed and his hip muscles strained against his frayed jeans. A beautiful boy, not as powerful-looking as Jack, but nice.

Oh, Jack! Why did he have to take that job way out in the Gulf of Mexico? She missed him so, left alone in this strange new town, and so soon after they were married. It wasn't fair! If he had only talked to her before he'd taken the damned job, maybe she could have gotten him to look for something here in Waycross. They'd hardly gotten settled and he was gone. Why, they still had stuff in the attic that they hadn't unpacked from the move six months ago.

Danny came toward the house with his coltish, clumsy walk, wiping his face on a bandana pulled from his pocket, running his fingers back through his hair. She really should offer him something to drink. He was a good worker, and she needed him around to help with the yard work now. She rubbed the dishtowel over her moist face, across her throat and down between her full breasts.

God, it was hot! How could anybody stand a Georgia summer? A fat fly buzzed arrogantly past her face and zoomed back fearlessly close, as she slapped at it with her dishtowel. She felt sick with futility.

Danny tapped at the back door.

"Through already?" she asked, shaking out the towel.

"Yes Ma'am." He looked up the steps at her. She was always a little surprised at how blue his eyes were.

"Come on in and let me get you something cold to drink."

"Thanks, I sure could use a glass of water."

She pushed the screen door open, out over the steps, and held it back to let him in. He came up, stumbling a little as his face passed close to her breasts. It occurred to her briefly to wear something more modest when he was around, instead of the short-shorts and halter-top she had on now. She knew that Danny and his friends had peeked at her from behind the lace curtains next door—watched her sunbathing. The first time, it had irritated her, and she'd thought about talking to his mother, Madge, about it, but Madge obviously didn't like her, going so far as to pretend she didn't see Christine when they were both out in their yards at the same time. Madge was weird. And anyway, what harm was there in giving the boys a little excitement sometimes? Who cared?

Danny came into the kitchen now, eyes turned self-consciously toward the floor.

"How much do I owe you today?" she asked as she opened the freezer door and started putting ice cubes into a glass. She wondered what he would do if she rubbed an ice cube over his flushed face, to cool him. She turned and looked at him.

He was leaning toward her with a paralyzed look of helpless yearning on his handsome face. He blushed, looked down and stammered, "Huh? Uh... I don't know. Whatever you think."

She turned quickly to the sink and filled the glass with water as a sweet wave of sympathy for him washed over her. She held out the glass to him. He hesitated a moment and wrapped his long fingers around the bottom of the glass, being careful not to touch her hand when he took it. The ice clattered as his hand shook. His face was still red and his voice squeaked a little as he mumbled his thanks.

Christine felt a weakening rush of tenderness for him, spiced with a warm contraction of the muscles between her legs. Knowing she had this power over him was heady stuff, but her better instincts prodded her to defuse the situation for him. "Okay," she said briskly, "How's ten bucks sound?" A quarter would probably have been fine. She wanted to pat him on his blond curls and tell him how cute he was. She pretended not to notice the bulge in his jeans.

"Yes, Ma'am, that's fine." He gulped the water, coughed and said, "Well, I'd better be going now."

"Okay, let me run get your money." She had an irrational fear that he might follow her into the bedroom—irrational and exciting. She shook it off and confronted herself in the mirror. Her heart was pounding and there was a strange glow on her face. "What are you doing?" she whispered to the vibrant face. Grabbing a ten from her wallet, grateful that she had the right change, she took a deep breath and hurried back into the kitchen. Danny had recovered his composure and was closely examining his fingernails with a bemused look.

"Here you go. Thanks, Danny. You do good work. See you next week?"

"Yes, Ma'am."

"And do me a favor, Danny? Don't call me 'Ma'am.' It makes me feel... well... old. Call me 'Christine', all right?"

"Okay, uh... *Christine*. Well, bye now. See ya." He hurried out stumbling a little down the steps.

She probably shouldn't have said that, she chided herself, but she really didn't like being called "Ma'am."

*Wonder if he's still a virgin...*

She picked up the glass he had left on the counter. After taking a slow sip, she wriggled her fingers in the cool water and picked up an ice cube which had probably touched his lips only a moment ago. She ran it slowly over her temples, across her cheeks and onto her lips, sucking in the melting ice water. Holding it to the small cradle at the base of her neck, she let the water run down her chest and trickle into the cleft between her breasts. She unfastened her halter-top, let it fall to her waist, slid the fast dissolving ice down to a reddening nipple and circled it until the ice had disappeared against the now stiffened flesh.

"Oh, Jack, I miss you so." She looked down at herself. "Super-tits," Jack had called her.

She wondered how Danny's boyish hands would feel holding her breasts. She stroked them now, closing her eyes and picturing Danny's face close to her, his mouth moving across her chest. She pinched the hardened nipples and imagined his full, moist lips touching first one, then the other. Danny?! Good Lord, what was the matter with her? She was married to the world's sexiest man, and he adored her. Yes, he adored her, and he was a man, not a boy! And she adored him right back. Yes. She leaned over the sink and splashed her face and chest with cool water and re-tied the halter top over her wet skin.

The tightness between her legs subsided.

"Well Christine, you sexy wench," she scolded herself with a laugh, "I think it's time you scrubbed your kitchen floor."

## Chapter 2

The rhythm of the soapy mop, gliding in orderly paths across her floor, had a calming effect on Christine. Sometimes she enjoyed doing housework. It numbed her mind and imparted a sense of accomplishment, especially when the work being done was for her own house. A clean and comfortable house was important—no, *necessary* for her. Her mental processes seemed to reflect her surroundings. When she was in a clean, orderly, comfortable place, her brain functioned better. She was sure of it.

When she finished and stood back to admire her neat little kitchen, she smiled with satisfaction. The sheer dotted-Swiss curtains she had made for the windows and the glassed section of the back door created a cozy, secure atmosphere. How could there be a wolf at the door of such a neat little house? She guessed that her mother must have instilled this attitude in her. Lord knows, her mother had kept a clean house. It was her only real skill, let's face it.

Her poor mother. She hadn't really wanted children, as she hinted on so many occasions. Christine had come into this world with great difficulty, entering via a breech birth, causing her mother twenty hours of unforgettable pain and leaving her unable to have more babies. Her mother harbored a deep resentment against Christine born of this pain, and often accused her of "doing everything backwards." Her gentle, ineffectual father was never able to achieve real financial stability, and his low-paying assembly-line job kept the little family in a state of nervous insecurity. She was only fourteen when his beat-up old Ford was front-ended by a drunk driver, and he died on the way to the hospital. Most of the small insurance payment from his union was consumed by his modest funeral, leaving his widow and daughter destitute.

Her mother sank into a quagmire of despair and self-pity. She just couldn't cope with paying the bills, and Christine had to quit high school in her junior year and go to work in a fast food horror house. She hated it. She hated her officious boss barking coarse orders at her, borne on waves of bad breath. She hated the sleazy, orange polyester uniform with its little pointy maid's cap. She hated the ugly male customers, who didn't know the difference between crude sexual allusions and wit, and thought that she was fair game. She hated her father for dying and leaving her in this mess. She hated herself for hating her father, the dearest, sweetest man in all the world. He had always worked so hard, and his failure to achieve financial success did not dim her admiration of him. From him, she had developed a deep regard for the old-fashioned virtues of labor and responsibility, and she stuck to her dreary job in respect for his memory.

After several years, she was made manager of the restaurant, an honor which did nothing to dispel her distaste for the job, and very little to increase her income.

Her trim body, curly red hair and pretty face got so much unwanted attention from her crude customers, that she more or less lost interest in male companionship. Although she did date occasionally, she found little pleasure in her shallow, self-seeking escorts. Her greatest pleasure became getting home, kicking off her shoes, going to bed and escaping into some Jane Austen or Bronte sisters.

And then, to make things worse, her mother had found the Lord. Found Him in a storefront church, in the balding, pot-bellied personage of Reverend Rufus J. Peabody. A fat fly. It wasn't long before his ministrations became private therapy sessions in her living room, usually administered after a hearty meal served by her mother, and involving a great deal of laying on of hands. His prayer technique often required that the recipient kneel before him while he stroked and patted her about the head and shoulders, as he lifted his supplicant face toward the ceiling and rambled aimlessly through his limited store of religious entreaties.

Next thing Christine knew, he had moved right in, to be available during her mother's frequent nighttime plunges into the Slough of Despond.

Christine's thinly disguised distaste for the Reverend just spurred him on to ever more zealous employment of the Gospel in her behalf, involving more and more application of pudgy hands on her reluctant body. She began to stay away from home more and more.

Then Jack Radford came into her life; her hero, a cowboy riding high in his eighteen-wheeler, coming to rescue her from the sad, grimy muddle her life had become. At first, he made her laugh. He came in regularly for breakfast, called her "Red", and kept his hands to himself. He wasn't much of a tipper, but on the other hand, he never pressed her for extra service and was generally easy to get along with. She liked his rough good looks, his short-cropped black hair, his muscular arms and chest, his way of looking down with amused tolerance from his six-foot-three onto her five-foot-four. Even in the morning, he had a hint of a beard. He stood out from the splotchy red-faced regulars she faced across her breakfast counter, with their bleary eyes, clumsily slicked-down hair, and bad teeth. He looked... well... healthy and clean. And the hint of a beard? Maybe he shaved at night. Anyway, it made him look tough.

One morning, she was having particular trouble with a surly trucker who appeared to have slept in his rig. He was angrily protesting the amount of the check, which he was waving in her face. His hands were shaking uncontrollably and he was having trouble focusing his blood-shot eyes. Christine never backed down from these confrontations, knowing that any hint of softness would be an invitation for more abuse. But she was afraid that this one was getting out of her control when Jack had intervened. In calm, soothing tones, belied by the the cold steely look in his eyes, he convinced the offensive man that paying the check was a whole lot better than "eating a fist sandwich" out behind his truck. Then he had waited until she finished her shift and walked out to her car with her, just in case the disgruntled customer had not completed his complaint.

After that, they began spending a lot of time together. Jack was so much fun to be with—sure of himself—mature for his 34 years. He had "been around" and knew how to please women. There were lots of envious female glances at them when he took her dancing the Texas two-step at the Wild Horse, a truck-stop where he knew everybody, and everybody seemed to like him. She had always loved to dance. Music had a way of entering her and moving her in its easy rhythm. When the multi-colored lights were flashing all around her, Jack's strong arms were whirling her around, and the whole room was pounding with the rhythm of a hundred feet, she was happier than she had ever been. No unpaid bills, no gray-faced depressed mother, no pudgy Reverend Peabody could touch her. Jack told her she was a real "looker," and whirling in the dazzling lights, she thought maybe she was.

Sometimes, late at night after they had been out dancing and having a few beers, she was overcome with a sick feeling of fear when she got home, slipping quietly into the house so she wouldn't wake the Reverend. She fought the sleep which might bring bad dreams or terrifying visions of her empty, going-nowhere life. The ominous feeling that something terrible was going to happen would bring on a night of miserable nausea, sometimes vomiting and diarrhea. Panic.

When she was with Jack, she felt safe. His arms were impregnable around her, his callused hands slow and gentle with her, his mouth sweet. She didn't care that they never went anywhere except to the truck-stop bar for beer and dancing. It was comfortable.

His friends there accepted her, welcomed her, made her feel at home. She liked the kidding they got about being "Love-birds." She liked it that his friends said "Jack and Red" as if it were a hyphenated word. In just a few months time, they had drifted into the assumption of impending marriage. She didn't encourage it, but she didn't discourage it, either.

In a desperate attempt to escape the orange polyester fast-food job, Christine had enrolled in the Moore School of Business for a night course in "Office Skills." The classes were boring, her classmates dull and the instructor surly. When Jack asked her to marry him, she accepted gratefully, never returning to a single class.

And now, here she was, all alone in this strange new town. Oh well, she guessed that things could be worse. At least she was away from the depressing self-pity of her mother and the fat little hands of the Reverend. And she had no more problems paying the bills, what with the checks Jack sent her twice a month. She'd just stay busy, and not start feeling sorry for herself.

*Hard work—that's the trick!*

She took the broom out to sweep her tiny little front stoop.

## *Chapter 3*

Danny ran home after cutting the grass next door, slipping the ten into his back pocket, and bolted up the stairs to his cluttered room. He pulled off his shirt and threw it onto a pile of clothes that submerged his chair. Looking down at his groin, he was glad to see that the bulge was subsiding. Shit! He hoped she hadn't noticed. He suffered from increasingly frequent embarrassment around women, as his body betrayed his prurient thoughts. He had begun to wear shirts that hung down over his fly, and resorted more and more to a kind of clumsy, loose-legged walk, leaning forward slightly in the hope that the protuberance would not be so obvious. Lord knows he tried to control his thoughts when he was around females, but no use, he just couldn't help it.

He pulled off his jeans and headed for the shower. It wouldn't be so bad if he was the size of Mark or Jimmy, his two best buddies. They kidded him mercilessly about his huge dick. They were probably just jealous, but he would gladly have traded places with them to avoid the attention the damned thing caused him.

"Ohhh," he groaned into the warm water hitting him full in the face, "she's fuckin' awesome!" His nostrils were still tingling from the sweet scent of her perfume, all mixed with that intoxicating female smell she always had. It had been all he could do to keep from putting his hands around her tiny waist, in those little bitty shorts. He turned the shower handle to "Cold."

"Danny," Madge called up stairs. *Oh, Shit, Mama's home.* "Danneee! How long have you been in that shower? Don't use up all the hot water, now. Your father has to get in there as soon as he gets home, you know. I don't know why you always have to stay in there so long, anyway." The nasal sound of her voice was a metallic taste in his mouth.

*Jeez, Mama, can't you ever leave me alone? Keep on treatin' me like a baby...*

A baby! He had a flashing vision of Christine holding him in her arms, against her bare breast, his mouth on her nipple.

"All right, all right, Mama! I'll be out in a minute," he shouted.

He turned off the shower, grabbed a towel and started rubbing it vigorously over his body. With his face close to the medicine cabinet mirror, he checked for signs of any developing zits. So far, so good. He felt his upper lip gingerly for any increase in the number of tiny stiffening mustache hairs. Not much change there, and the little hairs were so blonde anyway, that Christine probably wouldn't notice. Oh, well. He looked straight into the deep blue eyes and promised with conviction, "I'm gonna drill her. I don't know how, but I'm gonna." He felt the familiar hot thrill in his pelvis.

He stepped back and flexed his biceps, turning around to get a better view of his muscular back, tapering down to his lean waistline. Yeah, he'd pump her good, one of these days. He gave his hips a few forward thrusts. Yeah!

He'd had his share of making it with girls, much to the admiration of his friends. He had started early, getting busted in the fourth grade when his teacher had intercepted a note he had written to Loreen Hardigree. "Want to fuck?"

Then he'd pumped his skinny little cousin, Doris when he was just twelve. Poor little dumb Doris would do just about anything he wanted her to do, she had such a big crush on him. But he had felt kind of let down after he'd lured her into the basement and talked her into taking off her clothes, letting him get on top of her, letting him feel of her little titties, and poking her. He knew she was pretty miserable, thinking about what she had let him do to her, and he felt vaguely guilty about the whole thing. After that, he had concentrated on girls that dressed and acted sexy: short skirts, lots of make-up, flirty eyes, big boobs. All that stuff. He'd managed to talk a few of them into messing around with him, and had gotten a lot more sexual experience than any of his friends. Still, he mostly limited himself to one-on-one sessions with a dog-eared issue of "Club" magazine hidden under his mattress.

And then last winter, *she* had moved in next door! He thought about her all the time—all the time! And he hadn't been able to do anything about it so far, except to cut her grass and rake her leaves. She never talked *down* to him, like he was a kid or something, and then today she'd told him to call her "Christine" and not "Ma'am." Wow! That must mean something...

He wrapped the towel around his waist and went into his room, locking the door behind him. "Mama, I'm out of the bathroom." He reached under the mattress for the faithful ragged magazine, loosened the towel and fell back onto the bed. Stroking his swelling penis with one hand, he opened the magazine to the familiar "The Perfect Housewife" spread. It was easy now to imagine that the alluring wet mouth and full breasts of the model belonged to Christine. She even had red hair! He savored each picture. First, the exaggerated innocent look on her face as she tested the steaming soup, her lips pursed, little curls escaping from under her frilly cap, unaware that her firm, round buttocks were showing beneath her brief black French-maid's skirt. Then, a hint of lust on her pretty face as she slipped the maid's uniform off a creamy shoulder and breast. Turn the page. Danny's dick was hard as a rock, now. The black uniform on the floor, and with nothing on except the sheer white ruffled apron and perky white lacy cap, with open mouth and moist lips, she opened the door to a man (a next-door neighbor?). Next the man was nude, seated with legs spread wide apart as she leaned over him, serving him champagne on a tiny tray. He sucked at her nipple as one of his hands probed between her beautiful legs. He was erect (oh, and so was Danny). Turn the page. Now she knelt in front of his chair and her tongue licked the tip of his penis. At the same time, she dusted a small table with a gaudy pink feather-duster. She had a look of ecstasy on her pretty face. And the last picture, ohhh... she was bending over with her back to him, her luscious rounded rear straining upward toward him, peeking over her shoulder at him with pursed lips and big eyes innocent with happy surprise, she washed a window as he plunged his huge dick into her from behind. "Ohhh, ohhh, Christine!" Danny came into the towel.

Then, from downstairs, "Danneee, want something to eat?"

*Oh, yes! Pussy! A sweet little pussy. Christine. Christine's pussy!*

"Sure, Mama." His voice broke. "I'll be right down."

*I don't know how, but I'm gonna drill her.*

## Chapter 4

Sex was the enemy for Madge.  Her mother had told her often enough how her unfortunate birth was the consequence of silly romantic fantasies, virtue sold out for a mess of pottage; a handsome, sweet-talkin' man who had disappeared as soon as he had heard the bad news of her pregnancy.  Madge's mother had learned her lesson well enough and did not again succumb to such folly.  For little Madge, no siblings came along to diffuse the bitterness, and her frail shoulders bore all the weight of the wronged woman.  She was taught that the smart thing, the *only* thing, a woman should do was to marry a plain, hard-working man who was not a sex maniac, like most men were.  And above all, not to soil herself by yielding to the sexual urges of any man.

She had reached maturity with her virginity intact, partly due to her strict training, but mostly due to a total lack of feminine charm.  She didn't waste a lot of time trying to improve her plain, square face with cosmetics and primping.  Her short, stocky body didn't justify the purchase of a lot of fancy clothes, either.  She perfected her domestic skills, however, and it was her comfortable, neat apartment and luscious biscuits that really won the heart of the plain, hard-working man she finally got to know through the Calvary Baptist

Singles Club. Both she and Harland were virgins when they married after a four-year courtship, and the consummation of their union was something of an embarrassment to Cupid.

When she became pregnant, all her mother's old fears and aversions were alerted, and swarmed over her vulnerable spirit, occupying her brain with the totality of a Philistine attack. She hated her swelling belly and fruitlessly beat on it with clenched fists during many secret crying sessions in the bathroom. She would have terminated the pregnancy except for the strong anti-abortion sentiments of her church. She finally accepted her situation as an incurable disease, and took comfort in silent Christian martyrdom. And kept her legs crossed.

She gave birth with a terrible labor; hours and hours of intense pain—expression of the accumulated anger and indignity of the preceding nine months. She vowed that she would never go through this again! She hated it when Harland started that embarrassing sex business with her, anyway. Harland would just have to understand.

The beautiful little boy put into her arms by the beaming nurse was a strange alien to her. His soft murmurings could not penetrate the wall of aversion Madge constructed between them. She was determined to do her duty by him and be the best mother she knew how, but her heart never warmed to him. To make it worse, her mother confirmed her worst fear—her son looked just like his no-good, dallying grandfather. He was beautiful.

*   *   *

Harland, on the other hand, was immediately captivated by this remarkable new creature. In his clumsy way, he gave the tiny person all the affection his cautious heart could muster. He was in awe of his own child, and secretly agonized that this undeserved prize might be taken from him at any time. To allay his fears, he worked harder at everything, went to church with alarming dedication, and lived as frugally as possible. He accepted Madge's ban on sex as the price he must pay for this small wonder. He even endured her two and three day silences, when the anger poured off of her in tidal waves of door-slamming, pot and pan-banging and excessive vacuuming. He seldom knew the cause of these episodes, but was sure that somehow it was his fault. But he had his son.

He watched in wonder tinged with disquietude as his baby developed into a beautiful, quick-witted boy. Would he be able to keep up? Would his son be ashamed of his dull, unattractive father? His feelings of inadequacy made him handle this sturdy, healthy little creature with inordinate care. He suppressed his strange, unfamiliar urges to hug his son, fearing that physical contact with him would be as repulsive to Danny as it was to Madge. At little-league games, he marveled at the joyous ease with which other fathers punched and wrestled with their sons.

Harland felt the most comfortable with Danny when the two of them were out in the Okefenokee together. He loved the swamp: its peace, its slow pace, its indestructibility. He felt connected out there. He took Danny fishing or hunting whenever he could, along Gum

Swamp Creek or Alligator Creek. He felt more at ease with his little son then than at any other time.

Most of the rest of the time, he didn't know what to say to Danny. Well, he'd just have to show his love by providing the best and most secure home imaginable for his boy. That was something he could handle.

## Chapter 5

Damn! Danny couldn't believe it. Mark, quarterbacking the other team in the sand-lot football game, had handed off to Pete! Sissy little Pete. It was too easy. Danny charged through the line and hurled himself at Pete's mid-section. He almost hated to do it. He knew Pete was afraid of him, and he didn't want to scare him off completely. After all, it was Pete's football they were playing with. The momentum of Danny's drive took them back a couple of yards. He had to help Pete to his feet. Second and fifteen.

It was twilight on a Friday evening, and the game was breaking up in spite of everything Danny could do to keep it going. He loved crashing into the line of boys in front of him, bringing one of them down with a thud. The football felt good in his fingers when he caught a pass, and the flow of strength in his legs was satisfying as he ran with it toward the imagined goal posts. He liked to hear Mark's complaints that he was playing too rough, and to see the unwavering admiration in Jimmy's eyes at his daring athletic power. But now it looked like the game was over for today, and one by one, his buddies were leaving for homes and suppers.

When there weren't enough players left for a real game, Danny threw the football to Pete and with a slight tilt of his chin signaled

Mark and Jimmy to follow him, which they did without question. They started off at a fast clip towards home.

"Hey, Mark," Jimmy panted as he caught up, "Reckon we can git ya brother's car tomorrow, to do a little fishin'?"

"Hell, Jimmy, ya know how Bubba is about that car. Like it's made outta glass, or somethin'. Ya know, last time—"

Danny interrupted, "Give it a try, man. We haven't been out to Alligator Creek for months. Catfish supposed to be running real good out there, now."

Mark grumbled, "Okay, okay, I'll try, but I can't promise anything." Then, to change the subject, he winked at Jimmy and nudged Danny, "So, anything new with your sexy neighbor?"

Jimmy sniggered.

"Whadaya mean?" Danny examined a small scratch on his arm with exaggerated interest.

"We know you've been over there, cuttin' her grass or whatever. Sniffin' around…," Mark laughed.

Jimmy threw an imaginary pass toward a telephone pole, "I saw her sittin' at the counter at Woolworth's yesterday. Man, she's sure got a cute little ass! I'd sure like a little feel of it, I'll tell ya."

Unexpectedly, Danny felt an angry rush. He punched at the air. "Yeah, I guess she's okay for her age." What business was it of theirs? God, sometimes they were so dumb they made him *sick*!

"I'll bet she'd like some action, what with her old man gone such a long time. I'll bet he's gettin' himself plenty, down there with those hot little Mexican women," Jimmy mused.

"Hey, why don't we just stop by and see her for awhile?" Mark amazed himself with his own boldness.

"Sure, Stupid! For what?" Danny snarled.

"To get a look at those tits!" Mark whooped.

"Yeah, great. I kin hear us now. 'Good evening, Miz Radford. We thought we'd just drop in to take a look at your world-famous boobs, Ma'am.' You got class, Mark, you know that?" Danny forced a laugh. Why was he feeling that ache? He wanted to hit Mark. "Hey, I gotta get on home. See ya tomorrow?" The ache was in his loins.

"Sure, why not?" Mark didn't know what was getting into Danny. Shit, you could always count on him for a sharp comeback, especially anything about a chick. But not lately. Maybe Danny's weird mother was on him again about something. Mark tossed his head to get his soft dark hair out of his eyes. His family kidded him about his resemblance to Elvis, and he loved it. He had even perfected a rubber-legged impersonation of the King, wildly strumming an imaginary guitar. The success of the act depended heavily on a series of forward pelvic thrusts, which Mark believed were the outer edge of sexual aggressiveness. He was good at other impersonations, too, and had a running comedy routine going with Danny that never failed to send their peers into roars of boisterous laughter.

But now, Danny's participation was half-hearted, especially when the humor was about girls. He had even stopped the Saturday morning sun-bathing show without comment.

Jimmy ambled alongside Mark, oblivious to the unusual tension.

*Alligator Creek* 25

He wanted to talk about Mrs. Radford some more, or about any female, for that matter. He wasn't ready to do anything about it yet, but he loved the feeling he got when they talked about women, especially about tits and asses. "Yeah," he mumbled without conviction, "I'd sure like to get me a piece of that cute little ass."

Danny turned back and called, "So, are we goin' fishin' this weekend or not?"

"Sounds good to me," Jimmy answered. He was back on solid ground, now. Fishing was something he knew. "You getting' Bubba's car, right, Mark?"

"I said I'd try, but he's gettin' kinda pissed about us askin' him so much." Mark called back to Danny, "Why can't you git your old man's car sometimes, Danny?"

Danny answered in a half whisper, looking over his shoulder toward his house, "He'd probably want to come with us if I asked him. You know how he loves that swamp, 'specially if we're goin' to Alligator Creek. You try Bubba first, Mark."

"Okay, okay. See ya tomorrow."

Danny felt a little guilty about not wanting his dad to go along. Harland was the reason that Danny loved fishing, loved the swamp. He had taken Danny out into beautiful, secret places and sat with him for hours, watching his drop lines, mostly silent, as far back as Danny could remember. Out in the swamp, you didn't have to talk, anyway. It was better to listen. There was so much always going on around you, if you just listened. But, to tell the truth, Danny was sort of ashamed of his dad, now. He was so...well, *dumb*. He'd rather be with his buddies. He couldn't help it. That's just how it was.

## *Chapter 6*

Danny ran up onto his porch, forcing himself not to look over at *her* house. He knew without looking that the warm pink light was on in her bedroom, and he imagined her inside, moving softly around the room. He shook the image out of his head as the screen door slammed behind him.

"That you, Danny?" his mother called.

"Yeah, Mama. What's for supper?"

"It's not ready yet. Anyway, that Mrs. Radford next door wants you to come over and help her get something down out of the attic. She said she'd pay you. Why don't you go over and see what she wants before we start to eat? I sure don't want her callin' back and interruptin' our meal. She's a brassy thing. You never know what she might want next."

Danny hadn't heard a word past "…wants you to come over…" He felt his face reddening and turned away quickly. "Okay, Mama. I won't be long."

*Thank you, God, thank you, thank you.*

He ran, he flew down the porch steps and toward Christine's house, but suddenly realized that he was dirty and had on a stupid, sweaty T-shirt with the sleeves cut out and "Africa, USA" printed above a faded lion on it. He stopped dead. He couldn't go back home and change. How could he explain it to his mother? Frantically, he tried to smooth his hair with his grimy hands. He blew his breath into his cupped hands to check for bad breath odor. Well, nothing he could do about it now. He trudged on, subdued.

She answered his knock immediately, agitation showing in her glittering green eyes. She was wearing blue jeans and a man's shirt, the tail of which was tied up in a knot in front. The tight points of her nipples pressing against the shirt made Danny weak. A bandanna was tied around her head, but curly tendrils of auburn hair had escaped to frame her flushed face.

"Oh Danny, I'm glad you came over." She whirled away from him and turned back into the house, leaving him to follow her. "This junky piece of...," she snarled through clenched teeth. She turned on him, eyes flashing. "If there's anything I hate, it's..." The helpless dismay engraved on his face stopped her. She took a deep breath. "I've made a mess of trying to get my old waterbed down out of the attic. You won't believe what a mess!" she laughed, with a sudden change of mood. "Come see!"

The small hallway was blocked by the jumble of a wobbly folding stairway, two long side panels of the frame of a waterbed, and the misshapen plastic form of a deflated water mattress. The wooden side panels were wedged between the wall and the stair. A pungent odor of moldy plastic tickled Danny's nostrils.

"Well, there it is! My exotic waterbed. Looks pretty inviting, doesn't it? Uh, I mean..." She blushed and turned away.

Danny laughed. "Hey, everybody should have one."

She smiled at him gratefully. "Well, I'm throwing this one out. It's too hot in Georgia for a waterbed, anyway." God, he was cute! Even in that silly shirt. "Can you help me get it down?"

Danny grinned, "Sure. Where do we start?"

*Why not help you get it down? You've sure helped me get it up!*

He bent slightly forward over his pelvis, hoping she wouldn't notice.

"I don't know. Let me get up to the top of... No, we'd better start by getting the mattress out of the way. Maybe if we pull together..."

Trying to control the excitement her nearness stirred in him, Danny concentrated on the fine moldy powder which drifted from the mattress over his hands as he pulled on the plastic. His body sang with strength and purpose as he yanked the mattress loose, and it crashed down, bringing an unexpected box along with it. He caught the errant box just before it hit Christine's head, but in doing so, he knocked her off balance, and she fell back against the wall with a shriek.

"Oh, no! Oh, I'm sorry." Danny was stung with embarrassment. She was crumpled against the wall, knee deep in wrinkled plastic, but she was giggling helplessly. "Are you okay?" He took her hand and helped her to her feet, pulling her toward him. But then her hand was so small and so soft, he couldn't release it for a minute. She stopped laughing and looked into his eyes with a worried look which *acknowledged his desire.* For a moment, his passion transfigured their relationship into hunter and prey, and he, *he* was the hunter. A primitive power stirred within him.

She pulled away and quickly restored order with a "Well thanks, Danny. Yeah, thanks a lot!" She forced a small laugh, brittle with tension. All business now, she looked away from him at the wooden bed slats and added, "Now for the hard part."

But it was too late. At the moment, nothing was too hard for him. He knew a significant step had been taken. His nebulous dream had taken a shape for itself, and had become a tremulous goal. It was now just a matter of time.

He took over. "Why don't you climb over these slats and work them loose from the top, while I push them toward you from the bottom? Here, I'll help you up." He boldly took her waist in his dusty hands and lifted her over the rails onto the flimsy ladder. His heart pounded at the feel of her skin, her warm bare skin touching his hands.

She pushed his hands away, angrily. "Danny, for God's sake!" The ladder buckled under her, and she fell onto him, knocking both of them onto the crumpled pile of plastic. "Great move!" Her face was red with a kind of desperate anger which didn't make sense to him.

"Look, Danny," she said, "I appreciate your help, but I think I can finish it by myself now. Thanks anyway." She turned away briskly, went into the kitchen and poured herself a glass of water, without even offering any to him.

He got up slowly, in confusion and disappointment. The sweat and grime of the football game were now dusted with the powdery mold from the water bed. He felt a rush of disgust at his appearance. A lot of help he had been, too.

As he started toward the door, she called to him from the kitchen, "Hey, what do I owe you?"

He was speechless for a minute as the insult washed over him. Then with acid bitterness he answered, "Nothing, Christine. Just forget it!" He was surprised at the depth and resonance of his voice. Thank God it didn't break like it usually did when he was up-tight about something. He left without answering her as she stammered, "Well, gosh, I didn't mean to... I hope you didn't..."

A few minutes later, as the hot water of the shower eased him and erased the traces of grime and insult from his face, he smiled with the memory of her body in his hands. Maybe it hadn't been a total loss, after all. He felt rejuvenated as he stepped out of the shower and wrapped a towel around his loins.

*Watch out, woman. I'm gonna fuck that sweet little ass. Count on it, I'm gonna drill ya, Baby.*

Suddenly he realized he was ravenously hungry. "Hey Mama!" he shouted through the bathroom door. "Dinner ready yet?"

\*   \*   \*

Christine surveyed the chaos in her hallway. She turned away and pressed herself against the wall in frustration. Unexpectedly, she began to cry. She beat her fists helplessly against the wall and allowed herself to sink into self-pity. It wasn't fair! Life just wasn't fair! She tried so hard to keep things going, be a good wife, work for the future. What was the matter? She was miserable. Just miserable! Maybe she needed to get a job, take a class, go somewhere, anywhere! She stumbled into the bathroom and splashed her face with cold water. Well, the first thing she had better do was to get the dammed waterbed down and clean up the mess in the hallway. She took a deep breath and returned to the scene of the disaster. Ugh, why had she run Danny off like that? She could sure use his help now! His strong, muscular arms… Oh, God! What was she going to do?

When his warm hands had circled her waist as he lifted her up onto the ladder, she felt panic and feigned anger in a desperate hope to change the frightening direction in which she was plunging. Danny's lack of experience saved her from revealing the turmoil boiling up inside her. When they had fallen onto the heap of plastic, she was all but overwhelmed with a sweet yearning to relax on top of him, press her mouth against his, and feel his chest against her breasts. But he was still innocent of the depth of his effect on her, and of the powerful reality of female sexual desire, and so she was able to pretend anger, extricate herself from the primordial jumble they were in and pull herself to her feet. If she had just given in and…

She had to stop thinking about him like this! She grabbed a bed rail and pulled it loose with an astonishing burst of strength.

The whole business came crashing down around her, one of the rails slamming into her shin, breaking the skin. Blood poured out of the wound as she furiously kicked the moldy mattress and the bed rails. "Fuck this! Fuck this! I'm sick of being alone, trying to do a man's work. I'm going to..."

But there it was. There was really nothing she could do. So she washed and bandaged the wound, dragged the waterbed parts onto the back porch, made herself a sandwich, and turned on the television. His hands had felt strong and rough like Jack's. But something more, something electric had left a lingering warmth on her waist. She could still feel it now, as she bit into her sandwich.

*Wonder if he has a girlfriend? If he knows how to make love, what to say, what to do? I could show him a thing or two. As a public service. Ha!*

Sinking back onto the sofa cushions, ignoring the earnest news commentary, she gave free rein to her imagination. She could start with dancing lessons, show him just where to place his hand on her waist to lead her effectively, let the music move him. They would sway together, their bodies in perfect accord. Then she could teach him how to kiss, how to take it slow, his lips soft, his tongue just in her mouth, to taste her, to move his lips gently, sensuously against hers. She untied her shirt and ran her fingers across her breasts as she gave in to the fantasy. She could teach him how to undress a woman, to stroke each uncovered part in its turn, to take a nipple in his teeth with a little bite just hard enough to hint at suppressed savagery. He would spread open her legs and experiment with the mysterious, tender, responsive flesh. She unfastened her jeans. Oh, she would have to struggle against her own insistent passion as he explored hesitantly, and then with increasing confidence he would discover her secrets as her body strained toward him, shuddering with yearning, wet with wanting.

He would learn the techniques of controlling a woman through irresistible pleasure. She could show him all the positions his strong, supple body could perfect. She could introduce him to the agonizing rapture of oral sex, oh God, yes, yes! He would learn when to be tender and when to be fierce.

She stroked her pubic hair gently, rubbing her fingers across the moist lips.

*Danny, do you want me? Do you want your fingers here, where mine are? Oh, do you want me, Danny? Want to watch me, watch me get myself off? Imagine your dick up inside me, Danny. Up inside me, here, in here. In hard, out slow, oh slow. Ohhh, what if I, what if I kissed your hard stomach? I want to kiss your hard stomach. What if I ran my tongue over the smooth head of your penis, up and down the whole length of it? Took it into my mouth, deep, deep. What if I sucked you, Danny?* Her mouth watered. *Oh, Danny, Danny, I want you to fuck me! Fuck me, fuck me!!*

She heard her own voice; foreign, hoarse. "Fuck me, Danny!" Her hips convulsed as the blessed relief came, and then she was left with futile feeling of deprivation. She turned off the neglected television and headed for the shower. Well, that was pretty stupid. No more of that, she promised herself.

Yeah, she'd look at the want ads tomorrow. Maybe a job, new friends, getting away from the house would be the answer. She wished she'd finished that secretarial course, instead of quitting to marry Jack. She wished that Jack were here.

Well, a job would solve more than one of her problems; get her out of the house, make new friends, give her a little financial independence. Maybe she could save up her salary and buy herself an air-conditioner! She certainly needed cooling off! Ha!

She'd start checking into it tomorrow. For sure.

## *Chapter 7*

Danny woke up the next morning with the nebulous feeling that something good was about to happen to him. That "Saturday morning with money in the pocket" feeling. Well, hey! It *was* Saturday morning... But then the memory of the waterbed fiasco dampened his good spirits. There wouldn't be any money in the pocket either, unless he could cut the grass next door, and he was reluctant to even go over to ask about it. He felt a rush of the humiliation of last night, but it was quickly replaced by the memory of Christine's body in his hands as he lifted her onto the ladder. She probably was just frustrated by the whole situation. Maybe she wasn't mad at him, at all. Anyway, he needed the money. He had to get over there and check it out. You just never knew about women or what they might do next. Didn't his dad warn him about that all the time?

He moved his face close to the mirror for the morning zit check. No problem. He stepped back, flexed his muscles, caught a profile view, and decided he really didn't look all that bad. Too bad he hadn't had a chance to shower and change into some better looking clothes last night before he went to help Christine. Maybe he'd wear his muscle shirt over there today. Yeah, he could do a couple of dozen push-ups to pump up the biceps right before he went over.

He'd figure some way to touch her again. Oh, yeah.

He moon-walked backwards into the kitchen, executed a triple twirl to face Madge at the stove. "Gooood morning, little mother of mine. What's for breakfast? I'm starvin'."

Madge sighed in resignation, "You'd better save that energy for helping your daddy get that ol' Mercury runnin' again. I'll swear but whut he'd be better off to give the thing away!"

"Dammit, Mama, he knows how much I hate gettin' that black grease all over my hands. Why can't he take it to a garage? Or fix it by himself?"

"You ought to be ashamed of yourself, Daniel Wilkins! After your father works his fingers to the bone for you, you're afraid to get a little dirt under your fingernails! I swear, it makes me sick how ungrateful children can be. When I was your age—"

"Aw, come on, Mama," Danny interrupted, "gimme a break. I'll go help him soon as I get something to eat, okay?" No matter how much the whiny nasal voice irritated him, he didn't want to get into a wrangle with her. He needed quiet to hear the song in his head.

*I'll touch her again, today. Just touch her hand or something.*

"Well you better eat fast and git out there. It looks like it's gonna rain."

He wolfed down two eggs, sausage, biscuits and gravy, and hurried out to the garage for the Saturday morning duty call. Harland was bending over the engine, humming aimlessly, his knarled hands smeared black with oily grime. He likes it, he really likes it, Danny thought. He could taste his own aversion to this familiar scene.

"So, Dad, you need some expert help?"

*You dim-witted clumsy fool.*

Harland extricated his skinny body from the engine with a satisfied grunt, wiping his hands on his filthy worn undershirt. "Ohhh, my achin' back," he moaned happily. "It's about time you got your lazy butt out here." His brief glance at Danny glowed with affection. A brown dribble of spit and tobacco juice traveled down his chin from the corner of his mouth as he handed Danny the greasy wrench.

*   *   *

Later, Danny scrubbed angrily at his hands, working the rough Lava soap into the skin around his fingernails. Well, at least he hadn't cut himself this time. He was getting better at this, he guessed. The hot water poured from the shower head onto his face as he sang tunelessly into the stream, "Baby, Baby, Baby, I'm a-gonna git ya, Oo-ee, yeah, yeah, yeah." He didn't even notice the erection rising hopefully into the steaming shower.

He dried himself quickly, dropped his nude body onto the floor, and began a series of 50 push-ups. A few minutes later he stepped into white cotton Jockey shorts and pulled a sleeveless undershirt over his freshly pumped muscles. He thrust his long, muscular legs into a clean pair of jeans, buttoning them tightly across his hard, flat stomach. He checked himself out approvingly in the steamy mirror. He was ready.

What if she wasn't at home?

But she was. She answered his knock, wearing a prim little cotton suit, her hair pulled back into a lush, round bun. She looked almost school-teacherish to him. He wanted her more than ever.

"Cut your grass, Lady?" he asked with a cocky little grin.

She didn't smile. "No, Danny. I don't think it really needs it today."

"Hey, you don't want to mess up the look of the whole neighborhood, do you? It looks pretty bad. You're gonna be gettin' complaints from the Ware County Civic Association and all."

She laughed. "Oh, all right. Cut it. I think you're trying to take advantage of me, though."

"Don't worry. I'm cheap." He smiled at her last remark.

*And if you only knew how hard I'm trying to take advantage of you...*

She didn't give him a chance, though. He had just finished when it began to rain. He flexed his muscles as unobtrusively as possible, and ran up onto the back stoop, laughing and pushing his wet hair back from his face. Pumped-up shoulders and arms gleaming with sweat and raindrops, face flushed, blue eyes bright with anticipation, he looked up at her and opened the screen door.

She handed him a ten-dollar bill and said, "Thanks, Danny. I'm in a hurry. I've got an appointment. Job interview. See you next week?"

"Uh, okay. Thanks."

*Bummer!*

He stood there in the rain a minute, his hopes shattered. Well, he'd just have to try something else besides this handy-man shit. But what? He shrugged his shoulders and turned toward home. He'd think of something.

\* \* \*

Christine turned away quickly, so he couldn't see the toll this little performance had taken on her. Her hands shook as she locked the back door. She wondered if he deliberately wore the tank top to show off his muscles.

*Little devil!*

She'd really have to watch herself.

## Chapter 8

Jack shifted irritably away from the sweaty Mexican field worker seated next to him in the garishly painted jitney. He was exhausted from the last two weeks' non-stop work problems; bad weather, inept work crews, boring food. He was ready for a little time off in Tampico, that was for sure.

*Why does everybody on this thing smell so bad?*

He had been pleased with himself for managing to get onto this drilling rig job. These guys had so much money they didn't know what to do with it. His supervisor on the big mall framing contract in Waycross had called him in when that job was winding down. He was expecting to be offered something after the mall job. He knew he was good: always showed up on time, worked harder than anybody, kept his nose clean, and had a natural talent for construction work. Back in Allentown, he had decided that being on the road three weeks out of four wasn't a good idea for a married man, so he had sold his semi and applied for construction work. Big sacrifice! He took a hefty cut in income and had to start on the ground floor, taking orders from dumb-asses he didn't respect, but he did it for Christine, for Red. To spend more time with her; be home every night. The money from the sale of his semi was plenty for a good-sized down payment on the little house.

What he hadn't figured was that he would get so bored in such a short time. Red was great, it wasn't that, it was just that he wasn't used to doing the same old thing day after day after day. And it was kind of hard coming home to the same house, same woman every day. Red was always after him to talk to her; tell her what had happened that day. Nothing much ever happened. He got tired of her questions when all he wanted was a beer, his dinner, television and a little peace and quiet. And a good fuck...

So, when his super said he would recommend him for a contract working on a drilling platform off the Mexican coast, he jumped at the chance. He'd be a "weevil," an unskilled beginner, but he knew he could learn quickly, and the big oil companies were desperate for workers. He liked the idea of becoming a "roughneck," a skilled rig worker. The very danger associated with the job enticed him. Good money, adventure, new faces.

Shit! He was already bored with it.

\*   \*   \*

The battered mini-bus bounced dangerously along the crumbling road, the very picture of unjustified faith. Faith that it would reach its destination in spite of all the failures of an abandoned infra-structure. Faith as illustrated in bright primary colors covering the outside of the bus in pictures of Christ, the Holy Virgin and various saints and angels, competing with religious slogans and names of children and relatives dear to the driver's heart. Faith that the valiant engine and thread-bare tires would survive for another day. Faith that the total of the small fares from the jitney clients would cover today's expenses.

The jitney stopped with a cough in a rakish little cloud of dust. With relief, Jack swung down from the high step onto the rubbish lined, pot-holed street, and into the alternating blue and red flashes of the neon parrot beckoning him into the familiar smoky dive. Just three months ago, on his first free weekend, one of the younger guys from the rig had introduced him to the seamy pleasures of the Blue Parrot, and now he entered with a feeling of going home.

As Jack stepped inside, Rosita "Rosie" Valdez was on the bar, doing her sensuous twists which passed for dancing; doing them recklessly to the blaring music of the mariachi band, and she didn't see him come in. He looked for an empty table as the music stopped and the band went into a long snare-drum roll. Rosie began to lower herself, legs spread apart, hips rotating suggestively, concentrating on a silver dollar standing on edge on the bar between her bare feet. She lifted her full, ruffled cotton skirt as she got closer to the coin, revealing her generous, bare buttocks and a thick, curly black mass of pubic hair. As she neared the coin, she changed the rotating motion to slow, pelvic thrusts, in line with the coin. Carefully, she aligned the lush red slit in the black bramble between her legs with the coin. Slowly lowering herself, she sank heavily onto the bar, moaning with pleasure as she rubbed herself provocatively backward and forward a few times, and then rose up triumphantly. The band broke into a joyous trumpet fanfare. The coin was gone!

Jack had seen her perform this trick, her only theatrical skill, many times, but he still got a hard-on every time he saw it. She twirled once more on the bar, spotted Jack and held out her plump, brown arms toward him. Then, with a lascivious smile, dark eyes locked on his, she raised her skirts with one hand, and ran the other hand slowly up the inside of her bare thigh and caressed her genitals, inserted a finger into her vagina and retrieved the silver dollar. After holding it up for everyone to see and laughing with the applause, she dropped it into a pocket in her skirt, jumped down from the bar and worked her way through the crowd to Jack, as he nonchalantly took a seat at an empty table.

"Jah-kee!" She wrapped her arms around his neck and slipped herself onto his lap, straddling his legs. She wriggled her bare thighs and buttocks against him happily. He slid his hands under the full, bright-colored skirt and fondled her, pressing her harder against his swollen penis and covered her laughing mouth with his. All this was avidly watched by the other bar patrons, much to both Jack's and their enjoyment.

After the two Tecates he had ordered were sloshed onto the table, he threw down a five, grabbed the beers in one hand and Rosie's chubby hand in the other and headed upstairs, accompanied by grunts of disdain and sighs of envy from his fellow carousers.

Entering her tiny room, he was as usual both repelled and stimulated by the bawdy smell of cigarettes, stale beer, onions and cheap perfume. He fell backward on the dingy spread on her narrow bed. He held up the beers, signaling her to take them from him and put them on the bedside table. He tried not to look at her. She fastened the little latch on the door and moved seductively across the room toward him, untying the cord in her peasant blouse, slipping it off one shoulder to reveal a voluptuous breast. He wished her nipples were pink instead of brown.

She took the beers from him and bared her teeth in what she considered a sensuous smile. "Wotcha wan, Babee?" She pursed her lips. "Jah-kee wan some good Rosie blow-job?"

"Yeah, Rosie. A good Rosie blow-job! C'mere."

She put the Tecates on the table and leaned over him, bare breasts now swinging free. She removed his shoes, unfastened his khaki oil-stained work pants, pulled them down and threw them across the room with a happy shout of "Ole!" He closed his eyes and blocked out everything except the contact of her warm, wet mouth against his most sensitive body parts.

When it was over, he was sated and relaxed. He liked it that she swallowed his semen, like she was hungry for it. These Latin bitches really liked sex a lot. He opened his eyes and looked up at the ceiling, stained yellow with the smoke of so many cigarettes of so many men; hombres, caballeros, roughnecks, roustabouts. The plaster was cracked and large chunks were missing, leaving an insane map of states, countries, continents: Texas, Australia, Hudson Bay. Georgia? Naaah. He reached for a beer.

"Jah-kee, was good, no?"

"Oh, yeah! Good, Rosie. Good job." Maybe after he finished his beer, he'd sit on her face.

He wondered what Red was doing. She'd better be behaving herself. He'd give her a call first thing in the morning.

## *Chapter 9*

Christine held her eyes wide open and looked up at the waiting room ceiling, fighting tears. It was coming, she knew it. The third humiliating rejection today. She had seen it as the coldly superior personnel clerk glanced over her application, in the almost imperceptible shake of the head; heard it in the little sniff of disdain.

"I'm sorry, Mrs., um... Radford, we don't accept applications for clerical positions from anybody without at *least* a high-school diploma." With a tight, forced smile, the clerk looked up at Christine and added, "But you could apply for a job on our assembly line." The smile dissolved into pity as Christine shook her head and a tear rolled down her cheek. "I'm really sorry, ma'am."

"Thank you for your time," Christine said as haughtily as she could manage, as she turned and walked out of the office.

*Damn! I don't want pity! I want a chance, that's all, just a chance!*

Her miserable three months at the Moore School of Business were not even worthy of consideration, it seemed. She didn't need work desperately enough to work on an assembly line or to go back to waitressing. Maybe she should just give it up. Or maybe just get that damned diploma. She couldn't wait to get home.

Back in the safety of her kitchen, she sipped a life-saving glass of iced tea and collected her thoughts. She needed some job skills. She hated being in this helpless situation, totally dependent on Jack. But what could she do? Nothing. Maybe she should learn something about computers. Ugh! She picked up the Yellow Pages and turned to "Schools."

*   *   *

The Thomas School was not all that prepossessing from the outside. Christine hoped maybe this meant that their focus was on academic excellence, not just appearances. The location was good; close to a bus line that ran only a block away from her house. The administrative offices, as well as the six grimy classrooms, were on the second floor of a two-story brick building in a strip mall, above a check-cashing company, a pawn shop, and a discount shoe store. She climbed the stairs with determined hopefulness. The dirty beige hallway was posted with promises of high school diplomas, exciting career training and job placement opportunities. What more could you want?

If it was too bad, she could always quit.

So began a routine. Getting her G.E.D. was relatively easy; a couple of weeks of study and a long Saturday morning's exam. But the remedial English and Math classes were something else. Tedious. They sank her into a vague, gray world with only the resistance of fatigue and boredom to define her direction and imply progress. She became enchanted with the very bleakness of the quest, and relied on dogged determination. And it began to pay off. Her grades were good—head and shoulders above the rest of her class of mostly surly, apathetic kids, there to please a social worker or a parole officer.

Coming home from the grime and tedium became a real pleasure. Almost every night Danny was either playing ball in the street in front of her house with his buddies, or hanging out by himself, waiting for her at the bus stop.

"Carry your books?" he would laugh, and follow her into the house. He was a good listener, and she began to unload on him, her successes as well as her failures. She had never had anyone to talk to who was so attentive. Besides that, he was funny, and always so… so *upbeat.*

Like all good confidantes, Danny shared his own thoughts and feelings with her: how he felt so embarrassed when his parents made their obligatory visits to his school for teacher conferences, how it irritated him that his dad let his mother bully him around, how much he hated having to work on the old greasy car.

"It's like every Saturday—like a ritual or something, working on that old car," he complained. "Look at my hands, all banged up. You can't get that grease out from under your fingernails, either. See?" He held his hands to her.

Christine turned away quickly, fighting the urge to take those strong, working-man's hands into hers. "Well, at least you have a father. I wish I still had mine. Of course, he didn't ask me to work on any old greasy cars." She laughed and then turned to him with a serious look. "But I miss him, Danny. He was a good, hard-working man—like your dad."

When she was "down," Danny could always cheer her up with an impersonation or a raucous story about the boys. He could tell when she had done something outstanding at school, and would tease the story out and congratulate her.

So the time passed, through the blessed cooling of October, through a lonely Thanksgiving, and on to a short Christmas visit from Jack. The work on the off-shore rig had made him even better-looking, muscular and tan.

The visit was distinguished by a remarkable lack of conversation and an amazing concentration on sex. Jack laughed that he had had "blue balls" since his brief visit last July. She responded eagerly at first, to his strength and rough virility, but after a few days began to tire from the sheer energy requirements. She wanted to hear about his experiences on the rig: the danger and excitement, the sunsets on the warm Gulf waters, the men he worked with. He didn't want to talk about it, beyond the bare facts of dirt, grease and long hours, summed up in one or two sentences.

Cuddled up to his broad back after the usual evening's sex, she tried to tell him about school. "Jack? Honey, are you awake?"

"Hmmm?"

"Guess what. I got a hundred on my last two English tests. I'm pretty sure I'll get an 'A' in math, too. Both my classes. Aren't you proud of me?"

No response.

"Jack?" He was asleep.

When she brought up the subject of school at the dinner table, he didn't show any interest beyond two questions: when she would be through and what kind of job she would get. The trouble was that she couldn't answer either question with assurance. And, anyway, he never did talk much at mealtime.

She missed her talks with Danny, who had completely avoided her since Jack arrived.

So she just satisfied herself with Jack's physical closeness and his insatiable need for her body. Her cheeks became red and tender from the fierceness of his unshaven face, her legs were sore and trembly and her arms were bruised from the ferocity of his desire. She tried not to worry about the increase in his drinking, but two or three beers before lunch seemed unhealthy to her.

She felt a guilty sense of relief when the airport taxi took him away. She hoped Danny saw his departure.

He did.

\*   \*   \*

By February, she had completed the boring remedial English and Math classes and entered the dreaded Electronic Data Processing course, EDP 101. Much to her surprise, she found the alien new world of computers stimulating. The introductory class was exciting to her. She felt proud as she mastered each new step up this challenging ladder, and took pleasure in having to exercise her brain for the first time. She began to feel some curiosity about programming. When she wrote her mother about her new interests, including a modest mention of her high grades, she got an unusually prompt reply; a "What in the world do you think you're doing?" reply with advice not to get too smart for her own good because, "No man wants a wife that thinks she's smarter than him."

Danny, on the other hand, seemed to be impressed with her progress. He met her almost every day at the bus stop, and she began to rely on seeing his smiling face as she descended from the bus. He automatically took her books now, as they poured out to each other the events of the day they had been storing up.

"Well, how'd it go today?" he would ask.

"Great! We're learning how to flow-chart. It's a way to plan out the steps you'll have to take to solve a problem. It's fun. I'll swear, Danny, it's like a game, figuring out the best way to do a job—the most efficient way to use the computer. Sometimes I think I can feel the wheels turning in my brain!" She laughed. "That sounds silly, doesn't it?"

"Maybe not silly, but kinda weird. I guess I'm not smart enough. I've sure never felt any wheel turning in *my* brain!"

"Oh, Danny! Of course you're smart enough. You're like me. The way I've always been before. I've never had a chance to really use my brain, I guess. I never thought it would be fun to learn something as new and different as programming, but believe me, it is!"

They would go over the little victories and defeats they had experienced during the day. She felt perfectly at ease with him and comfortable with all subjects except one—she never mentioned Jack.

In her letters to Jack, she was careful not to mention either Danny or her excellent grades. She did keep him informed about her general progress. He never wrote to her, but in his weekly telephone calls, while he didn't express any interest in the content of her classes, he didn't object to the idea of her getting a job and helping him with the finances someday.

Mostly, the subject of Jack's calls was sex. At first the husky-voiced dirty talk was exciting, but she soon began to feel cheap, as if she were being used for relief of an itch. She felt guilty for not enjoying his calls. She knew how hard he was working, and how rough the conditions were that he had to live with. But she couldn't help it. She had to hold the phone away from her ear when he started talking about all the erotic things he would like to do to her. He would begin to breathe heavily, talk in disjointed sentences and make obvious grunting and groaning sounds. She didn't know quite how to respond. She didn't want to imagine what he was doing to himself during these segments of his calls.

But the checks kept coming every two weeks. What was the matter with her? She remembered the dreary struggle her poor father had endured in his attempt to support his little family. She really shouldn't complain. Jack was a good provider, and good-looking to boot.

And she continued to make progress in school.

## Chapter 10

"Get up out of that bed, boy! You're going to be late for school, and it won't be *my* fault!"

Danny was jarred awake by the sound of his mother's crashing entry into his bedroom. She didn't just open the door, she collided with it in mid-sentence and swung it open with a vengeance. He moaned and pulled the pillow over his head. Why did she have to wake him up like *this* every morning? What was the big deal? He never got used to it. In fact, it irritated him more every day.

"Aw right, aw right, aw right," he mumbled from under the pillow. "I'm practically up."

"If you'd get to bed at a decent hour, you wouldn't be so sleepy in the morning. What's gotten into you lately, anyway? You were hanging around next door last night until all hours—*again*."

"Oh, Mama, I was home by 9:00. That's not so bad."

*Man, I wish I could've just stayed there all night. For more reasons than one.*

He thought he might lay out of school today. Have a stomach ache. But the prospect of staying in the house with his mother's voice nagging at him all day made school seem not all that bad. He dragged himself out of bed and into the shower.

By the time he sat down to his huge bowl of sugary cereal and gulped about a pint of orange juice, his natural good spirits had taken over again. He polished off the cereal, tipped up the bowl to drink the last drop of milk and grabbed his untouched homework assignment and books. He'd be early enough to make a stab at the homework, a stab which, accompanied by his winning smile and glib tongue, he knew would keep him snugly in the good graces of his teachers. After a hopeful glance at *her* house, he joined Mark and Jimmy at the regular corner, and they headed for the bus stop, Mark twanging an imaginary guitar, Jimmy feigning passes with his invisible football, and Danny doing scathing impersonations of their English teacher.

\* \* \*

Madge wielded the vacuum cleaner against non-existent dirt like a bayonet against a loathsome foe. Each vigorous thrust was a blow at the despised image of her next-door neighbor. And why in the world was Danny hanging around over there so much? She had tried to talk to Harland about it, but the wimp just wanted everything to be peaceful and nice, no trouble please. He didn't see anything to be worried about. Well, it was plain to her that any woman that wore the kind of clothes *that* woman did—lack of clothes would be a better way to put it—was up to no good. Going around with her titties showing, and her butt hanging out of her shorts! Well, only a pure fool wouldn't know she was asking for trouble. And of course a kid like Danny would be taken in. He had a wild streak in him anyway, from his grandfather of course, and it wouldn't take much to get him going full steam ahead down the road to Perdition! The Whore of Babylon, that's what she was! Madge wanted to scream. Her head was beginning to ache again, and she had already taken three aspirins.

"Oh, damn that woman! Damn her!"

If there were only some way she could get rid of her…

"She's a devil, that's what! A witch! Evil, evil!"

\* \* \*

Danny, Mark and Jimmy were passing through the front door of the school, jostling each other, when Mark brought up their favorite subject.

"So, where were you last night, Danny?" Mark asked, tossing his hair back out of his eyes with an Elvis-like twist. "Back over at your neighbor's again, trying to grab a little feel?"

"Yeah, I went over there for a few minutes. So what? She had something she wanted to show me." Danny knew he had blown it before he even finished the last sentence.

"Wooeee, I'll bet!" Jimmy hooted.

"Hey, tell her we'd all like a look," Mark spread out his open hands, palms up, with an exaggerated look of innocence.

"You guys can go fuck yourselves," Danny growled. "It's the only way you'll ever get laid!"

Mark and Jimmy roared with laughter as they cavorted down the hall, punching at each other with friendly abandon.

He would never tell them that Christine had wanted to show him her EDP mid-term exam. She had made 100 on the multiple-choice section, and had gotten A+ on the small COBOL program making up the second section. Her instructor had written "Good going!" with conspicuous red letters across the top. She was glowing with pride when she showed it to Danny. He was able to give her a congratulatory hug without crossing the bounds of allowable behavior which had evolved between them. He knew exactly how long the brief contact could last and exactly how close it could be. These rules had never been spoken of. Speaking of them would require that they acknowledge the sexual tension between them, and Danny lived in constant fear that the acknowledgment of *that* would sever the delicate, erotic thread between them.

"Let's celebrate!" she had laughed. "How about a little glass of champagne? Would it be all right with your folks, you think?"

"Sure," Danny swaggered his shoulders slightly in an I'm-a-man-of-the-world pose, "Uncork that sucker."

*Champagne, huh? If Mark and Jimmy could just see me now!*

She handed him the frosty bottle and said, "Here, you do the honors. Women aren't supposed to open champagne, you know. I think it's against the law."

"My pleasure."

He had never even seen a bottle of champagne uncorked, but hey, it couldn't be all that difficult, could it? He tilted the bottle and analyzed the venture. Christine was getting wine glasses down out of the back of a cabinet, so he blessedly had a minute to figure out how to accomplish the task without embarrassing himself. After turning the bottle up and down a few times, he began untwisting the little wire holding the cork in place. With a resounding bang, the cork exploded from the bottle. Christine screamed and then laughed helplessly as the foam spewed from the bottle, ran down over his hands and began a widening puddle on the kitchen floor. She tipped a wine glass against the bottle and tried to salvage what she could of the erupting liquid, as he stood frozen with surprise and embarrassment. She grabbed a dish towel, bent over and started to wipe up the puddle, but looking up and seeing his distress, she stood up, put the wine glass down, took the bottle from him and began to clean his hands tenderly.

Recovering quickly, he laughed, took the dish towel from her and took her hands in his. He leaned his face down close to hers and said in an exaggerated French accent, "Madame would like zee champagne in zee *glass*, no?" His lips moved close to hers and an electric silence enveloped them, broken only by the diminishing fizz of the champagne still escaping from the open bottle. She pulled away from him, and began to pour champagne into one of the two glasses.

"For you," handing him a glass, "and for me," as she poured one for herself. She lifted her glass toward his in a toast. "Here's to…" she faltered.

"Us," he said, his voice husky and deep, "You and me…"

Silently, they both sipped at their champagne, unable to think of anything normal or sensible to say. Danny's eyes were locked on her flushed face. Her eyes, full of concern, roved the kitchen desperately for some object on which to focus. She seemed dazed.

She shook her head. "Danny," she said softly, taking the half empty glass from him, "I... I think you'd better go home now."

Had he crossed the line? "Oh no, Christine! Why? I thought we were going to celebrate you acing your test. You deserve a little pat on the back."

"Well, thanks buddy," she smiled. "I'll, uh, we'll talk about it tomorrow, okay?" She led him toward the door.

He started out, hesitated, turned and kissed her delicately on the cheek. "Way to go, Christine," he whispered.

\* \* \*

She closed the door quickly and leaned her forehead against the cool wood. His lips had been unbearably sweet on her cheek. My God, what was she going to do about *this*? She pressed her body against the door.

\* \* \*

The weird thing the next morning, was that Danny didn't want to tell Mark and Jimmy about the tender little encounter. He knew they wouldn't understand. Hell, *he* didn't understand it himself. But it sure was nice. Real nice. He ran the scene over and over in his head as he headed for class with a happy little smile on his face and a familiar bulge in his jeans.

## Chapter 11

It had been over a year now since Jack had taken the first boat trip out to the offshore rig. That had been an exciting trip, when he had been full of anticipation and proud of himself for landing a really great job. Now he hung over the rail as he headed back out to the rig once more, sick with too much booze, dope, shame and worry. Damn! How could he have let himself get into this mess?

It had started innocently enough, by his standards. He was upstairs at the Blue Parrot, feeling no pain, fucking Rosie's brains out, and somehow things just got out of hand. They had been drinking beer and smoking some really bitchin' hash when he had decided he just had to try some of that tequila that he had heard had a *worm* in it. He had stepped out into the hallway in his skivvies and shouted downstairs, "Hey, Pedro," (he called them all Pedro), "bring me up a bottle of tequila, and be sure it's got a worm in it!"

It had taken an hour before the sweaty little bar assistant arrived with a bottle of Mezcal, some limes cut into small wedges, a shallow bowl of salt, and two Margarita glasses. Rosie had been thrilled. This was expensive booze. After she made an amateurish attempt at making a Margarita, he grabbed the bottle, put a pinch of salt into his mouth, followed that with a squirt of lime and turned the bottle up for a big swig. Rosie joyously followed his lead, and soon the bottle was almost empty. She began trying to explain the use of the worm in the bottle. She pointed first to the worm and then to his penis. Rolling her eyes rapturously, she stretched her hands apart, indicating a huge increase in size. "Beeg man, Jah-kee!"

He got the idea. She poured out the last of the tequila, shaking out the worm into her glass. She delicately lifted the ugly little thing in her fingers and held it above his lips. He thought, "Hell, why not?" and swallowed it. She squealed with delight, threw herself onto the bed, spread her legs apart and beckoned him toward her. She was as hot as he was, or so it seemed to him. He blindfolded her and spread-eagled her on the bed, tying her wrists to the head board posts and her ankles to the foot board. "Fuck it, Rosie! You're a feast, you know that, you fat bitch!" he snarled through clenched teeth. With his feet against the head of the bed, he crouched over her, a knee on each side of her head, facing her feet, and rubbed his engorged penis over her eyes, cheeks and lips, as her tongue reached out for him. He teased her, inserting himself into her eager mouth in small, shallow dips, laughing when she lifted her head and blindly searched for him with her open mouth and busy tongue. He finally leaned forward and plunged the full length of his penis into her mouth, forcing it down her throat as far as he could. She gagged, but kept on sucking noisily, trying to swallow him. He pinched the little points of her big, brown nipples, and twisted them harder and harder as both his anger at their color and his animal passion increased.

When she stopped sucking and cried out at the pain he was

inflicting on her breasts, he slapped her thigh, hard, and it felt good to him. As he rubbed his genitals back and forth across her face, he reached for a half empty beer bottle, poured its contents out onto the floor, and began to force it up into her vagina. At first, she strained upward against the bottle, but as he became more and more violent in plunging it into her, she began to struggle against him, thrashing heavily from side to side, turning her head away from him. His slaps became blows and she yelled at him, "Basta, basta, Jah-kee!" and tried to fight him off. He jumped away from her, flung the bottle across the room and began to strike her with his fists.

Her screams brought two huge, gorilla-like Blue Parrot bouncers charging into the room, followed in a few minutes by several Mexican policemen in their silly-looking, gaudy uniforms. They shoved him around, handcuffed him and took him to a foul-smelling Mexican jail. They left him there in a cage with three drunken locals until the next afternoon, with nothing to eat or drink. He was finally brought before a judge and charged with assault and battery, as well as a whole list of minor misdemeanors. He reluctantly telephoned the platform for his drilling supervisor, Tony, the closest thing to a friend that he had down here. A grim-faced Tony came to the jail and bailed him out. The bribe required by the judge to keep Jack out of the miserable jail until his court appearance was more than a month's salary, which the furious Tony advanced to him. His salary was now docked for two months. God knows what would happen to him when he had to go back for his court appearance.

Now, on his way back out to the rig, Jack looked down at the undulating water and thought for a moment how easy it would be to just jump in. Instead, he leaned out a little farther and retched.

*Mother-fuckin' Mexican police! They'll take me for all they can get.*

What would he tell Red? How would he explain where all that money went to? Shit! Tony was still so pissed off that he wouldn't even talk to him yet about how they were going to handle things.

*What a fuckin' mess!*

\*   \*   \*

Christine took the letter out of the mailbox and stared at it in disbelief. A letter from Jack! Her first. She hurried into the house, threw her books down on the sofa and ripped it open with a little thrill of excitement. She was glad Danny hadn't met her tonight at the bus stop.

"Dear Christine," it started.

*Whatever became of "Red"?*

She felt a chill. "I had some trouble down here and I won't be able to send you any money for a while. Sorry, but I guess you'll have to use some of the money we got in the bank. I'll send you something if I can. Don't worry, I'll have it all fixed up before long."

*Fixed up?*

"Love, Jack."

She read it through carefully several times. Had she missed something? What in the world was he talking about? What kind of trouble? Oh, God, was he sick? Had he gotten hurt? It must be really bad if he couldn't tell her. *Trouble?* Did he know about Danny? Impossible! But what now? She didn't even know how to call him. Phone service, he had told her, was limited and difficult on an offshore drilling platform, and it had been up to him to call her every weekend. She began to panic. What if he needed her? Cold nausea clutched her stomach. She'd have to do something, but what? The nausea took over. She ran to the bathroom, leaned over the toilet and gagged. Her whole body was trembling and felt cold.

*No, no. Please no, no.*

She took several deep breaths and tried to get control of her mind, which was beginning to jump from one irrelevant picture to another: a dead dog beside the road, piles of broken pipe, a tree crashing down toward her. Why did her brain do this to her? "No, no, no," she cried aloud. "Come on, Christine, get a-hold of yourself. Oh, please!" The familiar panic was taking over. She shook violently as she pulled herself up from the floor and leaned over the sink. *Another deep breath.* She splashed cold water over her face and began to calm down a little. *Damn these spells, these panic attacks.* She recognized them for being irrational and knew the feeling would pass after a while, but couldn't keep them from sweeping over her sometimes. It was awful!

After the panic subsided a little, she sat down at the kitchen table, still shaking, and gathered her thoughts. She'd get the offshore telephone number from the home office of the oil company. She had their address in Dallas. It was on the check stub from the last payroll check he had sent her directly. Now if she had just kept it...

*Oh Jack, am I making too much of this?*

She realized that she needed to be able to get in touch with him, anyway. What if she had an emergency, herself? It was really ridiculous that she was so cut off from her own husband. Well, that was the way he had wanted it. Okay, she had a plan. She'd wait until tomorrow, during business hours, and she'd call company headquarters and find out what was the best way to get in touch with him. It was embarrassing, but she would do it. She went to her desk and began to look for the check stub.

The next day, she made the call to the home office, convinced them that she had an emergency and got the coveted telephone number on the oil rig. Jack wasn't there, but she remembered the name "Tony", his supervisor, and asked to speak to him. After a long wait during which each minute ticking by pushed up the cost of the call, she finally heard Tony's gruff and irritated voice.

"Yeah?"

"Is this Tony?"

"Yeah. Who's this?"

"This is Christine Radford. I'm real sorry to bother you, but I'm worried about Jack. I got this letter from him, and I'm real worried. He said something about some trouble down there. Is he hurt or sick or something?"

Tony laughed. "Naw, he ain't sick or nuthin'. He got in a little trouble with the Mexican police. They're always tryin' to git us on somethin'. It's the way they pay their bills."

*Trouble with the Mexican police?*

"Oh, no! What happened? He's not in jail or anything, is he?"

"Naw, he ain't in jail, least I don't think he is. He's in town now, prob'ly havin' to pay a whoppin' fine." Tony laughed. "I'll let him tell you about it, Ma'am. Ain't nuthin' unusual. Happens all the time down here."

"Oh dear. Well, uh, is there anything I can do? I could…"

"Naw, don't worry, Ma'am. Listen, I'll git him to call you soon as he gits back, okay?"

"Yes, please, I'd really appreciate that. And look, if there's any, uh, problem, could you call me and let me know?"

"Sure thing. Hey I gotta go now, but don't worry. I'll make him call you."

"Thanks, Tony. Bye."

She got a dial tone as Tony hung up.

*Now what? Did he get into a fight? Tony said he wasn't hurt. Why wouldn't he tell me what happened?*

Christine took a deep breath and tried to make a calm assessment of the situation. She was probably just exaggerating the whole thing. Jack was okay. If anybody could take care of himself, it was Jack! Okay, she wouldn't worry about it, but she sure hoped he would call her soon and explain. The uncertainty about how much money he would be able to send her just pointed out how much she needed to get a job. She was really glad she had been smart enough to start a small savings account in her own name. She probably had enough money to tide her over for a month or two.

But a job was definitely in order. Maybe they could help her down at the school. She'd look into it tomorrow. For sure.

She wished Danny would come over so she could talk to somebody about it. She went out and sat on her small front stoop. It was a soft, warm June night, with a honey-suckle flavored, light cool breeze. A little personal breeze. Lightning bugs were twinkling all through the bushes and up in the trees. The nearly full moon was rising through the tall, skinny pines, up into small clouds, flirting with her. She rubbed her hands gently over her thighs and up across her chest, crossed them in front of herself, and gave herself a little hug.

*Danny, where are you? I need you.*

## Chapter 12

The receptionist at the front desk of the Thomas school was sorry, but the job placement clerk wouldn't be in until after 5:00 that afternoon. It was now 4:15.

When Christine replied, "I'll wait," she was ushered into a cluttered office and offered a seat.

*Not in until after 5:00? Hmmm... Probably can't leave her day job for the few likely job candidates from this Mickey Mouse School.*

Christine moved some papers from the scarred-up chair, settled in and opened her "Business English" textbook.

At 5:30 the office door opened and a disheveled young woman bustled in, arms full of folders, an enormous handbag suspended from her shoulder, chewing gum popping in her heavily lipsticked mouth. She was short and buxom, with startling large pointed breasts. Her abundance of tousled, dark-at-the-roots blond hair supported a watermelon pink bow. She was resplendent in a flower-splashed dress with flowing sleeves, one of which was bunched up in the handbag straps on her shoulder. Her high-heeled white boots were studded with little chrome stars and crescent moons.

"Hullo, Honey," she greeted Christine. "Wat-cha want?" Her voice was loud and flat, slightly nasal.

"Are you the job placement clerk?"

"Well, yeah, I guess so. Among other things," she laughed. She dumped the papers in a heap on her desk, swung the huge handbag onto a filing cabinet and plopped down into the chair behind her desk. "I'm Bessie Tanner. Who're you?"

"I'm Christine Radford, and I need a job. Bad." Christine was relieved at how easy it was to talk to this woman. She felt an immediate rapport with her, like she'd known her all her life.

"You a student here?" Bessie asked.

"Yes, a freshman."

"Well, what can you do?"

"I'm interested in computer programming, right now. I think I'm pretty good at it, or will be as soon as I finish EDP 101."

"Oh, wait a minute. Christine Radford? You're the gal that scored so high on that IBM Programmer's Aptitude Test, aren't you?"

"Uh, I don't know. We never got our grades back. I thought…"

"Yeah, that's just like Bruce." Bessie leaned down and tugged at a boot. "Probably didn't want to admit that a woman outdid all the young male hot-shots in his class. Well, you did. You blew 'em away." The boot flew off her foot and bounced off the wall, and Bessie threw her arms out in an expansive gesture that knocked a few folders off her desk. "But you can't get a job programming yet. You've gotta finish a few more classes first. You taking COBOL any time soon? That's where the jobs are at." She began working off the other boot.

"Gosh, I'm signed up for COBOL next quarter, but I need a job *now."*

The second boot followed the same path and joined its companion against the wall. "Oooo, that feels good," she said as she massaged her foot. "I have to keep these damn things on all day. I work in a law office, and they sorta frown on going barefoot in the office, you know." She laughed and winked broadly at Christine, then continued, "COBOL next quarter, huh? Tell you what. Maybe I can get you going in a data entry job. You up for that?"

"Sure, I guess so…"

*This woman is going to be fun, but…*

"Got a resume on you?"

*A resume! I never needed one for waitressing…*

"No, do I have to have one?"

"Yeah. Get one to me tomorrow, and I'll see what I kin do for you. Just leave it on my desk, with your phone number and all, and I'll get back to you."

"I, uh, haven't written a resume before. Do you have a sample or something?"

Bessie laughed. "Boy, we're starting out from scratch here, aren't we? Hey, that's fine." She opened a dusty filing cabinet and started rummaging around in a drawer stuffed with papers. She extracted a folder and held it out toward Christine. "Here's something on how to write a good resume, samples and all. Take it home and work on it. Can you type?"

Christine took the folder and absent-mindedly began straightening out the jumble of paper in it. "Not really. I'm learning, sort of, in the

EDP class."

Bessie whistled and scratched her head with a long fingernail inserted carefully underneath the pink bow. "You've got some work ahead of ya, Honey. Never mind, with the grade you got on that Programmer's Aptitude Test, we'll find ya something to do on a computer."

"Well, thanks a lot for your time. I'll go home right now and start work on my resume. Are you here about the same time every day?"

"Yeah, unless I get lucky between my day job and coming here." She leaned back in her chair, put her feet on the desk, locked her hands behind her head and looked up at the ceiling. A blissful smile lit up her face. "Oh, that'll be the day, that'll be the day." One brightly polished toe-nail stuck out through a hole in her stocking.

Christine didn't quite know what to say. "Well, thanks again. I'll see you soon, maybe tomorrow?"

*Interesting, but can this person really help me to find a job? Kind of unlikely...*

Waiting for the bus she wondered what in the world she could put on a resume. No real high school diploma, just a G. E. D. The only job she had kept for any time at all was as a waitress, well okay, a manager in a really junky restaurant. Never mind, she had to get started somewhere. She'd take anything she could find. But that still didn't settle what she'd put on a resume. *"Best lay in town?"* That's what Jack had told her she was. She was so out of practice now, that she probably couldn't even claim *that* distinction any more.

And Jack? What was happening to him? Nothing to be done

about that now. She put Jack firmly out of her mind.

Later, on the ride home, she guessed that she wouldn't see Danny waiting for her at the bus stop, since she was so late getting home. Oh well, maybe she could call him up and ask him to come over and help her with something. The oven door was sprung and wouldn't close completely, and the faucet in the bathroom sink was dripping. She felt a happy little shiver, as she remembered the soft, sweet kiss on her cheek.

*No, I can't call him. I can't. I'd be asking for it.*

She hurried from the bus to her house, worried now that she *would* see him, and unlocked her door with shaky fingers. A sense of relief swept over her as she closed the door behind her and sank breathless onto the sofa.

Almost immediately, he knocked on her door. She recognized his distinctive, rapid tap. Maybe he wouldn't even remember kissing her. It probably didn't mean a thing.

With her heart pounding, she opened the door. He was standing there with a small, knowing smile on his face. His eyes said it all: that he knew that the kiss had been a significant step, that he knew that she was thinking about it. Her resolve collapsed under the assault of his self-confident, predatory look. She wanted to pull him to her and really taste his sweet mouth, and in spite of her resolve, she knew her eyes communicated this to him.

"Danny, I…" she stammered.

"Got any of that champagne left? I need to wash my hands."

She had to laugh. "Come on in, you idiot!" She stepped aside to let him pass. He smelled like Ivory Soap. "I've got work to do, but maybe you can help. Ever write a resume?"

*You good-looking devil.*

"No, 'fraid I can't help you there. What's up? Are you looking for a job?" and then, before she could answer, "Look, Christine, I really wanted to come over last night. We had a family thing come up. Mama insisted that I had to go. I didn't want to, but..."

"Of course. I was busy anyway, and... To tell you the truth, I did want to talk to you last night. I got a letter from Jack that's got me worried. He's in some kind of trouble with the... with the Mexican police."

"Bummer!"

"I don't know exactly what happened, but his boss, Tony, told me they arrested him for something. Wouldn't tell me what. Can you imagine?" Unexpectedly, her voice quavered, and her eyes welled up with tears.

Danny stepped closer and patted her on the shoulder. "It's gonna be okay, I'm sure. If it was anything really serious, you'd have heard more about it, don't ya think?"

Instead of turning away from him and changing the subject, the way she always did when their conversations got too personal, she surprised him by leaning toward him with her head almost touching his shoulder, and covered her face with her hands.

"Oh, Danny, I don't know what's the matter with me." She began to cry. "I'm such a baby, lately. I'm so afraid of... I don't know *what* I'm afraid of. I just feel like something terrible's about to happen. I just..."

He pulled her to him and began stroking her hair. "Hey now, don't worry. Nothing bad's gonna happen to you. It's gonna be okay."

She collapsed onto his chest and let the tears flow. He wrapped his arms around her and rocked her gently from side to side. "There, now. It's gonna be okay." He kissed her on the neck and whispered over and over into her ear, "Now, now. It's okay, it's okay."

She turned her face up to him with a look of utter helplessness. He tightened his arms protectively around her and murmured, "I won't let anything bad happen to you. Please, I don't want you to be afraid or sad or..." He kissed her wet eyes, her temples, her cheeks. With a moan, she found his mouth with hers, and kissed him with all the pent-up longing she had struggled against for the last year. He clasped her hungrily against him as her lips parted and her tongue touched his. With his mouth still on hers, he moved his hand down her back and pressed her into his body, against his erection. Feeling the affirmation of his desire, she locked her arms around his neck and lifted herself closer to him, opened her legs and wrapped them around his hips. He staggered slightly, then carried her across the room to the sofa and laid her down gently, lowering his body onto hers.

Christine traced the muscles in his back and arms with her fingertips, the muscles she had watched moving under his skin as he worked in her yard, the muscles she had tried to imagine flexing in her own body. They felt better, warmer, stronger than they had ever seemed in her imagination; graceful, powerful. His lips were moving downward from her face, past her neck, across her chest, toward her breasts, as he unbuttoned her blouse.

Suddenly, she was jolted back to reality by the very depth of her feelings. "Danny, Danny, Sweetheart. We can't do this. This can't happen. Oh, I'm sorry, I'm sorry I let it go this far. You know this won't work. Danny, Sweetheart, stop. Stop, Precious." She struggled up into a sitting position, took his hands in hers and kissed them tenderly.

Her blouse was open, her cheeks flushed, desire and frustration burned in her eyes, and she was telling him to stop. He stood up and looked down at her with confusion, close to anger. "What's wrong? You know how I feel about you, don't you? I'm... I guess I'm in love with you. I can't help it. I don't wanna be, but I can't help it." He turned away, shaking his head in frustration. "Don't you feel it too? Don't you... Please...What's the matter?" He turned back and took her hands and pulled her up close to him.

She tried to pull away. "Danny, Sweetheart, you're seventeen. I'm thirty-three. I'm twice your age. I could be your mother. Danny, I'm married. I love my husband. I want to be your friend, and this would..."

"Would what? You don't seem that much older to me. You're just right. You're..."

"Danny, you're important to me. I guess you're my best friend. I don't want to mess that up. If we started... If we ever... It just wouldn't work. It wouldn't be right!"

"Who cares if it's right or wrong?" He slipped his hands into her open blouse and caressed her breasts, lowering his lips toward them.

She took his face in her hands and kissed him again, the taste of him making her senses reel. "Please go home now, Sweetheart. Please. This won't work. I don't want to lose you. I don't want to hurt anybody. Please." She backed toward the door, pulling him along with her.

He shook his head in bewilderment, speechless as she maneuvered him to the door, opened it and gently forced him through it.

"Good-night, Danny. This was crazy. I'm sorry. Good-night."

Outside, he took a step toward her, but the door closed, barring his impulse to take her into his arms' to crush her resistance. He stood staring at the door for a minute before turning toward home with an audible sigh.

## Chapter 13

Christine awoke the next morning with her stomach in the clutches of a cold terror—the result of the unbelievable encounter with Danny last night. She was emotionally drained by the episode, and physically drained from the devastation of the panic attack which had followed it. She dragged herself into the bathroom and surveyed the damage in the mirror. She looked awful: face a ghastly white, eyes red and swollen from crying herself to sleep. And she still didn't know what was going on with Jack.

*I really don't want to live.*

She brushed her teeth, took a shower and dressed for school. Trying not to think of anything, she struggled into the kitchen and made herself a cup of coffee. She had to keep going. Sometimes you just had to keep functioning, even though you might not know why at the time. Things had a way of working out.

But *Danny*! What was he thinking? What was he doing? Had she ruined their friendship?

The coffee tasted good; the cup warm in her hands. She went out and sat on her back steps and sipped pensively as she stared out into the morning haze hanging quietly in the tall, slender pines. A mockingbird's brilliant song split the gray silence with a fissure of color. In spite of her mood, she shivered with bliss at the sheer beauty of the song.

She took a deep breath and stood up. She'd just keep on with what she'd started. Get herself in a better position to deal with things. Get a job! She'd at least start on the cursed resume, and go on to class. It'd be all right. Danny had said so last night.

*Danny, Danny, Danny!*

She felt dizzy.

*   *   *

Working on her resume was the hardest thing Christine had ever done. To begin with, she didn't have a single job experience that she was really proud of. She had heard that "everyone lies on a resume", but she couldn't even consider doing that. She would be sure to be found out if she got a job based on some lie or exaggeration, and wouldn't that be a mess? She didn't have any education worthy of mentioning. She couldn't even type. The whole prospect was really depressing.

And to make things worse, she couldn't concentrate on *anything* with the sweet memory washing over her, wave after wave of the memory of Danny's body pressing on hers last night. She had never felt such desire. And she had sent him away! But she *had* to. When he left, she had felt like the front of her body had been ripped off, and she had pressed herself against the door to stop the bleeding. And she knew he was standing right on the other side of the door! She could feel his presence. She heard him when he sighed, turned and headed for home. Oh God, what had he thought? It was unbearable to think how she must have hurt him. She wanted him here now, to yield to him, yield everything: marriage, school, reputation, future. And he said he was in love with her! She had enough experience to know the difference between a crush and a vital passion, and *this* was passion.

She needed help. If only Jack were here, it would be easier to think of herself as married, to concentrate on practical things, to at least have some vision of the future. The way things were now, she was being tossed all around on a sea of uncertainty. A *stormy* sea. Panic gripped her again. She needed help, all right.

Following the resume samples she had gotten from the school, she forced herself to write a brief chronology of the pathetic jobs she had held and a description of her "career" goals. She laughed derisively to herself at the term "career" as applied to her undistinguished life. She decided she would throw herself onto the mercy of the job placement lady. She smiled, remembering the happy disorganization of Bessie Tanner's office. She had really liked that woman's irrepressible attitude.

*Keep functioning! That's the thing.*

\* \* \*

Danny woke up with the usual sticky wetness on his belly. It had been a wonderful dream. He had been all over Christine, and she was loving it! He didn't want to wake up, but he knew his mother would bang his bedroom door open in a few minutes if he didn't go on and get up. He didn't want *that* to happen this morning! Not on this beautiful morning!

Holy shit! She had kissed him last night, I mean *really* kissed him, wrapped her legs around him, let him feel her up. Oh, those awesome boobs! His hands tingled with the memory. She wanted him! He wanted to jump up and down on the bed. It was too good to be true. He couldn't wait to tell Mark and Jimmy! He could hardly keep his feet on the floor on the way to the bathroom. She wanted him!

*She wants me!*

\* \* \*

Christine sat in the school's front office and read the want ads while she waited for Bessie. *Receptionist.* Maybe that would be a good place to start. She knew she could get another hash-house waitress job, maybe even at a management level, but she was determined to get an office job, dress up every day, meet interesting, successful people, go out for lunch in nice restaurants, get waited on, not do the waiting-on herself.

She was glad to have a reason not to go home at the regular time. She was terrified of seeing Danny. She didn't want to see hurt, rejection or embarrassment in his beautiful blue eyes. And she knew she couldn't trust herself to keep a respectable distance between them.

*Stop thinking about Danny! Concentrate on the task at hand.*

*Where is that nutty woman?*


\*   \*   \*


Bessie blew cheerily into her office at 5:30, leaving a trail of papers, brochures and candy wrappers behind her. "Well, you're back! Serious about getting that job, huh? I thought you might be, so I picked these up for you." She dug deep into the cornucopia of her huge bag and brought out several brochures from the U.S. Department of Labor and the Thomas School: How to Write an Effective Resume, Successful Interview Techniques, Current Job Opportunities, Careers in Technology and several others.

Christine was impressed, and her face showed it. "Wow! Thanks a lot, Bessie. Uh, is it all right if I call you 'Bessie'?"

"Sure. Did you have to ask? So, how'd you do on your resume?"

"Not so good. That's really why I'm here, to ask for your help. Could I, uh, pay you to help me to write it?"

"Well, it's not in my job description, but I think I could handle it. Maybe we could meet for lunch or dinner. That's about all the free time I have."

"Oh, that'd be great! How about dinner tomorrow night? When do you get off here?"

"Around 8:00. Why don't we meet around the corner at the Tasty Burger?"

"Sounds great! Meantime, I'll read through some of this stuff, uh, *information* you gave me."

"Okay, I'll see ya there at 8:00. Bring anything you've already done on the resume, and we'll take it from there."

Christine left with a good feeling that things were going to get done. Wonder how much she should offer Bessie?

She realized that she hadn't thought about Danny for several minutes. Good!

On the way home, she was afraid to look out the window of the bus as it approached her stop. With palpable relief, however, she saw that he wasn't there. Was he angry at her? Maybe that wouldn't be so bad, anyway.

*Think about the resume. Think about working in a nice office somewhere.*

She walked as fast as she could to her house. She was shaking so much that she dropped the keys to the door and spilled her books and job information as she picked up the keys. The skin on her back felt all prickly when she finally got inside and took a deep breath.

She had made it all the way into the kitchen before she heard his knock.

## Chapter 14

Christine held onto the counter top. Her heart was pounding dangerously. She couldn't open the door. But he knew she was at home. The lights were on in her living room, and... Who was she kidding? He had been watching for her, of course. He had seen her come in. She'd have to face him and send him away.

*Oh, Danny, I want you so much, but we can't, we can't.*

She took a deep breath and went to the door. "Who is it?" she said through the closed door, in a thin, high-pitched voice.

"You know who it is," he said with a soft chuckle.

Had he actually *laughed*? How could he be so unconcerned? Was it just *her*? Maybe they could go on as if nothing had ever happened.

"Danny? I don't feel so good. You'd better not come in."

"Oh, come on, Christine. I need to talk to you. Open the door. Please?" A little silent pause. "Please?"

She opened the door hesitantly. "Well, just for a minute."

He stood there for a second with a small questioning smile on his face. Then, with a shake of his head and a shrug, he strode into the room, picked her up proprietarily, kicked the door closed behind him and kissed her. The kiss was so perfectly right, so natural, so normal, that any thought of resistance on her part seemed laughable. She relaxed her body against his, completely.

*I can't fight this any more, God help me.*

With his mouth still on hers, drinking her in, he carried her into the bedroom and laid her on the bed.

"Danny, I…"

"Shhhh, don't say a thing." He bent over her and began to undress her with trembling fingers.

She moaned a despairing little sigh, heavy with guilt, yielding to what she knew would be inevitable pain, as she pulled him toward her and kissed him hungrily. She sat up and finished unbuttoning her blouse, shrugged it off her shoulders and reached around to unfasten her bra.

"Let me do that," he said huskily. He reached around and fumbled with the tiny hook on her bra. It didn't yield. After a few tense moments, he laughed and moved around behind her to accomplish the task.

She giggled at the sudden interference; the interruption of so much passion by a tiny little hook and eye. He laughed, too, but swiftly solved the problem and the bra loosened away from her breasts. He moved back in front of her and pulled the bra straps off her shoulders. "Oh Christine, Christine, oh shit Christine, oh God you're so beautiful." He cradled a breast in each hand and kissed first one, then the other.

The funny, clumsy moment with the bra had released the tension for Christine, and the easy way he had dealt with it seemed to prove how *right* they were together. She began to undress him.

She unbuttoned his shirt, her fingers jerky with impatience, kissing his chest with each new opening, biting at his neck and earlobes. She moaned with the sadness of her surrender, her guilt lending the deadly sweetness of over-ripe fruit to her hunger for his innocence and virility. She pulled his shirt back over his arms, making him helpless as she pressed her breasts against his chest.

He was deliriously happy. No moth ever flew more joyously into the flame. He stood up, shook the shirt off wildly, and pulled her forcefully up to him, bending his face to hers and forcing open her mouth with his. Her fingers worked frantically at his belt buckle. She dropped to her knees, pressing her face against the bulge in his jeans, wrapping her arms around him and caressing his strong, tight buttocks. She blew her hot breath through the pulsing blue denim as she finally opened the buckle and carefully lowered the zipper and pulled down his shorts.

There, straining toward her, finally, finally, was the smooth, red head of his magnificent penis. She kissed it lovingly. A drop of sweet nectar passed her lips, a covenant of his desire. She licked the tip with a delicious release of pleasure. Danny's knees buckled and he sank to the floor with a groan. She pushed him back onto the floor and crawled on top of him, rubbing her body against his and panted hoarsely in his ear, "Get those pants off before I rip 'em off!" She sucked at his ear lobe, ran her fingers through his hair and pulled his face toward her, kissing his mouth, eyes, temples, as he struggled out of his jeans. She backed down over his body, leaving a glowing wake of little kisses as her mouth moved toward his penis again. She kissed the smooth head, gently probing the small opening with her tongue. Then she slowly licked the full length, cradling it in her soft hands. "Oh, Danny, you're so big. You're wonderful. I can't believe it," she whispered. She circled the skin around the head with the tip of her tongue, and then with a feral groan, pushed her face against his groin as she plunged his full length down her throat.

Danny's thighs trembled as hot waves of rapture radiated from his groin and washed outward to his fingers and toes. *Jesus, what's happening to me?* He began to weep with the intensity as she moaned with a hypnotic mixture of pleasure and pain, now sucking hungrily, now gasping for breath

Christine raised her head and looked *through* his eyes with a dizzying sensuality. She lifted herself slowly to straddle him, spreading her legs apart, taking his penis in her hand and gently stroking her soft, soft pubic lips with the smooth head. She lowered her breasts to his chest and pressed herself into him with a circular motion. He strained toward her, as she, whimpering with desire, lowered herself onto him and pressed her body against his as he penetrated her. *Oh, at last, at last, the sweet fulfillment.* She was complete, she was connected, she was part of him. She writhed against him, arching her back, pumping her body up and down, pressing her soft breasts painfully against his chest, savoring the pain. She sucked at his bottom lip, tasting the nectar of the Gods. She was crying, mumbling, "Darling, you precious darling, you sweet, precious darling…", crooning to him in little whispers and sighs. She couldn't tell where her body ended and his began. Ancient magic, ancient magic.

Danny clasped her body to his and rolled over on top of her. His strength soared with his passion. He lost all sense of time and space and rose ecstatically into a strange musical rhythm, swimming around in his own atoms, lost in the flow of everything around him. He was invincible. He was weeping. His powerful hips forced her upward into a new ecstasy with him. Soon he felt the overwhelming tide rising in him, a gathering of pure force, more right than anything he had ever imagined. *Oh, Jesus! Oh, I'm coming* "Christine, Christine," he cried out with the sweet release of all his dammed-up longings. She screamed and dug her nails into his back as she took the power of his youth, and joined him in a blaze of rapture.

As the blissful flood subsided, they clung to each other in awe, fearful of the return to reality. "Oh God, Christine. Jesus, I love you. I love you *so much*."

"No, Precious. You mustn't say that," she whispered. "It was wonderful, mmmm, it was *wonderful*", she murmured dreamily, "but *love* is something else again." She kissed his eyelids and then his lips tenderly, awash in his sweetness. But another wave of desire turned the gentle kiss into a passionate yielding, and she forced her tongue into his mouth. He pressed his pelvis against her, and she was thrilled to realize he was ready for more.

She lay back and held out her arms to him.

Later, as they lay exhausted in each other's arms, she began to feel nasty little probes of guilt, nudging her toward a panic attack.

She knew it was coming, she felt the nausea and her head swam. Her hands began to shake and the silent cry of "No, no, no!" rose from her belly to her brain. She had to get him out of here before she succumbed. "Danny, you've got leave, please. Oh Lord, what have I done?"

"I don't know, but I sure hope you do it again," he laughed. He got up and began putting his clothes on. As he zipped up his jeans, he turned to her, his face radiating affection, and was shocked to see her agonized expression.

"What's the matter? Are you okay?" he asked with concern.

"Just go, please. I'm so sorry. I can't believe I let that happen." A wave of nausea. "Oh, Danny, I'm sorry. You've got to get out of here and not ever come back again." She began to cry and turned her face into the pillow.

He sat down on the bed beside her, lifting her into his arms, as she struggled against him. He stroked her tousled hair and kissed her wet eyes. "Are you crazy? That was wonderful. *You're* wonderful. I couldn't stay away from you before! You think I'm gonna stay away from you *now*?"

She pushed him away. "You have to." She really felt sick. "We can't go on with this. It's all my fault. I'm sorry. Please go now, NOW! GO!" She turned her face back into the pillow.

"Okay, but I don't think we did anything wrong. Hey, it sure seemed right to me, ya know? Listen, everything's going to be okay. I'll see you tomorrow. And stop worrying." He bent down and kissed the back of her neck.

"No, no!" She beat her fists in futility against the mattress. "Get out!"

Danny left in a joyous confusion. He was King of the World and he loved everything in it. He'd done it! It had happened! He'd drilled her! My God, so *that* was what it was all about. All the times he'd done it before were nothing, *nothing* like this. Mark and Jimmy were never going to believe it. He'd *drilled* her!

\*   \*   \*

When she heard the screen door slam shut, she put on a negligee and hurried shakily to the front door. As she closed and locked the door, her hands felt numb, the cold nausea took over, and she knew she was in for a good one, a full blown panic attack. Oh, shit! She ran toward the bathroom and knelt before the toilet. Thank God he left before he saw *this*.

*Oh, Jack, forgive me, forgive me!*

## Chapter 15

Next day, Christine used the word processor in the lab at school to write her resume, in preparation for her meeting with Bessie that night. It took her most of the afternoon, what with figuring out how to use the software and trying to get the grammar right. She was delighted to find the spell checker and frustrated by the formatting problems.

She fought thinking about Danny, without success. She had buried her face in the bed-clothes that morning, breathing in his lingering aroma. There had been a strong smell of semen in the bedroom last night after he left. My God, such virility! She had never imagined that kind of elemental passion. She had thought that Jack was a good lover, but his rough pursuit of sexual satisfaction was nothing like the primal masculinity of Danny's desire. And Danny had been so tender with her. Tender but completely overpowering. She longed to be with him now. She wondered what he was doing, thinking. She pictured him in class, walking across the school yard with his springy step, jostling with his friends. Her hands still felt the smooth, strong muscles in his arms, back, buttocks. She still tasted the sweetness of his mouth.

*How is this possible? He's just a boy! I don't care. He's*

*wonderful!*

After spending half of the night throwing up from a panic attack and lying on the bathroom floor exhausted with guilt, the reality, the basic good sense of Danny's irrepressible spirit had taken over in her mind. It had happened. She couldn't change that. And it had been the purest joy and most profound pleasure she had ever experienced. Crazy! She concentrated on the beauty of the thing, the undeniable sense of *rightness*, and tried to forget the immorality and the shame. What was morality, anyway? A set of rules arbitrarily laid down by some old codgers thousands of years ago, often in conflict with the strongest and best features of human nature. She bet they'd never experienced what she had last night!

And so now, at an unbearable slow pace, she completed a draft of the resume. She was ready to meet with Bessie at the Tasty Burger.

*Will he come over tonight? Will he be watching for me to come home?*

\*　　\*　　\*

At 8:00 that evening, the Tasty Burger was roiling with clamorous teen-agers. Christine felt decidedly out of place as she waited for Bessie. She couldn't believe that Danny was a contemporary of these noisy aliens. The odor of rancid grease and grilled-dry hamburgers competed for irritation value with the general racket. She really wanted to be at home in the order and quiet of her living room.

*Danny, are you watching for me to come home?*

\* \* \*

Bessie came in. She had her tousled mane pulled up tonight, into a sort of leaky fountain hair-do, which displayed her large, complicated dangling earrings to great advantage. They clattered from her earlobes and brushed against her fleshy shoulders with every movement of her head. Her big, warm brown eyes sparkled with animation. As she wound her way through the crowd, she was followed by a syncopated chorus of "Hiya, Bessie", "Good to see ya", and "Lookin' good, girl". She responded happily, calling an amazing number of the pubescent patrons by name.

*How does she tell them apart? Are they students at Thomas?*

"Hi, Christine! Ready to go to work? On the resume, that is." She laughed as she dropped heavily into the booth. "Hey, mind if I call you 'Chris?' 'Christine' sounds too prissy for me."

Christine smiled. Her name did sound funny when spoken in that loud, flat voice. "Why don't you call me 'Red'? That's what my husband calls me."

"Great, Red." She called out across the room, "Hey Billy Joe, bring me my regular, and an extra Bud for Red, here," then to Christine, "You want a beer, don't you?"

"Sure, thanks, but I'm buying."

"Suit yourself. Well, let's see what you got."

Christine reluctantly pushed the draft of her resume across the table to Bessie. "This is all I have so far. Uh, you come here a lot?

Everybody seems to know you."

"Yeah. Nuthin' better to do, dammit." Bessie rummaged deep into her bag, retrieved a large pair of red-rimmed glasses and put them on with a flourish. She began to read.

A singularly unattractive, gawky young man approached with a tray with two frosty beers and a large chili cheese steak sandwich. The sandwich was as lush as he was spare. He gave Bessie a warm smile as he wiped a soiled rag across the table with one hand and deposited the tray on it with the other. The beer bottles teetered precariously. He grinned fondly at Bessie. "Here you go, Bessie. You keepin' them lawyers straight?"

"You better believe it. Thank you, Darlin'," she replied without interrupting her reading. Then to Christine, "You didn't tell me you've been a manager." She took a swig out of the beer bottle and pointed it at Christine. "It don't pay to be too modest when you're lookin' for a job, Honey. Remember that."

"Well, I wasn't what you'd call a *real* manager. I just tried to keep things going behind the counter."

Bessie raised an eyebrow and aimed the beer at her menacingly, "Red, what did I just tell you?"

"Oops, you're right. Okay, I had six or eight people reporting to me for about five years."

"That's better. Write that down. That's your best sellin' point." Bessie took a big bite out of her sandwich. Melted cheese dribbled down her chin. "I know a place right now that could use somebody like you."

Christine felt a rush of excitement. "Really? That's great! I want you to know, I'm a real hard worker."

Bessie made a few more suggestions about additional information needed on the resume as she polished off her sandwich in record time. With her last bite, Billy Joe appeared back at the table. "Everything all right here? Ya need anything else, Bessie? *Anything*?"

"Naw, everything's fine. Bring us a check, Sweetie."

When Billy Joe brought the check, he beamed another smile at Bessie and asked, "Hey, tell Laura Mae I said 'Hi,' okay?"

"You can tell her yourself. You're in the office often enough!" Bessie chuckled. Billy Joe blushed.

Christine took the check from him without protest from Bessie, and realized that she had never been given a chance to order. She was too excited to eat, anyway. As Billy Joe left the table, he gave Bessie a shy little pat on the shoulder. Bessie didn't acknowledge it.

*He's looking at her like she looked at that sandwich. And she doesn't even notice.*

"Who's Laura Mae?" Christine asked.

"That's his cousin. She's our receptionist at the law office." Bessie laughed. "Everybody's kin to everybody down here." She added in a half-whisper, "I think he's got a little crush on Laura Mae."

Christine thought it was more likely that the poor kid had a crush on Bessie, but she kept that thought to herself. She paid the check and they left together under a shower of farewells: "See ya Bessie", "Take care, now", "Be good".

Billy Joe blew Bessie a kiss when she turned and waved good-bye to the room.

Bessie walked Christine to the bus stop. "I'll make a call or two tomorrow and let you know what I come up with. Stop by my office again tomorrow night. And hey, thanks for the sandwich."

"My pleasure. Thanks for your help. I really appreciate it. I can't … Oh, I almost forgot. How much do I owe you?"

"Forget it. See you tomorrow, Red."

Christine rode home on the bus in a happy fog. Bessie was fun to be with. Her first real friend in this one-horse town. Her mind was a chaos of lustful thoughts of Danny, hopeful excitement about a possible job, and worried doubts about Jack. She was exhausted from the warring passions. She laid her head back, closed her eyes and abandoned herself to sweet thoughts of Danny.

## Chapter 16

Harland was getting worried about Madge. She was as mad as a wet hen most all of the time, now. She had gotten up at 3:30 this morning and started taking down the dining room curtains. When he had dragged himself groggily into the dining room and asked her what was she doing up at this time of morning, she had snapped at him, "I'm spring cleaning! What do you think I'm doing?" He had urged her back into bed with the promise that he would help her the next Saturday. He wouldn't work on the car or go hunting or fishing. He would have time to help her. She snorted at him derisively, "You? Help me with spring cleaning? You wouldn't know where to start! I would get Danny to help, but you know where he always is—over next door at that whore's house!"

"Now, Madge. You shouldn't talk that way about Mrs. Radford. It don't sound like you."

"Well, what do you want me to think? He hangs around there all the time. She's nothing but a witch, that's what! A red-headed witch!"

"Now, now, Madge. That's enough of that kind of talk. Come on back to bed now, for a little while, anyway." He gave her a sympathetic pat on the shoulder which resulted, as usual, in her tensing her muscles and pulling away from him.

"You've got to talk to him, Harland! Tell him to stay away from over there. You mark my words, there's going to be trouble about this!"

"Not unless we make it ourselves. Danny's a good boy, and he's smart. He's not gonna get into trouble over some old married woman. He's just tryin' to help her out, and Lord knows she needs it, what with her husband gone so long, and all that."

"You call a red-headed hussy like that an 'old married woman'? She sure don't dress like one. Sounds like maybe you want to go help her out a little, yourself!"

"Now Madge, don't you carry on so. You know I got enough to do without goin' over there and takin' on more work. Come on back to bed, now. And quit your worryin'."

\* \* \*

Madge had become the center of attention at her church social gatherings. Her stories of the latest breach of Southern etiquette committed by her Yankee neighbor had elevated her to a new height of interest among the ladies of the Calvary Baptist Church Thursday Night Circle. They were delightedly appalled at the descriptions of the laundry hanging out on her neighbor's clothesline: matched sets of hot pink or black underwear and skimpy little bras and panties you could fit into a teacup. To make it even more sinful, the washing was often done on Sunday. No God-fearing woman would ever hang out washing on Sunday.  Strains of the blues and of Southern rock from the local black radio station often floated out of her windows, and she could even be seen dancing around the house to this awful music, wearing her skimpy little shorts.

It didn't help that she frequently cooked hamburgers or steaks on a dinky little grill out on her back porch, which she then ate at a lantern-lit table in her yard and washed down with *beer*.

Madge neglected to mention that her son spent a lot of time over there.  She did mention, however, that she wondered sometimes if this neighbor was some kind of a devil worshipper, or something.  Well, she certainly wasn't a Christian woman, that was plain to see.

Something had to be done.  She wished the witch would just move away.  Go out into the swamp and never come back again.  That's where she belonged.  Out there with all those other nasty critters.  Yes, she liked that idea.  But she was smart enough not to share *that* with her Thursday Circle.  Not yet…

She had another splitting headache.  She'd thought about going to the doctor and getting some pain killers, but she didn't want to spend the money, and besides, all she needed was a good night's sleep.  For weeks now, she'd been waking up several times during the night, yanked into a fearful, wide-awake state which would keep her up for several hours.  She would sneak out of bed without waking Harland.  The big lump wouldn't do her any good, anyway.  Let him just snore away.  She'd get some cleaning done.  Take the stove apart and clean under the burners.  Scrub around the edge of the kitchen sink with a toothbrush.

Her head throbbed.

\* \* \*

That morning, Danny had gotten up early, showered and was having his breakfast well before his usual wake-up time. When Madge had charged into his room to wake him up, she had been stunned to find it empty, his bed was made up, and most of his clothes put away. Then, when she came into the kitchen and saw him actually studying his geometry while he ate, she really started to worry.

Her eyes narrowed. "What's the matter with you, Danny? Are you in some kind of trouble?" she asked.

"No way, Mama. I just feel real good this morning. Thought I'd try bein' nice for a change."

"Well, somethin's up with you. You can't fool me."

"Oh, Mama, relax. You worry too much." He finished his cereal, put his dishes in the sink, picked up his books and tried to give Madge a good-bye kiss as he started for school.

She pushed him away and said, "Git on outta here, Boy. Don't try that mushy stuff on me. I know you too well." She softened her tone, however, and the corners of her mouth lifted imperceptibly.

\* \* \*

Danny had never been so happy in his life. He had been early getting to the corner where he usually met Mark and Jimmy, so he had run up to Mark's house and joined him as he came out.

"Whut's hap'nin', buddy?" he greeted Mark.

"Nuthin," Mark answered sleepily. "Whut's up wi' you?"

"Oh, not much… Except that I drilled her."

"You *what*?" Mark was now wide awake.

"You heard me, Stupid. I *drilled* her! I *did* it!"

"You're *lyin'!*"

"Naw I'm not. I'm serious!"

"Fuckin' awesome, Man. You serious?"

They had reached the corner, and Danny took a running leap and slapped the street sign with a resounding smack.

"I'm *serious*, Man."

"Damn! How was it?"

"It was awesome! Fuckin' awesome!"

"Holy shit!"

"It was wonderful, Mark. Wonderful. Totally fuckin' wonderful! You wouldn't believe it! She's fuckin' awesome!"

Jimmy had joined them. "Whut's so fuckin' awesome?"

Mark answered, his eyes wide with admiration, "He *drilled* her! Danny *drilled* her!"

"You're lyin'!"

"I'm serious!", and so on, and so forth…

## Chapter 17

The bus rumbled along, taking Christine home from her meeting with Bessie at the Tasty Burger. The rough ride usually irritated her, but tonight it seemed to rock her gently. Every inch of her body felt warm, relaxed and contented as she indulged herself in thoughts of Danny. His sweet-smelling, smooth skin, his soft, warm mouth, the strength in his arms, the depth of the blue in his eyes darkening with passion. She felt a little shiver of delight remembering how his long legs had shuddered with rapture. She almost missed her stop.

She was relieved that the meeting had taken as long as it did. Maybe this would keep her from having to struggle against her lust tonight.

She hurried from the bus to her house. Surely it was too late for Danny to come over. She could postpone the miserable, draining battle between her conscience and her libido for tonight, at least. After all, she had told him last night that he should go and not come back.

*Oh, Danny, don't listen to me. Come over here right now! I want you.*

She put her books down on the kitchen table and got a Coke out of the refrigerator. The house had never sounded so quiet. She sat down at the table and took a sip of Coke, listening for his tap on the door.

When it came, about five long minutes later, she jumped so violently, she knocked the Coke can over, spilling the bubbly liquid all over the table and herself. She grabbed a dish towel and wiped her skirt frantically as she hurried to the door. Her legs were shaking. She wished she had combed her hair and put on a little lipstick. She opened the door.

He stepped in quickly, kicking the door shut behind him and lifted her up into his arms and kissed her thoroughly. Without even the semblance of a struggle, she wrapped her arms around his neck, her legs around his waist, and melted herself against him. He staggered to the wall and pressed her back against it, as he lifted her skirt, pushed her panties aside and stroked her soft, wet lips with his finger tips.

"Danny, oh my God, Danny!" she half whispered, half moaned.

He covered her mouth with his and muffled any possible objections with the sweetness of his desire. Supporting her weight with one strong arm, he unzipped his jeans and guided his erection into her, radiating tremors of rapture throughout her body. The dish towel dropped to the floor.

\* \* \*

Later, while she cleaned up the spilled Coke, Danny sat at the kitchen table and watched her lovingly. "We sure seem to be spillin' a lot of stuff here lately, don't we?"

Christine laughed and yanked at his ear as she passed him, going toward the sink. "It's all *your* fault! I never used to spill things before *you* came along."

He grabbed her and pulled her onto his lap. "Is it worth it?" He nuzzled his nose against her neck.

"Oh, no question. Absolutely." She kissed him. Funny how she just couldn't get enough of the taste of him. She got up and went over to the sink. "But Danny, we've got to talk some sense about this. We can't hide this forever from your folks, from Jack. Everybody's gonna figure it out." She leaned over the sink and shook her head hopelessly.

"Who cares about them? It's *us* I care about. You and me."

"Jack'll kill me!" She whirled around, "and maybe kill *you*, too!" She was approaching hysteria. Her voice rose, "Oh, God, what are we gonna do?"

He stood up and took her gently in his arms. "Hey, Baby, calm down." He stroked her hair. "It's gonna be all right. I'll never let anything bad happen to you. Never! I love you. We'll figure out something. Maybe we can meet somewhere. If I only had a car..."

She looked up at him, "Does anybody know about us? Do Mark and Jimmy know?"

"Yeah, they figured it out. Well, actually I told 'em. I couldn't help it."

She bit her lip and pushed away, pressing her forehead into her hand. "Oh, God..."

He pulled her back to him. "Don't worry, they won't say

anything. They're cool. Look, I'd better go now, before Mama starts gettin' ideas. And remember, I love you." As he kissed her goodbye, her whole body trembled with both fear and passion.

She waited until she heard the door close before she sank helplessly onto a kitchen chair and lay her head on the table. She couldn't expect him to understand the seriousness of this. He really thought he could protect her, bless him. Bless him.

She abandoned herself to tears.

\* \* \*

Next day Christine finished typing the resume at school. She was getting a lot better at using the word processor. She read the document over with pride.

Later, she was waiting again in Bessie's office and jumped up to meet her when she came bustling in.

"Hiya, Red!" Bessie dropped a large shopping bag as she made for her desk.

Christine picked up the bag. It was full of paper-back romance novels. "Hi, Bessie, any news about my job?" Christine's face shone hopefully with a mixture of affection and trust.

"You betcha!" Bessie rummaged around in the pile of paper on her desk and extracted a note pad followed by a pen. "Here's where I want you to go," she continued as she wrote directions, "This is a really nice guy. A little old-fashioned, but bright enough as men go. He's got a little trailer plant, excuse me, a *mobile home plant* out towards Waresboro, and apparently it's startin' to make money, and he needs some help. Bad."

"Out toward Waresboro?"

"Yeah. You're gonna need a car."

"Oh, but I…"

"Listen, it'd be worth it. He's willing to pay for good help. More'n you could make anywhere else around here."

"Well, I guess I could…"

"Say, what's going on with you? You look great. Kinda like the cat that swallowed the canary. Got a new boyfriend or somethin'?"

Christine blushed furiously and looked down into the bag of paper-backs. "Uh, what do you mean? I, uh, I'm just excited about getting a job, I guess."

Bessie ripped off the top sheet of the little note pad and handed it to Christine. "Here's the number. His name's Stan Taylor. Call him in the morning and make an appointment. Take a copy of your resume with you. He's pretty sold on you already, just from what I've told him. When he sees you, well, you'll be a shoo-in. Better wear somethin' conservative. And look, don't be so apologetic about yourself, okay? Remember, you got a lot to offer."

"Okay, if you say so," Christine said, laughing, "but can I get out there without a car?"

"Yeah, there's a bus goes out there. Just a couple a day, though. Not enough to use it to get to work on a regular basis. You'll have to call Waycross Transit and get their schedule." Bessie reached across the disordered desk and dismissed her with a handshake. "Good luck!"

"I don't know how to thank you. Maybe, if I get the job…"

"There you go again! Whaddya mean, '*if* I get the job'?"

"Oh, yeah! *When* I get the job, maybe I can take you out to dinner or something."

"Sounds good. Now how about lettin' me get some work done here?"

\*     \*     \*

All the way home, Christine's thoughts kept straying to the heap of romance novels in Bessie's bag although she was trying to plan her approach to getting the job. What to wear, how to get out to Waresboro, how she could make a good impression on Mr. Taylor. She tried to muster every fact she might have dormant in the back of her brain about mobile homes. But Bessie's loneliness, as evidenced by the cheap paperbacks, kept pushing out her responsible thoughts and making her sad. She remembered the kid at the restaurant and his obvious adoration of Bessie, and guessed that he was lonely too. How sad that people can't get together better, to care for each other, to fill the empty places. Her eyes filled with tears as she thought how lucky she was to have Danny.

Danny! She could be put in jail for what was going on between them. Oh Lord, what was she going to do about this? Why did he have to be so beautiful? Why did he have to smell so good? Why did he have to be so sweet and so easy to talk to? Why couldn't Jack be more like Danny? Why couldn't Jack be *here*?

She hadn't heard from Jack since she had gotten that strange little letter. Her concern was turning to anger as she thought about it. It had been over 3 weeks, and no word. He *had* to know she was worried about him. She guessed he didn't even care how she was working out paying the bills, much less what she might be imagining the "trouble" could be. How could he be so, so *inconsiderate*? She would never, never put him through anything like this! She just might call him again out on the drilling platform. She remembered Tony's irritated, brusque voice and decided against that course of action. Damn Jack! He just didn't care. He...

*Okay, Christine. Hold it in the road. Get that job, take the money out of the bank and get yourself a car. You can take care of yourself!*

She took a deep breath and looked out of the bus window. She felt better. She'd just forget about school tomorrow and work on getting the job. She tried to imbue herself with the confidence that Bessie seemed to have in her. She pictured herself in a business suit, hair done up on top of her head, driving a car. Her own car. A shiny, sleek little red car.

Would Danny come over tonight? Of course he would. How were they going to keep this from blowing up in their faces? Her mind went blank. Danny...

\* \* \*

Arriving home, she couldn't believe it, but she had another letter from

Jack! Thank goodness. Now, maybe she'd find out what had happened. She ripped it open at the mailbox and started reading:

"Dear Christine,

Send me $750.00 soon as you can. I had to get a lawyer to get this stuff settled down here. Get it out of the bank and get me a money order. I need it by Friday." *My God! Today was Tuesday!* "Don't worry, I'm fine. These bastards just try to take Americans for all they can get.

Love, Jack"

She felt the familiar sick panic. She'd have to get to the bank first thing and get the money order in the morning mail. Maybe she should wire it to him. No, she'd just do what he asked. But they had less than $2,000.00 in their checking account. How could she buy a car, now? What about her job interview?

She hurried in, sat down at the kitchen table and started a "To-Do" list for tomorrow: First, the bank and the money order. She'd take stamps with her and get it right into the mail. Next, call Mr. Taylor and set up a job interview. Then call Waycross Transit and get a schedule of busses to Waresboro.

No! First the bus schedule, then the interview appointment, and *then* the bank. It was pretty clear now, how important it was for her to get a job. She wasn't going to let *anything* mess that up!

*I can't believe Jack still hasn't told me what the "trouble" is.*

Instead of the pretty, shiny little car she'd been picturing herself driving around, she'd just have to settle for an older, cheaper one. If she couldn't get anything for the small amount she had in savings, she'd use most of what was left in the joint checking account after she sent Jack the $750.00 he needed. If necessary, she'd try to borrow some money. She had good credit. Luckily, she had always paid the mortgage note on time. If she had a job, she could probably borrow what she needed. And she'd start her own checking account.

Yes. She had a plan now. She changed into a little silky robe and had already started to relax a little when she heard Danny's tap at the kitchen door.

She welcomed him in without hesitation or guilt; with the comfortable familiarity of a trusted old friend. "Hello, Sweetheart. I've missed you. What took you so long? And what's this coming in the back door about? Has anybody said anything... You're not ashamed to be seen coming here, are you?" She realized that that was an inane question as soon as it was out.

"Are you kiddin'? I wish everybody knew! My girl! Look at you - the best lookin' woman in town. But Mama's buggin' me a lot... I just thought it'd be better if..."

"I know, Sweetheart. You're right, you're right. That was a silly question. Come here to me and let me make up for it." She wrapped her arms around him, kissed him, gently sucked at his ear lobe and then whispered, "How long can you stay? I've got a little surprise for you."

"Oh, Jesus! As long as you want, you sexy..."

She led him through the bedroom and into the bathroom. She had placed candles of all different sizes, scents and colors around the bath. She lit them now, turned off the light and turned on the water in the bathtub. She unfastened the robe and turned to him. The steam began to rise from the tub. She unbuttoned his jeans and lowered the zipper as he pulled off his tee-shirt. Her robe slipped from her shoulders as she knelt before him and pulled his jeans to the floor. The peach-colored skin of her shoulders and breasts glowed in the candlelight. She rose slowly, rubbing her breasts against his muscular thighs, the bulk of his penis, the smooth, hard flatness of his stomach and chest. Her nipples were red, the little points erect. Looking up at him with eyes unfocused by lust, she raised her arms, removed a clip from her hair and let it fall around her shoulders.

"You're the most beautiful thing I've ever seen," he muttered hoarsely. He picked her up as the robe fell to the floor, held her to his chest and let her slide slowly down his body until his penis, now hard as a rock, was thrust between her legs.

"Wait, wait, Sweetheart. I'm not through. We're taking a bubble bath." She turned and poured thick pink liquid from a little bottle into the steaming water, as a mountain of inviting white bubbles began to rise from the water. She picked up a puff of the foam and divided it into two equal parts, and placed one carefully on the tip of each breast before she looked up at him. "Whaddaya think?" she asked him with a wicked little smile.

"I think I'm losin' my mind. I think I'm gonna eat you alive."

She tested the temperature of the water with one small red-tipped toe and stepped in, pulling him after her. The world fell away and there was nothing beyond the flickering warm lights of the little candles and the magic of touching each other.

## Chapter 18

Next morning, Christine skipped school and followed her plan. Sure enough, Stan Taylor was waiting for her call, and said he'd like to see her that afternoon. She made the appointment for 1:30, allowing herself 15 minutes from the scheduled arrival of the Waresboro Transit bus at the intersection nearest the Taylor-Made Homes plant.

She dressed carefully in her most business-like little navy-blue cotton dress with its wide, white collar. Very lady-like. As she put on her make-up, Danny's voice sang in her head, "You're beautiful, woman. You're the most beautiful thing I ever saw." She did feel beautiful. Her face was more alive, her green eyes brighter than ever before. Her whole body still tingled from their love-making last night. It had been slower and more deliberate. They had both held back just enough in the exquisite sensual indulgence to build the intensity to an almost unbearable level of desire. She had been lost in time and space, in a quintessence of pleasure. When he erupted inside her, she was catapulted into an orgasm frightening in its power.

She had never imagined that someone would savor every inch of her body the way Danny did. She stepped back and checked herself out in the mirror. She *was* beautiful! She'd just never really known it before. She pinned her lush red curls up into a bun, fastened on her small pearl earrings and sallied forth with happy confidence.

Before she caught the Waresboro bus, she was able to stop by the bank, get the money Jack needed and put a money order into the mail. He'd never get it by Friday, but so what? She had done just as he asked.

\* \* \*

She got the job, starting the next Monday! She couldn't believe how easy it was. Bessie had done such a good selling job for her that Mr. Taylor acted like she was doing him a big favor to come to work at his plant. He did seem like a nice man, and he talked about his business with a child-like enthusiasm. He needed her to do some relatively simple office tasks right now, while she learned the business. Later, he planned to buy a computer, and hoped she would be able to set it up for him and automate most of his accounting functions. Christine was excited and scared at the same time, more scared than excited. Well, like her daddy told her, you never knew what you could do until you tried. Right? She wished she could talk to her daddy right now. She knew he would tell her that she could do it. She'd call her mother and tell her all about it, but she knew she wouldn't get much encouragement from *that* source.

*Danny. I'll talk to Danny about this. He'll be excited and proud, I'll bet.*

Now she just had to get that car. She'd do that tomorrow. She still had the rest of the afternoon to check into where the used car lots were and how to get there. Then she'd go by the school and see about taking night classes. She'd check in with Bessie and see when she could take her out to dinner. She really owed that woman a lot.

She was on her way. It felt wonderful. Tomorrow, the car!

Tonight, Danny!

*He'll be impressed, I'll bet.*

\* \* \*

Danny had left home that evening, headed again in the opposite direction from Christines's house and circled around through the tall pines, before he tapped on her back door. His mother had really been getting on his case the last few days about how much time he was spending next door. He had just about given out of excuses as to why he was over there so much, too. In a way, he wanted to tell the whole world about what was going on between them; his *conquest*! But he had enough sense to keep his mouth shut, except for daily, enthusiastically received reports to Mark and Jimmy.

His dad had been asking him stupid questions, too, like, "Son, is there anything you want to talk to me about?"

Of course the answer was always, "Naw, Dad. Whaddaya mean?"

\* \* \*

When Christine opened the back door, Danny knew immediately that something good had happened.

"Guess what? I got the job." She threw out her arms in an exuberant gesture. "I got it!"

"Way to go, girl!" He grabbed her, and with her arms still spread out and her head thrown back in laughter, he whirled her around the room. After knocking over one kitchen chair and breaking a glass, they collapsed onto another chair into a riot of laughter and kisses.

Then, of course, one thing led to another…

\*   \*   \*

Later, back home in his room, Danny lay in his rumpled bed and thought about how proud he was of Christine and how happy he was about her job. Yeah, but he was *really* excited that she was getting a car. Now they could meet somewhere, go places together, do things without everybody having to know about it. They could go fishing. He'd show her the Okefenokee. She'd love it! They'd go down Alligator Creek one night, put out some drop lines, wrap up in a blanket and make out. She might be a little scared if they heard a bobcat yowl or an alligator bellow. He'd laugh and hug her and tell her there wasn't anything to be afraid of. If they caught any fish, he'd scale 'em, gut 'em and filet 'em on the spot. They'd cook 'em over a campfire. It'd be great! He couldn't wait.

He punched his pillow into a lumpy shape, hugged it to himself and fell asleep with a smile on his face.

\* \* \*

A few days later, Christine headed for school after work, driving her little car, her used Volkswagen Bug. It was yellow, had a dented right front fender, a rear bumper slightly askew, and it could've used a new coat of paint, but she loved it. It ran like a top. It was like her, she thought; slightly used, full of spunk, and zipped around everywhere. It got the job done.

She stopped for a hamburger and then arrived at school at 6:30. Just the day before, she had arranged to switch from day to evening classes, three nights a week. Now, she headed directly for Bessie's office for a quick chat before class.

"Hey, Bessie. How's it going?"

"Hey, Red. Great! Say, how does it feel to be part of the work force? Stan tells me you're just what he's been looking for."

Christine laughed and shook her head. "I don't know what makes him think that. I haven't done anything, yet. Answered a few telephone calls, sorted out some papers. He's got a real mess out there."

"Guess he needs a housekeeper first thing."

"Either that, or an inventory system. He doesn't even know what he's got. Listen, how about coming out to my place for dinner? Then we could maybe take in a movie or something."

"Sure, I could do that. When?"

"This weekend? Saturday night?"

"I'll be there. What time?"

"How about 7:00?"

"I'll be there."

"Great."

After giving Bessie her telephone number and directions to her house, Christine headed for her new class in high spirits. Bessie would be the first real guest she'd had since she moved to Waycross. She'd been a fool, hanging around her house, feeling lonely all the time except when Danny was around. She'd already met a couple of potential new friends at Taylor-Made Homes, too. With a little shiver, she realized that she was already stepping into that picture she had had of herself, a business woman with an office job. A job that was going to give her a chance to use her brain. That'd be a switch!

She slipped into class and took a back seat. It'd probably take her a while to catch up to wherever they were, but she knew she could do it. "*Would* do it," Bessie would say.

\* \* \*

Saturday night was a lot of fun. Christine splurged on a couple of steaks that she grilled on her dinky little charcoal grill out in the back yard, while she and Bessie had a beer. She had baked some potatoes and made a salad and they had a modest feast, seated at the rickety table by the grill. They topped it off with an apple pie which Christine had baked, much to Bessie's amazement. They swapped some good girl-talk and laughed heartily at Bessie's many jokes about the frailties of men. The conversation was so lively that it got to be too late for a movie, so they just washed up the dishes and lounged around in the living room until they had finished off a six-pack. Bessie left at about midnight, after several minutes of loud good-byes and see-ya-Mondays followed by a bravura of squealing tires.

They would have been astonished to know that for much of the evening, they had been watched with smoldering female malice from behind the neat lace curtains of the house next door.

\*   \*   \*

Danny had really been disappointed that Christine made plans for Saturday night that didn't include him. She had explained how much she owed Bessie, and how she had promised her a dinner as soon as she got a job.

"Besides," she added, "you need to spend time with your friends, go out with people your own age."

"You sound like you're my mother."

"Oh, Lord, not that! It's true, though. We've got to keep up our separate lives, just like we would have if this had never happened."

"Well, maybe…"

"We do, Sweetheart. I love… I really care about you, and I can't stand to think that I'm doing you any harm, interfering with your life. I want to make your life better, not worse."

"Then let's do something Sunday. Wanna go see the Okefenokee? Do some fishing?"

"Oh, yes! I've wanted to get out there ever since I came here. Let's do it!"

\*   \*   \*

So now it was Sunday morning. She was to pick Danny up at the Seminole Avenue bus stop, on the south-west side of Waycross at 10:00. She danced around the kitchen singing "Ah-louie-lou-way, a-wee, a-wee-de-lou, de-lou de-ay" and other unintelligible non-words, as she packed a picnic lunch. She made ham sandwiches, potato salad, deviled eggs and a thermos of lemonade. She packed a big bag of potato chips and a bag of devil's food squares, as she changed the words to "I really feel good, oh yeah, oh yeah, I feel so devilish. Ya-ya-ya-ya-ya. A-louie-lou-way…" and so on. She had already put her beach towel, some paper plates, forks, cups and napkins, and a can of bug-spray in the car. Danny said he would take care of the fishing equipment.

She added a couple of apples to the picnic basket. She hadn't been on a picnic since she was a kid, before her daddy died. Her eyes welled up with tears. Oh, thank God for Danny.

She'd washed her hair that morning and it shone like newly polished copper as she brushed it out. She was careful putting on her makeup, making sure she looked as fresh and pretty as possible, without looking "made-up." She put on her flattering white halter top, a tight-fitting pair of soft old jeans, and a plain cotton blue work-shirt over the seductive little top. She checked herself out in the mirror. Perfect! She looked natural, like she was going fishing, not too fancy, but still sexy. She put on her most glamorous sun glasses, grabbed the picnic basket and danced out the door.

"Ah-louie-lou-way…"

\*   \*   \*

Danny was waiting at the bus stop. Good! Nobody was in sight. The only building nearby was the corrugated-tin-roofed shed of the Williams & Johnson Lumber Mill, which naturally was deserted on a Sunday morning. "Smart guy!" she thought, about Danny's choice of meeting places. Then, out of nowhere, with a wrenching sense of doom, she realized that she *loved him*! She was *in love with him*! She trusted him and depended upon his judgment. She would put her life in his hands if need be. Her head whirled with the unreality of the thing. How had this happened? A boy. She was *in love with a boy.*

She got out of the car slowly as he strode confidently toward her with his springy, athletic step. Her heart swelled with tenderness as he moved closer. She wanted to devour him, to take him wholly into herself, or conversely, to be absorbed by him. She steadied herself against the car as her knees started to buckle under her.

"Hey, woman! Let's go fishing!" he said as he opened the door on the passenger side of the car. "There's a big, fat catfish calling my name out in Alligator Creek."

As quickly as it had come, her sense of doom evaporated, and a flood of joy took its place. "I'm there. Just tell me which way." She jumped into the car, slammed the door with a flourish, started the engine and turned to him with eyebrows raised high in an exaggerated questioning look.

"You're my honey, you know that?" he said and took her face in his hands and kissed her.

As she pulled away from him, she patted the accelerator with her foot—vroom, vroom—and rolled her eyes.

"Which way?"

They both laughed as the little car lurched forward in the direction in which Danny was pointing.

## Chapter 19

Danny directed Christine down a series of narrow roads that changed from asphalt to gravel, then gravel to dirt, and narrowed with each change. The roads began to be bordered with still black water, serene with creamy white water lilies. The farther they went into the piney woods, the more mirror-like standing water she saw, the more she felt the nearness of the great swamp.

The narrow road ended in a small group of unpainted buildings. There was a ramshackle cabin with a sagging front porch. The porch was furnished with several worn-out rocking chairs and an ancient wringer-washer. Close by was a shed-like building with a hand-painted sign hanging at an angle above the door saying "Miltons Bate Shop." An empty pig-sty with a broken fence was near-by, as well as several other unidentifiable buildings, probably chicken houses or storage sheds, Christine thought.

No one was in sight.

"We're here," Danny announced joyfully.

Christine looked around nervously to see if there might be any threat to either their safety or their anonymity. Danny saw her worried look and gave her a reassuring wink.

"Don't worry, nobody comes here except the old swamp families. I had a terrible time talking them into renting us some fishing gear and selling us some bait. If we're lucky, we might talk them into renting us a canoe."

"How'd you know about this place?"

"Oh, my dad brought me out here a few times when we use to go fishing. He knows some of the old swampers."

"Oh no! What if they tell your dad we were out here together?"

"Hey, I told you not to worry. These folks don't have any truck with the town folks. Besides that, they don't talk much about *anything* to *anybody* ." He got out of the car.

"If you don't mind, I think I'll just stay in the car."

Danny ignored her and lifted the picnic basket out of the back seat. "Come on. Let's walk down to the creek. That's where they prob'ly are."

"Well, I…"

"You're gonna love Alligator Creek."

She reluctantly picked up the bag containing the beach towel and other picnic stuff and followed Danny. He was peering into the dark interior of the "Bate Shop" and calling, "Hey, anybody home? It's Danny Wilkins. Olin? Harry?" The small building had a jumble of fishing poles, boxes and oil drums scattered around on its dirt floor. Along one wall were some wooden structures which looked like bunk beds, except that they were covered with moss and mud. Danny pointed to these and explained, "Worm beds."

Christine shuddered and whispered, "Gee, I hope they're all asleep."

He wiggled his fingers at her menacingly and took her hand and led her down a winding path behind the building, calling out every few seconds, "Yoo-hoo! It's Danny Wilkins." Then softly, to Christine, "They're nice folks, but sometimes if you come up on 'em too fast, they might shoot first and ask questions later."

"Oh Lord, Danny, what're you getting me into?"

"You're gonna love it!"

The path led to a shaky-looking dock built out into a small dark river.

"There she is, Alligator Creek," Danny said, beaming. The movement of the water was so slow that the surface had the same glassy mirror-like quality that Christine had seen in the standing water beside the roads. The thick greenery on the opposite side was perfectly reflected in the dark water. Two figures were bent over a wide, flat boat, loading something into it. A long pole rose out of the black water and leaned onto the deck next to the boat. A large hunting knife was lashed to the end of the pole.

Danny shouted, "Olin, is that you?"

One of the figures stood up slowly. "Yeah, Danny. Look, y'all jes git yer fishin' stuff outta the shed, and leave the money on the porch, under the warsher. Me'n Harry's goin' after Slewfoot."

"*Slewfoot?*"

"That sorry bear kilt my best hawg last night."

"But, Olin, you can't hunt him down in the swamp. You know the Feds'll get you for that."

"They'll hafta find us first. The women and liddle-uns is gone over to Ma Chesser's, they be so scairt that bear's a-comin' back."

Neither of the men had acknowledged Christine's presence. That was fine with her. The second man, Harry, hadn't even looked up or spoken to Danny. They were loading rolled-up sleeping bags, a large beat-up cooler, several rifles and a metal box Christine guessed was filled with ammunition. She was relieved when they pushed the flat boat out into the water and began to move it downstream, Harry hunched over in the front of the boat and Olin standing in the back, pushing effortlessly on the pole.

Danny called after them, "Okay if I use the canoe?"

"Jes leave another five under the warsher."

Harry swung his head slowly in their direction and turned his scarred face up toward them. He was the ugliest man Christine had ever seen. One milky blank eye stared vacantly into the pines, the other focused vaguely somewhere near their feet. His mouth opened into a menacing, toothless grin. "And be keerful ya don't git offen the main creek. Ya might git ya-selves shot." He spit a stream of brown liquid out into the water and returned to his original slouch. "That's accident-ly, of course. Heh, heh, heh."

The boat disappeared around a bend.

"*Shot*? Get ourselves *shot*?" Christine shuddered.

"They got a still or two back in the woods. It's okay, though. They know I'm not gonna go looking for it. That was Harry's idea of a joke."

"And did I hear them right?" Christine asked. "Are they really going out to kill a *bear*?"

"If they can find him, I guess."

"What did you mean about the 'Feds' getting them?"

"You can't hunt in the swamp anymore. It's a wildlife preserve or something. Come on, let's get the canoe and get going." He held his face close to hers and said in a deep, conspiratorial voice, "It's just you, me and the swamp."

"Oh, boy! Just you, me and the swamp…" *…and the bears, and the alligators, and some crazy guys with guns…*

"Come on, help me with the canoe and the fishing gear. Time's a-wastin'."

"Oh yeah, time's a-wastin', time's a-wastin'."

Christine followed Danny back up the twisting path to where a scarred old canoe was resting upside down on two sawhorses. "Wait here a minute," Danny said, and bounded up to the shack with the porch, pulled some bills out of his pocket and put them under a rock lying under the beat-up old washing machine. .

"I could help pay—"

"No, no," Danny interrupted. "This is my treat. You can help me with the canoe, though." He bent under one end and lifted it easily. "You get the other end, okay?"

Christine stooped under the other end of the canoe and, placing a hand on each side, took a big breath and pushed upward with all her strength. It was much easier than she had expected.

*Okay. So far so good.*

They carried the little craft down to the water's edge, turned it upright and returned to "Miltons Bate Shop" for the fishing poles and bait.

Christine volunteered, "Tell you what. I'll get the poles and you can get the bait."

Danny laughed. "You're not afraid of a few wiggledy little worms, are you?"

"Well, I..."

He grabbed her off her feet and spun around with her. "Don't worry. I'll protect you from the bad old worms." And then, with real feeling, "This is so great, getting you out here. Believe me, you're gonna love it!"

She brightened with determined new resolve. "Well, come on then, silly. Let's do it!"

They loaded the picnic things and the fishing supplies: poles, line, hooks, a can of worms, a bucket with holes in it to submerge in the water to keep alive the fish that they caught, a couple of red bobbers. Danny helped her into the front of the canoe and pushed it out into the smooth, silent black water. He got into the back as it glided gracefully forward and turned it toward the great swamp with a gentle sweep of his oar.

*He's so happy out here. He wants me to love it like he does.*

Christine forced herself to relax and began to open her senses to the reality of the Okefenokee. She leaned back against the picnic basket and looked up into the tops of the tall pines rising behind the thick bushes lining the creek. A hawk swooped down across the water ahead of them and disappeared into the trees on the other side. Satiny white water lilies rested peacefully on their dark green leaves on each side of the boat. Elegant gray draperies of Spanish moss lent an air of wisdom to the swamp. It was a living, breathing thing. It had been out here, so close to her, quietly following its own purposes for all the time she had been struggling to survive in her small, insignificant life. It had been out here like this for thousands of years.

"It's really beautiful, Danny."

"Yeah. Look up ahead—cypress trees."

A small group of the courtly old trees rose mysteriously from their perfect reflections, from their cone-shaped bases in the dark water, their languorous branches heavy with moss. Behind them, the massed undergrowth was speckled white, lavender and pink with a variety of small blossoms. The two-toned whistle of a bob-white was followed by a cascade of melody from a mockingbird. Then, from the undergrowth close to the canoe, Christine heard a chorus of little clucks.

"Oh, Danny, slow down. I think there's some baby ducks back in those bushes! Do you hear them?"

Danny laughed. "They're babies, all right, but not ducks. More like baby *alligators*. Calling their mommy."

"Oh my God!" Christine jerked herself up into an alert sitting position, dangerously rocking the frail canoe. "What'll we do?" Her face was ashen with fright.

"Hey, just don't rock the boat! She won't bother us if we don't bother *her*. Just stay cool." He guided the boat away from the clucking sounds and sped up slightly. "Don't worry. We're headed for a hammock. No alligators there, I promise."

"A hammock?"

"A little dry island. 'Gators like the water. You don't see 'em all that much on dry land."

Christine took a deep breath and willed the peace and beauty of the swamp to reclaim her. She turned and smiled at him. "Okay, if you say so. My big, brave swamper." She leaned back against the picnic basket again, looked up into the cypress trees and whispered, "Okefenokee, Okefenokee," as if it were an incantation.

"It's an Indian word. Means 'land of the trembling earth'. There's little islands out here that float on the water. You can feel them trembling under you when you walk on them."

"You're kidding me."

"No, it's the truth. You'll see."

By the time Danny pulled the canoe up onto the grassy bank of the hammock, Christine was completely under the spell of the Okefenokee. They unloaded the picnic basket and fishing tackle, and she spread the beach towel and began to lay out the delectable lunch while he baited the hooks from the repugnant can of worms. He set the two poles in the dense undergrowth beside the water. The lines stretched gently downstream in the slow-moving water, with the little red "bobbers" resting on the surface to let them know when they got a bite. He came back just as she was coring and slicing the apples.

Pulling the can of insect repellant out of her bag, she turned to Danny. "Come here, Honey, and let me spray you with my bug-spray."

"I don't need that. It's too early in the spring for flies and gnats, and there aren't any mosquitoes in the swamp."

"No mosquitoes in the swamp? You're kidding me, of course."

"No, really. Something in the water kills them. We've got bobcats and bears, but no mosquitoes. You don't need that stuff. It won't keep the alligators and bears off you, anyway."

"Danny, stop that! You're trying to scare me." She punched at his arm, but he grabbed her wrist and pulled her to him. "And you're doing a pretty good job."

"It won't keep me off, either."

"Oh, you're hopeless," she said. She sat down and tried to regain a little control, asking, "Are we in the wildlife preserve?"

"No, it starts about a quarter mile further downstream. Man, this looks good." He sat down beside her and began to unbutton her shirt.

"Danny! What are you doing?"

"Just trying to make you comfortable." He gasped when he saw the sexy little white halter top she was wearing under her work-shirt. The same revealing little scraps of material she was wearing on the day she had asked him to call her "Christine" instead of "Ma'am." He remembered it well.

"Oh, man, you don't know how many times I've wanted to get my hands inside this." He untied the halter straps at the back of her neck and let it fall to her waist. He moaned, "Look at you..." and gently stroked her breasts with his finger tips. He kissed the little cradle at the base of her neck, and began making a warm path of small licks and nibbles down to the deep pink nipples straining toward him. She arched her back and lay back on the beach towel with a delicious sense of abandonment. He slipped his hands underneath her back, untied the bottom of the halter and threw it aside. The sun was hot on her bare skin, and a whisper of a cool breeze touched her gently.

*I'm his. He can do anything he wants with me.*

He unfastened her jeans and lowered the zipper as his lips moved down over her belly. She lifted her hips to help him slip off her jeans and little pink bikini panties, exposing a fluff of coppery hair. Deliberately, he kissed the inside of one thigh and then the other.

"Oh, that sweet pussy, that sweet little pussy," he murmured.

She stretched voluptuously back, naked. It occurred to her briefly that they might be discovered, that the strange Olin and Harry might return, but it didn't matter. She was riding a continuum of beauty, mystery and pleasure which flowed through this place—which had for thousands of years. The warm sun, cool breeze and rivulets of birdsong bewitched her and lulled her into a deep contentment.

Danny rubbed his head gently on her belly and nuzzled her belly-button with his nose.

She giggled. "Oh no! I'm ticklish there."

"How about here?" He kissed her lower abdomen.

She ran her fingers into his hair and pressed his face harder against her. "Oh, that's good, that's so good."

"How about here?" he continued as he kissed the inside of her thigh again, this time moving up slowly toward the puff of red hair between her legs. She moaned, no longer able to talk.

*   *   *

Later, Christine lay blissfully in the warm sunshine as Danny gathered up their clothes and began to dress himself. They had walked barefoot, naked, hand in hand back to the dark water and bathed each other in the cool, pure water which was cleansed and colored by the tannin from the roots of the lush aquatic plant life.

From her peaceful languor, Christine looked up at him dreamily. "You were right. I felt the earth tremble."

Danny laughed. "Me too, and this island doesn't even float."

A serious look passed over her face. "Danny, you know what? I love you. I'm really in love with you."

"Well, it's about time you admitted it."

"So that's all the response I get for making that, that *momentous* declaration!"

"Well, let's face it. I kinda guessed it a long time ago." He kneeled down and kissed her cheek. "I love you, too. You're the best thing that ever happened to me."

She began to get dressed as he turned his attention to the picnic lunch.

"I'm starving," he growled as he popped half of a deviled egg into his mouth and unwrapped a ham sandwich. He looked up at the sky, "Mmm, hmm... And she can cook, too." He heaped a big mound of potato salad on a paper plate and crunched a handful of potato chips into his mouth.

Christine started loading up her plate with exaggerated urgency. In an affected southern accent she drawled, "Lordy, mercy! There won't be a *thang* left for poor lil' ol' me if I don't hurry!"

*Life is so good. Thank you, God.*

After a minute she asked, "Do you still come out here with your dad?"

"Naw, I haven't for a while. I usually fish with Mark and Jimmy, but not out here. We mostly go down Gum Swamp Creek. It's closer. Dad wants to come, I guess, but, I don't know, he sorta gets in the way."

"What do you mean?"

"He's just a stick-in-the-mud. And he, well, he embarrasses me. He's got such old-fashioned ideas, and he's always got that wad of chewing tobacco in his jaw—spitting all the time. Mark and Jimmy make fun of him. He *embarrasses* me."

"You said he knew some of the old swampers."

"Yeah, he does. His grandmother was a Chesser. He knows the swamp, all right."

"Well, he seems like a nice guy to me."

"He's nice enough, all right, and a damned good fisherman. Used to like to take me hunting, too. He's a real good shot. I just wish he could be more—you know—cool."

"I guess my father was kinda like that. Real quiet and easy-going. Working hard as he could all the time, but never really getting ahead. You're lucky you've still got your father. I wish I still had mine. I wish I could tell him what a great guy he was. I don't think anybody ever told him that." Christine's reached down into the picnic basket and brought out the devil's food squares as her eyes filled with tears. "Mark and Jimmy ought to be ashamed of themselves, making fun of him! And you shouldn't let them get to you." She paused. "Want a cookie?"

Danny was gazing thoughtfully out over the water. He took the little chocolate square without looking at her. "You're right, you know. I guess I don't give him much credit. He's really..." He dropped the cookie, jumped up and scrambled to where he had set the poles. "We've got a bite!" One of the little red bobbers was doing just that, bouncing up and down in the water.

* * *

Later, as the sun was sinking behind the mossy trees, filling the sky with color, turning the air a soft pink, they paddled leisurely back upstream. Christine had actually caught two fish, an ugly catfish and a jackfish. She had felt excitement and pride as she brought the fish in, and then as she watched them thrashing so desperately to free themselves and return to the water, she felt sorry for them. She had killed two blameless creatures that wanted so much to live. Danny laughed at her for her sentiment, then hugged her and called her his "little bleeding-heart."

Now, Christine relaxed into a deep sense of fulfillment, as her paddle slipped smoothly into the easy flow and helped move the canoe back upstream. She did love this place, just as Danny had predicted. She felt at home. The ancient and beautiful swamp had accepted her, and the fears she had felt earlier had evaporated.

*"Alligator Creek." It sounds like music.*

## Chapter 20

Jack had just about worn out his welcome with Tony. He had managed to get into a big fracas with Rosita's father in court. There had been a loud, confusing argument when Senor Valdez had tried to get some pesos to compensate for his daughter's terrible experience. Jack stated flatly that he had relieved himself of all responsibility with the fine imposed by the court. Senor Valdez disagreed. A chaos of multi-lingual insults and threats resulted, accompanied by a melee of menacing finger-pointings, fist-shakings, red faces and necks with protruding veins. An ineffectual interpreter tried to impose some calm and logic onto the situation, but managed only to add to the confusion.

Unfortunately, this sorry drama took place in the courtroom, over the tearful wailings of the wronged Rosita and under the cold intolerance of the judge. The result was another fine for Jack, for contempt of court, as best Jack could understand. Tony was not amused. He suggested that Jack would do well to start looking for employment elsewhere.

The additional fine now meant that Jack wouldn't have *any* money to send to Red. He'd just about quit worrying about Red, anyway. He had enough troubles of his own. On top of everything else, he felt sick and even feverish a lot of the time. A few days after one of his visits to the Blue Parrot, he had noticed a small blister-like bump on his penis, accompanied by an unpleasant discharge. He decided he'd better see a doctor next time he was in Tampico, and stay away from the Blue Parrot, but the problem went away after a few days and he put it out of his mind.

On his next visit to the Parrot, he had gotten into the mess with Rosie and the Mexican Police. As if that wasn't enough to worry about, he now had a big swollen lump on one side of his groin. It throbbed, it interfered with his sleep at night, and the damned thing just kept getting bigger. A couple of new "weevils" from Jamaica had noticed it in the shower, and had laughed at him.

"Hey, mon, you got one helluva *bubo* there. Who you been messin' 'round wit'? You better get youself to the doctor befo' it start turnin' blue!"

"Mind your own fuckin' business," Jack snarled.

"No problem, mon!" The weevils laughed and exchanged knowing looks as they left the shower.

Their warning stuck in his mind. Maybe he'd better see a doctor. Shit!

His work began to suffer. He had always been proud of his physical strength and quickness. Now, he was making foolish mistakes, dropping things, feeling dizzy. When he continued having trouble sleeping at night, he started taking sleeping pills when he was able to sneak them from the first-aid cabinet without anyone knowing about it.

After about a month of this, when Tony couldn't ignore the problems any longer, he called Jack into his small, messy office. "Look, buddy, I've done about all I can to git you through the stupid mess you got yourself into, but I can't put up with sloppy work. You're costin' me money, man. I think you oughta take a little vacation, a few weeks off, go home and get yourself in shape. You're takin' a leave of absence till you can git your ass in gear. Then come on back and we'll try agin'."

"But, Tony, you know I'm the best man you got out here..."

"You might have been *once*, but you sure ain't *now*!"

"You tellin' me to take some vacation?"

"I'm tellin' you to take some *leave* - without pay. You already used up most of your vacation with this Tampico shit!"

"But, Tony, gimme a break. I'll straighten up. I been good for you. I've..."

"And see a doctor soon as you git home. You don't look so good."

Jack was close to punching Tony's lights out, but he managed to control himself until he got back to his bunk. Shit! Things just went from bad to worse. Well, what the hell, he was sick of the whole damn oil business, anyway. He hadn't known when he had it good, driving his own semi, pretty much setting his own hours, seeing something different every day, sleeping with a different broad any time he wanted to. He'd been a fool, all right. A fool for a pretty face. Him! Big, tough Jack Radford. He'd never thought any female could get to him, but he just hadn't been able to keep his hands off

Red's hot-looking little body. Well, she was different from his other women. Smarter. More fun.

Maybe going back to Waycross was the right thing to do, anyway. Go back and get Red and head for home, for Allentown. Sell the damned house for what he could. Try to get himself a rig and get back where he belonged—trucking. Fuck Tony, anyway. So, he was going to do him a big favor and give him another chance, huh? Like hell! He was through with the whole oil thing.

Yeah, he'd call Red tonight and tell her he was on his way. She'd be tickled to death to see him by now. Come to think of it, he kinda missed her, too.

Maybe he should try to see a doctor down here, in case his medical insurance wouldn't cover it when he was on leave, or laid off, or whatever the hell it was that Tony had in mind for him. *Then* he'd call Red.

The bubo throbbed.

\* \* \*

Tony agreed to keep Jack on for two more weeks, until he could get his "business" taken care of. The "business" was a trip to a doctor in Tampico. Jack was wary enough to want to find out what was the matter with him before going back to Waycross. The visit confirmed his worst fears—he had a sexually transmitted disease, an "STD." Damn! They had more initials to identify the STD. They called it "LGV", which he guessed sounded better than "Lymphogranuloma

Venereum", or even "tropical bubo", the street name for it. Disgusting! He thought of it as the plague. The doctor started him on tetracycline, with a strong lecture about how important it was to keep taking it in the right dosage for 3 weeks. That would get the filthy germs out of his system and the bubo would start to go away, but he still might have some other nasty long-term side effects later on. Shit! You didn't even know when they might show up: scar tissue that could "tie the organs in the pelvis together", whatever *that* meant, or "thickening of the skin and tissue of the genitals," and worst of all "some decrease in sensitivity in the area". Damn that filthy slut, Rosie! If he was going to have something wrong with his dick for the rest of his life, he'd kill her!

It had taken Jack a week to get the appointment with the Mexican doctor and get started on the antibiotic. He just had a week left to get rid of the damned bubo before he went back to Waycross and Red. He couldn't let Red know about it. How could he explain to her how he got it? The doctor had assured him that the only way you could get it was by "direct sexual contact." No, you couldn't get it off a toilet seat or a door-knob. No, you couldn't get it by drinking out of a public water fountain or even being in a hot-tub with somebody. Maybe Red wouldn't notice. But what if he started having some of those "long-term" effects? Shit!

When he called Red a few nights later, expecting her to squeal and carry on about how glad she'd be to see him, he got another kick in the head. She didn't act excited at all. In fact, she was a lot more interested in what had happened, why Tony wanted him to take some leave, what kind of trouble he had had the month before. She even had the nerve to ask him what he needed the money for—his own money. She had written him about getting herself a job, and about using all the money they had left to buy herself a car, without even asking him what he thought about it. He could have raised hell with her for buying a car without saying shit to him about it, but he hadn't. He'd had too much else on his mind at the time. Now, when he *needed* a little money in the bank, she'd spent it all. Left him broke. Women!

So, she had gotten herself a job. Big deal! He didn't mention his plan to sell the house and move back to Allentown, though. She had sounded so excited and proud of herself, that he didn't want to talk about *his* plans yet. He wasn't sure now how she'd feel about leaving Waycross and this great new job of hers. He'd take his time and check out some of the details of his plan before he told her about it.

\* \* \*

Jack took a fleeting look out the ferry windows at the furious gray waves of the Gulf and quickly looked back at the floor. Just what he needed! He shook his head in disbelief. A damned hurricane coming into the Gulf just when he had to make his last trip from the platform back to Tampico! He hadn't had a choice, anyway. He was *out*, and another weevil was already moving into his bunk. Now, here he was, looking out at some *big* fuckin' waves, towering over the ferry, smashing down on the deck. He didn't scare easy, but he was scared shitless, now! He hoped they got into Tampico before the airport shut down. As much as he wanted to be on solid ground right now, he damned sure didn't want to get stuck in *that* place.

He had a sharp yearning for the gentle rolling hills of Allentown. Home!

He made it to the airport in time, and the plane to Dallas was waiting for departure on the tarmac, its wings buffeted around by the gusty wind. Jack had a heavy feeling that something terrible was going to happen. He was really afraid to get on a plane in this kind of weather, but once again, he didn't have a choice. Maybe that was what was making him feel so *down*. He wasn't used to being boxed in, not having any choices. He wished he could go back a year or two, when he was driving his own truck, making plenty of money, partying with old friends, free of responsibility. He wouldn't have gotten married, for one thing. He'd have just balled Red and had fun with her. She was a good sport. They'd have been fine without all this marriage shit! It had been his own idea, he had to admit. The first mistake in a whole list of mistakes. Well, he was going to put it right if he could just get back in one piece.

"Flight 287 for Dallas now boarding at gate 2."

*   *   *

As if the rough boat ride hadn't been bad enough, now he was being tossed all over the fuckin' plane. He tried as hard as he could not to let the big black guy sitting next to him know how terrified he really was. He forced himself not to hold on to the arm rests too tight. No white knuckles for Jack Radford! But every time the damn plane took a downward plunge, his stomach lurched up into his throat. After one particularly long plunge, he pulled the air-sick bag out of the seat pocket in front of him with a trembling hand.

"Quite a ride tonight," the guy next to him said in a calm voice.

Jack struggled to look unconcerned as he pretended to read the instructions on the air-sick bag. "I've seen worse." A drink. That's what he needed. "Where's that damned stewardess?"

"I think the captain's got 'em all buckled in till the turbulence smoothes out a little."

"Well, tough. I need a drink." Jack unfastened his seat-belt and started to get up, just as the plane surged upward wildly, throwing him back into his seat. "Shit!"

His neighbor's big, black hand patted him on the arm. "Hey, it'll be all right. We'll be outta this in no time, I betcha."

"Yeah, sure!" Where did this jungle-bunny get off, feeling sorry for *him*? He moved his arm away from the comforting pat.

He tried hard not to imagine what it would be like to dive sickeningly down, the plane screaming as it fell onward and onward. Helpless! He couldn't stand it! He didn't want to die!

He wished he knew how to pray. He wanted to straighten his life out: get well, go back to a job he knew and liked—trucking, settle down and be a family man, spend more time with Red, save some money. He might even go to church some.

He wondered if there were such things as heaven and hell. One thing was damned sure—he didn't want to die! Oh, if only he could be in Waycross right now, holding Red in his arms.

Gradually he realized the plunging, soaring and side-wise lurching were slowing down. He was afraid to let himself believe it though, until the captain's deep, slow-and-easy voice came on the intercom.

"This is your captain. Sorry you folks had to experience that little turbulence back there, but it looks like it's over now. We should have a smooth flight from here on into Dallas. We'll be arriving in an hour and 15 minutes. Weather there is calm and sunny, ground temperature a pleasant 82 degrees. Thanks for flying American, and we hope you'll choose us again next time you fly."

Jack was so relieved he wanted to cry. *Mr. Cool, that captain.* He was envious.

Then the stew's voice, "The captain has turned off the 'fasten your seat belt' lights, and you're now free to move about the cabin. We'll be announcing connecting flight times and gates soon."

*Great, bitch! But how's about a drink?*

The big guy next to him said, "Glad *that's* over. A little of that goes a long way!" He laughed heartily.

"You can say that again!" Jack was shocked to hear his own voice—weak, shaky. Damn! He hoped his neighbor hadn't detected the dredges of the fear he'd felt. He cleared his throat. "Guess I'm getting another damned cold." He got up and headed for the stewardess and a drink.

\* \* \*

Jack was almost back to his old confident self after having a few more drinks during the two hour layover in the Dallas airport, waiting for the flight to Atlanta, then on to Waycross. He felt at ease in the dusky bar, surrounded by weary-looking business men reading newspapers or staring blankly at a televised football game. He bought a local paper at the news stand next door and turned to the sports pages, but couldn't get interested in any of the stories there. They seemed silly after what he'd been through in the last few hours. The terrifying boat trip through the screaming wind and huge waves, and then the sickening flight through the edge of the hurricane had shaken him up pretty bad. In both cases, he thought he was going to die. And the worst of it was that there wasn't a damn thing he could do to help himself. He was used to feeling strong; being in control.

By the time the small commuter plane landed in Waycross, Jack had talked himself into a real hard-on for Red. He kept remembering the fun they'd had drinking beer and dancing all night, surrounded by his friends. The way Red looked up to him, like she knew he'd take care of her, had made him feel strong. She was so little he could pick her up with one arm and whirl her around the dance floor. He could still hear the sound of her laughter when he told a joke. He couldn't wait to see her.

Back in Waycross, as he came out of the plane and down the steps, his eyes scanned the small group of people waiting behind the fence, looking for the flash of her copper-penny hair. Where the hell was she? He had called her and given her his flight number and arrival time. He felt a stab of disappointment. Here he was, back from the edge of death, and she wasn't even there to meet him?

She was waiting at the baggage pick-up area. Damned if she didn't look gorgeous! She was wearing a plain little cream-colored silky blouse and black slacks and flat-heeled black loafers. She looked rich, classy. Her hair was redder and glossier than he had remembered, simple, smooth. Her skin glowed. She looked healthy and happy. He had expected to see her as he remembered her, in high-heeled shoes, skin-tight jeans, a bright sweater, hair teased up into a froth, and wearing lots of make-up. Instead, here she was looking like one of the models he had seen in a magazine on the plane.

She looked like the kind of woman that wouldn't want to give *him* the time of day!

She spotted him, waved and began to make her way toward him. He plowed his big frame through the crowd to her, grabbed her up off her feet and gave her a big bear-hug. Instead of hugging him back, giggling and squealing, as he expected, she seemed embarrassed by the display of affection, and wriggled out of his arms.

She gave him a sisterly kind of hug, patted him on the back and said, "Wow, Jack, you look great! You're so tan! Looks like you've lost a little weight, though."

"You don't look so bad, yourself," he answered warily. "Everything okay?" He looked toward the baggage carousel to hide his confusion at her cool reception.

"Oh, yes! Everything's great! Uh, how was your trip?" Her voice sounded tight. Kinda like that little pat on the back a minute ago.

"Shitty! We came through a damn hurricane. People were so scared they were throwin' up all over the fuckin' plane." He felt anger rising in his chest. This wasn't going the way he had pictured it.

He saw his two huge bags approaching on the carousel, pushed through the crowd, yanked them up easily and turned back to Christine. "Let's git outta here. I'm ready for a cold beer and a hot fuck."

"Oh Jack, hush!" She was blushing. "You're awful," she said with an unconvincing giggle. "Uh... Tell me about life on the oil rig. Was it pretty bad?"

*   *   *

They had a hard time getting Jack's huge bags and big body into the Volkswagen. After some uncomfortable laughter, they started toward home. Jack made another attempt at lighthearted camaraderie and said, "Hey, you know what? If you'da paid a few dollars less, you could'a got a *really* small car."

"It's all I could afford after... That is... Well, let's just say the price was right."

Jack looked out of the window at the alien pines and scratchy-looking palmetto bushes.

He felt sick. The bubo throbbed. *What a shitty homecoming!*

## Chapter 21

A sense of sweet satisfaction swept over Madge as she peeked through the curtains and watched Jack extracting himself from the cramped little Volkswagen. *Now, maybe that hussy will have to behave herself!* This guy wasn't somebody you'd want to mess around with. She had forgotten how big he was. And how rough-looking. She was glad he was back! She gave the dust-cloth in her hand a contented little shake.

She hoped this would put an end to whatever it was that kept Danny hanging around over there so much. Danny thought she didn't know that he was sneaking around through the woods, going in the back door of that witch's house. Hmmph! He thought she was a real fool, didn't he? She knew something was going on, all right. The trouble was, she didn't know what to do about it. Harland was no help, as usual. She couldn't bring herself to ask Danny if he was doing what she was afraid he was doing with that woman. She couldn't even think about it, much less talk about it. It made her sick. *Sick!*

She jerked herself back away from the curtains as Christine looked over toward her house. Had she been spotted? The look on Christine's face was worried, sad, like somebody had died or something. She should be happy to have her husband back home! The hussy!

Madge heard Harland coming in from the garage and crossed the room hastily, pulled a chair over to the tall glass-front cabinet that held his gun collection. She climbed on the chair and began reaching across the top of the cabinet with her cloth, dusting busily.

He called, "Honey, I'm home! What's for supper? Possum stew again?"

"It's on the stove. See for yourself." She was *so* tired of that old "Possum stew" joke, she could scream.

"Whoa, Miss Nellie! Turnip greens and cornbread! I'll go get washed up. Is Danny home yet?"

"No, not yet."

When she heard the shower start, she hurried back over to the window, but the Radfords were already inside their house, and she couldn't see anything that was going on.

She had tried to warn Danny about what kind of woman that Christine was, *a devil-worshipper*, but he just laughed at her. The little smart-mouth even said she was *crazy* to think stuff like that. *Crazy!* Well, he'd see some day. Hmmph. They'd *all* see someday!

\* \* \*

"I'll see about dinner while you unpack," Christine said briskly, "and I guess you noticed, I bought an air-conditioner." It was rumbling away heavily in the bedroom.

"Just a damn minute, Red, what about a little welcome-home? What's going on with you?" Jack grabbed her arm and spun her around and kissed her. She turned the kiss into a friendly little peck and patted him on the arm as she pulled away and hurried into the kitchen.

"I've made your Pennsylvania down-home favorites: pot roast with potatoes and carrots, green beans, spoon bread and guess what? Shoo-fly pie for dessert!" She began heating the dinner she had prepared earlier and setting the table with a kind of frantic good-will. "I almost forgot to tell you. Mother's getting married next month. Marrying that two-bit preacher. It's no surprise, but—"

"C'mere, Red. I got you a present," Jack interrupted from the bedroom.

"Oh, you shouldn't... Okay, I'll be right there." She took a deep breath and stifled the urge to run out the back door.

*I want Danny. What am I going to do? Danny, Danny...*

She released the deep breath with a sigh of resignation, turned and started toward the bedroom.

Jack was holding a yellowed plastic bag out toward her. "Here. This is for you. Try it on."

"Oh, Jack..." She opened the bag and pulled out a heavily embroidered peasant blouse, with a round neck gathered onto a string tie. The material beneath the elaborate floral embroidery was white and very sheer. "It's beautiful."

"Try it on."

"Oh, I'm sure it'll fit."

"Try it on, I said."

"Well, I…" She turned her back to him and with shaking fingers began to unbutton her silk shirt. She slipped out of it quickly and began to pull the peasant blouse down over her head.

"No. Take off the bra, too. I want to see those tits."

She looked over her shoulder and pleaded, "Oh, Jack… What about the dinner? I…"

"Take off the bra."

Really shaking now, with her back still toward him, she removed the bra and quickly slipped into the sheer blouse.

"Turn around."

"Jack, I…"

"Turn around."

She turned slowly, her unfettered, full breasts swinging slightly—clearly visible under the blouse. She desperately wanted to cover herself.

"Oh, *yeah*! There they are. Those pink nipples I've been missin'. Oh, yeah. Come here, Super-tits."

"The dinner's going to burn. I need to check the—"

"Come here. I'm havin' *you* for dinner. My sexy little wife."

She took a few hesitant steps toward him.

*Oh, God help me! Please help me. Please! I don't know what to do.*

He covered the distance between them in two steps, put a big hand on each defenseless breast and squeezed. She squirmed under the pain.

He squeezed even harder. "Feels like a perfect fit to me. What do you think?"

"Yes, yes, it fits fine. I..." Her eyes filled with tears.

He reached his hands up under the blouse and began to twist each nipple. "I've got something else here that oughta be a perfect fit for you. Take off those pants and spread your legs."

"Oh, Jack, can't we wait till after dinner? I need to go see about..."

"I'm havin' my dinner right here, right now," he said as he unfastened her belt and jerked her slacks down over her hips. "Lie down." He pushed her back onto the bed and pulled her slacks off roughly. His big body came down heavily on top of her as he pulled her panties off of one leg and forced her legs apart. His tongue plunged into her mouth as his penis scraped the walls of her vagina. He held her hips tightly in his callused hands and crushed her body against his with every hard thrust. She cried out in pain as he grunted, "Uh, uh, uhhhh," and came in her quickly. He collapsed on her for a moment and then rolled over.

"Yeah, that's more like it!" he growled. "Now you can go see about that dinner you're so worried about."

She forced back the tears as she gathered her clothes and staggered to the bathroom.

"Wear that new blouse, and I don't wanna see no bra under it!"

*Oh, Danny, Danny. What am I going to do? Please God, what am I going to do?*

## Chapter 22

Danny found himself in an unfamiliar state of shock. He had known all along, of course, that Christine, his own, his beautiful Christine was married—that there was a husband somewhere, but he had never pictured the actuality of another man in her house, touching her, lying in her bed. He lay on his bed now, staring at the ceiling, sick with frustration and helplessness. His life had ground to a halt. His arms ached with the need to hold her close to him, despair gnawed at the edges of a void in the pit of his stomach, and a hopeless weariness sapped the last drop of his strength.

If he just had somebody to talk to—somebody who would understand. He could talk to Mark and Jimmy, of course, but they didn't have the vaguest idea about how he felt. They thought it was all a great joke. He was pretty sure that both of his parents knew what was going on, but this wasn't the kind of thing you could talk to your *parents* about. Anyway, he had never been able to talk to his mother about anything important. It was like she was on another planet. A planet that had these tight rules—strict and stupid! Rules you couldn't bend, no matter what.

He was in a daze at school and couldn't keep his mind on his classwork. He was embarrassed several times when he was called on to answer a question he hadn't heard. Playing football in the afternoon, he had dropped passes, missed tackles, and miscalculated plays.

"Man, what's your problem?" Jimmy had asked, mystified. "I never seen you play like this before!"

"Aw, I'm not feelin' all that good." He left the game before it was over and went home to gaze blankly at the ceiling.

Christine had given him her number at work, and he had tried to call her from a pay phone after school, but she wasn't at her desk. He was afraid to leave a message, or even his name. Now he lived only to make it to tomorrow afternoon when he could call her again.

"Danny, supper's ready. Wash up and come on down, now."

"Sure, Ma. I'll be down in a minute." He didn't have any appetite, but he knew she'd nag him to death if he didn't eat. He dragged himself up and into the bathroom.

Maybe if he went out in his backyard and raked some leaves, he might get a glimpse of her inside her house. But what if he saw her husband? What if he saw him hugging her or something? He couldn't stand that!

He dried his hands and went downstairs, hanging onto the thought, "Tomorrow afternoon, tomorrow afternoon." At least, he'd hear her voice then—maybe.

At the table, he stared moodily at his country-fried steak and mashed potatoes.

"Gravy, Danny?" Madge asked, passing him the bowl of thick, greasy cream gravy. "*Danny*, what's the matter with you? It's your favorite. Are you *sick* or somethin'?"

He looked up, startled. "Huh? Uh, I'm sorry, Ma. Yeah, thanks." He took the bowl and tried to smile at Madge, but his mouth felt stiff.

"Son, how about let's do some fishin' this week-end? They tell me they're bitin' real good down on Gum Swamp Creek," Harland said with forced good humor. "We just need to git out, forget about our troubles sometimes, ya know?"

"Uh, gee Dad. I gotta go see about a… uh… getting a job. Mark said they're hiring down at the Piggly Wiggly."

*Of course, that's it! I'll get me a job, get me some wheels—a motor bike maybe, then I can get out to Waresboro and see her at work. Why didn't I think of that before?*

He brightened. "Yeah, I need to make some money." He heaped gravy into a well he made in the middle of his potatoes. "Mmmm, looks good, Ma."

\* \* \*

It seemed like Jack was drinking more every day. Christine now expected him to be drunk, often blessedly asleep, when she got home. He didn't seem to be making any plans to go back to work on the oil rig and he wasn't looking for another job in Waycross. He avoided getting into any real conversation with her, much to her relief. He side-stepped her questions about what had happened to him in Mexico and showed little interest in what was happening to her on her job and in school. Most of the contact between them had narrowed down to rough, drunken sexual assaults upon her.

Consequently, Christine took every opportunity to stay away from home, grateful for school three nights a week, grateful for all the overtime she could muster on the other two nights. Her afternoon calls from Danny and her visits with Bessie before class kept her from going completely out of her mind.

Her work was becoming more exciting, too, and helped keep her mind off her domestic troubles. Stan had screwed up his courage and bought a computer for Taylor-Made Homes, an IBM 360! He entrusted the operation of the alien genie to Christine. Gordon Palmer, the IBM Systems Engineer, the "SE", had included her in all steps of the installation and testing.

The installation was now complete. Now Stan, Christine and Edda-Lou, the bright young black student Christine had recommended for key-punch operator, were in a meeting with the SE. They reviewed the hardware, the preventive maintenance schedule, and the general plans for development of the applications the company would need in the future.

Gordon, the SE, said, "Christine's not going to have any trouble managing the inventory and billing systems we've installed, but she'll need some 360 Systems classes if you develop any in-house systems. With the COBOL training she already has, all she needs to get started is a few weeks in Atlanta, at the IBM Education Center."

Christine's heart began to pound with excitement. She looked down at her Sparco legal pad and began to make notes with the most business-like demeanor she could muster.

Gordon continued, "There's a class starting in 3 weeks, 'Intro to the 360'. She'll need that and '360 Operating Systems' for starters. They're taught back-to-back, one week for each."

Stan looked a little startled, but recovered from his surprise and asked Christine, "Can you go to Atlanta next month for two weeks?"

Her response was immediate and wholehearted. "Oh, sure. That won't be a problem. No problem at all!"

*Reprieve! Thank God. I can get away from Jack for a while. Wouldn't it be great if Danny could come up?*

Danny. A sharp pain stabbed her at the thought of him. She wished she could tell him about it right now, but it was past time for his afternoon call. She couldn't let herself think about Danny. She was missing a large part of herself, and she couldn't function if she thought about it too much.

*   *   *

She rushed into Bessie's office as soon as she got to school, but the sagging swivel chair behind the cluttered desk was empty.

"Damn! Where is that woman?" She scribbled a note on a yellow legal notepad she found among the scattered papers and stood the whole notepad up against the telephone. Bessie couldn't miss this one! The note said "Meet me at the Tasty Burger after class, if you can. I got some good news! Red."

Then on to class with a shiver of satisfaction...

In a few weeks, she'd be going to a real class—playing with the big boys! And no Jack for two weeks. What a relief that would be!

After class she passed Bessie's office where the lights were out and the door was closed. She hurried around the corner to the Burger Shack and found Bessie holding court. An adoring Billy Joe was bringing her offerings of food and drink, as a group of students regaled her with adolescent banter.

Bessie spotted her across the room. "Hiya, Red! What's up?" Then, to Billy Joe, "Get Red a beer, okay Sweetie?"

Billy Joe scurried to the bar. The students scattered.

"Hey, Bessie, guess what?" Christine said as she took the seat opposite Bessie in the grimy, graffiti-decorated booth, "I'm going to Atlanta for a couple of IBM training classes."

"Way to go, girl! Stan's paying for all this?"

"Yep! Hotel, meals, classes, travel expenses! Can you believe it?"

Billy Joe returned with a frosty Bud which he put in front of Christine with a big smile.

Bessie raised her bottle in a toast, "Here's to you, Red. You're on your way!" Then to Billy Joe, "Put this lady executive's beer on my tab, Sweetie. She's earned it!"

They launched into a lively conversation. It was such fun to talk to Bessie, and Christine was so excited about the Atlanta trip and so reluctant to go home, that she lost track of the time, and suddenly realized that the restaurant was nearly deserted.

"Shit, Bessie, look what time it is. Jack's going to be furious with me! He's mad enough already, at nothing, at everything. Just between us, it's gonna be great to get away from him for a while."

"What's the matter? You hardly mentioned him since he's been back. What's going on? Trouble in Paradise?"

"Oh, Bessie, it's just awful." Christine was vaguely aware that she had drunk a little more than usual, but she just didn't care. She needed someone to talk to. "He's like a different person since he came back from Mexico! Just lies around the house, won't get a job, drinking all day... I'm about out of my mind."

"So ya think he's not going back to the oil rig job?"

"Doesn't look like it. He won't talk about it. I think something bad happened down there. I think he got himself fired. And you know what else? I think he's got something wrong with him."

"Whaddya mean?"

"He, well, he... There's something wrong when he tries to..." Then in a headlong rush of words, "When we have sex, it's not *right*, not like it used to be."

"Ya mean he's *impotent*?"

"Well, no, I guess not *that*. He can still... He still gets it up, but he can't finish most of the time. He doesn't *get off* like he used to. Maybe it's me, I don't know. I can't help it. I don't want him to touch me anymore. It's awful!" She shuddered.

"Damn, Red! Sounds like you got a serious problem."

"Tell you the truth, I really think there's something wrong with him! I don't know what to do. I just want to get away from him."

Bessie reached across the table and patted her hand. "Look, I hope everything's gonna be all right, but if it's not, and you ever need me for anything, I'll be there. You can come over and stay with me if you ever have to. I mean it, Red."

Christine squeezed Bessie's hand. "You're such a good friend. Thank you. I'm probably just making a mountain out of a molehill. I'll bet he'll be just fine after he gets back to work—quits drinking so much." She took a deep breath, shook off her bad mood and got up from the booth with forced optimism. "And anyway, *I'm* off to Atlanta and the IMB Ed Center! Oh Lord, I gotta get outta here. I'll keep you posted."

She made her way carefully to the door with just the slightest stagger. "...And hey, thanks for the beer and for the *ear*."

Bessie shook her head, and her normally cheery expression turned to a look of concern as she watched Christine leave.

"Hey, Billy Joe, Honey. Bring me the check."

\* \* \*

Jack was slumped in his BarcaLounger with a beer in his hand, seething, when he heard the Volkswagen's sputtering little engine. The frenetic gaiety of a late-night television show poured out of the flickering screen and swept past him unnoticed. Red had called him before class and told him that she was meeting this girl-friend from the school for a short meeting after class. Short meeting! Right! That was four hours ago. No dinner, either. She had told him he could warm up some left-overs for his dinner! Fuck her! He had decided he'd just stick to a liquid diet tonight.

He didn't even look up when he heard her come in.

"Oh, Jack! You're still up! I'm sorry I'm so late. Bessie and I were talking and I just lost track of the time."

No answer.

She continued, "Guess what! Stan's sending me to Atlanta to the IBM training center for two classes on our new computer. Isn't that great? He's paying all my expenses. I'll be there for two weeks. I'll be taking…"

"You ain't takin' nothin'. You're my fuckin' wife, and you're staying here and actin' like a wife for a change."

"I, uh… I'm really sorry I was so late tonight. We'll talk about this tomorrow, okay?" She went into the bedroom and hung up her jacket. "Did you finish the macaroni and cheese?"

"Hell, no, I didn't eat no fuckin' leftover macaroni and cheese." He was sick and tired of the way she was acting since he got back. Some kind of wife! He pulled himself up out of the chair and followed her into the bedroom. "What's goin' on with you?"

"Nothing, Jack. I was just excited about going up to Atlanta, I guess. This is a big opportunity for me. I wanted to tell Bessie about it. She's the one that got me the job, remember? I'm sorry if I…"

"You're sorry, you're sorry, you're sorry!" He didn't think she was one bit sorry. "Just get me something to eat, dammit!" He came closer. It would be so easy to smack her across the room.

"Okay, Jack. Let's don't get in a fight, please."

He glared down at her menacingly for a minute, then whirled around and went back to his chair and stared vacantly at the television. He heard her go into the kitchen.

He knew he needed to do something about this damned disease. Something was definitely going wrong with the skin between his legs. He couldn't go to a doctor. He couldn't let anybody know what was wrong—what he *had* and how he got it! But he needed to know if there was anything he could do. He decided he'd ask the druggist tomorrow if there was some kind of cream or something he could use. It was a bitch trying to keep Red from noticing anything.

"Supper's ready, Jack." Her voice was calm, cold.

He turned off the TV set and went into the kitchen.

*Leftovers again!*

## Chapter 23

Christine made sure she was close to the phone all the next afternoon. She *had* to talk to Danny. She'd decided she wouldn't go another week without seeing him! She ached for him. She was afraid to close her eyes at night, for fear she'd call out his name in the black desperation of her fitful sleep.

\*　　\*　　\*

On Thursday, Danny called from the same phone booth in front of the Gulf station that he used every afternoon after school. Mark and Jimmy had even gotten tired of kidding him about it. They just kept walking. He'd catch up with them later.

"See ya in a few," Mark said over his shoulder and headed toward the park for their routine after-school football game.

"Yeah, in a few," Danny answered as he dialed Christine's office number. He had something good to tell her today, for a change.

*Please answer. Please be there.*

"Taylor-Made Homes, Christine Radford speaking."

"Ooooo. Hello, you sweet thing! I'm so glad you're there."

"Danny! Is everything all right?"

"Sure. I..."

She interrupted in an earnest whisper, "Oh, Danny! I don't think I can stand this anymore! I have to see you. I'm going crazy!"

"Hey! I know. Same here. But guess what! I've got a job, starting Monday. I'm gonna buy myself a motor bike. Then I can come out to Waresboro to see you after school every day."

"Wonderful! Oh, wonderful! What kind of job?"

"Bag-boy, at the Piggly Wiggly. It's out halfway to Waresboro, anyway. Is that perfect, or what?"

"Perfect, Danny. I'm so proud of you. But I can't wait till next week to see you. Why don't you come by the Tasty Burger tonight? I'll be out of class at about 9:00. I could meet you there."

"You're not afraid somebody'll see us?"

"Who cares? You're my next-door neighbor. We can just accidentally run into each other there. The place is full of kids. Nobody'll notice."

"I'll be there if I can. I'll take the bus or something. Oh Christine, I miss you so much!"

"Same here. Till tonight then, Sweetheart."

\*　　\*　　\*

After class, Christine rushed over to the Tasty Burger. It had become a haven for her by now, a place where she could talk to Bessie and forget for a while about her miserable marriage. The pungent odor of over-used cooking oil had even begun to be pleasant to her—cozy, predictable. Earlier tonight, however, she had avoided seeing Bessie at the school, hoping that later she might snatch a few minutes alone with Danny, but Bessie was already there, surrounded by her entourage. Christine had no choice but to join her.

"Hi, Bessie!"

"Hiya, Red! I didn't know you were coming over tonight. How's it going?"

Christine scanned the room intently for a curly blond head as she took her seat across from Bessie. "Oh, uh, it's going great." Then she spotted him and caught her breath. She felt dizzy. His back was turned to her. He was flanked by Mark and Jimmy. He was laughing and looking around—for her, she knew—and when he saw her, he was riveted into a gaze that blocked out the rest of the room. The look between them was an electric passageway of secrets and unfulfilled desires.

"Hey, are you okay?" Bessie asked in a worried tone.

"Huh? Oh yeah. I just saw my next-door-neighbor." She raised her hand and waved hesitantly at him. He said something to Mark and Jimmy, and the three of them started weaving their way through the crowd toward their table. Her heart pounded and her head swam. What would she say to him?

"Well, if it isn't Miz Radford!" he said as he approached the booth.

"Oh hi, Danny." She was relieved that her voice sounded normal, belying the turmoil underneath it. "What's up?"

"Scoot over," he said boldly, and sat down beside her in the booth. He reached across the table and extended his hand to Bessie. "Hi, I'm Danny Wilkins, Miz Radford's neighbor and yard-man." Mark and Jimmy smirked.

"Nice to meet you. I'm Bessie Tanner. I work at the school."

Danny continued, "And these bums here are my buddies, Mark and Jimmy."

As the group exchanged greetings, Danny slipped a hand into Christine's lap and wiggled a slip of paper at her. She briefly caressed his fingers as she took the little note in her own hand. She knew she that was blushing, and there was a roaring in her ears. The brief touch of their fingers had set hers trembling. She breathed in his heady aroma. He was so close! She pressed her knee against his thigh.

He was talking to her. "Any more yard work for me, Miz Radford? Now that Mr. Radford is back home..."

"Uh, no thanks, Danny. I guess maybe he'll do it now." She tried to laugh. "That is, if I can get him out of his easy chair."

"Well, good to see ya. Nice to meet you, Miss Tanner." He got up from the booth and started to herd Mark and Jimmy back across the room.

Bessie answered in her flat voice, now hesitant with confusion, "Yeah, good to meet you, Danny."

All of Christine's body cried out to follow him, to grab him, to clutch him to her. "Nice to see ya, Danny, Mark, Jimmy. Be good." They were gone.

She slipped the little note into her purse, and lifted her beer with a shaking hand.

"My God, Red! What's going on between you two?"

"Whaddaya mean?" She tried another unsuccessful laugh. "He's my next-door neighbor. He helped me with stuff while Jack was gone. He..."

"He's in love with you, and you know it! My God! The way he looked at you was plumb scary! And he's damned adorable, if you ask me."

"Oh, Bessie! You've got a vivid imagination." Christine got up shakily from the table. "I've got to go to the ladies' room." She dropped her purse and the contents scattered across the floor. "Shit! I don't know what's the matter with me tonight!" She frantically retrieved the little note and the other spilled items and stuffed them back into her purse. "I'll be right back."

"Nice going, Red." Bessie laughed her loud, raucous laugh and shouted across the room at Christine's back, "Hey, don't fall in!"

In the safety of the graffiti-covered walls of the ladies' room stall, she opened the note and read:

> "I love you. I miss you so much, I'm going crazy. Can you get away this weekend for another fishing trip? Meet me at the Seminole Ave. bus stop by the lumber yard? I'll call you tomorrow and we'll plan it.
> Love, You-know-who"

She read it through hungrily several times and then slowly and deliberately tore it into tiny pieces and dropped them into the toilet. After a lingering look at the little scraps, she flushed them away.

Three giggling girls came into the ladies' room as she came out of the stall. They were wearing short little skirts which showed a lot of legs which would have been better covered: one pair bulbous and fat, one pair thin and fragile, one pair bowed in lumpy parentheses. They all had the same hair-style—a short frizz perched above each forehead from which a long, outward swoop fell to their shoulders. Their faces were caked with make-up.

"My God, did you see the tall one with the blond hair? Those shoulders!"

"I'll take the Elvis look-alike."

"Okay, you two, leave me with the country bumpkin. I don't care. He's kinda cute in a sweet-but-dumb sorta way."

Christine washed her hands vigorously, splashing water onto the closest girl. "Excuse me!" she snapped, pushed past the girl and yanked several paper towels angrily out of the towel dispenser, on which some misguided aspiring interior decorator had pasted the picture of an elaborate bouquet of flowers.

*Ugly! Stupid! Hateful! Had Danny been flirting with these tacky tramps? Tacky, tacky!*

She glanced briefly at her face in the cracked mirror. It was flushed with anger, revealing her jealous rage. Worse, it showed her age. How stupid for her to be in competition with these silly girls! She took a deep breath, banged her way out of the room, and headed for Bessie's table, scanning the room for Danny on her way. There was no Danny, Mark or Jimmy in sight. Good! They had left! So, the girls were just being girls. There was no flirting going on. How could she have thought for an instant that Danny would be interested in one of those gawky girls with their tasteless clothes and excessive make-up?

As Christine gained the safety of the booth, Bessie leaned across the table and gave her a penetrating look.

"Okay, Red. What's between you and that tasty little boy-toy?"

"I, uh, we've gotten to be pretty good friends, I guess. He's really nice—easy to talk to. He's funny—makes me laugh."

"Looked like more than talk's been happening between y'all to me!"

"Don't be silly. He's just a good friend. He's helped..." She gave up the pretense. "Oh, Bessie!" She hid her face in her hands. "I don't know how this happened. I didn't want to start anything with him. It's crazy, but... but I'm nuts about him. He... he's my lover! I know it's awful, but I couldn't help it, I swear. He was over at the house all the time, and what with Jack gone so long, and..."

"Hey, calm down. I always say, 'Love is where ya find it,' right?"

"It's awful! Now that Jack's back, I miss Danny so much... I miss *being* with him so much. He calls me every afternoon after he gets out of school." She tried to laugh, but her throat was too dry. "Yes, high school! I know, it's nuts... He's my... He's the sweetest thing that ever happened to me! I'm crazy about him! And I can't *stand* for Jack to touch me any more." Christine reached for Bessie's glass of water, but had to put it down because her hand was shaking so.

"Whoa! Slow down, Red. This is serious. Sounds like big trouble to me!"

"I know, I know! Bessie, what am I going to do? I know you think I'm crazy, but I need Danny. I can't live without…"

"What'll Jack do if he finds out?"

"He'll kill me! He'll kill both of us! And that's another thing. He's mad at me all the time, anyway. You know what? I'm afraid of him! He's really been strange since he came back. And I'm sure something's wrong with him."

"Whaddya mean?"

"Well, he's lost weight, he's grouchy, he's not looking for a job, and he's… Well, all of a sudden he's *modest*. The other night he was taking a shower, and I went into the bathroom to take him some clean towels. He was coming out of the shower when I opened the door, and he jumped back into the shower and pulled the curtain closed and yelled, positively *yelled* at me to get the hell out! He's never been *modest* before. Something's wrong!" Much to her chagrin, tears began to well up in Christine's eyes.

Bessie patted her on the hand. "D'ya think it's 'cause he's drinking too much?"

"Well, I thought so at first, but now I think it's the other way around. I think he's drinking because there's something wrong with him. He won't talk to me. Not about how he feels, what happened on the oil rig job, when he's going to work—nothing."

"Maybe y'all oughta go to one of those counselors."

"Yeah, I suggested that a couple of days ago. I thought he was gonna *hit* me! He said, 'I ain't wasting my time and money on *that* crap.'"

"Well, if I can help you any way, just let me know. Maybe you could use my apartment to spend some time with your pretty boy."

"Oh, Bessie! You're so sweet! But I don't want to get you mixed up in this mess." She shook her head and looked down despondently at the table. "What a mess; what a mess!"

They both fell silent for a minute and then Christine brightened. "But I'm going to be out of it for a couple of weeks, anyhow! I'm going to Atlanta next Monday. Driving up Sunday evening. IBM classes start Monday morning. I can't wait!"

"Well, I hope you have some fun up there. And learn a lot, too, of course!"

"I'll stop by your office before I leave school tomorrow. Gotta run, now."

"Hold it in the road, girl!"

\*   \*   \*

When Christine got home, she slipped in as quietly as she could, turning the key carefully in the door. Her care was rewarded by the sound of heavy snoring from the lounge chair in front of the television set. She tip-toed into the bedroom and changed into the plain, sexless cotton pajamas she had slept in since Jack had come home.

Soundlessly, she sneaked into the kitchen for a glass of milk for her dinner, cautiously turned off the TV, gently placed the old afghan on the sofa over the sleeping hulk, and retired gratefully to the bedroom.

Tomorrow she'd talk to Danny and arrange to meet him Saturday, if he could get away. And starting Sunday afternoon, she'd be free of Jack for 2 whole weeks! She'd figure out something to do about all this. She'd be able to think better when she got away.

As she sank back exhausted onto the cool pillow-case and switched out the bedside lamp, she yielded to the fantasy Danny's nearness in the booth had spawned. She felt the weight of his muscular body on hers. She tasted his sweet mouth. She closed her eyes.

*Good-night, Danny. God bless you.*

## Chapter 24

Early on Saturday morning, Christine had clothes thrashing in the washer and tumbling in the dryer; fear and excitement thrashing and tumbling in her head. She was in a turmoil of anticipation. In spite of her chaotic thoughts, things were still getting done. She was packing, preparing to go to Atlanta, trying to soothe Jack's anger and convince him that her trip was in the best interests of both of them, and all the time disguising the intense joy she was feeling at the thought of seeing—of touching Danny in just a few hours. They had planned to meet at 10:00 that morning. She had told Jack that she'd promised to help Bessie get her car to the garage for repairs, and then to take her shopping. Bessie had agreed to take part in the deception, and was using the morning to visit friends in Valdosta.

How she wished she could take Danny to Atlanta with her! Romantic visions of the two of them strolling down busy city streets, laughing as they ate pizza in a little side-walk café, making love all night in the safety of a hotel room—all these fantasies and more kept popping up unbidden in her mind. In reality though, she was relieved that it was impossible for him to leave school next week. It was the last week of high school for him. He had finals, graduation practice, senior prom. Of course he couldn't get away. She didn't even mention it to him. It was out of the question.

Jack interrupted her reverie from the BarcaLounger, where he was watching an old re-run of 'Mr. Ed, the Talking Horse.' "How in the hell am I gonna get around while you're gone? It's still not too late to take a bus up to your big important school. How do you expect me…"

"Jack, please! We've been over this a thousand times. I've made the commitment, I've got my map, I need the car to get around."

"Man, you've turned into one cold-hearted bitch!"

"Jack…"

"Leavin' me for two weeks when I don't feel good, anyway. You're still my damn wife, ya know."

"Look, I've cooked you a freezer full of food and filled up the refrigerator with beer. There's plenty of Spaghetti-O's and canned beef stew in the cabinet. What more do you want?" Her irritation was showing.

"Well, I need the god-damned car!" His eyes never left 'Mr. Ed' during this exchange.

"You can ride the bus! I got around just fine without a car for a year while you were gone. And there's always a taxi if you haven't got time to wait for the bus."

She really thought he didn't have any reason to complain. After all, he didn't have to get to work every day. She was careful not to mention that she was the one paying the bills right now. She had every reason to do what she was doing! After all, she was getting paid her regular salary while she was in Atlanta.

Jack sank into a silent black mood, as Mr. Ed's mouth moved strangely from side to side, and his hoarse voice said, "Well, I guess that's a horse of another color."

By 9:30, she had all the necessities for her trip ready to be packed, and was ready to leave, ostensibly for Bessie's. Jack was still deep in his fuming silence as she started out.

"I'll be back in a few hours, Jack. I left some chili and cornbread in the oven for your lunch. Make yourself a salad." He ignored her completely. "See ya later." She was careful not to let the screen door slam behind her.

She controlled herself until she had turned the corner and was out of sight of the house before she broke into song. "I'll be down to gitcha in a taxi, Honey…"

He was waiting by the Williams & Johnson Lumber Mill and ran to the car and yanked open the door before she had come to a complete stop. He lifted her up from the seat and hugged her to his chest, moaning, "At last, at last!" For a minute, they both forgot where they were and just stood there, arms locked around each other, swaying back and forth.

Then, with a start, she broke away. "Come on, Sweetheart, get in the car, let's get out of here and go where we can be really alone. Oh, Lord, how I've missed you!"

They pulled into the gravel of a little one-pump gas station for something they could improvise for a picnic lunch. Christine was treated to her first sight of a two-gallon jar of pickled eggs sitting boldly next to a rack of beef jerky on the counter-top inside the tiny store. She rolled her eyes in horror at Danny, and he responded by licking his lips, rubbing his stomach and gazing at the ceiling with a look of rapture. She burst out laughing and punched him on the arm, just as a frail-looking elderly lady appeared from the back of the store.

The wizened face of the aged proprietress hardened with suspicion as she asked, "Y'all need some help?"

"Yes, ma'am, we sure do," Danny answered with a gentlemanly bow of his head, at the same time as he gave Christine a sharp pinch on her derriere.

"Danny!" Christine squealed and punched him again. The little lady scowled at them darkly. Danny looked at Christine with his brows raised in utter innocence and then back at the offended lady and shrugged his shoulders. Christine regained her composure and studied the strips of beef jerky thoughtfully, as she kicked Danny's ankle.

They bought several small packets of cheese and crackers, each with a flat little wooden stick enclosed for spreading the cheese onto the crackers, a couple of juicy-looking oranges, two Moon Pies, and two RC Colas. A Deep South feast!

They piled back into the car, still laughing, and were on their way again to Alligator Creek. Soon after they turned onto the gravel road, Danny pointed to an almost imperceptible overgrown two-track road into the woods.

"Turn off here."

"What for?"

"I want to show you something."

"Danny…"

"Trust me, you'll be glad you did."

She gave him a suspicious look, but turned onto the narrow, grassy tracks. "Where does this go?"

"You'll see. It's an old logging road. Nobody uses it anymore."

Soon they were out of sight of the gravel road, in a sparsely forested stand of young pines.

"Okay. This is good," Danny said, and reached over and turned off the ignition.

"Whatever you're up to…"

"I'm gonna make love to you, woman, till you turn blue!"

He leaned over and kissed her, wrapping his arms around her and pulling her gently toward him. His mouth was sweeter than she had been imagining. His clean, masculine aroma engulfed her. The gear shift poked her in the thigh.

"Mmmmm, ouch! The gear's poking into my leg. Here, let me…"

"Wait, I'll let my seat back." He fumbled his hand around under the passenger seat, found the lever and pulled it. The seat slid back with a thud. "Now, come here, you!"

She leaned over toward him. Now the gearshift pressed painfully into her side.

"Oops, that's not going to work," she said, suppressing a giggle.

"Let's try the back seat." He pulled his seat forward and stepped out of the car.

"So that's what that little back seat is for!" she said as she got out.

He was already in the back seat, holding out his arms to her. "Come here woman, you sweet little thing!"

She got out, pushed the driver's seat forward and climbed into the tiny back seat of the VW, easing herself slowly down onto his body. He moved his knees apart and she slipped between them. Her knees were bent sharply, her feet up and helplessly searching for a place to rest. Her right ankle hit the door frame. "Ouch!"

"What's the matter?"

"Damn! I hurt my ankle!"

"Poor baby! Let me kiss it and make it all better," he said. He tried to slide farther back onto the seat to give her more room. Her left knee struck the floor.

"Oh, no!" She started to laugh.

"Wait a minute. Maybe if I... Let me turn on my side." He was laughing now.

"Hold on. I know we can..."

"Oh, Rats!"

She collapsed on him, gasping now in helpless hilarity. They hugged each other, rocking back and forth, bumping into seat-backs, arm-rests, seat-belts, gear-shifts. Tears of laughter rolled down their faces. Christine finally caught her breath and pulled away from him.

"Okay, okay. Wait a minute." Another spasm of giggling. "I think your legs are too long!"

"No way! It's you! Your feet keep going everywhere!" Another paroxysm of laughter.

But their bodies soon surrendered to their yearning, and relaxed into the perfect harmony that was so familiar to them, so necessary for their survival. As they made love, the tiny, uncomfortable back seat became Cleopatra's barge, a magic carpet, cloud nine.

\* \* \*

Later, when they arrived at the compound of dilapidated buildings surrounding "Miltons Bate Shop", Christine was amazed to find it a beehive of activity. A sizable pack of lean hounds bayed a welcome; several barefoot children came running from behind the house; a tall, raw-boned woman in a faded cotton dress was feeding soapy garments through the slow-turning pair of rubber cylinders of the wringer on the front-porch washer; two big, scary-looking, bearded young men were playing horseshoes over by the pig-sty.

Danny sensed her misgivings and said, "Look, if you want to stay in the car while I go make the arrangements, it's OK."

"Yeah, good idea. Here, you need some money for the fishing stuff?" She gave him a ten dollar bill.

As he negotiated with the men, the smallest children gathered near the car, and Christine, leaning out the car window, managed to strike up a conversation. The dogs stopped barking and began to sniff the hand she cautiously extended to them. She felt considerably less threatened.

Soon they were floating silently downstream again, peaceful on the gentle black water. Christine sat on a small flotation cushion on the floor of the canoe and leaned back onto Danny as he let the slow movement of the water take them toward the swamp, using his paddle only to keep them in the middle of the little stream. She lay her head against his stomach and rested her arms on his thighs, re-connected to the order and beauty of the universe again through his body. He bent his head and gave her an upside-down kiss.

*Oh, yes. Life is good!*

"Wanna run away with me?" he asked.

"Why? I can't think of anywhere I'd rather be."

"You think I'm kidding, don't you?"

"Well, of course..."

"I'll graduate next month, and I could join the Army or the Marines, and you could come live with me wherever I'm stationed. We could get away from my folks and your husband, and this..."

"Whoa, Danny. Much as I love you and want to be with you, you know that's impossible."

"But why? I don't see..."

"For a million reasons. You're just starting out. Your whole life is ahead of you. You need a girl your own age, someone..."

"I've had girls my own age. Boring! That's not what I want. I want you!"

"...Someone you can settle down with someday and have a family. Someone you can take out on a date with your friends. Danny, Sweetheart, let's don't even talk about that. Let's just be thankful for what we've got, while we have it. We have to face it. This can't last long."

"You don't really mean that! You..."

"Let's just enjoy ourselves today. It's perfect right now."

"But I can't stand being away from you all the time like this! Thinking about you with someone else. Your husband..."

She turned to him and covered his mouth with hers. "Not another word," she whispered, and made it impossible for him to speak.

They ventured further downstream, passing the grassy "Garden of Eden" where they had picnicked before. A huge, immobile alligator dozed in the sun where their beach towel had rested.

"Danny, oh my God! Look! I thought you said alligators didn't like hammocks—that they stayed in the water!"

"Well, I said 'most of the time' they were in the water. They like a little sunshine now and then."

"But what if..."

"They won't come out like that if there's people around."

She shuddered. "Just think, we were lying there..."

"Look, I've been coming out here all my life, before I can remember, and I've never been threatened by an alligator. If you don't mess with them—they don't mess with you. Don't worry."

"Okay, if you say so... But are you sure *they* understand that?"

They drifted along for a while. The only sound they made was the soft whisper of Danny's paddle. Soon there was no bank on either side of their passageway. Cyprus trees and thick underbrush rose out of the smooth water, as far back into the mysterious woods as she could see.

"Where're we going?" she asked in the hushed tones of someone in church. She *felt* like she was in a vast cathedral. Beneath the high canopy of green was a dim, open, silent space, pierced every few minutes with the gleam of bright butterfly wings, or the clear ringing of a *kyrie eleison* of birdsong.

"We're going on down into the park a little way. I wanna show you something."

"But how do you know where you're going?"

"Oh, I've been out here lots of times. I know my way around. There's lots of landmarks. You can see marks on the trees, too. You're on the main highway to Chesser Prairie."

"Prairie?"

"That's just an open spot in the swamp, where fire burned out the trees a long time ago. Lots of flowers, lots of birds, real pretty. Daddy used to take me bird-hunting with him out in the prairies."

Soon the dense canopy above them began to open to more patches of sunlight, the trees were not as tall, and the undergrowth seemed thicker. Flowering shrubs lightened the dusky depths of the forest. Water lilies and ferns began to narrow the channel they were traveling, until they came out into a large, treeless area where the water was completely covered with a blanket of flowering plants. Flocks of birds swirled up from the dense growth, spiraled joyously and streamed downward again into the blossoms. Patient herons and ibises balanced delicately on their long, fragile legs and fed like upper-class Englishmen on the abundance at their feet.

"Oh, Danny! You did it again!"

"Did what?"

"Showed me something so beautiful... I don't know... I'd never imagined... Thank you."

"My pleasure!"

"So this is a 'prairie'! I never would've guessed."

She opened one of the little cheese-and-cracker packages, spread the cheese, softened by the sunshine, onto a cracker and turned to him. "Open your mouth." He ate it slowly, sensually, looking transfixed into her eyes. He took her hand and deliberately licked each finger, kissing each finger-tip, circling his tongue gently in the palm. She wanted to eat him alive.

"Danny, Danny! I'll never get enough of you!"

After they finished their picnic lunch, they sat silently a few minutes, feasting on the sights, sounds and smells of the swamp, sipping on their RC Colas. Suddenly, she turned to him with concern.

"Oh Danny, we'd better get back. Jack'll be wondering where I am. I told him I was taking Bessie shopping, and even *she* couldn't keep at it *this* long!"

"Sure, might as well. We'd have a helluva time trying to paddle through that stuff, anyway." He began to turn the canoe around. "Love me?"

"I adore you!"

"Run away with me?"

"No, Silly. Get that out of your head! That's a terrible idea!"

*That's a wonderful idea. A beautiful fantasy, that's what it is. Oh, just imagine...*

"We'll see about that," he murmured, unruffled.

\*   \*   \*

Jack had just about had it with this business of trying to make things work with Red. She obviously didn't give a shit about him, anymore.

He'd been contacting some of his good buddies from his old trucking days; trying to figure his chances of getting another rig. He'd left Pennsylvania with a good reputation for delivering his cargo on time, in good shape, and with a minimum of hassle. He was pretty sure that he could get back where he belonged by selling the house and using the money to buy another truck cab. He'd been worried about telling Red she was going to have to leave her precious job, but the way she'd been treating him lately, he really didn't give a damn anymore.

He looked up "Real Estate" in the Yellow Pages. Time to get moving. Time to get this damned house on the market.

\*   \*   \*

That morning before Danny left to go fishing with Mark and Jimmy, Madge had tried to convince him that he should take his father with him, but Danny had flatly refused. He had said that this was just for him and his friends, and they didn't want any parents or older people around, and didn't she understand that? The thing was, she wanted Harland out of the house. She needed to finish her letter and get it into the mail before she got caught. And then fate intervened...

Harland hung up the phone with a sigh and came into the kitchen. "I've got to drive over to Valdosta to get the derned part I need for the Mercury. I'll be back in time for lunch. Need anything at the store?"

"No, I gotta go myself, after you get back. Take yer time." She had God on her side, all right. This proved it.

As soon as Harland was out of sight, Madge ran to the bathroom, brought out the Kotex box and retrieved the folded piece of notebook paper she had taken from Danny's school things. She had already glued onto the paper, in a mixture of cut-out single words and combinations of unmatched letters, the following message:

"Dear Mr Radford
    Your wife is a devil worshipper. God will strike her dead. She has"

She laid the note on the kitchen table, got a tube of glue from the tool drawer, and a pair of scissors from her sewing basket. She began earnestly scanning the pages of a Good Housekeeping magazine for the remaining letters to complete her statement:

"sinned against God and you. She is the Whore of Babylon."

When she finished the note, she threw the magazine and the paper scraps into the garbage, and put away the glue and the scissors. Printing clumsily in block letters with her left hand, she carefully addressed a plain envelope with the information she had copied from her neighbors' mailbox. Her mouth was so dry, she had trouble licking the postage stamp. She put the folded note in the envelope, wrapped it in a paper towel and put it into her handbag, beneath her grocery list and stack of coupons. "Now," she said aloud, with a sigh of righteous satisfaction, "I'm ready to go to the grocery."

She felt happy for the first time in months. Maybe years.

## Chapter 25

Atlanta was all Christine had hoped for, and more. Not that it was easy. On the contrary, the all-day classes at the IBM Education Center on Peachtree Street were harder than anything she had ever imagined. She had never had to *really* concentrate on anything before. The schools she had gone to before were no challenge to her, but now she was stretched to the limit of her mental powers. It seemed as if her classmates all knew so much more that she did. At first, she felt intimidated, dumb, uneducated. Nevertheless, she made herself ask questions, even when she was afraid they might sound stupid. But the instructor always answered her with respect, and had a knack for making things clear. Her head was a-whirl with new ideas. She had a constant sense of awe at the technology being revealed to her.

Her luxurious hotel, the Fairmont, was on Peachtree St. just a few blocks from the IBM Education Center. The first morning, her walk through the balmy, late spring breezes on the way to class had set her heart pounding with excitement. The small, beautifully landscaped areas in front of the office and apartment buildings under the shade of the stately old oaks contrasted sharply with the heavy traffic, the purposeful looks on the drivers' faces and the intense preoccupation of the pedestrians. All these unfamiliar, urbane affections were exhilarating to her. She slipped into the role of a sophisticated career woman, forcing her face into the slight frown of concentration she saw on the faces of the people she passed. When she caught her reflection in the glass entry door of the IBM building, she burst out laughing at herself.

That evening, she walked briskly back to her hotel and rode up in the story-book glass elevator. She hurried into her room, hoping to see the little red light on her telephone glowing with the good news that she had a message from Danny. Happily, she did.

"Hello, you beautiful thing! I just wanted you to know I'm thinking about ya. Ahhh ... Nothing new here, just miss you real bad. Don't let any of those big-city guys steal you away from me. And ... hurry home. And ... yeah, I love you. Bye."

After savoring the brief message, she opened the curtains to the downtown lights of Atlanta twinkling like city-hardened fireflies. The eerie blue-domed flying saucer on top of the Hyatt-Regency floated in front of the great, glittering phallus of the new Peachtree Plaza Hotel. She drank in the cosmopolitan view for a few minutes, before falling exhausted onto the puffy quilted damask bed-spread. She closed her eyes and ran through the salient points of the day's class before changing into some comfortable shoes and going out for a bite to eat. After dinner, she returned to her room for a full evening of studying. She knew she should call Jack, but she put it off until tomorrow. After all, she had called him as soon as she arrived on

Sunday night, and had given him her hotel and room number. He could call her if he had anything to say.

*I've got to keep my mind clear for this class. Can't let myself get distracted.*

In class, her initial feelings of inadequacy began to wane, and she found the "Introduction to the 360" interesting and exciting. The good training she had already gotten from Gordon, the IBM SE, gave her a little head start, so she was able to make sense out of most of the technical discussions. She was pleased when some of her fellow students began to ask her questions during breaks, and seek her help on their assignments.

On the second day, one of her more adept classmates approached her when they broke for lunch.

"Hi. I'm Tim Cotter. Are you from the Atlanta area?"

"How do you do? I'm Christine Radford, and no, I'm not from Atlanta. I'm from Waycross, Georgia."

"I didn't know they had computers in Waycross!"

His eyes were taking her in with obvious admiration, making her feel as if she were back behind the fast-food counter, back in orange polyester. She turned her back to him, snatched up her purse and headed for the door. "You might just be surprised what we *do* have in Waycross. Electricity *and* running water…" She was out the door.

He followed her, laughing. "Hey, not so fast. I didn't mean to offend you. I noticed that you seem to have had some computer experience already. Guess I thought you must be from…, well, a big city," he finished lamely.

She pinned him with a cold stare. "Excuse me. I have some telephone calls to make."

"Sure. See ya later."

After lunch, they were divided into groups of four to work on an exercise. Christine was at first a little irritated to find herself in the same group with Tim Cotter. As the group worked on its assignment, however, she began to gain more and more respect for him. He was a good problem solver, and very knowledgeable about computers. Together, they made most of the decisions and answered most of the questions that came up. Their group was the first to complete its exercise, and was allowed to leave early. They were proud of themselves and decided, at Tim's suggestion, to celebrate with a happy-hour drink in the bar at the Fairmont.

Before meeting her new friends in the bar, Christine hurried to her room to see if there was a message from Danny. The little red "message waiting" light was dark.

Rats! Well, it didn't make sense for him to call her in the afternoon when he knew she was in class anyway, now did it? If she could just call him, or write him...

*Hey girl, take it easy. That's just the way it is!*

She changed into some comfortable shoes, freshened her make-up, ran a comb through her hair and went downstairs. The three other members of her group had been joined by several other classmates, all seated around a table loaded with happy-hour drinks and hors d'ouvres. Tim jumped up and waved at her as she entered the bar.

As she approached their table, she felt bathed in their acceptance and respect. "Okay you guys! What's going on here?" she asked cheerfully.

With a Sir Walter Raleigh flourish, Tim stood and offered her his chair. "Nothing so far, but now that *you're* here…"

She blushed happily, glad that the lights were dim enough that no one would notice, took her seat, and ordered a Heineken. No more Buds for her! She was moving up, wasn't she?

In the lively conversation that followed, she learned that Tim was manager of Information Systems for a nation-wide building maintenance corporation head-quartered in Atlanta. And better yet, his obvious interest in her was based at least partly on her computer skills, not just on her looks.

She was beginning to realize how hard it was to find trained computer technicians of any type: programmers, operators, systems analysts. The rapid growth of computers for businesses of all sizes was creating a real sellers' market for people with these skills. She felt the stirring of a sense of power. It felt good!

Tim leaned close to her ear and asked in a conspiratorial whisper, "How'd you like to move to Atlanta and come to work for me?"

She pulled back and studied him warily, without answering.

He nodded at the wedding ring on her finger and asked, "Is there a hubby back home?'

"Sure is! I'm married to a big, tough man with a short temper." *And I'm madly in love with a horny hunk I'm missing real bad right now.*

Still, she was flattered at the attention, and gratified to learn that she had value on the job market. She wished that some of those rude personnel clerks who had turned her down so flatly back in Waycross could see her now!

Christine settled into a comfortable routine of class during the day and study in her hotel room each night. She really missed Danny, but she forced herself to be satisfied with a cryptic little message from him on Wednesday night.

"Hi, Sweetie! I miss you real bad, but I guess you're learning a lots, and uh... behaving yourself!" A self-conscious little laugh. "I'm working all week-end, I mean, you not being here or anything. Sooo, see you next week-end, I hope. Man, I really miss you, big time! Bye."

She decided not to try to drive all the way back to Waycross for the week-end. Why bother if she couldn't see Danny, anyway?

On Friday evening, she called Jack. "Hi! How's it going?"

"Okay. What's going on with you?"

"Oh, everything's fine! I'm learning a lot."

"Hmmmm... Me, too. You might be surprised..."

"Look, if everything's okay there, I think I'll just stay here for the weekend. Stan said that'd be okay, with the hotel bill and all... Our study group is getting together tomorrow to work on our project. Besides, I could really use the time to study."

"Hey, it's fine with me. I don't give a damn if you come home or not."

"Oh, Jack..."

"I'm working on my *'career'* as well. I've got some plans..."

"That's good, Jack. I can't wait to hear about it. Look, we'll probably be out of class early next Friday, and I'll leave as soon as I can after that. I ought to be home Friday night, late."

"Suit yourself, Red. By the way, you got some enemies around here?"

"Enemies? I don't understand..."

"I got a really weird letter yesterday. Weird!"

"Whaddya mean? What did it say?" A paralyzing sense of doom washed over her.

"That you worshipped devils or something, and that God's gonna gitcha." Jack was laughing now.

Cold chills ran down Christine's back. *Oh, my God, is he just drunk, or has somebody said something?* She took a deep breath. Whichever it was, she decided she would have to ignore it now, and deal with it when she got home. What else could she do? She wanted to know what was in the letter, but was terrified to find out at the same time.

"Well, uh...all right, Jack." She forced a tentative laugh. "You never know about people in these small southern towns... Hey, you be good, and, uh... I'll see you next week, okay?"

"Yeah. Whatever..."

She hung up the phone, shaking with panic; relieved that the conversation hadn't gone any farther. She realized that at the very least she should have asked him more about his "career" plans. Oh, well ...

*Stop thinking about it!*

She went to the window and opened the curtains. The sun was setting behind the Atlanta skyline, painting a lush pink and orange backdrop for the shimmering lights coming on in the myriad windows of the tall buildings. The blue-domed saucer of the Hyatt-Regency and the austere slim rectangularity of Peachtree Center had a comfy familiarity now. It was strange but true. This could be her city if she wanted it. She could accept Tim's offer and be a part of this scene.

But what about Danny? She felt a pang of longing for him. How could she think of leaving him? Well, she'd just have to put him out of her mind for now. Right! Like she could do that! She turned away from the window and faced south, in what she thought was the direction of Waycross. With all the intensity she could muster, she willed her thoughts to reach him.

*Danny, precious, I miss you. I love you. I wish I could make things be different. I wish you were here. I wish I had you in my arms right now.*

She lay down on the bed and wrapped herself around her pillow, closed her eyes and let her mind drift out onto smooth black water. Into the Okefenokee. In a canoe. Into peace and tranquillity.

## Chapter 26

Madge was now almost totally preoccupied with watching for signs of some reaction to the anonymous note she had written to the big guy next door. She didn't know exactly what she was watching for; some kind of an explosion, maybe. She had seen him come out of the silent house several times, and head for the bus stop. She had seen him come home carrying a bag or two of groceries. Once, she had snorted with disdain as he came staggering past her house and stopped at his mail-box. As he reached in for the mail, he tipped the sack he was carrying, and a bottle fell out, breaking with a loud crash on the cement base of the mailbox. The cursing which followed both shocked and thrilled her with its vehemence and obscenity.

If only she could figure out if he had gotten the letter or not! Maybe she needed to send him another one. She wished she had some evidence of the whore's devil-worshipping. She really didn't know what that would be, though. Well, God would show her the way. He had chosen her to expose the evil. He would show her the way.

She thought she could figure it out if her head would just stop aching so much. The pain always started pounding inside her skull when she thought about that whore. It was like witchcraft. That was what it was! The whore knew she was on to her, and was making this pain in her head, so she couldn't think straight! She needed to get some help somewhere. When she tried to talk to the so-called "men" in her family, Danny laughed at her, and Harland just said, "Now, now, Madge. You know they ain't nothin' to this devil-worship stuff. You just relax now and don't worry so much. You just been workin' too hard."

*The fools! They'll see soon enough!*

She picked up a Ladies' Home Journal magazine from the coffee table, got her scissors out of the sewing basket, the glue out of the tool drawer, and sat down at the kitchen table. Now, what should she say? After several tries, she settled on:

"Dear Mr Radford

The hateful Whore of Babylon wilt get coals of fire heeped onto her head. That will stop her doing evil all the time. Amen"

She read it over a few times with great satisfaction. She loved the sound of it! If only she had someone to share it with, someone who could see how clever she was! Of course she couldn't let anyone know, not even her Thursday Night Circle, much as they relished her scandalous stories about the whore.

She wished she could talk Harland into joining the KKK, like her uncles had. They had invited Harland in as part of the family. He should've been proud, but he wouldn't even talk about it! If only they were members, maybe she could get the White Knights to burn a cross in the whore's yard. She shivered with delight at the thought. She could just see it; the huge cross ablaze next door, and the mysterious white-robed figures marching around it. She could feel the heat and hear the roar of the flames. She had heard that they let wives in now, as well. She could be marching in that righteous army, sharing in their power, keeping the niggers, Jews, queers and whores where they belonged.

Suddenly she had a frightening thought about the note lying on the table in front of her. What if the police were called in on this? What if they got her fingerprints off the note? Could they do that? She jumped up from the table and got a dishcloth. With shaking fingers, she began to wipe at the edges of the note, carefully holding down the pasted-on letters so as not to dislodge them. Then, with a shriek, she jerked her fingers off the letters as if they were being seared on a hot stove. She realized that the fingers holding down the letters would make perfect fingerprints. She put on her rubber gloves and started again, this time dabbing with intense concentration at each little letter.

The front screen door slammed.

"Hey, Mama, I'm home!"

"Danny!" She frantically gathered the note, glue and scissors in a jumble and pushed them into the junk drawer beside the sink. The rubber gloves snapped as she yanked them off. "Uh, what're you doin' home so early?"

"We were having graduation practice and we got through early, so they just let us go home." He opened the refrigerator and peered inside with great interest.

Madge turned to the sink and began to wash the spotlessly clean porcelain to hide her agitation. Danny poured himself a glass of milk, got a jelly donut out of the bread-box, and sat down at the kitchen table.

"Whatcha doing, playing paper-dolls?" he asked as he picked up the Ladies' Home Journal and dangled a well-shredded page.

"Give me that! It's none of your bizness, boy!" Madge grabbed the incriminating magazine from him.

"Jeez, Mama! What's the big deal? I was just..."

"You better get on upstairs and do your homework. Get out from under my feet!"

"Hey, I'm outta here, Mama. Whaddya so uptight about?" He stuck the donut in his mouth, put the milk bottle back into the refrigerator, took his glass of milk and headed upstairs, shaking his head. He mumbled from behind the donut, "Besides, we don't have any homework. We're practically graduates, remember?"

Her heart pounded as she listened to his footsteps on the stairs. As soon as she heard the sound of his door closing, she retrieved the note, hastily put the scissors and glue back into their places, folded the note and hurried into the bathroom, where she hid it for now in the safety of her Kotex box.

Back in the kitchen, she threw away the magazine and the little paper scraps surrounding it. She poured herself a glass of iced tea and, still shaking, sat down at the table to regain her composure.

*Close call! Thank you, God, for protecting me. I am your avenging angel. Praise Jesus!*

\* \* \*

Upstairs, Danny locked his door, put the donut and glass of milk down on his bedside table, retrieved the dog-eared "Club" magazine from under the mattress and settled back onto the bed. He hadn't had as much need for the faithful magazine lately, but what with Christine in Atlanta...

After he had eased his sexual tensions, his mind drifted back to his mother and her increasing strangeness. What in the world was she cutting up magazines for? It wasn't like she was saving recipes for her kitchen note-book, like she had in the past. There had been a whole bunch of little scraps of cut paper on the table. It didn't make sense. Maybe he ought to talk to his dad about it.

He missed Christine terribly. Not only was he hungry for her body, but he needed to talk to her. He couldn't decide what he was going to do after graduation. He sure didn't want to spend the rest of his life as a bag-boy at the Piggly Wiggly. Mark was going off to Georgia Southern in the fall; Jimmy was going to work for his dad in the roofing business; he didn't know what *he* wanted to do. Maybe he should try getting into computers, like Christine. He needed her to talk to.

What if they moved in together? Boy, that'd give the whole town of Waycross something to talk about! They could make love all night every night. Wake up together every morning. Shower together. Have breakfast together. He could reach out and touch her any time he wanted to.

He knew she didn't love that husband of hers anymore. He desperately wanted to get her away from him. Although they tried to ignore the existence of the marriage and the hulking reality of the husband, he could see the horror deep in her eyes when Jack's name came up in their conversation. Something had to be done. Well, he was getting his used Honda 350 out of lay-away this weekend. That was the first step.

In the meantime, it was Friday and Mark had invited him, really had *insisted* that he come to a surprise birthday party for Jimmy tonight. He guessed Christine was right. He did need to spend more time with his friends. He'd kinda dropped out of the social scene since he started up with her. Not that he didn't love her more than anything in the world, more than anything he'd ever imagined, but still, he needed to get out and do more stuff with his friends.

He polished off the rest of the donut and the milk and headed for the shower.

\* \* \*

Next morning he was up earlier than usual. He dressed in work clothes and made his way out to the garage, where he knew his dad would be tinkering around with the cursed Mercury.

"Hey, man! You need some expert help here?"

"Danny! You're up early. Yeah! Grab a wrench. I kin use some good help, awright."

His old man's obvious happiness made Danny have to look away. It was pitiful how much he appreciated the little attention Danny paid him. It was enough to make anybody feel sick with guilt. He made a promise to himself to be a better son, to spend a little more time with his dad.

After a while, Danny got up the nerve to ask Harland about Madge and her strange behavior lately.

"Say, Dad... Uh, is Mama OK?"

"Umm..."

"I mean, is she sick or somethin'?"

"Naw. She's just fine as far as I know. Why'd you ask me that?"

"Well, she's been acting kind of funny lately; jumpy, nervous."

"Don't worry, Son. It's prob'ly jist a woman thing. She's gittin' to the age where women git, well, strange sometimes. You know, change of life and like that."

"I don't know... She scares me sometimes. She acts like she's mad all the time about something."

"Now, I told you not to worry. You got enough to do now, what with graduatin' and all."

"Maybe y'all oughta go on a vacation or something. Hey, I know! Why don't you take her down to DisneyWorld! That'd get her mind off whatever's bothering her!"

"Lord, where'd you git such an idear? She'd no more go down there with all them Yankee tourists everywhere, than she'd stand on her head and whistle Dixie!" Harland laughed heartily at the thought. "I told you not to worry! She'll be just fine. It's just a woman thing. Hand me that lug-wrench." He chuckled again at the idea of Madge in Disneyland, as he reached out for the wrench. "Say, Son, whatever happened to that purty little curly-headed Betty Sue Jamison you used to take to the movies and all?"

"Oh, she's OK. She's graduating next month, too. Going up to Athens. Wants to be a nurse. She was at the party last night."

"Don't you ever take her out no more?"

"Naw, she's got herself another boyfriend." Danny's face reddened. She'd been at the party, all right. She'd been all over him, flirting up a storm! He changed the subject. "You know, Dad, I been thinking about joining the Army, or maybe the Marines."

Harland dropped the wrench on his foot. "Dammit!"

"Whaddya think? Army or Marines?"

\*　　\*　　\*

*Army or Marines?* Harland leaned down and rubbed his foot. He hoped Danny hadn't seen the shock and despair on his face at the thought of his son joining one of the armed services, of his leaving home. Harland had tried not to think too much about it, about Danny graduating from high school, going off somewhere, to school or something. He was feverishly proud of his son, the first in his family to graduate from high school. He knew Danny deserved a good life, nice job, maybe even some adventure. He was such a smart boy, a good boy, and Harland had nothing to offer him. Nothing! He sure couldn't imagine Danny working with *him*, down at the machine shop, getting his hands all scarred and black with grease, just barely making enough to live on, but it broke his heart to think of being separated from him. Thinking of him out there somewhere that he couldn't see him every day, couldn't take care of him if he got sick or something.

Harland cleared his throat and straightened up. "Well, I don't know. Whaddya want to go off for, leave yer ma, git sent all aroun' from here to there? Back and forth. I don't know. I jes think you kin do better than that, don't you?"

"Well, Dad, I could get a good education that way, and it wouldn't cost me anything. I think I'd like to get a job in computers or something technical, ya know? They say the Army's good for that."

"Computers! Ya don't say! Computers!" Harland shook his head in wonder. "Well, if that don't beat all!" He could feel his son, his purpose for living, his center, slipping away from him. His head swam. "Look, I think that's enough fer today. Let's go see what yer ma's got goin' fer lunch." He slammed down the hood of the old Mercury, gave it a pat and turned his face away from Danny.

"Come on, Son, let's wash up," he said, his voice rough as gravel. He leaned over the garage's deep aluminum tub-sink and began to lather his hands vigorously with Lava soap.

*　　*　　*

Standing next to his father at the grimy old garage sink, Danny looked first at his hands, and then at his father's. The lather on Harland's gnarled hands didn't cover up the scars, the prominent veins and the age spots. His familiar pungent scent of chewing tobacco, grease, soap and sweat made Danny's heart swell with love. He wanted to hug his old man, but didn't know how to even approach it.

When he looked back at his own smooth, tanned, muscular hands, the lather on them took his mind back to bubble-baths with Christine. He could feel her silky, soft skin and the delicious swell of her beautiful breasts, as his hands slid over them. He felt the old, familiar throb in his groin.

"You know what, Son? Since you're out of school till graduation, you'n me oughta jes take off 'n go down Gum Swamp Creek, camp out, do some fishin'. Whaddya think?"

"Gee, Dad, I don't know. I'm s'posed to work, but…"

"Aw come on, now. You kin git off, I bet. I got a bunch of vacation time comin', and we ain't gonna be busy next week. I know I kin git off. Why don't you see if you kin, too. We ain't done nuthin' like that since you wuz a little squirt."

"Sounds like a good idea. I'll see if I can talk the boss into it tomorrow."

He rinsed the soap off and patted Harland on the back as they skirted around the Mercury and moved toward the kitchen.

"Come on, Dad, you really think you're ever gonna get that old bucket of bolts running?"

Harland grinned happily. "Any day now, any day!"

## Chapter 27

Driving home on Friday afternoon, Christine was as happy as a lark. Although no grades were given out in class, she knew she had done really well. And Tim Cotter had been serious about the job offer, too. In fact, he had offered her almost double the salary she was getting from Taylor Homes. She and Tim had worked well together as a team on several class assignments. He hadn't embarrassed her further with any more personal questions or sexual advances. Of course, she couldn't consider leaving Waycross and her responsibility to Taylor Homes, not after Stan had invested so much in her education. Most of all, she couldn't imagine being separated from Danny! But she felt real strength in the knowledge that she was so employable.

She had called Jack both Wednesday and Thursday nights, but didn't get an answer. She felt a little ashamed of how glad she was when she didn't have to talk to him. A good wife would be worried that something might be wrong, but she was just relieved.

She tilted the rear-view mirror and took a look at herself. "You're not a very good wife, are you? In fact, you're a *bad girl*," she said aloud to the smiling reflection, "but you've got yourself a *profession*! You can take care of yourself, woman!" She rolled down the window and shouted out at the passing cars, "Whoopee! I'm gonna make it! Yeah! I'm gonna *make* it!"

As she filled up the car with gas at a freeway exit, the aroma of barbecue drifted under her nose and got her stomach juices flowing. She followed the seductive smell to a small, low-ceilinged, pit-cooked barbecue restaurant, and pigged out on Brunswick stew, cole slaw, cracklin' cornbread and barbecued pork. It amazed her how southern her tastes had become! She realized with some surprise that it had been months since she thought about her family, friends, and old life back in Pennsylvania.

Back on the road again, she turned on the static-riddled little VW radio. Aretha Franklin was belting out, "R-E-S-P-E-C-T…" Perfect! She joined in.

*   *   *

It was almost midnight when she rolled into her driveway, and she was stunned to see a large "For Sale" sign in the middle of her yard. "For Sale?" She couldn't believe her eyes! Was this some kind of a joke? Maybe it was more craziness from the mysterious anonymous letter writer.

The house was dark. She expected to see the flickering bluish light of the television in the living-room, and was hoping that Jack would be snoring away as usual in front of the set. To her surprise, neither Jack, the TV nor the BarcaLounger were there. She tip-toed quietly into the bedroom. The bed was empty.

"Jack," she called, "where are you?"

No answer.

She turned on the light. The closet door was open, and she could tell from across the room that his half was almost empty.

"Jack?" she called even louder into the empty house. The silence was ominous.

On the kitchen table, she found an envelope with "Red" written in large letters on the front. Inside was a note to her:

"Dear Red,

I've gone up to Allentown. I got a good job offer with my old trucking company. I'll be staying for a while with your mother and the reverend, till I can find us a place to live. Mrs. Townsend with Mayberg Realty can tell you all about the sale of the house. Her number is 912-361-5592.

I'll call you Saturday.

Jack"

She felt as if she were made of glass, fragile, extremely breakable. There was a ringing in her ears. She sat down slowly and carefully at the kitchen table, dazed, shaking her head in amazement as she read through the note several times. This couldn't really be happening! What did he mean, "...till I can find us a place to live..."? Had he lost his mind? Was *this* what he was thinking about when he had mentioned his "career plans"? Well, he had another think coming if he thought she would just pull up stakes and move back to Pennsylvania like that. Just like that! The nerve!

And staying with *her mother*! The nerve!

She ran into the living-room, grabbed up the telephone and started to punch in her mother's number, but stopped and slammed down the receiver. He said he'd call her. Fine! She'd just wait till he did. That would give her time to think more rationally about how to handle this.

The very *nerve*!

Her hands shook as she unpacked. Furiously, she hurled each article of dirty clothes into the dirty-clothes basket, and then kicked the basket to boot. It tipped over, spilling its contents. "Dammit, dammit, dammit! Fuck you, Jack!" she screamed at the basket as she flipped it up with another hefty slam.

*OK, this is ridiculous. This is it! I'm through! Let him move back to Allentown. Let somebody else deal with him. I'm through! I mean it! I'm through!*

\* \* \*

Jack was pleased with himself. Red's mother and the reverend had welcomed him with open arms. Made him feel right at home. "Rev" was a real nice fellow, for a preacher. He and Red's mom both thought Red was pushing her luck, going off to school and leaving him at home, getting so tied up in her new job. Thought she should appreciate having a good man like him to take care of her. Her mom was downright embarrassed for her.

He had found out what he wanted to know about getting a rig, too. He could get a nice one for what he had in the equity in the house in Waycross, what with his good credit and all. With his contacts from his trucking days, he could get all the loads he needed to keep him busy. Back on the road again!

His buddies were glad to see him back at the Wild Horse, as well. He'd had the first real fun he could remember since he'd left Allentown for Waycross. He had a great time on Friday night, getting sloshed on beer and dancing with a bunch of different broads. He was sure glad to be home!

Then on Saturday afternoon, he called Red. Boy, was that a letdown! She'd sounded cold as a witch's tit in a brass bra. She said she couldn't leave that shit-ass job of hers because she "had an obligation to Stan" since he'd made such an "investment" in her education! She'd asked him not to sell the house for a while, until she could figure out some other place to live. Fuck her! He had to sell the house to get a rig, so he could get back to work. What was so hard to understand about that?

*Women!*

It made him feel good to tell her about the two crazy letters he had gotten about her. He told her he had left them on the top of the chest of drawers. She didn't even answer him for a second or two.

"Red? Did you hear what I said? You better read them letters. Somebody's out to gitcha for sure down there."

"All right, Jack, I'll read them… Listen, you just… you do what you have to do, and I'll do what I have to do."

"What in the hell does *that* mean?"

"I guess it means that I'm not moving back to Allentown. Not for a while, anyway."

"Suit yourself, bitch!" He slammed down the receiver.

*Women! Who could figure them?*

## Chapter 28

Christine was shaking with anger after her conversation with Jack. He had hung up on her! She hadn't even been given a chance to talk to her own mother. What a jerk he was! She got herself a Coke and went out to sit on her back steps and gaze out into the pines.

On second thought, it wasn't such a bad conversation, after all. Hadn't this really been what she'd been waiting for? A chance to get away from Jack and the impossible situation they'd gotten into? She could spend time with Danny now, on a more regular basis. Okay. If Jack wanted to sell the house, fine! She'd start looking for an apartment, maybe out near Waresboro. More convenient. She started to feel excited about the idea. Danny could come spend the night with her. Oh, luxury…

She watched the end of the day soften the streaks of gray and white clouds with pink and amber, as lightening bugs began to twinkle back in the palmetto shrubs underneath the tall, spindly pines. The little yellow sparkles brought back the view from her hotel window in Atlanta, as the lights of the tall buildings had twinkled on in the pink light of sunset. She felt the strength she had gained in Atlanta begin to return.

An apartment, of course. She could afford her own apartment. She could fall asleep in Danny's arms, make breakfast for him, kiss the back of his neck as he drank his coffee. They would be free to indulge their every fantasy.

Suddenly, she remembered the letters Jack had told her about. She yanked herself out of her reverie and ran into the bedroom. There they were, on top of the chest as Jack had said—two envelopes addressed to "Mr. Radford" in what looked like a child's large printed letters. How strange! They couldn't be from a child! She didn't know any children here, and she was pretty sure Jack didn't either. But of course, they weren't written by a child. They came from some adult, trying to disguise his handwriting. She almost laughed at the utter foolishness of such a thing, but instead, she shuddered as cold fear crept up her spine. She was afraid to open them. Well, they weren't going away if she didn't open them. It was better to know than not to know, right?

With a conscious forcing of false courage, she started to pull the note out of the top envelope. There was a soft tap on the back door.

*Danny!*

She hastily stuffed the note back into the envelope and put it with its companion back on the top of the chest. She rushed through the kitchen and, with her heart pounding and hands shaking, opened the back door.

There he was, even more beautiful than she had remembered! Was his skin really creamier, tanner? Was his hair really blonder? Were his eyes really that blue? Wordlessly, she took him into her arms and nestled her face against his neck, breathing in his scent. He picked her up and she wrapped her legs around his trim, hard waist. He was too good to be true. He carried her across the kitchen and pressed her against the refrigerator.

"God, I love you, Christine! I thought I was going crazy without you these two weeks. I never thought I'd want anything like I want you!"

"I know, I know." She slipped down to her knees in front of him and kissed the wonderful hard bulge, as she unsnapped and began to unzip his jeans. Waves of desire radiated from her pelvis out to her toes and fingertips. He lowered himself to the floor and pulled her onto him.

They undressed each other slowly, each unbuttoning, each unzipping punctuated with another caress, another tasting. They rolled over, changing positions, oblivious of the hard, cold kitchen floor. She was lost again in the out-of-focus dimension of ecstasy. Her vision blurred. For one brief moment, she imagined that she saw a white, stricken face at the back door, but when she raised her head and focused her eyes on the spot, there was nothing there. She abandoned her senses to the rapture that was Danny.

After the piercing urgency of their need for each other had been assuaged, they moved to the living-room and lay on the sofa, partially dressed, still satisfying their sensual thirsts.

"How did you know that Jack was gone?" she asked, as her fingertips traced the veins in the muscles of his arms.

"Dad and I just got in from fishin' all week down Gum Swamp Creek, just a little while ago, and when I saw the sign in your yard, man I freaked!" He laughed. "I had a helluva time controlling myself. Didn't want Dad to think I'd lost my mind."

"…Or that your lover lived in the house behind that sign!"

"You got the picture. So, soon as we got inside, I asked Mama if she knew anything about the sign. She said it'd been put up last Tuesday or Wednesday, and then Jack, she calls him 'the big guy next door', had driven off Thursday, pulling a U-haul trailer, and she hadn't seen him since. I saw your car in the driveway and took a chance. If he'd of been home, I was gonna ask for a contribution for the school band."

"Ooooo, I'm glad you took a chance!"

"Me, too," he whispered in her ear and moved his lips down her neck in a path of little kisses and nibbles. He looked up and asked, "So what's goin' on?"

The romantic spell was broken. "That sorry bastard took off for Allentown, staying with *my mother*. Can you believe the nerve? He thinks we're selling the house and moving back there so he can get another truck—go back to work for his old company. 'Course, he didn't bother to mention any of this to me."

"You're not *moving*?" he asked with alarm.

"No way! If he wants to go, so much the better, right? Me? I'm stayin' right here."

"But what about the house? Is he really gonna sell it?"

"Who cares? I guess he's got to sell it so he can buy himself another rig. I'm gonna rent an apartment, or maybe a little house—out towards Waresboro, if I can find something I can afford. Just think, then we could be together without worrying about anybody seeing us. It's a blessing in disguise. You can spend the night with me."

He took her gently in his arms and murmured softly in her ear, "I can fuck your brains out all night long…"

"Danny, you're such an incurable romantic! You know that?" She laughed and shook her head.

He continued, "…but I gotta go right now. I haven't even unpacked. I sorta slipped out while Mama was givin' Dad the what-for for something or other. I'm sure they've missed me by now."

"Maybe we can go somewhere tomorrow. We could go to a movie, if you've had enough of the swamp for a while."

"I'll go over to Mark's and give you a call after church. We'll sneak away somewhere."

"Okay, Honey. Good-night. I love you." She tousled his hair as he started out the kitchen door.

He stopped on the back steps and looked up at her. "…and I *adore* you. Good-night, sleep tight…"

"…And don't let the bed-bugs bite," they said in unison.

As soon as he left, she remembered the letters waiting for her on the chest of drawers. She marched purposefully into the bedroom and retrieved them.

*Just get it over with.*

They couldn't be as bad as her fear of them was, right? She took them into the kitchen, fortified herself with the last Coke in the refrigerator, and opened the first one.

The chaotic look of the different-sized letters and patched-up bits of words caused a wave of nausea to rush up from her stomach. This was really sick. *"Devil worshipper? Whore of Babylon?"* This had to be from some religious fanatic. Why would anyone hate her so much? She hadn't done anything bad to anybody in this town. It had to be about her relationship with Danny, what else?

Suddenly, the ghostly face at the kitchen door flashed into her memory. Oh my God! It was Madge! Madge knew what was going on! Of course she did. She had seen them making love on the kitchen floor. How humiliating! Christine's knees buckled under her. How awful! Oh my God! Their naked bodies! Exposed!

Madge must have known for some time. That would explain why she was so rude, why she always avoided Christine, why she always pretended she didn't see her. But even so, why would she do such a crazy thing as to send Jack a sick letter like this? Why didn't she just stop Danny from coming over? Settle it within her own family? Maybe even take it up face to face with *her*? Christine shuddered at the thought. She read over the pasted-up letters carefully. This was serious. She was dealing with a real nut-case here.

In a panic now, irrational, she ran around the house, making sure all the doors and windows were securely locked. Maybe she should get some help, call the police. But then, Madge would see the police car, and really get mad. And what would the police do, anyway?

They'd take the letters down to the station and forget about them, most likely. And what if they started investigating what it was that made Madge so mad? They'd have to know about Danny, about their relationship. Would they accuse her of contributing to the delinquency of a minor? Or something worse? Statutory rape? She wished that she could call Bessie, but it was almost midnight. She just couldn't wake her up so late. And what could Bessie do anyway? What could anybody do? Dear God, she had brought this all on herself! She began to shake violently, as the cold nausea swept over her. She ran to the bathroom, sobbing.

*God help me! God forgive me! Somebody help me, please!*

\* \* \*

Early the next morning she staggered to the kitchen, drained emotionally and physically, and made herself a pot of coffee. It was only 5:30, but she had given up on any real sleep. After a cup of coffee and a bowl of cereal, she showered, dressed and finished unpacking. Back in the kitchen, she watched the clock hand move at a glacial pace until it finally reached 9:00, the time she had decided she could call Bessie.

"Hello?" Bessie answered the phone in a sleep-thickened voice.

"Bessie, it's Red. Can I come over, or can you come over here? I'm in deep trouble. I need a friend, bad." To her chagrin, she began to cry.

"Oh Lord, Red. What's happened?"

"First of all…" she sobbed, "…when I got back last night, Jack was gone…"

"Well, that's not so bad now, is it?"

"…and he's put the house up for sale!"

"Now *that's* serious!" Bessie admitted.

"And somebody's sent him these awful, *hateful* anonymous letters about me. Poison pen letters about *me*!"

"You're kidding."

"No, I'm not! Two of 'em! Bessie, I'm scared. Can I come over and show 'em to you?"

"Of course you can! Right now, if you want to."

"Oh, thank you, Bessie, thank you."

"Hey, what're friends for?"

Christine hung up the phone and finished her coffee in a gulp. She was ready to go, car keys on the table and the letters in her pocket-book. She wanted to be back home by noon, so she wouldn't miss Danny's call.

*Danny's call…*

"Christine," she said aloud to herself, "you've got your priorities right!" She had to laugh at herself in spite of everything.

## Chapter 29

Madge had watched Harland and Danny leave for their fishing trip last week with mixed emotions. In a way, she was glad to get them out from under her feet, but at the same time she resented how they could just take off like that, so easy. Harland had asked her to come along. Hmmph! Like he thought she'd want to go wallowing around in a muddy old swamp, getting eaten alive by bugs, maybe even snake-bit! That sure wasn't her idea of fun.

She felt sick to her stomach, too. She'd felt sick ever since she'd seen those naked bodies, rolling around on the kitchen floor. Nasty, nasty, nasty! And one of them was her son! She didn't know him any more. How could he do such a thing? The whole thing was so filthy. Filthy! She wished she could get it out of her mind. She tried to concentrate on her housework.

She had had a bunch of things she wanted to get done, with the men out of the way. New kitchen curtains for one, and cleaning and re-organizing those messy shelves in the garage where Harland kept all his precious junk, for another. But that only took up the first day and a half, and then she started getting bored. She had spent a lot of time watching the house next door for signs of immoral behavior, imagining what evil, Satanic things could be going on. But there was no sign of the whore or of her tacky little foreign car. Madge hadn't had anything to keep her going except looking forward to the Thursday Night Circle meeting.

But then the real estate lady showed up next door, and staked out the "For Sale" sign in the front yard. What could that mean? They probably couldn't pay the rent, or mortgage, or whatever, what with the big guy just lollin' around the house, not working any that she could see. Well, she was glad they were moving! Maybe she could get some decent, God-fearing neighbors for a change. And the sinful fornication that was keeping Danny over there all the time—well, that would come to a stop. And about time, too! Hmmph! She'd be glad to see the back of both of them.

The long, dark nights alone in the house were another matter entirely. She began to hear suspicious noises every once in a while: scratches, thumps, snuffling sounds. She was afraid that some of the niggers down at the machine shop would know that Harland was gone for a week, and that would just be an invitation for people like that to come break in and rob her, or even worse. Oh Lord, she couldn't even think about it! She kept all the windows closed and bolted every night, hot as it was. A couple of times, when she was really frightened, she took one of Harland's rifles out of the gun cabinet, and went from window to window with her heart pounding, peeking through the glass and pointing the unloaded rifle out at the empty yard. Oh, how she wished she knew how to load and shoot the thing. She vowed that when Harland got back, she'd make him teach her how.

At the Thursday night circle meeting, she refreshed the thirsty ladies with news of the deplorable goings-on next door. After the clucking had subsided, she told them how her husband and son had gone *fishing* and left her all alone for a long week. They discussed at great length how dangerous it was for a white woman to be left alone at night now-a-days, and they all agreed it was heartless for Harland to have done such a thing.

By the time Harland and Danny got in on Saturday night, she had worked up a full head of steam, and she really let Harland have it! She wouldn't let up until he promised to take her out on Sunday afternoon and teach her how to shoot.

\* \* \*

Bessie rushed around, straightening up her apartment. Red was on her way over to talk about that son-of-a-bitch she was married to, and some nasty letters somebody had sent him. Bessie threw dirty clothes into the closet, stacked magazines in a pile on the small remaining empty space on the coffee table, gathered up dirty dishes from tables and, yes, even from chairs, and dumped them in a tottering pile in the sink. She pulled the bedspread up over the rumpled sheets, pillows, over-due library books and Speigel catalogues that festooned the bed. She zoomed into the bathroom, splashed some water on her face and gave her teeth a vigorous, 21-second brushing, then back into the bedroom where she plunged her body into a caftan and her feet into fuzzy little slippers. All of this was accomplished in the 17 minutes that it took Christine to get over to her house.

She answered Christine's knock with her usual aplomb, eyelids back at half-mast, and drawled, "Well, get yourself on in here, Red. Wanna cup of coffee?"

"Thanks, Bessie. Look, I hope I'm not intruding, inviting myself over like this, but…"

"Forget it, Red. You're welcome any time. You know that!"

The truth was that Bessie was delighted to have Christine turn to her for help. She thought of Christine as her best friend. Bessie knew a whole slew of people, but there weren't many she could actually call "friends". She knew that a lot of folks thought of her as "trailer trash", and it hurt her, but she couldn't be anything other than herself. She'd made a couple of attempts to dress and act in a more conservative manner, but it just didn't work. She felt like a fool dressed in a plain little gray suit, and looked about as dull as yesterday's mashed potatoes. Besides that, it was a strain, holding back, trying to act all prissy, prim and proper. Anyway, Christine accepted her the way she was, respected her, trusted her.

"Come on in here and tell me what's happened."

Christine hugged her and said, "Thank you for being such a good friend." She shook her head and stammered, "I…I really don't know where to start."

"Let me see those letters. We can start there."

Christine pulled the two letters from her purse as if they were slimy, and handed them to Bessie with a mixture of shame and worry.

Bessie led her into her remarkably messy kitchen, cleared a small space at the table with a sweep of her arm, poured Christine a cup of tepid coffee and refilled her own cup. "When did Jack get these things?" She opened the first one and began to read the vicious little message. "Jesus, Red! This is sick!"

"I know, I know. Jack got 'em both while I was in Atlanta. He told me he'd gotten 'em, but I guess I didn't take it seriously. Guess I was too busy to think about it."

"You got any idea who'd do something this stupid to you? I mean, this is seriously *stupid*!"

"The only person I can think of who dislikes me enough to do something like this is...I hate to accuse anybody... Anyway, I'm probably wrong..."

"Okay Red, quit beating around the bush! Who?"

"Well, maybe it could be Danny's mother, Madge. I know this sounds crazy, but I thought I saw her peeking in the window in my back-door last night."

"Git outta here!"

"Well, maybe I just imagined it... Oh, Bessie! I was so happy driving back from Atlanta! I thought I had the world by the tail, you know?"

"You did good, huh?"

"You better believe it! I got offered a job in Atlanta—making almost twice as much as Stan's paying me. I learned so much, had so much fun... Then I get home to all this: Jack gone, the house up for sale, poison pen letters, threats aimed at me!"

"Maybe it's time you moved on—took that job in Atlanta…"

"No, no. I'm not ready for that. I couldn't leave Stan right now. He hasn't got anybody to take over and run his new computer system, and he's been so good to me, invested so much in me, I couldn't take off now. Not to mention… Well… I couldn't leave Danny! You wouldn't believe how bad I missed him while I was in Atlanta. And you, my best friend! My *only* friend, besides Danny." Christine was shaking by now, and tears were streaming down her face.

Bessie hurried over to her, wrapped her big, soft arms around her and let her sob it out against her shoulder. "Okay, Red, cool it. There's ways we can deal with this. First off, why don't you move in with me for a while—till you can figure out what you want to do?"

"My gosh! What a nice offer! I might take you up on it, if I have to. I mean, if the house is sold before… I'm gonna start looking for a place out near Taylor Homes, tomorrow. I've made up my mind that I'm *not* going back to Allentown with Jack. No way!" Christine jumped up from the table and started pacing around the kitchen. "But what am I gonna do about those letters?"

"Well, I guess there's not a helluva lot you *can* do. You got no proof where they came from. And, now don't take this wrong, but you don't wanna stir up a lot of talk—attract any uh, undue attention to your situation, if you know what I mean."

Christine sat down at the table and shook her head in resignation. "I know, I know, but it's so…it's so *unfair*!" She jumped up again and started pacing. "And what if she reports me to the police—decides to take some legal action against me—accuses me of contributing to the delinquency of a minor, or *statutory rape*? Oh God, what if—"

"Hold on, now! In the first place, I don't think you've done anything illegal. I'll ask one of the lawyers about that tomorrow—one of the advantages of working in a law office. In the second place, if it's Madge that sent these letters, I don't think she's gonna want to broadcast it all over Waycross. She'd of done that already, if that's what she wanted."

Christine sat down again, somewhat calmer. "Well, whaddya think I ought to do?"

"If I was you, I'd put these stupid letters in a drawer and try to forget about 'em. Then, I'd call the real estate company tomorrow and find out what's going on. Then I'd start putting the stuff I wanna keep into storage somewhere. If you want to, you can put it in my name. By the way, is your bank account in Jack's name?"

"No. We've got separate accounts. I opened my own when I had to send him that money in Mexico—when I first went to work for Stan. I didn't want any of my paychecks going to Mexico, if I could help it."

"Sounds like you're in good shape. And just in case, I'll start cleaning up the spare bedroom. I've been looking for an excuse to do that, anyway."

"Bless you, Bessie! I feel a lot better about everything. Oops, look at the time! I've got to go." Christine giggled and looked a little sheepish. "Danny's gonna call me when he gets out of church."

"You're a wild woman, Red! Damned if you ain't!"

## Chapter 30

In church that morning, Madge felt a thrill when they started singing "Onward Christian Soldiers." *She* was now one of God's Christian soldiers! She would march on, fearless, and proudly carry the banner of His vengeance. Her face glowed with an unaccustomed fervor. Last night, when she saw the disgusting sight on her hated neighbor's kitchen floor, she heard God command her to get rid of the pestilent whore. She would save her son and the rest of the world from that evil woman!

When the song ended, she bowed her head briefly and prayed silently, "Jesus help me to be the sword of your righteous vengeance. Amen."

As Harland drove them home after the benediction, Madge said, "The pot roast'll be done by the time we get home. Soon as we finish dinner, we can go out for my first shootin' lesson."

"Well, sure, Madge. That'll be fine," Harland answered. She ignored the twinge of concern in his voice.

After their Sunday dinner, which Danny had gulped down like the house was on fire or something, she stacked the dishes in the sink, leaving them for later, and hung up her apron. Danny had already rushed off to Mark's house, and Harland had just settled down into his easy chair with the Sunday paper and rested his head back onto the little crocheted antimacassar, when she appeared in the living room, hands on hips. "Well, are we goin' out shootin' or not?"

He jerked himself to attention. "Sure! If you really want…"

"How many times do I have to say it? Yes, Harland! I really want to learn about them guns and how to use 'em!"

Harland put the paper aside and got up with forced enthusiasm. "Well, let's just do it, then," he answered as he opened the glass doors on the gun cabinet. As he stroked the long barrel of a large old gun lovingly, he seemed to warm to the task. "This is my grandpa's old goose gun. You sure don't want to use *it*. I just keep it here for looks. It's dangerous—hadn't got no safety on it. Ya better stay clear of it!" He laughed. "Course, it ain't loaded."

"Whut's the best one to use if ya need to kill somebody a ways off from ya? Uh, like across the yard?" Madge's eyes had a hard-edged gleam.

"I reckon that'd be this one," he said, taking out long, slim rifle. "This here's a .22. Won't knock ya down when ya shoot it, but it'll do the job." He pointed it out the window and sighted down the barrel. "Ka-pow!"

"So, is that one loaded?"

"Lord no, Madge! I wouldn't keep a loaded gun in the house. You oughta know that!"

"Well, kin ya please load it, and let's git out back an' start showing me how to use the thing?" Why was he piddlin' around so much over this?

Harland couldn't help wondering why Madge had all-of-a-sudden gotten so interested in learning how to shoot a gun. She'd always had a real low opinion of guns, hunting and the like. It was nice to have her treating him like maybe he knew something for a change, but a little worrisome at the same time. Somehow, the story about how scared she got while he and Danny were out fishing didn't ring true. She's been alone before when they went hunting or fishing, and she hadn't been particularly scared.

"You better go change clothes 'fore we go out into them woods. You'll git mighty scratched up if you don't."

"But I did change! Why d'ya think I got on these pedal-pushers?"

"Well, Madge, I think maybe ya'd better put on some of *my* pants—cover up your whole legs. Then flimsy little pants are purty, but they ain't gonna do ya much good out in the palmettos!"

"Your pants? Lord help me, Harland! They ain't gonna fit!"

"Jes try on them overalls I paint in. They're hangin' on a hook in the closet."

A few minutes later, Madge returned to the living room wearing his paint-spattered overalls and an expression of embarrassed resignation. She wouldn't look at Harland, but kept her eyes mostly on the ceiling. "Well...?"

Harland chuckled. "I do declare, Madge, but derned if ya don't look kinda cute in them overalls!"

"Oh, stop talkin' like a fool and let's git out there and start shootin'!"

Was that a *smile* he saw on her face?

He poked his arms through the open sleeves of his hunting vest, dropped a couple of handfuls of .22 cartridges into a pocket, and a few minutes later they were making their way through the thick brush behind their house. Harland led the way, carrying the Winchester, trying to open up a path for her, but succeeding only partially. She was gamely following him, punctuating almost every step with an "Ouch!" or an "Oh!"

Soon they came to a swampy opening in the pines, where the dense underbrush stopped.

"Okay," Harland said, "I think it'll be safe to do a little target practice here. First, ya need to know how to load." He removed several .22 rim fire cartridges from a large pocket in his vest. "First off, make sure the safety's on. See that li'l dot? When it's red, the safety's off, and you kin shoot yerself in the foot. Ya really don't wanna do that!" He laughed at his own little joke, beginning to enjoy himself immensely. Madge did not laugh.

He twisted open the tube below the barrel, the magazine, inserted the cartridges, reinserted the spring-loaded rod and twisted the magazine closed. "Didja watch that?" She nodded. He twisted open the magazine, emptied the shells into his hand and handed her the gun. "See, the safety's still on. Now you load it!"

She took the shells one by one from his hand, dropped them into the magazine and twisted it shut. "There!" she said with a grunt of satisfaction.

"Well, ain't you somethin'?" He took the gun from her and said, "Okay, Miss Smarty-pants, now watch this carefully." He raised the gun and tucked the stock snugly into his shoulder, steadying the barrel with his left hand. "Be sure ya got the stock, uh... the handle here, good and tight into your shoulder." He wiggled his right-hand index finger. "When ya put this finger on the trigger, be sure ya squeeze, not pull. *Squeeze*, not *pull*. Got it?"

"Got it!"

"Okay, here." He handed her the rifle. "Now you do it just like I did, but don't squeeze the trigger yet."

Madge copied his stance and handled the rifle just as he had. She looked through the gun's sights and pointed the barrel across the little clearing. "Bang, bang!" she said, "You're dead!"

Harland was really surprised. That was the nearest thing to a joke she had made in too many years for him to remember. This was fun! "Okay, Annie Oakley, now push your right thumb forward on that little button there and it'll take the safety off."

She did as he said and, with a strange little smile, put her finger on the trigger.

"Good. Now, that finger you got on the trigger? Squeeze it real slow and easy-like."

"All right, I'm squeezin'!" The rifle discharged with a loud "crack". Madge jumped and let out a scream.

Harland steadied her. "Good girl! Now do it agin, and this time aim it at that big pine over there. Just line up that little point stickin' up on the end of the barrel in the center of the notch here and put both of 'em on the target, hold the gun still, and remember, *squeeze*, don't *pull* that trigger."

She gave him a dirty look which made him chuckle contentedly. She squeezed the trigger with a cold assurance.

For over an hour, Harland led her gently through the skills of killing something with a rifle. It was the best exchange of friendship they had experienced since they had been married. Madge concentrated with great determination, listening carefully to everything Harland told her. By the end of an hour or so, she was splattering pine cones off a log where Harland had set them up as targets for her. He wanted to hug her, but decided he'd better not push his luck.

They continued the practice until he was out of bullets and then walked back on the rough pathway like a couple of pals. Harland was indeed a happy man!

*   *   *

Christine was just leaving to meet Danny at the Madison Theater when she heard the sound of gunfire. It sounded like it was coming from the woods behind the house. She had a moment of cold fear, but convinced herself in short order that there must be someone hunting back in the woods. Anyway, she was driving all the way to the other side of Waycross to a movie selected on the sole merit of its being the farthest from their neighborhood, with less likelihood of their being seen by anyone they knew.

She ignored the continuing gunfire. She had other things to worry about besides being accidentally shot by some near-sighted hunter!

Danny was waiting for her as planned, sitting in the center of the back row, munching on popcorn from a large bucket-sized container. He was slumped down in his seat with his feet propped up on the back of the seat in front of him. After a brief glance in her direction, he looked back at the screen, where a huge, jelly-like substance was oozing down someone's staircase. He tilted the popcorn bucket toward her. "How're ya doin', cutie-pie?" he drawled, as if this meeting were an every-day occurrence.

She giggled and felt like a high-school girl again. Like the carefree and confident high-school girl she had *wanted* to be, but never really was. She slipped her hand through the space between the arm-rest and the seat and ran her fingertips provocatively up and down his thigh. He moaned softly through his mouthful of popcorn.

She decided to wait until after the movie to tell him about the letters and her suspicions about their source. She got some popcorn out of the bucket with her free hand, settled back into her seat, and watched the slime move further down the steps and engulf a poodle.

## Chapter 31

Bessie was worried about Red. It was bad enough to be taking a roll in the hay with a teen-ager, but taking it with a teen-ager with a crazy mother, now that was just plain dumb. Add to that a big, hard-drinking, old-fashioned, male-chauvinist husband, and you've got a recipe for disaster. Bessie really liked Red, and felt like she had a stake in her future, since she had launched her, so to speak, on her career. How could such an intelligent woman be such a fool over a horny kid? Of course, he *was* a *hunk.* Oh, yeah, no doubt about that!

When she got to the office on Monday morning, she checked with Laura Mae to see which lawyer, if any, had some free time.

"What's up?" Laura Mae asked. "You need some free legal advice?"

"As a matter of fact, I do. I've got this friend who's havin' a... uh, *flirtation* with a guy a lot younger than she is. A *lot* younger."

Laura Mae arched her eyebrows. "Mmmm... For a *friend*, huh?"

"Yeah. A *good* friend!"

Laura Mae snickered and looked down at the appointment book. "Looks like Sidney has a free hour after lunch." She rolled her eyes and then gave Bessie a lurid wink. Bessie wondered what in the world had gotten into her. Could Laura Mae suspect that she had a little crush on Sidney Haynes, the youngest and nicest of the three lawyers in their office? She had been very careful to conceal it, always treating all three with the same respect and consideration.

"Thanks, Laura Mae. Would you buzz me when his last client before lunch leaves?"

"Sure. Glad to help." More bizarre eyebrow-raising and eye-rolling.

Later, when she asked Sidney if it was illegal for an older woman to have sex with a teen-ager, a high-school boy, he laughed.

"Tell your '*friend*' that she doesn't have anything to worry about. The age of consent in Georgia is 13. Can you believe it? And statutory rape is a 'spit-on-the-sidewalk' thing. It's never charged unless there's some real element of rape in the relationship. As for 'contributing to the delinquency of a minor', as long as you don't get him drunk, do drugs with him, or rob a filling station, you're okay. I'd say just have a good time and don't worry about it." He winked at her.

Bessie felt an unaccustomed blush rising from her throat to her face. She turned away quickly and started out the door. He had winked at her. He was behaving almost as strangely as Laura Mae had. At the door, she turned and, in her most business-like voice told him, "Thanks, Sidney. My friend will really appreciate this."

"Hey, tell her I said 'Go for it!'" He chuckled.

*Amazing...*

As she passed the receptionist's desk, there was Billy Joe again, the kid from the Tasty Burger, lounging against the desk. He whirled around and sputtered, "Uh... Hiya, Bessie. You're lookin' good. How's it goin?"

"Busy, Billy Joe, busy." she answered with a half smile, hurried into her office and closed the door, still a little flustered from Sidney's wink. She wondered if she should speak to Laura Mae about Billy Joe hanging around the office so much. Of course, he *was* Laura Mae's cousin and all that, but still...

But Sidney had *winked* at her!

When Bessie arrived at the Thomas School later that evening, there was a note from Red standing up against her telephone, asking if they could meet at the Tasty Burger when she got out of class. Good. She'd tried to call Red a couple of times after talking to Sidney, but Red had been in a meeting or something all day.

Red was already seated in their regular booth when Bessie made her customary celebrity entrance into the Tasty Burger. She hurried over to the booth and got there just as a beaming Billy Joe did. She tossed her order to him over her shoulder, "Hi, Sweetie, bring me my regular."

"Comin' right up, Bessie," he said. His face was flushed.

Bessie didn't even look toward Billy Joe. She said to Red, "So, where you been all day? I've been trying to call you."

"Hi, Bessie. I've been real busy. You wouldn't believe how far behind Stan got on everything while I was gone. Boy, were they glad to see me back!"

Bessie lowered her voice. "Well, I got some good news for ya. I asked one of the lawyers about Georgia laws about sex with minors, and he more-or-less said not to worry. Said to tell you to 'Go for it.' I'll swear."

"That's encouraging, for sure."

"So, you decided to come back to school?"

"You betcha. I'm sticking to my guns, getting back into classes, getting my Associate's degree if I can, in spite of all this other stuff."

"Good for you. Don't you let anything stop you!"

"I'm not, Bessie. I'll swear, I'm gonna make this all work out. You'll see."

"Hey. I believe you."

They chatted cheerfully, Bessie putting away a chili cheese steak sandwich, and each of them having a beer, the only change in their routine being that, since Red got back from Atlanta, she always ordered Heineken instead of Bud. As they headed out, Red took one of Bessie's round hands in hers and squeezed it. "You don't know how good it is to have somebody I can talk to, be honest with, confide in. Bessie, I really…"

"Oh, cut it out, Red. You're gonna make me cry. Smear my mascara. Maybe I'll see you tomorrow at school."

"Sure. I'll stop by before class. Night, Bessie." Red gave her a hug as they parted in the parking lot. "Thanks again for checking with your lawyer friend."

"Forget it. Night-night." Bessie felt a surge of affection for her friend. It really felt good to be able to do something nice for somebody who was trying as hard as Red was.

When Bessie got into her car, she was annoyed to see a folded piece of paper stuck behind her windshield wiper. "Shit," she snarled, "another stupid advertisement!" She stepped out, grabbed the paper off the windshield, wadded it into a ball and threw it in the general direction of the dumpster behind the Tasty Burger. Then, as she started back into the car she stopped abruptly. Was that her name she had seen on it? She walked over and picked up the little paper ball and unfolded it. Yes, her name was on the front, and little hearts were drawn before and after it. Hearts? How weird! She looked around the parking lot. Red had already left, and no one else was in sight. She got back into the car, turned on the interior lights and read:

> *Bessie, Bessie, girl of the hour.*
> *To me you are a pretty flower.*
> *I think about you night and day,*
> *And hope you like me the same way.*
> *~From Your Secret Lover~*

She searched the note front and back, but couldn't find any indication of its source. Her heart fluttered for a moment as she let herself imagine that it might be from Sidney. Quickly, she dismissed that thought. He wouldn't come into a place like this, and surely, he'd write a better poem than this. Besides, he didn't have any way of knowing she would be here, anyway. She looked around the parking lot again, but still didn't see anyone, so she tucked the note into her voluminous purse and chuckled to herself as she drove toward home.

Intriguing… Probably one of the kids from school, playing a joke on her. Well, if there was one thing she knew how to do, it was how to take a joke.

\* \* \*

Christine arrived home exhausted. Things had really been in a mess when she first got to the office this morning. There was no doubt in her mind now that Stan really needed her.

She made up her mind to start training Edda-Lou to take more responsibility in operating the accounting systems. Christine had met Edda-Lou in Cobol class at Thomas, and had recommended her for the part-time key-punch job. Edda-Lou was young and bright and was already able to bring the system up and run some of the simpler jobs, following the detailed instructions Christine had carefully written for her. The experience of the last two weeks had convinced Stan that he needed to hire a computer operator as well as a key-punch operator. Christine wanted to see Edda-Lou promoted to the new position.

She kicked off her shoes and collapsed onto the sofa. What a day! She hadn't had a second to catch her breath. She had managed to get in a call to Mayberg Realty and left a message for Mrs. Townsend to call her ASAP. She had also brought home the Waycross Chronicle. She opened it now to "Apartments for Rent" and scanned the approximately two dozen ads for something near Waresboro. This wasn't easy, since she didn't know the names of many of the streets there, and didn't recognize any of the streets mentioned in the ads. She'd have to get some help. She bet Danny would know where these streets were. If only he would come over.

*Danny, come here to me. I want you. I need you. We could—*

The telephone startled her out of her reverie. A syrupy sweet southern voice oozed out of the earpiece.

"Miz Rad-fud? How're you doin' tonight? This is Ellie Townsend with Mayberg Real-ity Comp'ny?" she whined. "I've been talkin' to that big, handsome hus-bun' of yours."

"Who? Oh, you must mean Jack." Christine couldn't help herself. The vibrations of that high-pitched voice sent an irritating current from her ear-drums out through her whole nervous system.

"Yes ma'am, that's the one aw-right." Ellie Townsend giggled.

"Well, Mrs. Townsend, I need to meet with you as soon as possible to discuss the terms of the sale of my house."

"Of co-us, Miz Rad-fud. How's about I take you to lunch tomorrow?" she cooed, the invitation sticky with honey. "They's a real nice place out there near where you work, that has the best fried 'tater logs you evah ate. It's 'Josie's Kitchen.' You know the place?"

One more minute of this and Christine would scream. "Yes, I know the place. Meet you there at 11:45?"

"Wunnerful! I've reah-ly been lookin' fard to meetin' you, Miz Rad-fud."

"Tomorrow at 11:45, then. Good-bye."

"Bye, now!"

Well, she'd have to steel herself for this one. She hoped she wouldn't show her intense irritation at that voice. Not to mention the sale of her house, right out from under her. Punching out the silly woman wouldn't help matters a bit, though.

"Aw-rat, Christine," she drawled aloud. "Y'all jes git you-seff to the kitchen and git you-seff a li'l ole bite to eat, now, ya heah?" She had picked up a barbecue sandwich on the way home. Much as she loved barbecue, she had a fleeting wish that she had a nice New England pot-roast sandwich in the bag, instead. She got a Coke out of the refrigerator. Perfect with a barbecue sandwich. Yeah, she guessed she'd sold out to southern taste.

*When in Rome...*

Next day, when she walked into Josie's, she immediately spotted Mrs. Townsend. The aging southern belle personified. She was seated in a booth by a window overlooking the asphalt parking lot, the pot-holed highway and the seedy strip mall across the street. Her faded pink-champagne-blond hair was teased to perfection into a dry, balloon-like froth which added a good four inches to her height and bobbed with frantic good-will above the back of the booth. The sparkling frames of her multi-colored rhinestone-studded glasses swept jauntily upward at the corners, and were attached to a thin chain which looped down over her shoulders. There was even more froth at the neck and wrists of her pink polka-dot dress.

As Christine approached the booth, the foamy apparition turned toward her expectantly, her mascara-heavy eyelashes batting madly.

Her bright red mouth opened into a big smile, revealing a broad smear of red lipstick on her teeth.

"Mrs. Townsend?" Christine asked, extending her hand. "I'm Christine Radford."

Ellie Townsend bubbled up out of the booth and met Christine's handshake with a plump little hand tipped with brilliant red fake nails. The thumbnail had been lost, most likely in the storm of ruffles at her wrists. The handshake was disconcertingly limp, belying her overdone facade of enthusiasm. The exposed thumbnail was bitten down to the quick, and had a yellowish, unhealthy look.

"Weh-ull, weh-ull, weh-ull! It's a real pleasure to meet you, I'm sure. That big ole good-lookin' hubby of yours didn't tell me he had such a purty wife. My goodness? I always did jes *love* red hair!"

Christine coughed as she took her seat, choking on the thick scent of Tabu.

*Will I live through this?*

She cleared her throat. "Well, Mrs. Townsend, what arrangements did you make with my husband about the sale of the house? He's in Pennsylvania, and we haven't had a chance to talk about it."

"Whut all do you need to know?"

"What will you be expecting of me? Will you be showing the house any time soon?"

"Now don't you worry one little bit about that. Mr. Rad-fud said you'd be movin' ever-thing up north with him real soon? I'll jes wait till then, fore I start bringin' folks in."

Why did the voices of southern women always curve upward at the ends of their sentences, making everything they said tentative? "But I may not be moving to Pennsylvania anytime soon. I'm looking for an apartment here, uh, until I can get some things in order at work."

*Why do I feel like I have to explain any of this to this ... this frou-frou?*

"Oh, dearie me, now that might be a little *prob*-lim. Mr. Rad-fud promised me a *bo*-nus if I kin git your purty little house sold befo-ah the end of the month. I've awready got two *re*-al inter-rested parties. I'll need to git 'em in for a little look-see real soon?"

"How soon?"

"Weh-ull, this comin' week-end'd be jes fine!"

"This week-end? Sorry, no way. I can't possibly be out for a month or so."

"Weh-ull ma'am, you better take that up with yoah husbun'? It looks like to me he's in a big hurry to sell it."

"Okay, Mrs. Townsend. I'll call him tonight and see what I can find out. I'll call you back tomorrow or the next day." Christine got up to leave. She certainly couldn't stomach having lunch with this woman.

"Weh-ull goodness me, it's been a *re*-al pleasure to meet you, Miz Rad-fud. You jes give me a ting-a-ling tomorrow and let me know if this week-end's okay? Co-us, I could show it while you're still there. I kin call you—"

"Don't call me. I'll call you by Friday. Good-day Mrs. Townsend," Christine said as she hurried toward the exit.

She stopped by Burger-King and picked up a hamburger, some fries and a coke on her way back to the office. Her anger at the whole situation was boiling up into her brain, making it hard for her to think clearly. She clenched her teeth.

*That sorry bastard! Thought he could have me out in a week or two? He's got a lot to learn!*

## Chapter 32

The phone was ringing when Bessie arrived home, tired and irritable after a long day of frustrating problems at the law office and then again at the school.

*Damn that phone. What now?*

"Hello," she barked.

"Bessie?" a tentative adolescent male voice cracked.

"Yeah?"

"This is Billy Joe Reeves."

"Who?"

"Billy Joe Reeves. You know, from the Tasty Burger?"

Bessie held the phone away from her ear and looked at it incredulously. What in the world was he calling *her* for?

"Oh, yeah. Uh… how're you doing, Billy Joe?" *How'd he get this number?*

"Jes fine, jes fine! Uh… So, yer doin' good, huh?"

"Yes, Billy Joe, I'm fine. Fine! What-cha want? I just got in, and I'm real tired."

"Oh, gee, I'm sorry to bother ya, but I, uh… I'd like to talk to ya 'bout sumpin'"

"What is it, Billy Joe? Get to the point."

"Uh, well..."

"Well, what? Look—"

"I know you git jobs for people down at the school, an' I wuz... uh, I wuz jes wonderin' if maybe..."

"Maybe what? For goodness sakes, Billy Joe!"

In a rush now, "Maybe you could git me a new job somewheres."

"Oh, for goodness sakes. I get jobs for students of the school, not for the general public. Besides, you already got a job."

"But, cain't we even talk about it? Waitin' on tables at the Tasty Burger ain't no decent kind of job."

"Listen to me, Billy Joe. You come down and enroll in the school, take some technical courses, get yourself some skills. *Then* I'll help you get a better job, okay?"

"Could I come over 'n maybe we could jes talk about it?" A sad little note of pleading had crept into his already unsteady voice.

"Sorry, but... Look, I don't mean to be rude or anyothing. Tell you what. Why don't you stop by my office at the school some evening? We can talk about it then, okay? I gotta go right now."

"Sounds great, Bessie! I'm off on Tuesdays. Kin I come by next Tuesday?"

"Yeah, I guess that'll be all right. About 6:00?"

"It's a date, Bessie. It's a date. Thanks."

*It's not a date, Billy Joe. Lord, what have I got myself into now? That kid is weird!*

"Good-bye, Billy Joe," she said firmly.

She hung up the phone, shaking her head, feeling a slight sense of apprehension. Still, it'd be good if she could help a kid like that get a little more education, give him a better chance in life and all that. Riding on this little surge of altruism, she decided to unload some of the junk in the spare bedroom, just in case Red might have to take her up on her offer.

"You're a good woman, Bessie Tanner," she told herself fondly.

* * *

Lunch hour had become a test of endurance for Christine. Every day she ventured out into the oppressive heat to look at another apartment for rent in the Waresboro area. One dreary, cramped little box after another assaulted her senses with garish colors, deteriorating plumbing, or the acrid smell of mildew. One bleary-eyed or surly landlord after another discouraged her in her quest. One after another of the want ads that Stan and Edda-Lou had circled for her, indicating that they were reasonably close to the office and fell within her price range, were crossed out. One whiny phone call after another from the ruffled and polka-dotted Mrs. Townsend reminded her that she needed to get out of the house, one way or another.

She was so discouraged, she had almost made up her mind to move in with Bessie when it happened. She found it!

She was drawn by a romantic sense of mystery down a winding dirt driveway into the dusty yard of a large old two-story frame house, hidden from the road in a grove of stately live-oaks, curtained with

Spanish moss. A wide, two-story porch stretched across the front of the house. White paint was peeling from the walls, and several of the green shutters hung askew. She was enchanted. The heavy, intoxicating aroma of magnolia blossoms enveloped her, making her giddy. Sounds of the road she had just left evaporated, and her tensions were lulled by the brief, sleepy melody of a finch. The only sign of human habitation was on the lower porch—a row of well-worn, inviting rocking chairs, faintly moving with the slight breeze which was also teasing the veils of Spanish moss in a light little dance in the heavy branches of the oaks. She sat in the car for a minute, afraid of breaking the mystical spell by getting out. She checked the circled want ad. Yes, that was the number she had seen on the rusty mailbox out on the road. She got out slowly and stood for a long moment in the yard, yielding herself to the musty magic of the place.

Taking a deep draft of magnolia-laden air into her lungs, she walked up the wide stairs and tapped the ornate brass door-knocker.

"Just a minute, please. I'll be right there," sang a fragile voice.

A minute later, the door opened, and a tiny lady with wispy white hair peered up at her with intense concentration. She was wearing a long, flowered chiffon dress, and a pearl necklace and earrings glowed softly by her face. After a few moments of silent scrutiny, she stepped back, opened the door wide and motioned for Christine to come in.

"You've come about the apartment, I 'spose?"

"Yes, ma'am," Christine said with a little bow of her head. She had an irrational urge to curtsy. She followed the flowing chiffon into a formal parlor and took a seat as indicated, on a red-velvet cushioned chair.

The spacious, high-ceilinged room was fitted with Victorian furniture, satin brocade drapes and oil portraits of stern patriarchs looking down from heavy, ornate golden frames. The air was cool, sweet with the scent of magnolia, spiced with furniture polish. A sense of mystery, of troubles suffered and resolved, of generations of love, jealousies, joys and tragedies endowed the room with an impregnable peace. The imposing portrait of a handsome man in a Confederate uniform hung over a long, carved mantle, and was crowned by a pair of crossed swords. Dusty yellow tassels hung from the sword handles.

"I'm Eufalia Worthington, that's *Miss* Worthington, and you...?"

"I'm Christine Radford. Nice to know you, Miss Worthington."

"All right, then. Tell me all about yourself," said her frail hostess, sweetly.

To her surprise, Christine found herself telling this enchanting little stranger all about herself: where she was born, how she came to Waycross, where she worked, what she did, why she needed an apartment, what the status of her marriage was—well, almost.

Christine talked for some time, encouraged by slight nods and vague smiles from Miss Worthington. Christine didn't mention Danny, of course.

After a while, Miss Worthington said, "Well, I like what I've seen and heard so far. I think I might show you the apartment, now."

Christine felt like she had gotten sanctification from the Pope. She followed Miss Worthington out of the house and into the side yard. A flight of stairs led to the upstairs porch. Miss Worthington's layers of flowered chiffon, puffed and swayed by the gentle breeze, led Christine up the steps to the upper porch where two more old rocking chairs stirred invitingly. In the center of the porch were French doors leading into a wide hallway bisecting the second floor. At the far end of the hallway, through open French doors, Christine could see across a screened porch, out into the lush green and gray of more huge oaks and Spanish moss. The breeze flowing through the long hall was cool.

*Lovely. Too good to be true. What's the catch?*

"The north side, on our left, will remain closed off. It hasn't been occupied for over 40 years now, since my dear papa died, right in that first room, as a matter of fact. The apartment is here, on the south side," she said, unlocking the first door in the hall.

The door swung open to a large, high-ceilinged, musty room, darkened by heavy drapes drawn over the windows. Ghostly pieces of furniture, covered with dusty sheets, crouched menacingly in the semi-dark. Paint was peeling away from the walls, yielding to an overwhelming sense of decay. Christine had a hard time subduing an impulse to rush over and open the windows. The air was hot and stifling.

*Okay. You were wondering what was the catch?*

"There's a fireplace in the parlor here, and another in the bedroom." Miss Worthington smiled sweetly as she led Christine on to the next room. A deep bay window reached out into the trees. In its center was a tall, four-poster bed with a canopy of heavy brocade. Cob-webs stretched across the corners, barely perceptible in the dim light. More furniture lurked around the room under graying sheets. Christine was speechless.

"And here's the bathroom." Miss Worthington led Christine into a small hallway and stood discreetly aside to let Christine peer into the bath. An over-sized claw-foot tub stood in porcelain majesty on the white-tiled floor. Christine hadn't seen those small, hexagon-shaped tiles since… she couldn't remember when. Across the little hallway was a large walk-in closet.

*Nice!*

The hallway led into the last room, a big, square kitchen with dark-green painted cabinets on two walls and lots of windows on the other two. A door with a large wavy glass window led onto the screened porch. A faded brown and orange linoleum curled up at the corners. A dingy-looking refrigerator and stove, and a long, divided chipped porcelain sink completed the kitchen furnishings. The walls were a dreary, mottled yellow.

Miss Worthington stood silently and watched Christine's every reaction.

"Oh, my! It's…uh, so big! And your ad didn't say that it was furnished."

"Yes, but you still may need some of your own things. And I could store anything you didn't want across the hall. Papa won't mind, I don't think," she assured Christine with an angelic smile.

"It's, uh … it's lovely, and…gee, it's really roomy, and… Would I have the use of the porches?"

"Certainly. There are steps leading down from the screened back porch. Papa and I used to sleep up here on the porch on hot summer nights when I was little."

"Would you have any objection to a little…uh…redecorating?"

"No, not a bit. I would have to approve your plans, of course."

"Uh…Miss Worthington, it looks like the apartment has been vacant a long time."

"You're right. About fifteen years."

"Do you mind telling me why? I mean, it's so, uh…nice and all."

"I just haven't found anyone I thought I should rent it to."

"Oh, really?" Christine turned and studied the small, impassive face.

"Yes. I'm quite particular about whom I allow in my house, you see. When I saw you standing out in the yard, taking everything in, so to speak, I decided you had the right sensibilities for this old place. Otherwise, I never would have come to the door."

"Oh, my… Well, I'm certainly glad you did!"

"So, am I to assume that you want to take it?"

"Yes, I think this is exactly what I've been looking for, even though I hadn't realized it before."

"Good. Let's go downstairs and have a sip of sherry and talk over the details, shall we?"

\*   \*   \*

Betty Sue Jamison had stepped up her campaign to get Danny's attention. When she asked him to the senior prom, he'd been kinda relieved that he wouldn't have to worry about a date. People were wondering why he'd stopped chasing around after the girls like he had last year, and he felt like he ought to take somebody to the prom, at least. Betty Sue was all right—a good buddy. Trouble was, now she kept calling him up, even coming out to buy stuff at the Piggly Wiggly when she knew he was working. He'd had to run her off today when he went on break, so he could call Christine.

It was a regular thing now, calling Christine every afternoon at about 2:30. She'd started trying to stay at her desk then, so she could talk to him. He knew because she had told him so.

"Hello, this is Christine Radford."

"Hey, Baby! How'd the hunt go today?"

"Oh, Danny, you're not going to believe it. I think I've found the perfect place. It's upstairs in a great old house, off to itself, private. I can't wait for you to see it."

"Why don't I come by your office when you get off today, and I'll follow you over there?"

"Aren't you working today?"

"Yeah, but I can always take off on some excuse from this shit-job."

"Oh, Honey, don't do that. You're gonna need a good work record, so you can get a good recommendation when you go looking for another job. Besides, the landlady and I have a few more details to work out before I'm sure I'll get it. It doesn't look so good right now, but with a little paint and new curtains... Oh, it's gonna be wonderful!"

"Okay, then. I'll be over later tonight if I can sneak away."

"I'll leave the back door unlocked. Hey, I love you."

"I love you too. Later."

"Later."

\*   \*   \*

When Christine got home, there was a letter from her mother which she assumed was another appeal to quit her silly job and get up to Allentown where she belonged, and to try to be a better wife to good old Jack. There was also another letter from Mexico to Jack from Dr. Hector de Santos. She had already forwarded several letters from the doctor on to Allentown. Each time she did, it gave her an uncomfortable feeling. In one of Jack's tense and infrequent telephone calls, she had asked him what the letters were about, and if he had any medical problems. He had told her curtly that it was none of her business, and certainly nothing for her to worry about, and that he was in perfect health.

This time, she looked at the envelope from Dr. de Santos for a long time, struggling with temptation. Finally, with an "Oh, what the hell?" she ripped it open. It was an overdue bill for medical services—examination and treatment for LGV, whatever that was. Her fears about his health returned in a rush, and with a shudder she remembered his strange behavior after he returned from Mexico: his attempts to cover himself as he stepped out of the shower, the awful rough, thick feeling of his skin during sex, the way he didn't seem to get satisfied like he had before.

A wave of nausea washed over her, and she dropped the invoice onto the floor, as if it were crawling with germs. What if he had gotten some awful disease while he was gone, and hadn't told her about it? No, that was silly! Why would he do such a thing? Unless it was something he thought he had to hide from her? What if...?

*Stop it! This is silly. I'll ask Dr. Fish about it next week when I go in to get my birth control prescription refilled.*

She picked up the invoice, put it back into the envelope, folded it and put it into her purse. She'd worry about it later. Right now, she'd just get out of these hot clothes and into her sexy little shorts and white halter top that Danny liked so much—just in case.

The sound of gunfire started again in the woods behind her house. Once again, she thought about calling the police, but she really hated to stir up trouble. Anyway, she guessed it was poor old Harland, out target shooting. That guy sure needed to get a little fun somewhere.

Maybe Danny would know something. She'd try to remember to ask him about it if he came over tonight.

He did come over. She was at the stove, making a white sauce when the back screen door squeaked open. "Come on in, Honey. I can't stop stirring the white sauce."

"No problem. You just keep on stirrin'," he said, as he wrapped his arms around her waist and began kissing the nape of her neck.

"Oh, you…" she groaned and moved her body sensuously against him. She didn't interrupt the rhythm of her stirring, though. "And by the way, do you know what all that shooting is that's going on back in the woods?"

He let her go and began to set the table for two. "Yeah, that's Mama. Can you believe it? She's decided she wants to be an expert marksman, now."

"Madge? I can't imagine!"

"Well, she does. Dad's been teaching her. He thinks it's great."

Christine added grated cheddar to the white sauce and stirred it thoughtfully.

*Why in the world does she want to learn how to shoot?*

The hair stood up on the back of her neck.

## Chapter 33

By Tuesday, Bessie had completely forgotten that Billy Joe was going to stop by her office, and she was startled when he tapped lightly on her open door to get her attention.

"Oh... Billy Joe! Come on in and take a seat while I finish this stuff, and then we'll... uh, talk about what you want to do. With your life, you know." She motioned him toward the empty chair and turned her attention back to the paper work piled in front of her. Why had she told him he could come here?

"You just go right on with your work. I ain't in no hurry to go nowhere." He smiled nervously, sat down and began to pick at a hangnail. She tried to ignore him as she struggled to concentrate, but his fidgeting distracted her.

He cleared his throat several times and finally blurted out in a voice that squeaked, "You sure look nice today."

"What?" She cleared *her* throat. "Uh... thanks." This was embarrassing. "Hey, listen Billy Joe, I think you need to talk to the counselor here, instead of me. I can give you some information on the courses of study, but that's about all." She rummaged in a drawer in her desk for a moment and handed him the current quarter's bulletin of classes. "I think you're real smart to decide to improve your education, and I'll be glad to help you get a job when you graduate, or at least have picked up some skills. Why don't you look at the technical section and see what you might be interested in?" Why did he look so distressed? She relented a little. "Look, come in during regular hours tomorrow and ask the desk clerk when we're giving the next General Aptitudes Test. That'll be a good place to start." She nodded encouragingly, forced a smile, stood up and extended her hand for a dismissal handshake.

He took her hand shyly and mumbled, "Maybe after you git off tonight—"

"Lord, Billy Joe!" She hadn't even heard him. "You'll never get anywhere with a wimpy handshake like that! When somebody shakes your hand, you ought to give them a nice, firm, friendly shake. See, like this..." She tightened her grip slightly and pumped his hand with confidence.

He blushed, but returned her handshake with a little more assurance.

"Now, that's a lot better," she said. "Come on in tomorrow and see about that test."

"Thanks. I... uh, well..."

"And hold your shoulders up! You gotta at least look the part, you know." She turned her attention back to her paperwork.

He straightened up to his fullest height. "Good night, Bessie. I... uh... Thanks agin." He was gone.

*That poor kid. I hope I wasn't too hard on him.*

\* \* \*

Well, now she knew! Christine beat the steering wheel with both fists at the first red light after leaving the doctor's office. She had kept up her courage and asked her gynecologist about LGV. He had confirmed her ugly suspicions. *Jack had a venereal disease.* It was one that could only be caught through direct sexual contact. The disgusting thickened skin in his genital area was indeed caused by the nasty disease.

While she had been eaten up with guilt about her passion for Danny, he had been merrily screwing around with some woman in Mexico! The irony would be a good joke if it all weren't so horrible.

Dr. Fish had taken a blood sample and sent it off to Atlanta for testing. She would have to wait at least a week before finding out if she had the infection. He didn't seem to be too concerned about it, but still...

Her initial panic congealed into a cold aversion to Jack and a calm, firm resolution to sever all ties with him. His utter disregard of her, his obnoxious forcing of his disease-infested body upon hers, his deceit—all sank into the depths of her reason with an icy finality. She never wanted to see him again. She didn't want to hear his voice again, and she dreaded his next telephone call. What could she possibly say to him?

And what could she say to Danny? *Oh, Danny!* Had she unwittingly contaminated that sweet, beautiful, healthy body? They would have to abstain from sex until she got the results of her test back.

*Damn Jack! Damn him! Damn him! Damn him!*

He had smeared a nasty coarseness over the mystical perfection of her love-making with Danny. He had fouled the purest and best thing that had ever happened to her. She hated him! And how could she tell Danny?

Dr. Fish had told her that she probably didn't have anything to worry about. The disease was spread when the infected person had an open sore. As far as she could remember, that hadn't been the case with Jack. But she couldn't be sure. She had dulled her senses as much as she could when Jack was forcing his unwanted attentions on her. Why had she let him use her like that? She shuddered. Why in the world hadn't she said "No!" Why had she thought that just because they were married, she had some stupid obligation to let him satisfy his loveless, carnal desires with *her* body? The memory of his assaults upon her washed over her in a wave of disgust. In her imagination she smashed her fists into his face, over and over.

But for now, she had to calm herself. There was nothing more she could do until she got the report from Dr. Fish's office. But in any case, she had to tell Danny. She owed it to him. Oh God, how awful!

She pulled into her driveway, cut the engine and gave way to tears of rage, frustration and humiliation.

*I know. I'll call Bessie. She'll understand.*

She got out of the car, straightened her shoulders and marched into the house. She slammed her handbag onto the sofa as hard as she could, went to the bathroom and blew her nose, took a deep breath and splashed cold water on her face.

*I'll get through this. At least this has made it clear that I have to divorce that son-of-a-bitch. That low-down, dirty son-of-a-bitch!*

\*   \*   \*

When the phone rang, Bessie was afraid to answer it, afraid it would be Billy Joe again. He had called her twice since their meeting this afternoon; once at the office and again right after she got home. He didn't seem to have anything to say, not really. He just rambled on about nothing in particular; how he hated his boss at the Tasty Burger, how Laura Mae was doing so well at the law office; how nice Bessie was to help him. Well, she certainly didn't have to worry about whether she had been too rough on him with her criticism earlier today.

She answered brusquely. "Hello?"

"Bessie, are you busy? It's Red. I—"

She softened her tone. "Oh, not a bit, Red. Glad to hear from you."

"I've had some bad news. Can I come over? Maybe we can go out and have some dinner?"

"Sure. Sounds good. Come on over."

"Okay. See you in about 20 minutes?."

"The sooner the better."

"Hey… Thanks, Bessie."

Bessie shook her head as she hung up the phone. More bad news? That poor woman sure had more than her share. She rushed around the apartment, throwing things into closets.

When she opened the door for Red, Bessie could tell she'd been crying. She patted her on the shoulder. "Hey, girl! What's the matter now? They throwing you out of your house?"

"No Bessie, it's not that. It's..." She pressed her lips together, her face turned red and her eyes flashed.

Bessie continued, "Cause if that's what it is, you can move in with me. I already got the spare room cleaned out, more or less."

"Thanks, Bessie, but it's not that. I think I've found an apartment. It's... It's that son-of-a-bitch, Jack!" She clenched her fists and growled in a hoarse voice, "I – hate – him!"

"Whoa... Take it easy. What now?"

"I found out he's got a... a *venereal* disease!" She shook her fists at the ceiling. "He got it while he was in Mexico. Oh, the bastard, the *bastard*!" In shame, she turned her head away from Bessie.

"Oh, my God! What's he got? Syphilis?"

"No, it's LGV. Wait a minute. I've got it written down." She got a slip of paper from her purse and read, 'Lymphogranuloma Venereum, also known as tropical bubo.' The 'bubo' is a big, horrible sore place that swells up down in your groin..." She shuddered. "...like a black plague sore!"

Bessie shuddered. "Shit! Sounds disgusting. I never even heard of it. Do you...do you think he...he passed it on to you?"

"Probably not, but I won't know for sure until Dr. Fish gets my blood test back, in a week or so. I'm gonna go crazy until I find out. Plus," her eyes welled up with tears and her voice quavered, "I've got to tell Danny!"

"Oh, you poor thing." Bessie put a comforting arm around her shoulders.

"Bessie, I've never really hated anybody before in my whole life. But I *hate* Jack! I *hate* that sorry son-of-a-bitch!" She stomped her foot. "How could he do this to me? I'm getting a divorce! I mean it!"

"Hey, girl. Take it—"

"I'm gonna kill him!" Christine's voice was shrill and rising. She began to pace the floor. "I'm gonna—"

"Hey, slow down. You better get yourself into my office and talk to a lawyer about this. Call and get an appointment with Sidney. He's the best in our office. Least, I think so. Not to mention the cutest."

"I'm giving that son-of-a-bitch his walking papers! I'm reading him his rights! I'm—"

"You're not telling him a thing, girl. Not until you've talked to a lawyer. You're not gonna talk to him at all. Not till you get ahold of yourself."

"Okay, Bessie, you're right as usual. What's this lawyer's last name?" She took a pencil from her purse and turned the slip of paper over.

"Haynes. Sidney Haynes. He's really a good lawyer. I bet he'd make a divorce feel like a picnic. Almost makes me want to get married so he can get *me* a divorce."

Red gave her friend a baffled look. Bessie realized she'd gone a little off track in her praise of Sidney. She just got carried away sometimes when she thought about him. She'd have to be more careful. "Come on, let's go down to Aunt Molly's Trolley and get us some fried chicken."

"Oh, Bessie…"

"Come on now, Red. Let's just *calm* down and go get us some dinner."

"Okay. I'm not really hungry, but I'll try. Calm down; eat fried chicken."

As she led Red to the door, the phone rang. "Dammit!" she said and gritted her teeth. "I hope that's not Billy Joe again."

"Billy Joe, the *waiter* at the *Tasty Burger*?" Red asked in disbelief.

"Yeah, he's making a real pest of himself. Wants me to get him a job. I'm trying to get him to take some classes. He hasn't even got a high-school diploma."

"I know how that is. Remember? I've been there, not too long ago, either. Go easy on him, okay? That's a bad situation to be in."

The telephone continued to ring.

"Don't worry, I'll give him some good advice. Hold on a second."

"Bessie, if anybody in the world can give good advice, it's you." Red laughed.

Bessie picked up the phone. "Hello?" Bessie looked at Christine and rolled her eyes toward the ceiling.

"Oops, sorry, Billy Joe. I'm just on my way out the door. Going to dinner with a friend…

"Naw, don't call back tonight. I'm, uh, gonna be real late. Gotta go, now. Bye."

She lowered the receiver onto its cradle, grabbed Red by the arm and pulled her toward the door. "Let's get outta here."

It really wasn't late when they got back from Aunt Molly's Trolley. Red had just pushed the food around on her plate, worried one minute and angry the next. Bessie had wolfed down her fried chicken, mashed potatoes and thick cream-gravy, corn-on-the-cob, two big biscuits and blackberry cobbler with ice cream. The only time Red perked up at all was when she told Bessie about the apartment she'd found. It sounded like a dump to Bessie, but she kept this thought to herself.

When they got back to Bessie's apartment building, Red didn't want to come in.

"I'd better get on back home. I've got a lot of planning to do." She hugged Bessie warmly. "Thanks again. You always come through for me."

"Any time. Be sure to call Sidney tomorrow."

"Don't worry, I will. Night."

"Night."

As she passed the oleander bushes in front of her apartment building, Bessie was sure she saw a figure hiding in the shadows. She was too frightened to investigate, but just hurried into the building and into her apartment, slamming and locking the door behind her.

*Don't be silly. It was probably just the wind.*

But there hadn't been any wind tonight.

## Chapter 34

Living with Red's mom and the Reverend Rufus J. Peabody was really getting on Jack's nerves. He was sick and tired of Rev's constant holy talk and all the Bible stuff. That religious shit was all so phony that he really had to work sometimes to keep from stuffing something down the pudgy little preacher's throat. Red's mother was fine, though. She treated him like somebody special and kept after Red to come to her senses and get on up to Allentown. But that preacher husband of hers...

Jack had found a great deal on a used rig, but the problem was he had to act fast. The owner was in some kind of big trouble and needed cash now. The bank was ready with a loan, but he needed the big down-payment he'd have when the house was sold. Mrs. Townsend had a buyer for the house, and all the paperwork was moving along okay. Now it was up to Red to get their stuff packed and get out of the house. He'd found an apartment for them. It was small, but it was out near the truck dispatcher's office where he'd be taking most of his jobs.

He tapped his foot impatiently as the phone rang and rang. Finally realizing that this was Wednesday and Red would be at that damned school, he slammed down the receiver. Oh, what the hell?

He'd call her at work tomorrow. Right now, he'd just go down to the Wild Horse and forget about Red for awhile. Forget about those super-tits with their pretty pink tips, and how that hot little red-haired pussy used to respond to him.

*Damn her!*

When he pushed into the crowd, into the flashing lights and loud music at the Wild Horse, he felt revved up for awhile. It didn't last long, though. The girls were crowding around him, as usual, wanting him to ask them to dance, but when he got them out on the dance floor, they always seemed heavy, clumsy. They all wore too much make-up, too. Their butts looked lumpy in their too-tight jeans. He tossed down a few boiler-makers, but that didn't help, either. Just made him feel down. Really down.

He gave it up and went home after the first set was over.

\*   \*   \*

Christine was taking Bessie's advice and postponing the inevitable talk with Jack. She still didn't know how to approach the subject of his venereal disease. What she *wanted* to do was to scream at him, to slap his face, to scratch his eyes out. Well, this wouldn't accomplish anything, so she was trying to put off the confrontation until she had her emotions under control and had a reasonable plan. At the office, she had asked the receptionist to tell any unidentified caller that she was in a meeting, and that she'd call them back later. She didn't return any calls from area code 610. At home, she didn't answer the telephone at all.

She followed Bessie's other suggestion and made an appointment with Sidney Haynes, to start divorce proceedings. She'd talk to Jack after this process had begun.

In the meantime, she had signed a solid rental contract with the ephemeral Miss Worthington. Her renovation plans—new paint, curtains, an air-conditioning unit, kitchen cabinet doors and drawer fronts, and new inlaid linoleum for the kitchen floor—all met with Miss W's approval. Danny had agreed, in fact was eager to help her. They were meeting for lunch today at Josie's Kitchen. She was taking the afternoon off so she could show him the apartment and then go by the hardware store and pick out the paint colors. She had brought broom, mop, cleaning supplies and work clothes along.

And she still had to tell him about Jack's awful disease.

She had just taken a seat in a back booth when the sputtering sound of the Honda 350 engine approached, circled around to the back of the restaurant and cut off. Her heart beat wildly. Her eyes were glued on the entrance when he came in, pulled off his helmet and ran his fingers back through his hair. She watched as his eyes scanned the room, waiting for the moment he would see her. When he did, his smile, like fireworks, lit the whole room and obliterated everything between them.

*He's worth it. All the worry, the guilt, the uncertainty, the danger. He's worth it.*

He came across the room toward her, with his athletic, self-confident walk, his helmet under his arm. He leaned down close to her and whispered, "Hello, beautiful."

"Hi, good-lookin'," she answered softly. For a split second, she thought he was going to kiss her, right here in public, and she didn't even care. But he took his seat across from her and opened the menu.

"So, tell me about the apartment," he said as he looked over the menu.

"Oh Danny, I've got so much to tell you—some good, some not so good."

"...Some not so good?" She had his full attention now.

"Well, first off, I think your mother knows about us."

"That's no big deal. She's been suspecting something all along."

"But now, I think she's... uh... sure of it!"

"Whaddya mean?"

"Danny, I think she saw us the other night—making love on the...on the kitchen floor."

"No way!"

"I thought I saw her face that night, peeking in the window in the kitchen door." Danny was stunned. "And somebody sent Jack some awful anonymous letters about me, saying I'm a... Saying I'm evil, and worse!"

"Oh, shit! What did the letters look like?"

"They were made out of little cut-out, glued-on letters. They were—"

"Fuck! *That's* what she was doing with those cut-up magazines. *Fuck!*" Danny buried his face in his hands in horror.

The waitress was standing at their booth. "Is ever-thing awright?" she asked, looking at Danny with concern.

Christine answered, "Uh, yes, everything's okay. We just need a little more time before we order, please."

"Of co-us, ma'am. Y'all just take your time." She smiled encouragingly as she left.

Danny looked up. "What did the letters say?"

"I can't remember the exact words. Something like I'm the whore of Babylon and God's gonna get me. I'll let you read them if you really want to know."

"Oh, Christine, I'm so sorry." He reached across the table and took her hands in his. "What did Jack think?"

"He acted like he thought they were funny. I don't think he took them seriously."

"Well, we're just gonna have to be more careful. *I'm* gonna have to be more careful." He patted her hand.

"And that's not all—"

"Why can't everybody just leave us alone? We're not hurting anybody!"

"Danny, listen honey. I've got something else I have to tell you."

"You're not leaving?" he cried out in panic.

"No, no." She lifted his hand to her cheek. "You know I couldn't leave you." He had tears in his eyes. "It's that… It's probably nothing to worry about, but—"

"What is it? Please…"

"I've just found out that Jack has a… a disease." She plunged on. "A *venereal* disease."

"Oh, no! Is it the—?"

"It's 'LGV', something he caught in Mexico. It's not very contagious, and if I *had* gotten it from him, I'd most likely have had some symptoms before now."

"LVG? I never heard of it. What does it—"

"I don't think we have anything to worry about. It's kinda rare, not that easy to catch. Dr. Fish took a blood sample from me and sent it off to Atlanta. It'll be a week or two before I find out for sure."

"A week or two?"

"I know. And in the meantime, we'd better not…"

"Oh, Christine!"

"I can still hold you in my arms, and kiss you." She stroked the back of his hand. "I can kiss you all over—"

The look of horror on his face melted into a slow smile. "Stop it. You're driving me crazy."

She licked her lips. "We'll have to find other ways…"

He closed his eyes and moaned. "Christine," he said earnestly, serious now. "I love you so much I'll do anything I have to, *anything* for us to be together. I'll leave home. You're gonna *have* to get a divorce, now. We can run away! We can move in together. I'll go anywhere you want to go."

"You know I love you the same way. But no, honey. Let's keep our heads now. We'll just have to cool it for a while. Be more careful."

"You still want me to help you paint and all?"

"Sure. No harm in helping an ex-neighbor paint, is there?" Her eyes welled up with tears. "Oh, Danny, I'm so sorry."

He squeezed her hands. "It's gonna be okay. Nothing's ever gonna come between us."

The waitress, reappearing at their table unnoticed, cleared her throat loudly. They broke away with a start. Danny looked up at her and smiled.

"I'll have a cheeseburger, an order of potato logs, and a large Sprite," he said with complete composure.

The waitress looked at Christine with her eyebrows raised in a question, and the corners of her mouth lowered in disapproval. Christine stammered, "Uh... I'll... Hmmmm." She cleared her throat. "Bring me a hamburger and a Coke." Then boldly, "I'll just have some of *his* potato logs."

*So there!*

"...And we're in a hurry," Danny added. The waitress turned away with a small snort of disdain. Danny grinned and took her hands again. "Let's eat fast and go see that apartment."

Christine relaxed. So what if the waitress thought that something was going on between them? So what if everybody around here thought the same thing? It couldn't be helped. It'd be such a relief if they could stop all this sneaking around and lying.

After they had finished their hurried lunch, they split the check and left Josie's together.

"You want to follow me?" Christine asked.

Danny took her hand and pulled her toward the back of the restaurant. "Sure, but first I got something I want to show you." He led her to where his Honda was parked next to the back of the building. "I bought you something." He un-strapped a second helmet identical to his from the back of the seat and held it out to her. "Now I can take you riding."

"Wow! This is great." She tried on the helmet, laughing. "Perfect fit." She took it off and handed it back to him. "Thank you, Sweetheart." She wanted so much to kiss him.

He put both helmets on the bike seat and turned back to her, his eyes narrowing with desire. "Come here…"

She backed away. "Danny…"

He moved toward her.

"Danny, we shouldn't… We can't…" Her back was to the wall. He put a hand against the wall on each side of her and pressed her body against the back of Josie's Kitchen, and kissed her. *Really* kissed her. Her head swam, and for a moment she forgot where she was. Helpless, she yielded, put her arms around his neck and pulled herself to him.

"Weh-ull, weh-ull, weh-ull! If it isn't Miz Radfud. My goodness? I wuzn't expectin' to see *you* here! And your young friend?"

*Oh my God, this can't be happening! Ellie Townsend! Oh my God!*

Danny had jumped back away from her. Now if the ground would just open up and swallow her...

"Uh... Mrs. Townsend. Uh..."

Danny stepped toward Ellie and extended his hand. "Mrs. Townsend? I'm Danny Wilkins, Mrs. Radford's neighbor...and *friend*. How do you do?"

Ellie was taken completely off-guard by his easy courtesy and apparent lack of concern. She batted her mascara-heavy eyes. "Weh-ull, I'm jes fine? And how are *you*?"

Christine recovered slightly from her state of shock. "Uh... Danny, this is Ellie Townsend, my uh... rather, *Jack's* real estate agent."

"Nice to meet you, Mrs. Townsend," Danny said, all cordiality. "Mrs. Radford and I are just talking about paint colors for her new apartment."

Christine gulped, on the verge of hysteria.

*Paint colors?*

Christine forced herself to look Ellie Townsend in the eye. "Yes, I'll be moving out of the house in about a week, if everything goes as planned," she said, marveling at Danny's coolness.

"Weh-ull, now that's re-al nice! And listen, I need to put a lock-box on your do-ah and start showin' the place as soon as I can? Would tomorrow be aw-right?"

"Certainly, that'll be fine with me."

*Anything you want to do is fine with me, you silly frou-frou. As long as I never have to see you again.*

"Weh-ull, good. Aw-right then." Ellie turned to Danny. "It sure was nice to meet *you* Mr., uh… whut wuz it now?"

"Wilkins. Danny Wilkins. Nice to meet you, too, Mrs. Townsend."

They parted: Christine shaking with guilt and fear, Ellie rumbling with the volcanic tremors of an eminent gossip eruption, Danny smooth and unperturbed.

Christine stumbled into her car as he swung his leg onto his bike and slipped his helmet over his wavy blond hair. He called across the parking lot to her, "Hey, I'll follow you." Like they hadn't already planned that.

*Had it really happened? Danny was so cool!*

She felt dizzy.

*Where am I?*

## Chapter 35

Christine was numb with dread as she drove from Josie's Kitchen toward the new apartment. The sounds of the street were far away and indistinguishable. She could see the motorcycle following her, but the figure with its dark helmet, bending over the handlebars, was mysterious, inscrutable, anonymous. Her hands on the steering wheel were foreign to her, deadened as she was with a sense of doom. She was aware that she was somehow functioning, heading toward something—the apartment? Yes. But she was disconnected from whatever force was moving her along toward her destination. What was the point, anyway?

She pulled into the long, winding, oak-lined drive, and as the sounds of the road faded away, the feeling that she was in a fantasy became more pronounced, but she felt the oppressive doom lifting. She leaned her head against the back of the seat and breathed in the healing, velvety aroma of the magnolias. She heard the Honda engine sputter up and stop next to her.

"Are you okay? Christine, are you all right?" He was leaning close to her, his hands on the car door, his face furrowed with worry. "Come on, honey. Come show me around this spooky old place."

His voice brought her back to reality. "Okay, sure. I guess I'm all right. Just kinda in shock from seeing Mrs. Townsend. Or rather from *her* seeing *us*!" She took a deep breath, shook her head and got out of the car. "Well, how do you like it? Isn't it beautiful?" She forced everything else out of her mind: Ellie Townsend, Jack, venereal disease, poison pen letters, Madge's stricken face at the kitchen door. She willed the magic of the old place to take over. "Come on, I'll introduce you to my landlady." She reached for his hand, but thought better of it, and motioned for him to follow her. Now another sickening fear swept over her. What would the elegant Miss W. think of *Danny*?

When she tapped the big brass door-knocker, the door opened immediately. Miss Worthington's bright face smiled up at her. "Do come in Mrs. Radford." Her eyes made a quick but intensive tour of Danny. "And who is *this* handsome young man?"

"This is Danny Wilkins, Miss Worthington, my next-door neighbor. He'll be helping me with the apartment redecorating."

Danny lowered his head in a bow as he stepped forward and shook Miss Worthington's hand. "Miss *Eufalia* Worthington? Wow! It's a real pleasure to meet you. I've heard *so* much about you—"

"You've heard that I'm a crazy old lady?" Miss Worthington had a twinkle in her eye.

"I've always heard that you're the first lady of Ware County," he answered, "and I'm right proud to meet you."

"Well, young man. You're quite the gentleman." She led them into the parlor.

Christine was dumb-struck for a moment by this exchange, amazed at Danny's old-world courtesy, and intrigued by Miss W's notoriety. How did Danny know about her?

Recovering, Christine explained, "I wanted you to meet Danny. He may be coming over to work sometimes when I'm not here, so if you have no objection, I'd like for him to have a key."

"Are you in school, Danny?" Miss W. asked sweetly.

"Not right now. I just graduated from Blair High—"

"Named for my great-uncle, Worthington Blair," she softly interjected.

"Yes ma'am, I know, and for the summer I'm working at the Piggly Wiggly, right up the road."

"And you plan to enter college in the fall?"

"Well, ma'am, I don't know as yet just what I'm going to do."

"Hmmm. We'll need to talk about that sometime soon." She reached a frail little hand up and patted him on the shoulder. Then to Christine, "I certainly don't have any objection to your giving Danny a key," she turned back to Danny, "as long as you understand that you must never bring anyone with you."

"Of course, ma'am. I understand." He bowed his head ever so slightly again.

Christine smiled with relief. "Thank you, Miss Worthington. I hope to move in a week to ten days. Danny and I are getting started today. We'll try not to disturb you too much."

As they started out of the parlor, Danny looked back and tilted his head toward the large portrait under the crossed Confederate swords.

"Is that the famous Colonel Worthington, ma'am, over the fireplace there?"

"Yes, that's my brave great-grandfather, a fine man!"

"And a handsome one, too," Danny added.

"He was the best horseman in Georgia, they tell me, before he lost his leg at Antietam. Still liked to ride, though."

"Well, he's a hero to my dad."

"Yes, and his spirit still lives in this house."

The three of them gazed at the portrait for a minute before Danny broke the silence. "Nice to meet you, ma'am." Yet another little bow of Danny's head.

"And a real pleasure to meet you, son."

As Christine led Danny up the stairs to the apartment, she told him, "You really charmed Miss Worthington. I'm proud of you. I've been wondering how she'll react to our, uh… friendship."

"She's gonna love us—" he said as he patted her rear.

She squealed, "Danny! Stop that!" and swatted at his hand.

"—unless she hears you yelling at me like that." He laughed and patted her again, trying to slip his hand between her legs.

She ran up the stairs away from him, turned, scowled ferociously and silently shook her finger at him.

As soon as they were inside, she shook her head and said, "Danny, we're really gonna have to be more careful, or—"

He took her in his arms and kissed her, squelching all of her objections.

They toured the dusty old apartment, Danny surprising her by pointing out the quality of the wood and the artistry of the carving on the fireplace mantles. He loved the high ceilings, noting that they would make the hot summers easier to bear. He opened the windows, cemented shut by layers of paint and years of neglect. An aromatic, refreshing breeze began to flow through the musty rooms. They took the covers off the chairs and sofas and shook them out over the front porch rail. They decided on paint colors, and Danny calculated how much would be needed of each color and type. A deep contentment enveloped Christine. They were home.

When Christine explained that the north side of the floor was shut off, Danny told her, "Yeah, that's probably because old man Worthington's body is still in there."

"Danny! What a horrible thing to say!"

He laughed and began to lurch toward her, his eyes rolled out of focus toward the ceiling, his body stiff as a mummy. "Oooo, I'm gonna gitcha."

"Stop it, you idiot!" She laughed and ran away in mock fright. "That's not funny."

Danny then told her a little of the history and mythology of the Worthington family and the old house. It used to be called "Magnolia Manor." It had been built soon after the "War Between the States," after their plantation had been burned by renegade Union soldiers. Colonel Worthington had returned from the war a broken man, as were so many Confederate soldiers; broken in both body and spirit. The family had managed to survive by harvesting turpentine and selling timber, but little by little had been forced to sell most of their original 12,000 acres. The Colonel's grandson, Paul, had married beneath him, to a high-strung beauty who provided him with his only child, Eufalia, a wild and fun-loving girl, cursed with her mother's breath-taking beauty. Eufalia was only 17 when her mother disappeared into the Okefenokee with a Yankee cypress timber entrepreneur. There were some who said that Paul had murdered his unfaithful wife in their bedroom, and disposed of the body in the swamp. Others claimed to have seen her floating away on a flat-boat with the timber salesman. Paul, himself, was seldom seen after that, and was said to be cared for by his daughter, Eufalia, with extraordinary devotion.

After the death of the last faithful old servant, Miss Eufalia's only contact with the outside world had been through her attorney and financial manager, the grocery delivery boy and an occasional delivery truck driver.

"Nobody ever heard anything about a funeral for old Paul Worthington, and some folks think he's still in his bedroom."

"That's ridiculous," she said with an involuntary shudder. "We'll just stay on *our* side of the house, anyway." Using the broom, she began to pull down cobwebs from the canopy over the bed.

"We'll show that old bed some love-making like it's never seen before," he said.

*Is this really happening? What about all of those problems; all those dangers? They just don't seem real anymore.*

"Yes, but not now," she answered. "Now it's off to the paint store. I can't wait to get started."

As they started toward the car, Danny said, "Just a sec. I want to ask Miss W. something." He ran up onto the porch and tapped the knocker. Miss W. opened the door immediately. He said a few words and was answered with a nod and a big smile.

He ran out and hopped into the car. "I just wanted to ask her if it's all right to leave my motorcycle here. You never know about these old folks."

"Well, you've certainly got her number. You've got her eating out of your hand."

In a short time, they were back from the hardware store with everything they needed. They replaced the furniture covers and began cleaning and preparing the walls for their cheery new colors.

When she looked out the windows, she saw nothing but comforting green leaves and ancient-looking lacy gray moss. It seemed that she was in an enchanted tree house, safe from the real world. She determinedly fought off the occasional nudges of panic that kept trying to remind her of all the uncertainties stalking her. Those nudges made her feel as if she were teetering along a path at the edge of a chasm. She couldn't afford to look down into its terrifying depth.

\*  \*  \*

Bessie had just gotten home when there was a knock on her door. She couldn't believe her eyes when she opened it and saw the lanky, waif-like Billy Joe standing there. She had thought this little problem was settled. What a bother!

"Billy Joe! What in the world are you doing here?"

"I brought ya somethin'." He held out a handful of oleander flowers. The branches had been broken off at different lengths.

"Flowers? For me? What's going on here? You got no call to be bringing me flowers."

*He broke them off the bushes in front of the building. Damn.*

"Uh... I wuz jes thinkin' about you," he stammered. "Kin I come in? Please?"

"Well, I—"

"Purty please?"

"I've had a rough day, Billy Joe, and..."

"Just for a minute?"

"Oh, all right." She stepped aside and let him in. "Did you sign up for that aptitude test like I told you to?"

"Uh, not yet. It costs twenty-five dollars! I just ain't had the money, ya know? Anyways, I think I know whut I'm good at. And it ain't on that test, either!"

He thrust the oleanders at her so that she had no choice but to take them. She carried them into the kitchen, rinsed out an empty mayonnaise jar, filled it with water, stuck the ragged bouquet into it and put it on the cluttered coffee table. "There!" She refused to thank him. "So, what is it you want to talk to me about?"

"Did you like the poem I wrote you?"

"The poem?"

"You know, the one I left on your car last week."

"Oh my God! Was that from *you*?

"I thought you'd know it wuz from me. You know I—"

"I didn't have any idea."

He plowed on clumsily, "You know I like you a lot." He took a few steps toward her. "And I think you like me, too."

"Billy Joe, I don't hardly even *know* you! This isn't—"

"And Laura Mae told me about how you ast the lawyer about us."

"About *us*?"

"Yeah, about is it legal when a woman is older then a man, and they still…"

"Good Lord, Billy Joe! I was asking that for a *friend*."

"You don't have to hide nuthin' from me, Bessie. I been wantin' you for a long time." He had backed her into the kitchen while he made this declaration, and cornered her against the cabinet. She tried to slip past him, but he took her by the arms and pulled her toward him. "Bessie, I—" He attempted a clumsy kiss on her neck.

"Stop this right now!" she shouted at him and tried to squirm out of his grasp. "There's been a big mistake." He was as strong as a mule. "I never meant to give you the idea that there was anything between us." With a surge of strength, she shoved his arms away and pushed herself past him into the living room. "I want you to leave right now!" She opened the apartment door.

"But Bessie, I thought… Don't be mad, please. I'm sorry if…"

"Listen to me. I'm gonna act like this never happened. And don't you ever do anything like this again."

"Please, Bessie. Cain't we—"

"Can't we *nothing*! Get on out of here before I have to call the cops or something!" she screamed.

"I'm sorry," he shook his head and stumbled past her, "but, dammit, you made me think that…"

She slammed the door in his face and closed the dead bolt with a resounding thud.

*Well, I reckon that's the end of my nights at the Tasty Burger. Damn!*

Shaking her head, she crossed the living room, grabbed up the mayonnaise jar of oleander flowers, took them into the kitchen, threw the flowers in the garbage and rinsed the jar out in the sink. She breathed a sigh with the finality of that gesture, but her relief was shattered by a banging on her door—a loud banging.

He shouted through the door, "Bessie, I ain't through! You made me think you had the hots for me. It ain't fair. Always callin' me 'Sugar' and all that. And Laura Mae said you liked me a lot. It ain't fair! I ain't goin' away so easy."

Bessie was getting really frightened, now. "Look, Billy Joe, I'm sorry if I made you think… Hey, I do *like* you, but not like a… I never meant—"

"Yes, you did! You was always comin' on to me, and you know it! You cain't jes thow me away like I was a piece of trash or sumpin'! I ain't no trash! I ain't!" He kicked the door, hard.

"Billy Joe, stop that! I'm sorry, but if you don't get out of here right now, I'm calling the police—"

"You wouldn't—"

"If the neighbors haven't already called them."

His voice dropped to a vicious tone. "This ain't over, Bessie. You cain't thow me away like a piece o' trash." His footsteps ran down the hall, down the stairs and faded away after a loud slam of the apartment building's front door.

*Oh my God. What have I done now?*

## Chapter 36

Madge was ready. She could blast nine out of ten pine cones off a log at a hundred feet. Now she had to decide when and where to enact God's vengeance on the evil that was living next door to her, that evil still walking among innocent people, spreading corruption like a pestilent disease. She could do it now, any time Harland and Danny were away from home and the whore was in sight. Sometimes she thought she should just go over there and do it and let the power of the Lord save her from any blame. But when she thought like that, the voice would come:

*Wait. Wait and you will be told the right time and place. Selah.*

She still had a fear of being arrested and having to go to a nasty, dirty jail; being locked in with criminals. So she just continued to practice out in the woods, and sometimes when she was alone at home, she would point the rifle out a window toward the hated house, and imagine the red-headed whore in its sight.

At least, Danny wasn't sneaking over there all the time, like he used to. He was working hard at the Piggly Wiggly, and she had felt right proud for a minute when he told her that he had taken a second job, painting for one of the ladies at the store.

That fool, Harland, was trying to get all the overtime he could, too. He was all down-in-the-mouth now because he hadn't been able to save enough money to send the boy to college. Big deal! If somebody really wanted to go to college, they could find a way to pay for it. Right?

Anyway, Danny didn't deserve all this fuss about going to *college*. She hated to think about him anymore. Every time she thought of him now, she saw the disgusting two bodies writhing on the floor, the nasty kitchen floor. How could he do such a thing? Just like his grandfather...

\* \* \*

Jack finally heard from Red. Yeah, great! Now she had it in her head that she wanted a divorce. She was using "infidelity" as her grounds. Said she'd found out that he had caught a venereal disease in Mexico, plus he had deserted her by leaving her and going to Pennsylvania.

It threw him off his feet for a minute, but he quickly recovered. "What the hell are you talkin' about? There ain't nothin' wrong with me! Where'd you get that idea?"

"Jack, how about skipping the act, okay? I saw the invoice from Dr. de Santos in Tampico. You got LGV while you were in Mexico. I asked Dr. Fish what that was and he—"

"Hold on a minute," he interrupted. "That invoice is just a Mexican scam to get more money from another American sucker—"

"And he said there's only one way you can get that disease."

"You don't know what the hell you're talkin' about."

"And you didn't even bother to tell me. You didn't care if I got it or not." Her voice was deliberate with aversion.

"Have you lost your mind? There ain't nothin' wrong with me! You gonna believe that *spic,* Dr. Santos, over me?"

"Oh Jack, give it up. I'm getting a divorce. I've already talked to a lawyer here. My mind's made up—"

"Listen, Red, you got it all wrong. We need to talk about this—"

"And all we gotta do now is to divide up the furniture and stuff. I want to be fair."

"You call this 'fair'? Springin' this on me without no warnin' like this? You been avoidin' all my telephone calls. Well, now I guess I know why!"

"Look, I don't want any alimony, or—"

"*Alimony?* Well, that's good 'cause you sure ain't gettin' a damned cent!"

"That's fine. All I want is the air-conditioner and the kitchen table and chairs."

"You ain't gettin' nothin', you hear? Nothin'!"

"I bought that air-conditioner with my own money, and I'm taking it." Christine spoke slowly now, her voice cold, controlled. "You're welcome to everything else in the house except my clothes, but I would like to have the table and chairs—"

"You ain't gettin' nothin'!"

"—and maybe the dishes and pots and pans—"

"Nothin'! Not a God-damned thing!"

"—because I really need them."

"You lost your mind?"

"Look Jack, it's over. I'm moving out next weekend, putting all your stuff in storage and mailing you the key. My lawyer, Sidney Haynes, will be in contact with you. You should be happy to get out of this marriage. It hasn't worked for a long time."

"Well, ain't you somethin'? You gonna make up your mind just like that! You gonna throw away our marriage just like—"

"Jack, you've never listened, and you're not listening now. I don't want to cause you any trouble. I just want out. *I want out!*"

She hadn't raised her voice, but the last three words, like dry ice, had burned into his brain. His head swam. "But you can't—"

"I'm hanging up now, Jack. I'd prefer it if the rest of our business was done through our lawyers. Good-bye, and no hard feelings, okay?"

He couldn't speak. He heard a click followed by the dial tone.

\* \* \*

Danny was really surprised how nice they were to him at the Marine Corps Recruiting Office. He didn't have to wait at all. The tough-looking, broad-shouldered Sergeant didn't actually smile at him a lot, but he sure was polite. "Respect" was the word. Staff Sergeant McCain had tremendous pride and self-respect, and he treated Danny with respect—called him "Mr. Wilkins". It felt great.

After establishing that Danny was 18 and a high-school graduate, the sergeant explained to him that he would have to meet the physical, mental and moral standards of the Marines. He said that their standards were the highest of any of the armed forces, but that he had no doubt that Danny could meet them. Danny's chest expanded with pride.

The benefits sounded great. They would teach him self-confidence, poise and discipline. He would have financial security and receive top-notch physical and technical training. After his honorable discharge, he could get funding for college up to $50,000.00, depending on his length of service. Best of all, he would wear the uniform of the best and toughest armed service in the world.

Christine would blow a gasket when she saw him in that uniform! And his dad would be so proud.

He got so revved up, he almost went for "late entry," where you could sign up now and actually enter a few months later. He decided against it though, until he could talk to his dad and to Christine. He couldn't wait to tell Mark and Jimmy about it, too.

He had just gotten home and was changing into his painting clothes when his dad pulled up in the driveway. He ran downstairs to tell him the news.

"Hey Dad, guess what! I went down to the Marine recruiting office today, and I think I can get in with no problem. They really liked me."

"Marines? Oh Danny, do you really think... I don't know... Marines?" Harland's face had paled. A look of anguish distorted its usually cheerful features.

Danny was stunned. He'd expected his dad to be thrilled for him, proud of him.

"What's the matter? Don't you like the Marines? The best armed forces in the *world*? I thought..."

"Oh, there's nuthin' wrong with the Marines. It's just that I was hopin'... I don't exactly know whut I was hopin'. We'll talk about it later, after supper."

"I gotta go paint, now. I'll see you later."

"Son, I..." Harland reached toward him, like he was going to hug him or something. "I just—"

"Gotta go, Dad. See you later. Bye, Mama!" He hurried out and spluttered off on the little Honda.

What in the world was the matter with his parents? Madge hadn't shown even the least spark of interest when he told her he might join the Marines. She'd just said, "Whut in the world would you want to do that for?" and had gone back to humming "Onward Christian Soldiers." She hummed that stupid song all the time. She was acting real spacey most of the time, now. He and his dad had kinda gotten used to it. At least she seemed happier than she used to.

Then this strange reaction from his dad. It was confusing. He wondered what Christine would think. He'd soon find out, as he was hurrying on his way now to see her at the new apartment.

*Paint a little, mess around a little. I love it.*

On a whim, he stopped at a 7-Eleven and bought a pint of peach ice-cream for Miss W. Last time he'd talked to her, she'd said something about how she hoped her old peach tree would have some decent fruit on it this year. She was such a neat old lady.

After giving Miss W. the ice cream and accepting her bright-eyed thanks, he ran up the steps, two at a time, to the apartment. Up to the "tree house," as Christine called it. She was up on the ladder painting the ceiling in the bedroom.

"So, there you are, you lazy-bones," she said to him, her face radiating love. "Where've you been?"

"Oh, I've got lots to tell you," he answered, lifting her off the ladder to slide down his body until their lips met. She held a wet paint-brush in one hand and a cleaning rag in the other, as he walked over to the newspaper-covered bed with her, still in the transport of the kiss, and laid her down.

"Wait, wait," she laughed as he began to unbutton her paint-splattered work shirt. "Let me put this paint-brush down, you nut."

He caressed her shapely little bottom as she bent over the paint can to clean the brush. "Damn, that's the cutest little booty I ever saw. Get out of those clothes. I'm gonna make you cry for more!"

And he did. He did.

\*　　\*　　\*

No matter how hard she tried, Bessie couldn't get Billy Joe off her mind for long. She'd given up the Tasty Burger and her well-loved chili cheese steak sandwiches, but she still saw him almost every day at the law office, as he lounged against the front desk talking to his cousin Laura Mae. She didn't know why the lawyers put up with him, hanging around like that. She had gotten jumpy; afraid to pass the oleander bushes in front of her apartment anymore, nervous going out to her car after work at the school. At home, the ring of the telephone would startle her and she would be afraid to pick up the receiver. All too often, there would be a menacing well of silence there when she did pick it up. She didn't know what to do about it. She couldn't go to the police. He hadn't hurt her or outright threatened her. Oh, how she wished that Red had moved in with her instead of getting that apartment!

One day, after he had leered and winked at her as she had passed him at Laura Mae's desk, she asked him to come into her office. Laura Mae looked up in surprise and grinned slyly. Billy Joe jerked to attention and followed her.

Inside her office, she sat on the edge of her desk, facing him squarely. "Close the door, Billy Joe," she said in a voice cold and flat with authority.

His face was flushed and his hands shook as he closed the door.

*How can anybody look clumsy just closing a door? Jeez!*

"How ya doin', Bessie?" he asked with a forced cheeriness, which was defeated when his voice cracked.

"Billy Joe, are you following me around?" she asked bluntly.

He sputtered, "Followin' you aroun'?" He squeaked out an embarrassed snicker. "No, whaddya mean?"

"You wouldn't be callin' me up and not sayin' anything, now would you?"

His face got even redder. "No, 'course not! Why would I—"

"—Because if you are, I wanna warn you, I'll go to the police if I have to."

He clenched his jaw and his watery little eyes narrowed. "You better not go to no police. I've been tryin' to be nice to you, and you keep treatin' me like a piece of trash. I ain't no trash, Bessie. You ain't thowin' me away like no piece of trash!" He was shaking, now.

Bessie was really frightened, but she kept her voice low and steady. "You'd better go now, Billy Joe. I don't want to cause you any trouble. Just please leave me alone."

To her relief, he started toward the door, but turned back to her with his hand on the door-knob. "You're gonna be sorry you treated me like this!" He started to say more, but apparently thought better of it, turned and lurched out the door.

*Oh, Lord. What am I gonna do? He's crazy as a bat!*

She sat down shakily at her desk and composed her thoughts. Maybe she should get away for a while. She had months of accumulated vacation on both her jobs. She'd been working her ass off for five years, saving every penny she could. Her dream was to buy a little place of her own, fix it up and still have enough money to invest for a secure future and maybe even some travel. Still, she could afford to take some time off. Maybe time would solve this problem. Out of sight, out of mind?

*But what if absence made the heart grow fonder?*

\* \* \*

Down on her hands and knees, scrubbing the white-tiled bathroom floor with Comet, Christine firmly put all her troubles out of her mind, and concentrated on the good things which were happening to her. The apartment was looking better than she had ever imagined it could. She saw Danny every day now, and was amazed at the knowledge and skill he showed in the renovation. And at his irrepressible good humor. He dealt immediately with the myriad problems they encountered: the broken damper in the bedroom fireplace, the hornets' nest on the back porch, the leaky faucet in the bathroom, the heavy bedroom door which had to be re-hung because it dragged the floor when you tried to close it, the broken window pane in the kitchen, the air-conditioner they had moved from the house, which didn't want to fit into the large old window in the bedroom. He solved these problems with unflagging industry and innovation.

Best of all, Dr. Fish had gotten the blood test results from Atlanta, and informed her that she was free of any infection. Now Danny kept her tingling with desire and laughing with joy. Life was a big game to him, and he carried her along into his happy world with the formidable force of his positive personality. They made love at least once every day. And she loved him more every day.

She had put the divorce proceedings into Sidney Haynes' efficient hands with complete confidence, and stopped thinking about Jack most of the time. She still avoided his calls. His presence in her life was dimming in her mind; his image blurring in her memory; his welfare fading from her concern.

At Taylor-Made Homes, Stan was pleased with her work, and grateful that she was training Edda-Lou in the operation of their computer systems. He had questioned the idea at first, but was now convinced that Edda-Lou was as capable and intelligent as Christine had predicted she'd be. He was getting his inventory under control, collecting on his accounts receivable, and paying his bills on time. The office was running smoothly and his business was expanding. He gave Christine a lot of the credit for his success.

Stan recommended a good, reliable contractor to install new linoleum in the kitchen, and to replace the fronts of her cabinets. He even cosigned on a loan with her to pay for all this. Now she was broke and in debt, but happier than she'd ever been.

She finished scrubbing the bathroom floor and looked at it with pride. It was gleaming white. She wished Danny were here to see it, but he wouldn't be here for another half hour or so. To celebrate her clean bill of health, they were taking the evening off from the renovation. He was taking her for a ride on his bike, out to Alligator Creek for a little, uh… fishing!

She decided to run downstairs before Danny arrived and tell Miss W. about the contractor who was scheduled to start work on the kitchen tomorrow.

"Oh yes," Miss W. purred, "I know the reputation of Ware Construction Company. Very wise choice. They're reliable people.

Actually, I'm related to the owner." She chuckled. "Just as I'm related to half of Ware County, as a matter of fact."

"Danny's taking me fishing this evening, out to Alligator Creek, so you won't be bothered by all the hammering and—"

"Goodness, gracious! You haven't bothered me one bit. I'm glad to have the old place taken care of for a change."

"Well, you've been awfully patient with us, and we appreciate it."

Miss Worthington looked down at her hands with a thoughtful expression. "By the way, Danny mentioned to me that he was thinking about joining the Marines. What do you think of that idea?"

"It worries me; it really does. When he told me about it, he was so excited and... Well I really didn't know what to say. I think it'd be better for his future if he went on to college somewhere. It's probably a matter of money. Besides, I'd really miss—"

"Yes, we'd both miss him, I'm sure. He's become like a son to me; the son I never had. I wondered if you'd mind if I talked to him about college."

"Oh, that would be so good, if you would! Of course," Christine blushed furiously, "I don't have anything to say about what he does with, with his, uh, future." Her voice faded away in confusion.

"I'm sure we *both* care about his future. He's such a lovely boy. And so much potential. Let me see what I can do."

"Thank you so much, Miss Worthington. You're such a good friend."

"And by the way," Miss W. continued serenely, "did you know that one of Catherine the Great's lovers was 41 years younger than she was?"

Christine was stunned into a frozen silence. Her eyes widened; her jaw dropped open. "I... Uh, what? I don't understand..."

Miss W. smiled sweetly. "I've never held with the limitations of convention, Christine. Fortunately, I've always been in a position that afforded me that option."

Christine backed toward the door, stumbling over a fringed, velvet footstool. She recovered her balance and stammered, "Uh, well, uh, I'd better be going now. Thank you again." She turned and hurried shakily out onto the porch.

As she closed the door, Miss W. looked up at Christine out of the top of her twinkling eyes. "Tell Danny to stop by for a little talk, soon. Good-bye, dear."

Christine climbed the stairs slowly, the magnolia-scented unreality of the place swirling around her. Could she have heard right? Did the aristocratic Miss W. know about her relationship with Danny? And approve? Maybe it wasn't all that bad, after all. She stopped and sat down on the steps as she heard the happy little spluttering sound of the Honda 350 approaching.

Danny skidded up to the foot of the stairs in a small cloud of dust, cut the engine and came up the steps two at a time, pulling off his helmet. He bent over her and kissed her with unabashed lust. She slipped her arms around his neck and spread her legs apart as he lowered his weight onto her. She tipped her pelvis up toward him and pulled him to her with wanton abandon. Who cared if anyone saw? The pressure of this passion, this feeling swept everything else away.

The wooden step pressed hard against her spine.

"Ouch! Let me up, Honey. The step's—mmm." He covered her mouth with his as he picked her up and carried her up the remaining stairs and into the parlor. Their own private little sanctuary.

He lowered her gently onto the sofa. "You beautiful little hussy. You drive me crazy! I'll never get enough of you, never!"

"Ooooo, I sure hope not."

It was almost an hour—an exquisite hour—before Christine slipped on her helmet and mounted the Honda behind him, slipping her arms around his waist, feeling the strength in those muscles that she knew so intimately, as he maneuvered the bike down the winding dirt driveway and onto the road. The late afternoon wind blew against her face and the throb of the engine made her tingle. Every cell in her body was vibrant with happiness as they headed out to Alligator Creek and the beautiful solitude of the Okefenokee.

## Chapter 37

"Miz-tuh Radfud? Weh-ull, how are *you* today? This is Ellie Townsend, the real estate lady?" The whiny voice trailed off into a giggle.

"Oh, Miz Townsend! Glad to hear from you. You got some news for me?"

"Yes sir, I sure have. Sure do! We got us a re-al buyer, already been approved for the loan and everthing. Yoah wife has moved out, and now all we gotta do is finish all the paper work and set up the closin'!"

"Sounds good, Miz Townsend. Do I need to come down for the closing?"

"Not really. Course I sure would like to see yoah handsome face," giggle, giggle, "but we can handle it by proxy."

God, how he hated that southern drawl and all that silly snickering. "Good! I'd just as soon not see any more of Waycross, if I can help it. Look, is there any way we can speed this thing up? I really need the money as soon as possible."

"Weh-ull, you know I'll do everthing I can to help *you* out. Oh, by the way, I saw yoah wife the other day. That's how I knew she'd moved out. She wuz... Weh-ull, I don't know how to say this, and I know it's none of my bizness, but I'll swear, I jes don't see how she could git herself tangled up with a kid like that, not when she had a big, handsome husband like *you*!"

"What? What are you talkin' about?"

"Oh my goodness. I thought you knew all about... I thought that's why you left... Oh, goodness. I'm so sorry if I've spoke out of turn. Oh, dear! I wouldn't have..."

"Miz Townsend, what are you talkin' about? What do you mean 'kid'?"

"Weh-ull, maybe it wasn't nothin'. Prob'ly I jes... No, to tell you the truth, Mr. Radfud, she wuz jes plain *smoochin'* with this kid, yoah next-doah neighbor, out behin' Josie's Kitchen, and that's the truth! It wuz awful!"

"What the hell—"

"I have to tell you, I was right disgusted. *Dis-gus-ted.*"

Jack's voice lowered into a slow growl. "Just what exactly were they doin'?"

"Oh, it wuz awful. He wuz jes mashin' her up against the back of the buildin', and they were kissin'! She was huggin' on him like... Like a... Weh-ull, it wuz jes awful!"

There was an extended silence before he said, "Listen, Miz Townsend, I think I'll come down for the closing after all. You just let me know as soon as you can set it up, okay?"

"I certainly will! And I hope I didn't say anything that—"

"Don't worry. You said just the right thing, Miz Townsend. Thank you. You did me a favor. A *big* favor."

"Weh-ull, I'll call you jes as soon—"

"The sooner the better."

Jack lowered the receiver carefully. It was all he could do to keep from yanking the phone cord out of the wall and throwing the phone across the room. The *bitch*! The god-damned mother-fucking red-headed *bitch*! He'd *kill* her. God-damn her! Acting so fucking high-and-mighty about him having a disease. Taking some fucking spic's word against his. Opening his mail. And all the time she was... He'd *kill* her! *Mother-fucking bitch!* And that little punk, that fucking cracker *punk*. He'd kill them both. *God-damn them! He'd kill them!*

No wonder she was hiding from him, not taking his calls at work, moving off somewhere so he wouldn't know where she was. He'd get her address from her mother. Her mother wanted them to get back together, anyway. He'd tell the old bat he was going down to talk Red into coming back to Allentown, where she belonged. Then he'd just go drop in to see her. Yeah, that'd be a nice little surprise, wouldn't it?

*The bitch!*

\*　　\*　　\*

Danny held the delicate china teacup in one hand and its saucer in the other. He really wanted one of the little square cup-cakes that were all covered with white icing and pink sugar roses, but he didn't know how to manage it with both hands already full.

## Alligator Creek

Miss Worthington smiled at him. "Just put your cup and saucer on the coffee table, Danny, and have yourself a petit-four if you'd like," she advised, lifting the plate in his direction.

Danny laughed, acknowledging that she had read his mind, and put his cup down gratefully and got himself a little cake. It was delicious. Inside the crusty white icing was a rich chocolate cake with an even richer chocolate-candy-like filling. Wow! This wasn't bad at all.

"Hmmm... This is really good, Miss Worthington. Did you make these things yourself?"

"Good heavens no." She laughed. "I order these from Bloomingdale's in New York. I never did master the art of cooking, I'm afraid."

She cleared her throat, tilted her head to the side and gave Danny a penetrating look. "Danny, are you still thinking of joining the United States Marines?"

"Yes, ma'am. I've already been down and talked to a sergeant at the recruiting office. He thought I'd make a good Marine. They don't take just anybody, you know. If you're a Marine, you're in the best fighting company in the world!"

"Is that what you want to do? To be a soldier? To learn to be a killer? But you would certainly be handsome in the uniform."

Danny flushed and quickly picked up his cup of tea and bent over it for a sip, so she wouldn't notice. "Well, I don't know about that. I'm not really all that sure I want to be a soldier. I don't like the idea of having to kill anybody. I could finish my education, though."

"What kind of education do you want?"

"I don't know. I like working with my hands. My dad says I'm good at working on this old car he's rebuilding. I'm good at math, too. Maybe I'll study engineering or something like that."

"What if you could finish your education at some school like Georgia Tech?"

"That'd be great!" Danny shook his head. "But I don't have much chance of that. That'd be way too expensive. My dad's a machinist and he doesn't make all that much money. He's a great guy, don't get me wrong, but—"

"What if someone were willing to pay for your education? Would that make a difference?"

"Oh, yes ma'am. But my grades weren't good enough to get a scholarship."

"Were they good enough to get you into Tech?"

"I don't know. Maybe, but I don't think so. Prob'ly not."

"Danny, before you join the Marines and leave us to go off and fight wars, why don't you find out just what the requirements are for getting into Tech, and see if you can meet those requirements. Check into a few other schools, too: South Georgia over in Douglas County, or perhaps Auburn, West Georgia, Southern Tech. Then come back and talk to me about it. I'd like to help an intelligent and serious young man to get a good education. I know you're intelligent, and I hope you're serious. Are you serious?"

"Oh, yes ma'am. Wow! I don't know what to say." Danny was flabbergasted. "That would be wonderful, Miss Worthington. I'd really be... Really... That's something I've never even thought about, well, not a lot because... I just don't know what to say, Miss Worthington."

"Just say you'll look into it, Danny. Then get all the information and come back to see me. If you'd like to enter school this fall, we'll have to hurry. We're probably too late for Tech, but maybe you could get into a junior college. Anyway, you do the leg-work, and I'll be here to help you when you're ready."

"I don't know what to say—how to thank you. I'll get started tomorrow. This is the biggest thing—the best thing anybody ever did for me. I don't know why you'd want—"

"I'm the end of the Worthington line, Danny. I have no children, no heirs. I think you're a fine young man, and I'd like to pretend you're the son I wish I'd had."

"You're a wonderful lady, ma'am. I'll try to... It would be such an honor to..."

"Go on now, Danny, before we both start crying and embarrass each other." She got up and led him to the door. "Get to work on this fast, now. It would be nice if you could start school somewhere this September." She extended her hand.

Danny squeezed the tiny hand, and leaned forward and kissed her gently on her cheek. "I'll make you proud of me if it kills me!" he said, his eyes bright with conviction.

"Well, perhaps we shouldn't go quite that far," she said, shaking her head, but her eyes, too, were shining with joy.

On the porch, he turned back toward her. "You don't mind if I tell Christine, uh, Mrs. Radford about this, do you?"

"No, but please don't talk about it to anyone else except your family. Of course, nothing has been decided yet, but I still wouldn't want this to be common knowledge around Ware County. Yes, let's be sure to keep this between us; Christine and your mother and father. And please ask them not to mention it to anyone else. Bye-bye, Danny." The door closed softly.

Danny stood transfixed on the porch a minute, then shook his head and took a deep breath. Christine was at school tonight, and he was burning up to talk to her about this. What a kick! His dad was probably still at work, so that left only his mother on the approved list of people he could share this with. He hopped on his bike and took off for home.

"Hey, Mama!" he called as he ran into the kitchen. "Mama! Where are you?"

"I'm here in the living-room. Did you wipe your feet before you came in? I don't want—"

"Mama, I've got some good news." He ran into the living room just as she was closing the glass door on the gun cabinet.

*Man, she sure has gotten interested in those guns, lately.*

"Guess what," he said, his eyes sparkling with excitement.

"What in the world's got into you, boy?"

"Mama, Miss Worthington's offered to pay my way to college, if I want to go. Can you believe it? To college!"

"Is that the old lady you're doin' the paintin' for?"

"Uh, yeah. That's her. Isn't that great?"

"Well, if you say so. I didn't know you wuz so all-fired up to go to college. Whut happened to those big idears you had about joinin' the Marines?"

"I don't know. I still might do that, but she wants me to get some information on engineering schools—see if I can get accepted somewhere. Man, I'd really like to get into Georgia Tech. Just think—"

"I thought you were gonna git yourself a job and help your father pay some of the bills around here."

"But Mama, I could make lots more money if I had an engineering degree. I could take care of the both of you when he gets too old to work, and—"

"Hmmph! I never had much truck with educated fools, but it's your life. Do whatever you want to do. That's whut you're gonna do, anyway." She sniffed loudly and shuffled into the hall-way.

Danny put his excitement out of his mind for a minute and studied his mother. Her hair had apparently not been combed today, and tangled pieces were sticking out at odd angles. Her dirty cotton dress was buttoned wrong. She had on one faded pink and one dirty white sock, and no shoes. Her shoulders were hunched, and she shook her head constantly. She had always been neat and clean and conservative in her dress, and her increasingly slovenly appearance was shocking to Danny.

"Mama, are you all right?" he asked with concern.

"I'm fine! Or I will be when I can get this filthy house cleaned up." She rolled the vacuum cleaner out of the hall closet and into the living room.

Danny looked around the spotlessly clean room. She had been running the cleaner in here when he left for work this morning.

"Mama, the house looks fine. Why don't you go take a little rest before Daddy gets home? You look a little tired." His suggestion was drowned out by the roar of the cleaner.

"There's a time to work, and a time to rest. A time to live, and a time to die. Blessed be the name of the Lord." She thrust the cleaner vigorously across the worn rug.

Danny gave up and went upstairs. He brushed his teeth and put on fresh deodorant before putting on his paint-splattered coveralls. Christine would be home in about a half hour. He couldn't wait to tell her the news. He hoped he could get to her before Miss W. did.

He heard his dad pull up in the driveway and barreled down the stairs and bounded out to the car. "Hey, Dad! Guess what! Miss Worthington has offered to pay my way to college, if I can get in somewhere. Can you believe it? Pay my way!" He threw his arms around Harland and rocked him back and forth.

Harland laughed and hugged him back, the affection quickly degenerating into playful punches. "That's great, Son. That lady must think a lot of you. She's a fine lady, and from what I've heard, she don't like all that many people."

"Well, I reckon she likes *me*!" He kick-started the Honda. "I'm on my way out there now. See you later."

Harland called out over the sound of the engine, "We'll talk about it tonight. Way to go, Son."

Danny started out, but got a worried look on his face and walked the bike backwards toward Harland. In a softer voice which Harland could barely hear over the loud noise of the engine, Danny said, "Dad, Mama looks terrible. Is she okay, you think? Maybe we should take her to a doctor or something."

Harland looked down and kicked at a rock. "I don't know what to do. She sure ain't herself here lately. I think she's just wore out from all that cookin' and cleanin'."

"But all that religious stuff—"

"I know. I'm tryin' to talk her into goin' on a vacation with me. Maybe one of them cruises, or somethin'."

"You and Mama on a cruise? That might help, but I don't know... I hate to say it, but sometimes I think she's, well, maybe goin' crazy."

"Now don't say that, Son. She ain't *crazy!* She's just havin' a little trouble with her nerves, that's all. Probably some kinda woman thing. Don't you worry about it. You gotta think about goin' to *college.*"

Danny caught his father's eye for a brief moment, and they exchanged a worried look—concern that neither could fully express.

Harland looked down the road after Danny long after the sound of the Honda had faded away.

## Chapter 38

Ellie Townsend had spread the word all over Ware County, clucking with righteous indignation as she shook her head and deplored the disgusting behavior of the red-headed Yankee. Seducing a little high-school boy! It was just the worst thing she had ever heard of in her whole life, and the most delicious gossip she'd ever distributed.

Madge had come onto the news a few days later than the rest of Ware County; a few days of abrupt halts in the conversations of her friends when she approached them, and nasty little snickers behind their hands. At her Thursday Circle, her devoted church friends finally told her. They had thought it over carefully and decided, for her sake, that it was their duty to tell her about the ugly rumors.

She was devastated. She should have acted sooner. Now she *knew* what before she had just *thought*, and the worst of it was that *everybody knew*. Here she had to sit like a dummy, with a smile on her face, and act like she knew it all the time. By the time she had left, though, she had convinced them that Danny wasn't having any part of that whore, and that it was all *her* chasing after *him*.

How could he have done this to her? The humiliation! The disgrace! She wished he'd never been born. She wished she'd never gotten married. She hated men. She hated sex. It was Satan's weapon for destroying the Good and the Clean. If she'd never had *sex* with Harland, all this would never had happened. She wanted to scream and cry, but the tears wouldn't come. Her eyes burned. Her brain burned. It had always been like this when she suffered. Alone and tearless.

In her shame and misery, she heard the voice of God again:

*Go ye and rid the earth of this pestilence, good and faithful servant. Selah.*

She was not alone. God was on her side. She would do His bidding. Tomorrow! Then maybe she could get the nasty picture out of her head. The filthy kitchen floor. The whore, with her red hair hanging down over her face, on top of Danny, pumping up and down. Pumping up and down!

God would work through her. Blessed be the name of Jesus. Tomorrow.

\* \* \*

On Thursday morning, when Bessie walked into the office she knew that something was wrong. It was in the air. Laura Mae was not at the front desk. There was no welcoming smell of coffee. In her office, the message light was blinking. She clicked the "Play" button and listened as she settled in; extracting the day's necessities from her huge bag, unwrapping her powered-sugar-covered donuts, and running a comb through her hair. To her dismay, the first message had been recorded last night and was from Billy Joe. He sounded drunk or drugged or something.

"Listen here, Bessie. I know you don't like me. Nobody does. But you shouldn't have called me 'Sugar' and all that. I thought you liked me. It really ain't fair how you built me up like that and then jes thowed me away. Well, I ain't gonna be around for people to step all over no more... I coulda been real nice to you, but... Uhhh... Anyway, I ain't gonna feel bad no more. No more... I'm sick and tired of feelin' bad. Good-bye, Bessie. I wish we coulda... Hmm... Bye, Bessie." The answering machine clicked with an awful finality.

The message was delivered in slow, slurred speech. His voice trailed off in mid-sentence several times, and the message was interrupted by several long pauses. At the end it degenerated into a mumble, difficult to understand. It gave her a deadly, eerie, helpless feeling.

She didn't know what to do, but she really needed to talk to somebody, quick! She hurried out of her office and found the staff gathered in the break room, wrapped in animated conversation. Laura Mae was not with them.

Bessie stopped in the doorway. "What's happened?" she asked.

Their conversation halted abruptly, and they all looked at her with embarrassment and concern. Sidney explained gently, "It looks like Laura Mae's cousin, Billy Joe, tried to kill himself last night. He's in the hospital now, having his stomach pumped. Seems he took a whole bottle of sleeping pills. Laura Mae's down there with him now, and probably won't be back in today."

"Oh, my God!" She swayed and hid her face in her hands. Sidney stepped forward and steadied her. She stammered, "Is he... Will he be all right?"

*Do they suspect that I had anything to do with it? Oh, please no! Oh, please!*

Several voices assured her that he was going to be just fine.

"Did he write a note or anything?" she ventured, afraid to hear the answer.

Nobody knew whether he had or not. At least they hadn't found one so far.

"Oh, that poor kid. That poor kid," she mumbled, shaking her head and looking at the floor.

Back in the sanctuary of her office, she forced herself to face the question. Had she had anything to do with Billy Joe's attempt on his own life? The pathetic and damning message on her answering machine sure indicated that she had. She knew that she should erase it immediately, but didn't know whether she could bring herself to do it. The pitiful self-revelation it contained was somehow sanctified by his suicide attempt. She felt sick with guilt and sorrow.

She clicked "Play" again on the incriminating machine. "Listen here, Bessie. I know—" She clicked "Delete."

The slow, flat voice came back, "One message deleted."

She felt even worse for a minute, and then took a deep breath and told herself, "Okay, Bessie. There's nothing you can do about this right now. Just concentrate on that pile of work on the desk." She would have to get through the day and talk to Red about it when she went to her new apartment for dinner tonight. She dove into the paperwork.

*　　*　　*

Christine and Edda-Lou left the office together, and now were scooting along in the VW, on the way to Christine's for dinner. Bessie was invited, too. Christine had wanted them to meet for some time, now.

She felt a warm glow of pride as they turned into the canopied driveway to Miss W's stately old house. Waiting in her refrigerator were a lasagna casserole, garlic butter for the Italian bread, home-made ranch dressing for the salad, and a yellow cake with fudge icing, all ready for her final touches for their all-girl dinner.

Edda-Lou said, almost in a whisper, "Gosh! How romantic," as they pulled up to the old house.

"It is, isn't it?" Christine answered happily. "I was so lucky to find this place. Wait till you see my tree-house apartment."

Christine had a right to be proud. The light, soft pastels of the new paint went perfectly with the gentle colors which had emerged from the drapes, rugs and upholstery when they were cleaned. Christine's few furniture additions had settled in comfortably with the antiques which now gleamed from the application of furniture polish and elbow grease. A pleasant light filtered through the huge old oaks into the tranquillity of the elegant rooms.

As she followed Christine in, Edda-Lou exclaimed in awe, "Oh my gosh. This is beautiful!"

"Make yourself at home," Christine sang, "Would you like some wine or sherry while I get out of this dress and into some shorts?" She hoped that Edda-Lou would choose sherry, as she had just bought some delicate little aperitif glasses.

"Sure, I'll have a glass of wine, if it's not too much trouble."

*Oh, well.* "Red or white?"

"White, please."

Christine poured Edda-Lou a glass of Blue Nun and herself a glass of Burgundy. She put out a wedge of brie and dumped some Waverly Wafers into a small basket, and led her guest out onto the screened back-porch. She had cleaned up the old picnic table and benches she had found on the porch, and now it looked absolutely festive with a blue checkered tablecloth and candles in empty Chianti bottles, and a bouquet of blue and pink corn-flowers and Queen Anne's lace in the center. It looked wonderful and gave Christine a little thrill of satisfaction. She lit the candles and went inside to change.

She had planned the little dinner, "hen party" Bessie had called it, when Danny told her he was invited to Mark's good-bye party on this evening. Mark was leaving for Georgia Southern next Monday. Danny was in the process of gathering information on technical schools, and had hoped he could announce to his friends that he, too, was going off to college soon. Danny had told Christine, in an effort to maintain the complete trust between them, that Betty Sue Jamison was "kinda sweet" on him, and that she'd be at the party. This news gave Christine a moment of jealous insecurity, but the moment was brief. She welcomed his confidence and told him that she understood that he needed to keep up his friendships with people his own age, both male and female. She didn't say it, but she was sure down to the marrow of her bones that he loved her, and she surely didn't want to diminish his life in any way. So, she planned the hen party. It would keep her from sitting around and feeling lonely and neglected.

Bessie arrived just as she had changed into her shorts and tee-shirt.

"Jesus, Red!" she exclaimed, "You done a lot since I was over here last week. It looks like a damn picture in 'House Beautiful'. Amazin'."

The three of them put the finishing touches on the dinner and sat down at the table amid a swirl of happy camaraderie.

At the table, Bessie leaned over toward Edda-Lou and confided, "Red tells me that you're a real comer in the computer business."

Edda-Lou looked down, embarrassed, and stammered, "Uh... well, uh... I wouldn't exactly say that." She looked up and nodded her head at Christine. "Christine's real patient with me. She's a good teacher, too. Makes it seem easy. I'm—"

Christine interrupted, "She's *good!* Pretty soon, if I'm not careful, I'll be out of a job."

Edda-Lou laughed. "That's not gonna happen. Mr. Taylor couldn't get along without Christine. You oughta hear him braggin' about how smart she is." She turned to Bessie. "And I hear that you're workin' two jobs and runnin' the show in both places."

"Oh Lord! Not hardly." Bessie shook her head. "But you know whut? I guess we're all pretty damned smart, around here."

"Here's to us!" Christine raised her glass. The Burgundy glowed a soft red in the candlelight.

"To us."

"To us!"

"And pass the lasagna!" Christine added. They all laughed.

Bessie got a serious look on her face then and said, "But I reckon both my offices are gonna hafta git along without me for a while. I've decided I need to take a long vacation."

"Well, you sure deserve it, Bessie," Christine answered, "but what made you decide to finally take some time off?"

"I gotta git outa town. Like *before sundown.*" Bessie's good humor evaporated suddenly, and her eyes became bright with tears. She dropped her fork on the table and looked down into her plate.

"Bessie! What in the world? What's happened?" Christine got up and went around the table and sat beside her friend. As she put her arms around her, Bessie began to cry.

"It's that Billy Joe! He's drivin' me crazy! He's been followin' me, callin' me and not saying anything. And now he's... he's..." She was sobbing now. "He's tried to kill himself!"

"Oh, Bessie!"

"And it's all my fault!"

"No, no, no, Bessie," Christine rocked her in her arms. "You haven't done anything to make him do something like that. No, no, no. You know better than that."

Edda-Lou was mute for a moment with embarrassment and concern. Then she patted Bessie on the back gently and murmured, "There, there, now."

"Oh, I'm sorry, y'all," Bessie whimpered. "I didn't mean to wreck the party. I just—"

"Hush, Silly," Christine comforted her. "What're friends for, anyway? Tell us what happened."

Bessie reached down into her huge bag and retrieved a slightly-used handkerchief. She blew her nose with a resounding "honk", wiped her eyes and explained to Edda-Lou, "This kid at the Tasty Burger somehow got the idea that I wuz givin' him the 'come-on' or somethin'. I'll swear, I wasn't! Then there wuz this mix-up at the office. His cousin is our receptionist, and she thought I wuz askin' one of the lawyers about…"

Christine frowned and shook her head tensely at Bessie.

"Uh… about… Well, anyway, she thought I wuz interested in the poor kid. You know—interested. It was crazy! Anyway, he started callin' me all the time—at home, at both jobs, followin' me aroun', scarin' me. I swear, he was hidin' in the shrubbery in front of my apartment one night, and I…" Bessie sobbed a minute and continued, "I mean, he got really furious when I told him to leave me alone, and I… uh… I finally told him I was gonna call the police if he kept botherin' me. That was a few days ago, and then today I found out that he ate a bottle of sleepin' pills." Bessie's voice rose up into to a wail.

Edda-Lou gasped, "Oh, my God! Did he—"

"Naw. He ended up in the hospital, gettin' his stomach pumped. He's gonna be okay, I think."

"Thank God for that." Christine said softly.

"But now, the whole office thinks I was mean to him. Maybe I was." Bessie lowered her face into her handkerchief and began to cry again. "I didn't mean to… I tried to… Oh, I just feel awful about all this!"

"Now listen, Bessie," Christine said firmly, "You didn't do anything wrong. You weren't *mean* to that boy. You tried to help him. I know you did. You gave him some good advice, about school and all. He was *so* lonely, he just misunderstood… Look, you're a really warm and friendly person. He probably wasn't used to that. He got a big crush on you, but it *wasn't your fault*. I know you feel bad, but believe me, it's gonna be all right. Maybe he'll get some help now."

Bessie sighed and tried a tentative smile. "Hey y'all, I sorry. I didn't mean to blubber like this. But anyway, that's why I thought maybe now'd be a good time to take a vacation." She looked from one to another with a naughty grin. "Hmmm, didn't I see a chocolate cake in the kitchen? A big ole slice of that oughta fix me right up!"

All three laughed with relief. They finished the dinner and began to clear the table.

Later, over cake and coffee, Christine confided to them that she had gotten a call from Tim Cotter in Atlanta that day, offering her a job again. His company was expanding, and they were desperate for experienced computer people. She was flattered, but not really tempted, although the money *was* good.

"I'm happy where I am right now, working with good people, and..." she winked at Bessie, "having a few really *good* friends, and living up here in my fancy tree-house."

All three were in good spirits when Bessie and Edda-Lou left. Christine finished cleaning up the kitchen and went to bed happy. She pulled the extra pillow over beside her, wrapped one leg around it and hugged it tightly to her body. It smelled like Danny. She breathed in deeply and imagined his body close to her.

*Danny, I want you. Mmmmm... Where are you and what are you doing?*

\*   \*   \*

Earlier, Danny had arrived at Mark's party with Betty Sue Jamison. She had called him and asked for a ride, and he didn't know how to refuse. His arrival caused an affectionate stir of back-slaps, punches and insults.

"Well, can you believe it? Look who's here. We all thought you were dead!"

"Or in jail, more likely."

"Hey, are we the lucky ones, or what? Where've you been, man?"

Danny reveled in the good-natured teasing, punched them back and laughed. "I decided to go slummin' tonight. So, here I am."

Betty Sue had hurried to the bathroom to comb her hair, the top mashed flat by the motorcycle helmet, and the ends blown into a wild dishevelment by the ride. Her cheeks were flushed with happiness. She knew she was the envy of every other girl at the party.

The party was taking place in the basement of Mark's house. A folding table with a paper table-cloth printed with balloons, fireworks and the words "Bon Voyage" in bright, primary colors, was set up with paper plates, cups and napkins. On the floor beside the table was a wash tub filled with ice and cans of Coca-Cola, Dr. Pepper and Sprite. On the table, little squares of cheddar sported multi-colored toothpicks, and a big bowl of potato chips sat close to the ubiquitous dip of sour cream mixed with Lipton's French Onion Soup Mix. The air was thick with cigarette smoke. There was heavy traffic in and out of the door leading out to the back yard cement patio, where Four Roses was available to spike the soft drinks in their paper cups. A portable record player sat on a chair, with a grand disarray of "45" records scattered all around it. Couples were dancing beneath the furnace pipes and plumbing j-joints that heavily adorned the ceiling. They clutched each other and swayed, hardly moving, to the slow music, and jumped and jerked wildly around the supporting iron posts to the fast music.

Danny was having fun. He was a good dancer, and was bombarded with shy flirtatious glances from girls wanting him to ask them to dance. Since school had been out, he hadn't seen much of Mark and Jimmy, and it was great spending time with them again. He stayed away from the booze though, taking just enough in his paper cup of Sprite to avoid being a "bad sport". Mark was drinking heavily, however; drinking right out of the bottle. Soon the Four Roses was gone, and they switched to King Cotton Peach Brandy.

Danny took turns dancing with every girl there. He didn't want to neglect anybody, and although Betty Sue was the best dancer, he didn't want to give her the wrong idea by showing her too much attention. He was really enjoying dancing and being with his friends again, though.

All of a sudden, Mark stood up on a chair and shouted for everyone's attention. "Hey, whaddya say? Les have some *real* fun!" He was slurring his words and having trouble focusing his eyes. "Les all go skinny dippin' out in Worthington Lake."

This suggestion was greeted with a whoop of approval from the male contingent of the party, and embarrassed but titillated snickers from the females.

"You know we can't do that," Danny admonished, "Worthington Park is closed after sundown."

A chorus of "So what?", "Who cares?", "Come on, let's go" erupted from the boys, and a few half-hearted "Yeah, it's too cold, anyway", "My daddy would kill me" and "That water's all muddy" protests came from the girls.

"Y'all are nuts," Danny persisted. "The cops patrol that place all the time."

Mark taunted Danny in a sing-song voice, "Whazza matter, Danny-boy? You scared your *old lady'll* git mad at you?"

Jimmy burst out laughing, spitting his King Cotton laced Dr. Pepper all over his date. "*Old lady!* That's a good one!"

Danny felt a hot flush of anger rising into his face. "What the fuck? Go on and get yourselves locked up! Who gives a shit?"

Mark wouldn't leave it alone. "Danny-boy's gonna be in trouble," he sang in the old "nya, nya, nya, nya, nya, nya" kind of child's song. "Old lady's gonna cut him off."

The boys roared with laughter. Danny's affair with Christine was common knowledge to them, but unknown to the girls, who now stood around with puzzled looks on their faces.

"Come on, Betty Sue, I'll take you home," Danny said, his jaw muscles working tensely. "That is, unless you want to go swimmin' with these idiots."

"Who the fuck you callin' a idiot?" Mark said, jumping down from the chair and muscling his way through the party, which was now alerted with excitement and fear. "You too damn good for your old friends anymore? Too busy with your new li'l piece o' ass?"

"Come on, Danny, let's go," Betty Sue pleaded. She tried to hold him back, but his body was now pumped with rage.

He lunged forward at Mark. "Shut the fuck up!"

"Make me, asshole!"

"You're asking for it, asshole!"

Mark's flushed face was just inches from Danny, now. "Fuck you!" He shoved Danny backward. "Fuckin' that old bitch!"

Danny's fist slammed into Mark's face. Mark staggered backward onto the silly festive table and crashed to the floor amid little cheese squares, potato chips and French Onion dip. Danny was immediately sick with guilt and wanted to pick his friend up, to apologize, but he knew that the best thing he could do was to get the hell out of there before things got any worse.

Betty Sue was crying and pulling at his arm. "Come on Danny, please. Please! Let's go. Please take me home."

He took her arm and started out the back door. They passed Jimmy, who was frozen in dismay. "Sorry, Buddy," Danny told him, with a pat on the shoulder.

Behind him, Mark had scrambled to his feet with a little help, and was lunging drunkenly toward him. "You fuckin' son of a bitch! Fuckin' stuck-up son of a bitch!" Danny and Betty Sue had made it to the patio when Mark smashed into him from the rear and they both went down onto the cement. Danny skinned both his hands and his cheek, and Mark lay groaning, holding his wrist.

Danny picked himself up, staring in disbelief at his bloody hands. "Shit, Mark! What's the big deal here? Look, I'm sorry…"

Betty Sue yanked on him for all she was worth. "Please, Danny! Come on!"

Mark rolled on the ground and moaned, "Oh fuck! My damn wrist is broke."

Danny yielded to Betty Sue's urgent tugs and left, calling over his shoulder. "Look Mark, I'm really sorry. I'll call you tomorrow."

The motorcycle ride to Betty Sue's house was wordless. He fervently wished he had gone over to Christine's instead of going to the disastrous party. What in the world had Mark gotten so mad about? Must've been the booze talking.

The way Betty Sue clung to him made him feel uneasy. It always felt so good when Christine was behind him on the bike, her sweet breasts pressing against his back, but this stiff little body behind him was a hindrance. Betty Sue didn't lean with him when he made a turn. She was a foreign object. Christine was like a part of him.

When they got to Betty Sue's house, he took her helmet and walked her to her door in silence.

"You want to come in and let me put some mercurochrome on that?" she said, reaching her hand toward his cheek.

He pulled back. "Naw. Thanks anyway, but I don't want your folks to see me messed up like this. And look, I'm really sorry things turned out like they did tonight. I don't—"

"Don't worry. I'm just glad you didn't get hurt too bad."

"Night, Betty Sue. I'm sor—"

"Good night, Danny. It's all right." She reached up and kissed him gently on the lips and then hurried inside.

He ran down her walkway to his bike, strapped on his helmet, swung his leg over the bike and headed for the tree house. For Christine, comfort, sanity, home.

He hoped Betty Sue hadn't seen him wiping his mouth after she kissed him.

## Chapter 39

Christine was drifting contentedly in a dream of Danny, fueled by his lingering aroma in the pillow she was clutching. He was in her arms and they were floating blissfully on the black water of Alligator Creek. He wasn't speaking, but he was telling her how much he loved her. He was dissolving into her body, enriching her, and she was absorbing him as part of herself. She knew that when they reached the heart of the swamp, the beautiful open "prairie," that they would no longer be separated from each other or from the mysterious life force around them. Their atoms would be swept upward with the scent of water lilies, into the graceful swirl of flying creatures; birds, butterflies, dragon-flies. Suddenly he was no longer in the canoe with her, but was approaching on a flat-boat powered by a gasoline engine. She could hear it coming. She lifted her head and realized that she was no longer dreaming. He *was* approaching. On the sweet, familiar sound of the Honda.

Still half asleep, she stumbled to the bay window and looked out into the moonlit yard, in time to see him pull up at the foot of the stairs. Joyously, she ran out onto the front porch, red-gold hair tousled, cheeks pink with excitement and green eyes shining. Her filmy white gown drifted back gently in the light breeze, molded against the soft curves of her body. Her white arms glowed in the moonlight as she held them out to him.

He ran up the stairs, picked her up and said with a small sob, "Oh my God! You're so beautiful it hurts." She lifted her arms upward toward the moon, and in her sleep-drugged mind she felt she was flying up into the bright stars above her, feeling the rush of space against her, comprehending the distances between the galaxies.

She brought herself back to reality and nuzzled her face against his neck. "Oh, I'm so glad you came over tonight. But what happened? It's so early. Did the party break up early?"

"I guess you could say that," he said with a wry chuckle.

Then she noticed the skinned place on his cheek. "Oh my gosh, Honey! What happened?"

He put her down and showed her his hands. "Nothin' to worry about. I just got in a fight with my best friend, that's all. With Mark."

"Oh no! I'm so sorry. Come on in and let me put something on it. You poor thing. What started it?"

"He had too much to drink, and we got into a stupid argument—about nothin', really."

"*Nothing?* You couldn't have—"

"Mark wanted everybody to go swimmin'...well, actually skinny-dippin' out in Worthington Lake. I said we shouldn't go. It's closed at night and they patrol it. I know cause—"

"And *that's* what you got into a fight about? Danny, I can't believe you would—"

"Well, then they started teasin' me about... about you. Mark said some things... made some... some crude remarks about *you*, and I guess I lost it."

"No, no! Oh, Danny! I wouldn't have you... I can't bear to think that I ever caused you any—"

"Hey, it's not *your* fault. Mark and Jimmy both thought you were the most beautiful, sexiest woman they ever saw. They thought I was the luckiest guy in the world, at first. Now they can't see why it's become such a big thing, you know; why I spend so much time with you. I think they're jealous. They just—"

"Of course, you can't expect them to understand how we feel about each other. Neither one of us meant to fall in love. It's crazy. I don't understand it myself."

"Well, I don't regret a thing. I mean, I still think I'm the luckiest guy in the world. I *am* the luckiest guy in the world! I don't care what—"

"We're *both* lucky, and I sure wouldn't change a thing. But come here, let me fix your poor skinned-up face and hands," Christine said as she led him to the bathroom.

As she gingerly cleaned and dressed his wounds, her voice took on an even more serious tone. "You know, Honey, this just tells us that we're right to keep all this to ourselves as much as possible. There're not many people who could accept our relationship, much less understand it. It would be silly for us to even hope for that. I'm lucky that Bessie accepts it. We're both lucky that Miss W. does. She's all for it, as a matter of fact."

"I know all that," he said, wincing from the sting of the antiseptic, "but it still gets away with me when they make jokes about us—especially in front of everybody like that."

"Danny, listen to me. This is important. I couldn't stand it if I thought that I caused any bad problems in your life. You don't know how much I want you to be happy; not just now, but for the rest of your life." She brushed a curly blond lock up off his forehead. "I can't bear it if this thing...this *wonderful* thing we have between us turned out to be bad for you."

"How could you ever think this would be 'bad' for me?"

"Well, like tonight. I don't want you to get separated from your friends, your family. I want you to fall in love with somebody your own age sometime—maybe not right now—" They both laughed. "And get married, have children, beautiful blond curly-haired children, and have a normal life."

"Yeah, but how about better-than-normal? That's what I've got now!"

"Well, it just can't interfere with the *rest* of your life."

"Christine, please. I want to spend the rest of my life with *you*, not anybody else! When you get your divorce—"

She put her smooth, cool fingers over his lips. "Don't even say it. This can't go on for the rest of our lives. Not that I won't love you for the rest of my life. I will! But we can't be a real couple, a socially acceptable couple—"

"Who gives a shit about being 'socially acceptable'?"

"You will, eventually. Maybe I will, too. It matters."

They looked into each other's eyes for a long moment, with feelings of tenderness, loss, love and hopelessness struggling for supremacy. Then the sparkle, always right below the surface, came back into Danny's eyes and he smiled. Hope took over, in spite of all Christine's good sense. Danny hugged her close to him.

"Your hands—" she cautioned.

"Don't worry about me. I'm a man, remember? We don't feel pain."

"Oh, you fool. I love you so much! What am I gonna do?"

"How about... um... spending the night with me? I'll call home and make up something and stay over." He kissed her.

She felt the dependable bulge swelling against her, and the thought of his body on hers banished all her rational concerns. "Oh, yes! Yes! Let's do it!" What were those trivial, mundane worries compared to *this*? This overwhelmingly sweet desire?

"I hope my dad answers," he said as he dialed. Then, "Hello, Mama. Me and the guys are going fishin', and we're gonna camp out, so I won't be home till tomorrow...

"Naw, don't worry. I'll just wear some of Mark's old clothes...

"No, ma'am. We gotta go now. I don't have time to come by the house...

"I *know* I gotta work tomorrow, Mama. I'll just go from here...

"It'll be all right, don't worry. I'll just come back here and clean up and change clothes. I'll get to work on time, I promise...

"Now, Mama, don't worry. We know right where we're goin'. Out on Gum Swamp Creek. We been fishin' there a million times.

We're not goin' all the way out into the park or nothin'. Don't worry."

This conversational vein continued for some time, until the passion he and Christine had felt when it began was drained away and replaced by feelings of guilt. When he finally said, "Look Mama, I really gotta go, the guys are waitin' for me. I'll be home tomorrow after work," and hung up, they looked at each other with faces tainted with chagrin. Danny shook his head and confided, "I'll swear, I think Mama's goin' crazy. She doesn't make sense half the time anymore."

Christine ventured uncertainly, "Maybe this wasn't such a good idea."

Danny said, "Are you nuts? This is a wonderful idea! I can't believe we haven't done it sooner. Hey, you got anything to eat? I'm starvin'," and the happy mood was restored.

She cut them each a piece of cake, and poured two glasses of milk. As she looked across the table at him, senses all heightened, the chocolate fudge icing melting in her mouth was the best thing she had ever tasted in all her life.

"Man," he said, "this is the best cake I ever ate."

She shook her head in wonder.

They made love all night, with sweet interludes of blissful sleep. Each awakening engulfed them with the wonder of finding themselves together, wrapped in each other's arms, in the exquisite comfort of their seclusion. There were times when the intensity of her ecstasy frightened her; made her afraid her heart might burst.

Next morning, he sang in the shower while she made breakfast. She served it on the screened porch, the blue checkered table cloth and the cheerful blue, pink and white flowers still remarkably festive. He wolfed down pancakes and syrup, bacon, two eggs over easy, orange juice and coffee. She was thrilled by his perfect ease, his enormous appetite, his very presence. It all seemed so *right*!

"See," he said as he left, "it oughta be like this all the time."

She waved good-bye to him from the front porch. She felt as if half of her body had been torn away as he disappeared down the tree-covered drive.

## Chapter 40

On Saturday afternoon, Madge headed for the grocery. Something was wrong, though, and she didn't know exactly what it was. Danny had called her that morning from the Piggly Wiggly and told her not to worry, that he got back from his fishing trip and made it to work on time. It didn't sound right for some reason. He was doing that thing that he did when he was hiding something—being too nice, too happy. She thought about going out to Waresboro to see if he really was at work, but decided it was too much trouble. Besides, she didn't want to drive that far. The car was low on gas and she didn't like going to the filling station. That was a man's job.

Harland had gone hunting with some friends from the machine shop where he worked. Fine. Good riddance! But he should have made sure the car had enough gas in it before he left. She felt sorry for herself. She did everything she could for those two, and what did she get in return? Nothing. Not even a "thank you."

As she drove, the hideous picture of Danny and the whore assaulted her mind again. And that fool, Harland, still thought the sun rose and set on his precious little boy. Especially now that he might be going to *college*. Hmmph! She just wished Harland could have seen the sight she saw—those naked bodies wallowing all over the kitchen floor. Pigs! Filthy pigs! She'd almost told Harland about it a million times, but she couldn't let anybody know that she'd been over there, spying. Besides, she didn't want anybody to know what she really thought of her ex-neighbor and maybe suspect *her* as being the one that finally got rid of her, so she couldn't say anything. She thought of Jesus's mother.

*And Mary kept all these things and pondered them in her heart.*

That's what she'd do. Keep it to herself.

In the A & P, while she carefully picked out the best pole beans—not like some people that just threw them in the plastic bag by the handful—she heard her name.

"Hello, Madge. Is Danny okay?"

It was Mark's mother. She never could remember that woman's name. "Well, I reckon so. I hadn't seen him since last night. He's not home from workin' at the Piggly Wiggly, yet." She forced a modest smile.

*My son is working. Too bad yours isn't.*

"I know you'll be glad to hear that Mark's wrist ain't broke. It's just sprained."

"Oh, did they have an accident? I tried to tell Danny that it was dangerous stayin' out in the swamp like that, all night."

"Whaddya mean 'out in the swamp'? They got in their fight in my basement; there and out in my back yard. Nobody went out into no *swamp*."

Madge turned back quickly to her careful selection of pole beans. "Oh, I guess Danny went with some of his *other* friends." Her heart was pounding, and she knew her face was red. "Those boys sure do love their fishin'."

"Well, I don't know who he went with. He left right after the fight, and I ain't seen him since."

Madge struggled to hide her agitation, examining each bean with intense concentration. The voices were screaming in her head, but the Lord made her voice calm and controlled as she said, "I'm sorry, but I'm kinda in a hurry. Tell Mark I'm glad he's all right." She sounded strange to herself, like somebody else talking. She twisted the top of the plastic bag tightly, threw the beans into her shopping cart and rushed away just like somebody who had important things to do. The voices screamed on.

*The filthy little liar! The devil! How can he embarrass me like this? He's got the Devil in him. She did it! She put the Devil in him!*

Lightening bolts of pain pierced her head. As soon as she was out of sight of Mark's mother, she abandoned her cart full of groceries in the frozen food section and hurried out of the store. She knew what she had to do.

She drove home wrapped in a rush of sound. Demon howlings and the deafening drum-beat of her own throbbing head almost drowned out her guiding voices. She was only vaguely aware of the angry honking of the horns of automobiles all around her.

*Jesus, help me. Gird up my loins with the power of God's righteousness. Help me to do Thy bidding. Amen.*

She went directly to the gun cabinet when she got home. Thank God, Harland had not taken *her* rifle. He had taken a shotgun and left her the weapon she needed. She took the gun out of the cabinet and stroked its stock lovingly. Suddenly she felt calm, alert, strong.

She had to have a plan. Where was the whore? It was Saturday, so she wouldn't be at work and Madge didn't know where she lived. How could she find her? She needed some aspirin. She took the gun into the kitchen and laid it gently on the kitchen table. There on the table, was a note in Danny's handwriting. A sign! She picked up the note and read:

*Dear Mom and Dad,*

*Sorry I missed you. We're going back camping again tonight after work. Don't worry. I'll be all right. I'll see you tomorrow.*

*Love, Danny*

He was with that whore! She knew it now without a doubt. He was either at her house, or they'd gone camping. Maybe they were out in the swamp, fishing. *Together*. Where, where? She knew what to do. She'd call Jimmy. If she was cagey enough, maybe she could get him to tell her where the whore lived.

She took her aspirin tablets, doubling her usual dosage to four, and looked up Jimmy's telephone number. Her fingers were shaking so much, she could hardly dial.

*Dear Heavenly Father, be with me and make me calm down. I am about to do Thy bidding. Make me stop shaking, so I can be about Thy business. Amen.*

She was in luck, and Jimmy answered the phone. God was with her again. Jimmy sounded groggy, like maybe she woke him up. Lazy thing!

"Jimmy, this is Mrs. Wilkins, Danny's mother. I need to get in touch with Danny. There's been a... uh, death in the family."

"Gee, I don't know, Miz Wilkins. He oughta be at work."

"No, he's off work by now. He left me a note sayin' he's gone fishin'. I think he might be with... with that Miz Radford. Do you know where she lives?"

"No ma'am, I sure don't, but if they've gone fishin', they're prob'ly out on Alligator Creek. That's where they usually go."

*Usually go? Usually go?*

Madge's head swam. She managed a polite, "Thank you, Jimmy," and carefully replaced the receiver. How long had this been going on? Seems like on Friday Danny had said they'd be out on Gum Swamp Creek. The little liar! So that's what was going on! Lies, lies, lies!

Hatred and frustration burned through her brain and cleared it of everything except revenge. Revenge and duty. She had to get that filthy whore out of her life. Out of decent society. Once again, she saw the abomination on the kitchen floor. Nude bodies sprawled on the floor, rubbing against each other, hips pumping, fornicating—fornicating!

*The time is here, good and faithful servant. The wrath of the Lord will cleanse this evil from our midst. Selah!*

She felt the strength of Jehovah fill her body and mind. She knew that this was the moment. The fornicators were in the swamp! She could imagine the feel of the gun kicking gently back against her shoulder, sending its cleaning missiles into the unclean body of the corrupter. She could imagine the thuds as the bullets tore into that hateful body. The body would sink into the mud and filth of the swamp, and be eaten by alligators. Nothing would be left. All this nastiness and sin would cease. It would be gone. Life would be clean and orderly again.

She hurried now, purposeful and happy: changing into Harland's old paint-splattered overalls, putting on his hunting vest and filling the pockets with .22 caliber cartridges. She knew exactly where to go. There was a Texaco filling station out where the road crossed Alligator Creek. She'd gone there once with Harland, back when he was always trying to get her to go out in the swamp with him, and they'd rented a flatboat. He'd showed her how to push on the pole that moved the boat along, so she knew just how to do it.

She had a little trouble convincing the Texaco man that she knew what she was doing, that she could handle the boat okay. He kept trying to tell her she shouldn't go out there alone, but she knew exactly what she was doing, and she wouldn't take "No" for an answer. She finally had to offer him twice the regular fee, before he'd say she could rent it. That was okay; nothing could stop her now. She pulled the car behind the station, slipped the gun out and went down to the boat as unobtrusively as possible and pushed off.

The flatboat was hard to guide. It kept running up under the branches of the bushes beside the narrow stream. Madge's face and hands were getting scratched up pretty bad. It hurt, but she could take it. Satan was trying to stop her. She wasn't surprised. This was a struggle between right and wrong, and she would win. *Right* would triumph!

As the slow-moving stream was joined by other small streams, the going got a little easier. Soon, she approached a rickety dock where several ragged children were fishing. She could see some shabby, unpainted buildings back under the tall pines. The children stood as she approached, staring at her in disbelief. One of the older boys ran excitedly from the dock toward the buildings, shouting, "Hey Ma! Somebody's comin'! Whut about Olin 'n Harry? Somebody orta tell 'em!" The other children just stood there stupidly, not saying a word. Madge ignored them. Poor white trash!

She poled her way slowly past without speaking. She could hear uneasy voices back in the woods, but they soon faded into the distance.

The stream widened and spread out into the heavy growth alongside. It became harder to tell exactly where the main channel was. Water stood around the bases of the trees and bushes on all sides of her. Knobby-toed cypress trees with moss dangling from their branches made the passage darker. The sky was darkening, as well. The late afternoon sun had disappeared behind gloomy, gray clouds. She fervently hoped it wouldn't rain.

She heard unseen creatures rustling and splashing in the dim woods around her. She knew they were slimy things: frogs, lizards, snakes. She felt something looking at her, and jerked her head around to see two impassive yellow eyes watching her, sticking up out of the smooth surface of the water—two deadly-still, threatening, gnarly globes. Silently, they sank into the water, leaving no trace of a ripple. An alligator! Had she really seen it?

She was venturing into Hell, and Satan was trying to scare her. She must not be frightened. God was with her! He would protect her from the evil around her. She expected to find the whore around every bend in the channel of black water. Black as sin, black as sin. She heard a rumble of thunder in the distance.

The sun set and the woods darkened, but her senses were sharper than they'd ever been in her life. Suddenly, she saw the faint flicker of a fire back among the dark trees. A narrow channel led off the main stream toward the fire. She'd found them! Praise God! Stealthily, she poled her way into the channel and stopped to check her gun. It was loaded and ready. *She* was ready.

As she drew nearer, she could see the silhouettes of two figures moving in the firelight: one tall, one short. She crouched down and slowly poled the flatboat closer, until she was about 50 or 60 feet away from them. With razor-sharp concentration, she watched the smaller figure. She steadied herself on one knee, raised the .22 slowly and took aim at the figure. As it rose from a crouching position to stand straight, its back to her, she centered the gun's sight between its shoulders and coldly, calmly squeezed the trigger.

The figure jerked wildly, clutched its right arm, and a hoarse, masculine voice howled, "Ow! Shit! I'm hit! I'm hit!" and crouched back down onto the ground.

Madge shuddered in horror at the deep, coarse, *male* voice. Dear Heavenly Father! Had she shot Danny by mistake? But the voice wasn't Danny's.

The other figure rushed over to the wounded man. "Harry! Harry! Stay down. Are ya okay?" This came from another gruff masculine voice, as the taller figure bent over the smaller one.

*Two men? Who were these people?*

"Hell, no, I ain't okay! I'm shot, God-dammit, Olin. I'm fuckin' shot!"

The taller figure barked, "Shut up!" and the voices dropped to whispers. She saw quick, furtive movements by the fire, and then the figures separated in opposite directions, moving quietly, bent over close to the ground. She could see that they were both carrying rifles. She heard muffled, rustling sounds coming toward her now from both sides, and in a panic, began to shoot wildly in the direction of first one, then the other. When the gun was empty, terror took over, and she dropped the gun and grabbed at the pole. Her shoulder struck the pole hard, and it slid away from her, into the water. She bent over and felt for it, her hand flailing around wildly in the murky black water, just as a shot whizzed past her head.

*God help me! Jesus help me!*

Ah! She felt the pole in her hand and, rising to her knees, frantically tried to push away from the bushes where the boat was now deeply entangled. Another shot flew past her, closer than ever. The flatboat turned slightly, but wouldn't come free. She stood then, and pushed the pole with all her might against the bank of the narrow channel. Just as the boat moved away, there was another shot, and a searing pain tore into her right thigh. She screamed as the shot knocked her off the boat, back into the black, infested water. Gasping at the pain, she brought her head just above the water. Her feet sank into vile, squishy mud, but the water was only waist-deep. She could see the two figures clearly now, close to the opposite bank of the stream, still silhouetted against the fire. She crouched low and kept her face just barely above water and moved slowly backward, underneath the thick underbrush.

"What th' hell, Olin? Warn't thet a *woman* screamin'?" whispered the short one.

"Shhh! I think I got 'er, but we gotta make sure. Git the gun offen thet flatboat."

"Hell, no! You git it! I'm done shot wunst already!"

The tall guy, the one called "Olin" grunted, "Shit!" and stepped carefully into the water and pulled the boat back toward him. He picked up the .22 and handed it over his shoulder to the one called "Harry", then shoved the boat back in the direction of the main channel as hard as he could. It began to float away sluggishly.

"Hell, Olin, thet there's a nice li'l boat, we oughta—"

"Shut up, stupid! We gotta git thet boat as far away from here as we kin! You don't want the fed'ral poh-lice findin' it 'n tromping roun' our still, do ya?"

"Well, les git on outta here! My arm needs fixin', bad!"

"First, we gotta make sure thet woman don't carry no tales outta here, okay?"

"She's done drownded by now."

"Well, I hope so! But les jes set here and listen fer a spell."

All this conversation was conducted in hoarse whispers, but Madge could hear it clearly across the narrow water. Now she would have to stay perfectly still in this position until the men left. Under the mucky water, her leg was screaming with pain, and it was all she could do to keep the scream from bursting up out of her mouth. She could see the shape of her boat slowly edging away from her.

There was another distant rumble of thunder.

*Please, God, don't let it rain! Oh, please!*

"Come on, Olin. Les git outta here 'fore it starts a-rainin'."

"Jes a few more minutes, now. Think ya kin go put out th' fire, 'n finish loadin' up?"

"I reckon so, but les hurry."

Harry moved cat-like, in a crouch, back to the fire, and began to cover it with dirt. Suddenly, his hunched frame was illuminated by a flash of lightning, followed by a deafening crash of thunder. He jumped in terror.

"Damn it all, Olin, les git outta here! I'd jes as soon git shot agin' as git fried alive by lightnin'!"

"Git thet fire out 'n thow some brush over the still, and we kin git away from here."

Olin shot twice into the water in front of Madge and twice into the brush near her terrified, trembling body. The pounding of her heart and her gasping for breath were so loud to her that she couldn't believe that the two men didn't hear her. The intense pain in her thigh throbbed down the whole reach of her leg, but she knew she had to hold herself perfectly still and keep submerged until they left.

*Christ be with me! Lord have mercy on me! God protect me from evil!*

It began to rain, first a few scattered, heavy drops, and then a downpour. Olin backed away from the water, watching carefully for signs of the person who had shot at them. Lightening cracked all around, illuminating the grotesque figures of the men and the eerie shapes of the moss-draped cypress trees. Thunder drowned out their voices, but their alarm was obvious as they hurried to cover the still and get away. After a few more minutes, which seemed like hours to Madge, their flat-boat approached her hiding place. She took a deep breath, sank beneath the water and held herself there as long as she could. She thought her lungs would burst, but she managed to stay under water until they had passed her.

As she brought her face carefully out of the nasty water, she heard Harry saying, "But I *know* it was a derned woman, Olin! I bet it was one o' them she-devil Indian sireens! I've heared 'em before, I tell ya! 'Specially right before a storm!"

"Shut the fuck up, Harry." Olin emphasized each word through clenched teeth. "They ain't no sich thing. How many times is I gonna hafta tell ya? They ain't no sich thing as them ghost women!

Anyway, you think thet ghosts go around shootin' guns? Pay attention now, 'n hep me git this other boat out inta the big channel so it'll float on down to the prairie. Somebody's gonna be out here a-lookin' for thet woman come tomorry, 'n we don't want 'em pokin' around the still!" Each word was a vicious dart at the hapless Harry.

"Don't git ya panties in a wad, Olin! I'm jes scairt! And besides, I'm bleedin' a lot!"

Olin pulled a grimy bandana from around his neck and handed it to Harry. "Here. Put this around it. Hit ain't nothin' but a little flesh wound! The bullet jes grazed by. Hit ain't no big thing."

Another blinding bolt of lightening illuminated the ghastly scene with the intensity of a strobe light, and Harry's grotesquely scarred face flashed in brilliant black and white contrast at Madge. His blank, milky eye was staring straight at her, like the Devil himself was pinning her with His look of pure evil. Harry's other eye was looking into the woods several yards away from her. But the Devil had seen her. He knew where she was! The Devil himself knew she'd failed, lost her gun, lost her boat!

*Oh, God! Deliver me from the power of the dog! Heavenly Father, deliver Thy faithful servant! Oh, please, God! Help me! Help me!*

The two men disappeared down the narrow stream, pushing Madge's boat ahead of them. When she was sure they were far enough away, she started to drag herself across the narrow stream toward more solid ground. At each step, her feet sank deeply into slimy mud, and roots and vines clutched at her legs. With a shudder of revulsion, she visualized all kinds of horrible things lurking beneath the surface of the water: snakes, frogs, lizards—*alligators*! She thrashed wildly the rest of the way to the low bank and dragged herself out. She tried to stand, but it was too painful, so she began to drag herself toward the still, the only man-made thing around, a dim reminder of civilization. The wound in her thigh was hot and throbbing, and she looked down to see a red stain widening on the right leg of Harland's overalls.

Then the air shook with a massive roar! A blood-chilling reverberation of savage power! The bellow of a bull alligator! She had heard it from a distance, years ago, when she was in the swamp with Harland. She had panicked then, and made him take her back to safety immediately, and promise never to take her back into the Okefenokee again. And now, here she was alone and helpless, with a monster close by!

She heard her own terrified voice screaming, "God help me! God help me! God help me!" Once again the brute's roar ripped the air. She collapsed next to the branch-covered still and sobbed, "Jesus save me! Jesus save me! Jesus save me! Please, sweet Jesus!" and slipped into blessed unconsciousness.

When she came to, the rain had stopped, and the thunder was rumbling away into the distance. It was pitch black. The only thing that connected her with reality was the awful pain in her leg. The far-away thunder had a strange, wailing tone. It was the ghost maidens! The lost Indian maidens who lured men to their deaths in the depths of the swamp. The mournful song grew louder, and swirled around her in the blackness. She began to cry softly, helplessly.

*My God, my God, why hast Thou forsaken me?*

She was wet, shivering with cold and terror. The eerie yowl of a bobcat lifted the hairs on the back of her neck. She was alone. She'd been shot. Nobody knew where she was. Things were crawling on her. Bugs were biting her. She was bleeding. She was dying!

She sank back into unconsciousness.

## Chapter 41

On Saturday, the time between Danny's departure for work that morning and his return that afternoon had seemed to Christine an aberration, like she'd been holding her breath. She'd showered with the old hand-held shower, and felt every part of her body still alive from last night's love-making. After rubbing herself all over with lotion, she had dressed in a pink and white halter-top sundress with a full circular skirt, little bikini panties and flat sandals with narrow white straps that criss-crossed her feet right above her painted pink toenails. Now it was Saturday afternoon, and Danny was coming to Christine's straight from work

They were going out west of Waresboro to a catfish and hushpuppy restaurant that Danny liked. A date. They were going to have a date! She checked herself in the mirror. Her animated face glowed like a teen-ager's! Then her happy smile turned into a lascivious grin. She reached up under her skirt and pulled down her little pink panties, twirled them around on one finger as she wriggled like a stripper into the bedroom and dropped them into her lingerie drawer.

"I'll see *you* later!" she told them as she made a voluptuous figure eight with her hips and closed the drawer with a ka-boom of her derriere.

When she heard the Honda approaching, she ran out onto the front porch, her heart beating wildly, the sweet weakness of desire radiating from the cool, tantalizing feel of bare skin between her legs. He jumped off the bike before it had completely stopped, dismounted and lowered the kick-stand almost in one motion.

He flew up the stairs, two at a time, pulling off his helmet as he came, lifted her in his arms and kissed her, drinking her in like a dying man lost in the desert who just found an oasis of fresh, pure water.

She wrapped her legs around him as he carried her toward the apartment without taking his lips away from hers. She reached back with one hand and opened the screen door. He made a deft little turn to get inside, and lay her carefully on the soft old Persian runner in the hall.

He growled, "I've thought about you every *second* since I left this morning."

She pulled him down to her and sucked gently on his lower lip. "Mmmmm... Guess what—" she murmured.

His hand inched up her thigh, and when it didn't encounter the expected panties, it stopped abruptly and then circled around behind her and clutched her bare hips against him. "Oh, my God!" he whispered into her ear. His breath was hot.

"—I've been thinking about you, too," she continued, catching her breath.

"I can tell."

He pulled up her full skirt and buried his face between her legs.

Later, as they gently washed each other in the big, old bathtub, they heard the distant rumble of thunder. Danny looked down in mock surprise at his stomach and said, "Wow! I must be hungrier than I thought!"

Laughing, Christine stroked the hard ripples of his abdominal muscles that she loved so much, and said, "Let's get out of here before it starts to rain. I'm hungry, too."

They dressed hurriedly, but just as they started down the steps, a blinding flash of lightening and an earsplitting crack of thunder sent them running back onto the porch. A sudden, vicious wind whipped the great branches of the oaks wildly against each other and howled furiously around the old house. Christine stretched her arms into the powerful gusts and let the wind whip her full skirt against her legs. Scattered drops of rain began to pound into the dry dust in the yard in little puffs, and ushered in a deluge of heavy rain.

"Oh, I love storms!" she exulted. "The power!"

Danny grabbed her from behind, lifted her off her feet and whirled around with her. "You crazy wild woman! I love *you*!"

They sat in the big, old rocking chairs and watched the storm rage around them. Christine's hair began to curl in tight little ringlets around her face. As they expected, the violent storm left as quickly as it had arrived, leaving the air clean, the oak leaves sparkling in the fading evening light, and the gray moss dripping lazily.

"Come on, let's take the Honda," she said. "I want to feel the wind on my face."

They flew along the dark road, past piney woods and scattered farmhouses with warm yellow light flowing out of their windows into the soft, pink early evening air. Little fizzes of joy kept bubbling up into Christine's chest, threatening to burst out into laughter. She knew she was a curious sight straddling the bike behind Danny, her full skirt wadded up in front of her, tucked under as much as possible, its pink floral pattern in frivolous contrast to the heavy-looking black helmet on her head. The very irrationality of it filled her with happiness, separated the two of them from the constraints of society, and freed them to meld into some greater, boundless reality. When they reached the restaurant and she swung her leg over the rear fender of the bike onto the ground, she felt strong, whole, invulnerable.

They ate with ravenous appetites, giggling helplessly as the stack of catfish bones grew on the discard platter between them. The crispy crusts and soft, crumbly centers of the hush-puppies were world-class gourmet delights to Christine, and even the Tartar sauce seemed to transcend the ordinary.

When she reached for the check, Danny snatched it from her. "You're my date, woman! You tryin' to embarrass me or something?"

"Okay, Mr. Macho-man."

Back home, they sat on the back porch and split the one remaining piece of cake. When the last crumb was gone, she sat in his lap and rested her head on his shoulder while he stroked her hair. In silence, they listened to the tree-frog and cricket symphony, their contentment deeper than words.

Next morning, she made omelets, using tomatoes, onion, basil and cheese left over from Thursday night's lasagna. She was washing up the breakfast dishes while he sat, still in his underwear, and read the Sunday funnies over his third cup of coffee. The phone rang. She dried her hands and picked it up.

"Hello?"

"Is this Christine Radford?" asked an unfamiliar male voice.

"Yes, it is." A cold fear gripped her stomach.

"Christine, this is Harland Wilkins. Is Danny there?"

"Danny? Uh..." Her head reeled.

"Don't worry. It's all right, I mean about Danny being there, that is... uh... if he *is* there."

"Well, uh..." She looked at Danny with panic in her eyes. When he had heard his name, he had dropped the paper and stood by his chair, his eyes riveted to hers. Now he silently mouthed the words, "Who is it?"

Harland continued, "Look, we've got an emergency here. Madge is missing. The police think she's out in the swamp—"

"Out in the swamp?" Christine sank slowly into a kitchen chair.

"I need Danny. We gotta go look for her. I talked to Mark and Jimmy and they thought Danny might be over at your place, otherwise I never would have…"

"Oh, Harland, I'm so sorry. I…"

"Can I speak to him, please?"

"Of course." Her voice was little more than a whisper as she handed Danny the phone. "It's your dad."

Danny shook his head and backed away. She extended her arm toward him, shaking the receiver insistently. He took the phone as if it were a ticking time bomb.

"Dad?" His voice sounded high-pitched, childish.

"Danny, you need to get home soon as you can. Your mama's missing."

"Mama? Missing?"

"I haven't seen her since yesterday. I called the police last night, and they've found the car out at the Texaco station on highway 84, where it crosses Alligator Creek. She rented a flatboat there yesterday, and went off down the creek. She ain't showed up since."

"Oh, no! What in the world…"

"If she's in the swamp, ain't no police gonna find her. We gotta git out there and look for her. Maybe git some of the Chessers to help us. Soon as we can. Course, the Chessers won't talk to the police, so—"

"I'll be right there. I can't believe… Hey, Dad, don't worry. We'll find her."

Danny hung up and stood immobilized, appealing to Christine with a look of dazed disbelief and terror. She had never seen fear or uncertainty on his face before. It chilled her blood, and she reached out to embrace him.

"Danny. Honey…"

"Mama's lost out in the *swamp*. I can't believe it. I gotta go."

"Oh, Honey, I'm so sorry. I know you'll—"

"What in the world got into her? What—"

"You'll find her. I know you'll—"

"But she's been gone since yesterday. She *can't* be in the swamp. She *hates* the swamp! You can't imagine. She *hates* it!" He stumbled into the bedroom and began to dress, shaking his head and mumbling, "But she couldn't… I mean she hates the place. She just couldn't…"

Christine made soothing noises, patted him on the back, helped him find his clothes. "You'll find her, Honey."

"Oh, Christine, I think maybe she's gone crazy! She's been acting real funny lately." His eyes filled with tears.

She wrapped him in her arms and rocked him. He was her baby. She couldn't bear to see him hurt. "It's gonna be all right. You'll find her. I know you will."

As he staggered toward the front door, Christine handed him his helmet and said, "Let me know if there's anything I can do to help. *Anything*." She took his face in her hands and kissed each wet eye, and then his quivering lips. "I'm right here if you need me."

"I love you so much, Christine." He clung to her; desperate—a drowning man clinging to a lifesaver.

"I love you, too, Honey. Let me know what happens. Now, go!"

He bounded down the stairs, jumped on the bike and disappeared down the driveway. She turned back into the apartment and collapsed onto the sofa, stunned. This couldn't be happening! It was a nightmare. How did Harland find her unlisted number? How did he know Danny was here? How much did he know about them? What did Madge know? Oh, God! Was this her fault? Had she driven Madge to this? Nausea and panic rose from her gut. A wave of guilt washed over her, draining away all her strength. The cold panic gripped her stomach. She stumbled toward the bathroom.

## Chapter 42

Danny flew home, bending low over the handlebars, focusing on driving the bike, trying to keep his mind clear of the murky swirl of unanswerable questions about how and why his mama was in the swamp. If she really was. It was so hard to believe.

Harland was waiting out front when he skidded into the yard. Harland had on his work boots and hunting jacket, and had two rifles resting on his shoulder. He looked calm, strong, purposeful.

"Oh, Dad!" Danny said, his voice almost a sob.

"Let's go, Son. We ain't got no time to lose. You gotta get us out to the Texaco station where the car is."

The ride was clumsy and taxed the little Honda 350 engine to its limits, but they arrived without any problems. A Ware County Sheriff's car was parked next to theirs. A Sheriff's deputy was lounging against their car, his hat pushed back on his head, chewing on a toothpick. A few small boys were wrestling around aimlessly, hoping for some exciting event to entertain them. They all looked up in anticipation as Danny and Harland sputtered up on the small motorcycle. Like two circus clowns on a tricycle, Danny thought.

All feelings of embarrassment evaporated as Danny saw the deputy's reaction to Harland, however. The Deputy spit out his toothpick and straightened up to a military posture, lifted his hat, ran his fingers through his hair and replaced the hat squarely on his head. He approached Harland and Danny respectfully. "Mr. Wilkins, Sir! I'm Officer Jenkins."

Harland extended his hand. "Good to meet you, Officer Jenkins. This is my son, Danny."

"Hello, Danny." The deputy glanced in Danny's direction and turned back to Harland. "I've been instructed to help you in any way I can, Sir."

"Good, good! How about fillin' me in on what you know so far?"

"Well, we found the flatboat Mrs. Wilkins rented. It was out in Chesser Prairie, and we towed it back. Didn't see no sign of your wife, though. We questioned the Chesser family, but they hadn't seen nothin'. The station manager here didn't know nothin'. We checked out the car real good, but we didn't find nothin' there, either. Sheriff Swain's gone over to Valdosta to see iffen he can get Bubba Tolliver's bloodhounds over here." He looked down at the ground. "Sorry, but that's about it." He looked up at Harland. "You want us to tow your car home?"

"No, thank you. I've got my own set of keys here. Danny and I'll just take it from here. Thank you for all your help. We'll prob'ly ride out to the Chesser place and see if we can find out anything. They don't feel all that... uh, *comfortable* talkin' to the police, you know."

Deputy Jenkins laughed. "Ooo-eee! You can say that agin'! Maybe they'll talk to you, bein' everybody knows you're such a big hunter and fisherman and all that. I've heard tell you know the swamp better'n most the old swamper families do."

"Well, I don't know about that, but thanks agin for your help."

They shook hands and the deputy left, rewarding the dusty swirl of little boys with two short wails of his siren as he pulled out of the Texaco station. The boys squealed and jumped up and down in appreciation.

"Come on, Son. Let's see what the station manager *really* knows," Harland said as he opened the patched screen door to the Texaco station office. Inside, he approached the manager good-naturedly. "Hi, I'm Harland Wilkins. You rented a boat to my wife yesterday?"

"Look, mister, I'm real sorry about what happened. I tried to talk her out of going out there all by herself, but she had her mind made up. Sure did." He shook his head disconsolately.

"It wasn't your fault, what happened. I just wanted to be sure you got your boat back okay, and that you got paid for your time and everything."

"Oh, yes Sir! Don't you worry about that! I just wish now that I'd stuck to my guns and not let her have it. Sure do."

"Well, like I said, it's not your fault. Did she say anything about where she was goin' or what she was doin'?"

"Naw, not really… But…"

"But what? Anything, uh… funny that you noticed about her? Did she look upset or anything?"

"She didn't look like she was upset or nothin'. She was real business-like. Sure was. But they was one thing..."

"One thing? What was it?"

"Well, I didn't want to say nothin' to the police, but uh... I think she had a rifle with her. She kinda tried to slip it outta the car, but..."

"Yeah, my .22's missing. I figured she had it."

"Maybe she was goin' huntin'?"

Danny blurted out, "Mama? Huntin'?" His face was contorted with disbelief.

Harland took Danny's arm in a gentle but firm grip, squelching this line of talk. He nodded reflectively. "Must've been. Well, thanks a lot. If you think of anything or hear anything, I'd sure appreciate it if you'd give me a call. I'm in the book. Harland Wilkins."

"Sure, Mr. Wilkins. I'll do that. Sure will."

"Thanks. Okay if we leave the bike here for a while?" Harland pushed open the squeaky screen door.

"Sure thing, Mr. Wilkins."

Danny rolled the Honda behind the station and followed Harland silently to the car. He was amazed at how easily his dad had handled both the deputy and the Texaco man. He avoided Harland's eyes as they drove down the narrow roads so familiar to him now since his romantic excursions into the Okefenokee with Christine had begun.

Harland was talking strategy. "She must've passed the Chesser place. If she'd had some kind of accident before that, the police would have found somethin'. Besides, a flatboat'd have a helluva time just driftin' past all the bushes along the side without nobody steerin' it. It'd get stuck somewhere for sure, before it got out to where the channel gits wider."

Danny was close to tears. "Oh, Dad, we're never gonna find her out there!"

"Them Chessers is bound to know somethin'. They know everthing that comes down Alligator Creek. They's somebody watchin' all the time, believe me!"

"Do you think she's... she's gone crazy? I mean—what in the world would she go out into the swamp for? You know how she hates—"

"Now, Son. We don't know what happened yet—what was on her mind. First, we'll just have to find her, then we'll let *her* tell *us* what she was tryin' to do out there. And no! She ain't crazy! She's just got herself over-wrought about somethin'. You know how she is."

Danny looked away in shame as tears began to roll down his face. "Dad, I'm really sorry I lied to y'all about goin' fishin' with Mark and Jimmy. I've been lyin' about a lot of stuff, lately. I feel so bad about—

"Look here, Danny. We'll have to talk about this soon as this here thing's over. Yeah, that's bad, you tellin' us lies, but I'm sure you thought you had your reasons. I just don't wanna talk about it right yet, okay? First let's find your mama—that's the main thing. Then, I reckon, we got a lot of things to talk over."

Danny slumped back in his seat and closed his eyes. The narrow shadows of the tall pines flickering past cast vertical streaks of black across the redness of the inside of his eyelids. It made his head hurt. He felt impotent with misery.

Harland was leaning forward, concentrating hard on the pot-holed road, and avoided looking directly at Danny. "Look, Son, I didn't mean to embarrass you, callin' over to Mrs. Radford's like that. I had to find you, though. I called over to Mark's, thinkin' his mama might know where y'all were fishin', and course, Mark wasn't fishin'. He was home. He told me you might be with…uh…Mrs. Radford."

Danny moaned softly, "Christine," without opening his eyes.

"So, I took a guess and looked up Miss Eufalia's address in the telephone book. I'd kinda figured you'd got to know Miss Eufalia so good because of Mrs. Rad…uh…Christine. Anyway, with that address, I got both their telephone numbers—Miss Eufalia's and Mrs…uh…Christine's. Got 'em from Sherriff Swain's office."

Danny didn't answer.

After a few uncomfortable moments of silence, Harland continued, "By the way, let me do the talkin' when we git to the Chessers', okay?"

"Okay, Dad," Danny answered, his voice flat with resignation.

They reached the shabby clump of buildings around the bait shop, heralded by a cacophony of barking dogs and the squeals of a bunch of animated children. When Danny got out of the car, the three littlest girls ran to him, their thin, fragile arms extended. He knelt and embraced them.

"Where's that purty lady?" the smallest girl asked him.

In a soft voice, Danny answered, "Shhh. She couldn't come today. Maybe next time."

Two women, working at the old wringer-washer on the front porch of the biggest building, eyed them suspiciously. Harland called to them in a friendly voice, "Good mornin', ladies. Is Olin here?" Neither woman answered, but one of them backed away a step and then turned and hurried into the house.

A few minutes later Olin shambled out onto the porch, yawning and scratching his arms absent-mindedly. "Harland? That you?" he said, squinting his eyes in Harland's direction. Then, smiling at Danny, "How're you doin', buddy?" Danny smiled and nodded in reply.

"Yeah, it's me," Harland answered. "It's been a long time, ain't it?" He gave Danny a questioning look. Why were they treating Danny with such familiar ease?

"Lord, yeah! Ain't seen you fer two or three years, not since you come out here to warn us 'bout them Feds gittin' ready to crack down on the white lightnin' business." Olin cackled with such glee, that it brought on an attack of coughing. He cleared his throat and spit dark brown phlegm off the edge of the porch. "Whut kin I do for ya, buddy?"

"I thought maybe y'all could help me out a little, here. Wondered if maybe y'all seen a woman goin' down the creek on a flatboat yestiddy," Harland answered, serious now.

"Lord, the poh-leese done been here this mornin', astin' bout that very thing. I tole 'em we ain't seen nothin'."

"Well, that's my *wife* they're lookin' for, Olin, my *wife*! I was hopin' maybe somebody in your family might have thought of somethin' after the police had left."

Olin had jerked to attention and his jaw had dropped open when Harland said "wife." Harry, who had been listening from just inside the screen door, stepped cautiously out onto the porch, his scarred face twisted with concern. His right upper arm was bandaged and hung in a faded calico sling.

"Your *wife*?" Olin gasped.

"Oh Lord, no! Was thet woman your missus?" Harry shook his head from side to side in a slow, exaggerated motion.

"Whut happened to you, Harry?" Harland asked.

"Oh, this here?" Harry raised his wounded arm and winced. "It ain't nothin'."

Olin turned to Harry and growled something that made Harry shrug and go back into the house. Olin spit off the porch again and turned to Harland. "Well, uh... Ya know whut, after them poh-leese had done left, some of the young'uns remembered they seen a lady goin' by on a flatboat. Must've been her."

"She was by herself?" Harland asked.

"Did she say anything?" Danny asked at the same time.

"I reckon she was by herself. Jes went floatin' by, the kids said. Didn't say nothin'."

"Lord help us, Olin," Harland said. "We gotta git out there and find her quick. The pore thing don't know nothin' about stayin' alive in the swamp. And we need help bad! Wonder if you 'n Harry could help us out any?"

"Why shore, Harland," Olin said, with a furtive glance at Harry, who had just stepped back out onto the porch again from where he had been standing behind the screen door. Harry was visibly worried; his good eye shifting anxiously between Olin and Harland.

Olin continued cautiously, "Whut kin we do?"

"First off, you kin let us have a boat, prob'ly the canoe, for a while. We'll take good care of it."

"Sure, that ain't nothin'."

"And any chance y'all could help us go lookin' for her? Ain't nobody in the world knows the swamp like you two."

Olin glanced at Harry and said, "That's the truth, ain't it Harry?" Then back to Harland, with some reluctance, "I reckon we kin hep ya out. Whaddya say, Harry?"

Harry kicked at a loose board on the porch and stammered, "Well, yeah. I reckon so."

"Oh, thank God," Harland said. "I won't never forget this, Olin."

"It ain't nothin," Olin said and started back into the house. "Hit'll take us a minute or two to git ready."

"And Olin?" Harland added, "I'd just as soon leave the police out of this if we can, okay?"

Olin laughed. "That suits *me* jes fine! But I reckon they's still some of 'em out pokin' around in the prairie. We kin steer clear of 'em. They don't know whut the hell they're doin', anyway."

Harland and Danny carried the canoe down to the water, got their rifles out of the car, took their seats in the canoe and waited.

About 20 minutes later the little party started down Alligator Creek, Olin and Harry leading on the flatboat, and Harland and Danny following in the canoe. Olin and Harry were also armed with rifles. They had hunting knives strapped to their belts, and a large knife fastened to the top of the pole Olin pushed to propel them down the stream. They had brought along a blanket and a jug of whiskey.

Harland called to the two men, "If we git separated and either of us finds her, shoot twice and then wait a minute and shoot twice agin, okay?"

Both men turned and looked hard at Harland before Olin shrugged and answered, "Okay, sure."

The air was clear beneath a protective dome of rich blue. The sun was bright and an uncanny, quiet peace had settled over the Okefenokee after the violent storm of last night. The swamp was clean and welcoming, gentle with birdsong, soothing with its glassy, smooth black water. It seemed unfair to Danny. How could it be so beautiful, so peaceful, so unconcerned, when his mother was lost out there in it somewhere in misery or terror—maybe even dead.

Olin and Harry set a slow pace in front of them. They seemed to be engaged in an intense discussion while Olin searched first one bank and then the other in a mechanical, systematic way, punctuated by sharp jerks of his head as he tossed short remarks over his shoulder to Harry. Harry was clearly agitated, and his shaggy head shook with disapproval as he looked back and forth between Olin and Harland.

Danny could hear his constant, whiny flow of words, but couldn't understand what he was saying.

"Looks like them two got some disagreement, don't you think?" Harland said to Danny in a calm voice. His eyes did not leave their concentrated search of the undergrowth on each side of the channel. "I think they know somethin' they ain't tellin' us."

"Like what?"

"Like they seen her. Like maybe they know where she is."

"But then, why wouldn't they have said anything to the police?"

"That's what's got me worried, Son. It don't look good. They got a reputation for—"

"—Yeah, I know, 'Shootin' first and askin' questions later.' Oh Lord, Dad! You don't think—"

"Well, I pray to God they ain't shot her, but somethin's goin' on. We gotta watch 'em real close. If they got somethin' to hide, they might be tryin' to lead us off in the wrong direction. I don't know. We just gotta watch 'em real close. Try to keep your mind open, you know?"

Danny felt an icy dread clutch his heart. He had never felt real fear like this before. He had always been stimulated by the challenges he met, but now he felt helpless, incapable of rational thought, impotent with so much at stake. He was sick with guilt. He took a deep breath and forced himself to concentrate on the search; keep his eyes sharp and his mind open—like Harland had said.

*Please, God! Let us find her. Please let her be all right.*

Danny decided to concentrate on Harry. He seemed to be the one least in control of his emotions—the easiest to read.

And so the little search party moved slowly and deliberately, deeper into the swamp. There was a flurry of excitement when the flatboat pulled to one side and Olin retrieved a small bit of faded, ragged cloth from the branch of a prickly hawthorn bush on the right side of the stream. It was obvious that the little scrap of material had been there for a long time—probably for years. It had faded to a colorless pale gray, and dissolved into tatters around its edges. Still, Olin and Harry showed it an inordinate amount of interest, held it up for Harland and Danny to see, and seemed to conclude that it meant that the missing woman had gone into the swamp at that point.

"I'll betcha she turned off right along here somewhere," Olin ventured, peering back into the brush with a sage nod of his head.

"Yep. I'll betcha that's where she is, back yonder somewheres," Harry agreed solemnly.

"Well, I dunno," Harland said to the two men, shaking his head thoughtfully, "then why was her boat out in th' prairie? Besides, there ain't no way she coulda got back through them thick bushes. I think we need to keep on awhile."

Olin gave Harry a worried look and said, "Well, iffen you say so."

They moved along, the flatboat staying closer to the right side now, and picking up speed.

Harland said to Danny under his breath, "You think they're tryin' to keep us away from the left side? Seems to me they's somethin' over there they don't want us to see. Whaddya think?"

"I think you're right, Dad," Danny replied in a whisper. "Look, they're really speedin' up now."

Now Harland and Danny both began to give particular attention to the left side, and soon saw a narrow channel leading into the swamp. The flatboat had moved some distance ahead of them by now, and was disappearing around a curve in the stream. Harland pointed to the channel.

"Look, Danny. Think we oughta check that out?"

"Sure looks like Olin's tryin' to steer us past it, don't it? Yeah, let's see where it goes to."

They paddled swiftly into the channel, ducking under overhanging branches, pushing through vines and lily pads. In just a few minutes, they saw a hammock on their right, with a well-worn path leading up from the channel. The channel itself disappeared into impenetrable growth past the path.

"Let's see what's up that path, Dad," Danny said, breathless with excitement.

"I reckon it's a still, but we can go see. That may be whut made them boys try to git us past here, if they been makin' likker back in here."

They pulled the canoe up onto the bank and hurried up the path. Around the first turn, they could see the still. It was partially covered with brush, but the rusty metal oil drum and the twisted pipes were still clearly visible.

"Come on, Son, let's go," Harland said and turned back toward the canoe. "We don't want them to ketch us lookin' 'round here. That'd be a big mistake!"

Danny, however, had broken into a run toward the still. "Just a minute, Dad. I never saw a still before. I'll just be... Oh my God! There's a body... Oh, God! It's Mama! It's Mama! Oh no!" His voice was high-pitched and frantic, now. "Oh, Dad, Dad! It's Mama! I think she's *dead*." He dropped to his knees beside the still body. "Mama! Mama! Please, Mama. It's me, Danny!" He was crying now. "What happened? Mama, say somethin'."

Harland had run back to Danny's side and was cradling the lifeless body in his arms. "Madge! Madge! We found you! We—"

"Look, Dad! She's all bloody! Oh, she's dead! She's dead isn't she?"

Harland laid her back down gently and pressed his fingers against her neck, close to her windpipe. "No, she's still alive, son. Thank God, she's still alive."

"But look at her; she's all skinned up. Her leg—it's all bloody! Oh, Mama!"

"Come on, let's get her in the canoe. We gotta get her to a hospital. Fast! Oh Lord, Madge. Whut' in the world were you doin' out here?"

Madge moaned softly as they lifted her limp body. "Careful, Son. Gentle, now," Harland warned. Danny was at her feet; Harland's arms supported her shoulders as they started down the path. "I sure wish we had that blanket and that whiskey Olin's got on the flatboat."

Then, leaning over close to Madge's ashen face, "It's okay, Madge. You're gonna be okay. We'll get you all fixed up, Hon. You're gonna be just fine."

They eased her into the canoe, and Harland pulled off his tee-shirt and made a pillow for her head. Danny followed suit and took off his shirt and stretched it over her chest. Tears were streaming down Danny's face. "Mama, I'm so sorry, I'm so sorry."

Harland aimed his rifle into the trees away from the canoe and shot twice, paused and shot twice again, to signal to Olin and Harry that they had found Madge. Then he stepped into the canoe and pushed off. They were soon moving up Alligator Creek with strong, clean sweeps of their paddles. Madge moaned intermittently and whimpered something that sounded like "Alligators, alligators." She was still alive, but almost unrecognizable underneath the blood, scratches and mud.

Danny's guilt, confusion and fear dissipated a little as all his resources turned to getting her to the hospital in time.

## Chapter 43

It was mid-morning and Christine lay on the bed with a damp cloth on her forehead. She was recovering from the attack of anxiety and nausea that had devastated her after Danny left to search for Madge in the swamp.

The telephone rang, jerking her to a sitting position. Maybe they had found Madge! But that wasn't possible, was it? Not enough time. Danny had been gone just a little over an hour. Surely not more bad news. The room reeled around her.

"Hello?"

"Hi, Red! You up already?"

*Thank God! It's Bessie!*

"Oh, Bessie! I'm so glad it's you. You won't believe what's happened, Oh, it's awful." Christine started to cry.

"Whoa, girl! What's it now?"

"Danny's mother's missing! Apparently she's out in the swamp, if you can believe *that*."

"Oh, Jesus!"

"And to make it even worse, Danny's father tracked him down and found him over here. Called him over *here*! Danny stayed over last night—"

"You gotta be kiddin'."

"—and we were having breakfast when his father called. Danny was out of his mind, as you can imagine. Oh, it's just awful!"

"Poor Red—"

"Poor *Madge*! And poor Danny! What a mess."

"Listen, why don't you come over? I got somethin' to tell you about, anyway."

"Why don't you come over here? I can't leave the phone. Waiting for news. Danny might need my help, or—"

"I gotta stick around here for a while. I'm waiting for a call-back from an Atlanta real-estate agent, but then—"

"From an Atlanta real-estate agent? What in the world?"

"Yeah, that's what I was calling about. Tell you what. I'll come over as soon as I can. I got lots to tell ya. And you just hang on till I can get there. It might be a little while, but—"

"Bessie! Are you telling me you're moving to Atlanta? What's happened?"

"Yep, I'm gittin' outta here. Should have a long time ago. This Billy Joe thing shook me up pretty bad. Helped me decide it was time, over-due even. I'll be over soon as I can, but it'll probably be a couple of hours, okay?"

"Oh, thank you, Bessie!"

"Let me know if you hear anything new. And look, I really hope everything's gonna be all right."

"Thanks, Bessie. Oh Lord, what'll I do without you?"

After Bessie's call, Christine finished cleaning up the kitchen and then took a shower and dressed in her best chino slacks and a black silk shirt. She made up her face carefully, her hands shaking, and pulled her hair up in a conservative French twist. She wanted to be ready for anything—police station, hospital, whatever.

She had just made up her mind to go down and tell Miss W. all that had happened, when she was startled by a heavy pounding on the front door.

*The police?*

"Who is it?" she called out, struggling to control the trembling in her voice. There was no answer. She opened the door to the hallway and saw standing on the porch on the other side of the front screen door, the hulking shape of the last person in the world that she wanted to see—*Jack*!

"Jack, is that you? I can't believe it! What are *you* doing here?"

He planted a hand on each side of the door-frame and leaned forward, pressing his face against the screen. "That my little wifey in there? Ain't ya gonna ask me in?" His voice was husky, and he was slurring his words.

Christine's knees buckled under her, and she had to hold onto the wall for support. For a brief, irrational moment, she started to just shut and lock the door, but she knew he wouldn't go away quietly. Besides, he was living with her parents, and they loved him. She needed to salvage what she could of these deteriorating relationships. "Well, gosh. Of course. Uh…" She un-latched the screen door. "Why didn't you tell me you were coming down? What's going on?"

*Be friendly. Keep it light.*

He stepped into the hallway. "I thought I'd just surprise you." He lowered his face close to hers and tilted it from side to side. "Surprise, surprise!"

She pulled back. His breath was heavy with the sour smell of prolonged drinking. His eyes were bloodshot and glazed over with the effort of focusing.

"Uh... Can I get you a cup of coffee?" she offered, as she led him into the apartment.

"How's about a beer?"

"Sorry, but I think I'm all out. Have you had breakfast?" She could have kicked herself. She sure didn't want him hanging around long enough to eat breakfast! How could she get rid of him without setting him off? He was staggering slightly as he walked, lifting his feet higher than necessary—obviously drunk, and it wasn't even noon!

"No, I don't want no breakfast. Ain't ya got anything to drink?"

"I have some sherry. Would you like—"

"*Sherry*? Shit no! You know I don't drink no candy-assed shit like that!"

They were in the kitchen now. She pulled a chair away from the table and offered him a seat. "I'll make us some coffee." He twirled the chair around, straddled it and sat down, leaning his heavy, muscular arms on top of the chair-back. She asked, "What are you doing down here? Closing on the house?" She poured water into the coffee-pot.

"Yeah, I'm down here closin' on the house. And while I was here, I thought I'd just drop in to see how my little wifey was doin'."

She got the coffee from the refrigerator and began measuring it out. "I'm doing fine, Jack. My job's going great, I'm feeling good—"

"And how's your *love life*?" He tilted his head down and looked up at her out of the tops of his eyes. His mouth curled to one side in a nasty sneer.

She could feel a tell-tale blush creeping up into her face, and she turned away from him and began to get cups and saucers out of the cabinet. "Oh, well... Come on now, Jack. That's not any of your concern now, is it?" She tried for a light-hearted laugh, but it didn't quite come off. "Hey! How's Mother and the Rev.?" She turned the coffee-pot on.

"They're fine."

"And how's *your* job? Mother said you got another rig. You doing all right with it?" The question sounded phony, even to her.

"I ain't gittin' rich, but I'm doin' okay. So how's your little boy-friend?"

"Boy-friend?" Her heart began to pound. The cups rattled in their saucers as she carefully set them on the table.

*Don't let him see how scared you are.*

"Yeah, I know all about you robbin' the cradle with that little piss-ant from next door. You oughta be 'shamed of yourself!"

"Please, Jack. Let's don't talk about our private lives."

He mocked her in a falsetto voice, "'Let's don't talk about our private lives.' I guess you *don't* want to talk about *your* private life, Miss Stuck-up!"

"I don't want to get into an argument with you, Jack. I was hoping we could… could be friends."

He mocked her again, "'I was hopin' we could be friends' she says. Little Miss Stuck-up, fuckin' the high-school boy next door! You're really somethin', ain't you?"

"I think you'd better go, Jack," she said in a tight, controlled voice. "Right now." She picked up the cups and saucers and returned them to the cabinet.

"I ain't goin' nowhere, you little bitch!" He stood up, stumbling a little over the chair, and kicked it across the room. "I'm getting' me a piece of that ass you're passin' around. You're still my wife, you know." He staggered toward her, bumping into the table and knocking over the sugar bowl.

Christine had whirled around to face him and cried out when he kicked the chair and started toward her. She held her hands out in front of herself now and started backing toward the door. "Jack, calm down, now. You don't want—"

"Don't you fuckin' tell me what I want, you stuck-up bitch!" he yelled. He lunged at her as she broke for the door. She almost made it, but he caught her arm as she yanked open the door and dragged her back into the kitchen.

She screamed, "Jack, stop it, stop it!"

He slapped her hard across the face and yelled, "Shut up, bitch!" The combs flew out of her hair and it fell down around her shoulders. He grabbed a handful of it and yanked her head back while his other hand clutched her between her legs. "You fuckin' bitch!"

She screamed again and brought her knee up, hard, into his crotch and tried to twist out of his grasp. He doubled over, grabbing her shirt and shouting, "Owwww, God-dammit!" Her shirt ripped open as she broke loose from his grasp and ran out onto the back porch. The screen door to the back steps was latched! She fumbled at the latch, her hands shaking violently, and got it open just as she heard him charge out onto the porch. She ran wildly down the steps which were shaking with his heavy, stumbling footsteps behind her. Out in the yard, she screamed, "Help, Miss W.! Help!" Her heart sank as she realized she didn't have the keys to her car, and she hesitated for a fatal second—*where to go*? His heavy body crashed against her and drove her to the ground. She thrashed wildly, trying to get up, and managed to roll over, scratching at his face. He was on top of her again, but she was able to sink her teeth into his arm as she kicked against his legs. She saw his fist coming at her face and tried to pull away, but it caught her with all its force on her cheek. She tried to scream again, but could only make a gurgling sound. His hands were on her throat and she went limp, gasping for breath, as everything got dark, all sound drifting away, drifting away...

Suddenly, he released his hold on her throat, and she heard a primal, "Arrrgh!" as he fell to her side. Her eyes came back into focus and she saw, silhouetted against the sun, the tiny form of Miss

Eufalia Worthington, chiffon floating gently from the fragile arms which were raised above Jack's hulk, Colonel Worthington's Confederate sword raised over her head, ready for another blow. Jack clutched his shoulder and tried to scramble away, but the sword descended on him a second time, slashing into his upper arm. Blood was everywhere. Jack screamed in pain. He struggled to a crouch and dove at the little figure wielding the long sword, but this time it came down on his other shoulder and he dropped to the ground with a feeble moan.

Miss Worthington still held the sword aloft with one hand as she reached down with the other, and helped Christine to a sitting position. "My goodness, such a violent man!" she said sweetly, "Are you all right?" Christine couldn't speak from the intense pain in her throat, but she nodded weakly. They both turned to stare at the widening pool of blood around Jack's body. "Oh, my! Such a mess," Miss Worthington said, shaking her head with distaste. "Don't worry, I called Sheriff Swain before I came out here in the yard. I suggested that he call an ambulance as well, as I thought we might need one. Do you think you can stand up, Dear?"

Christine tried to stand up, but was overcome with dizziness, and sank back to her knees on the ground. The sharp, metallic taste of blood filled her mouth, and the hand she raised to her cheek came back bloody. She spat out blood and almost fainted at the sight. There was a terrible pain in her throat. Her blouse was torn and hanging in tatters from her shoulders.

"Come along, Dear, if you can," Miss W. encouraged her, "before this Yankee comes to and starts on another rampage. Come inside and let me clean you up a little."

Christine could hear the approaching wail of sirens now, and she made another attempt to stand, but couldn't. She sat back and tried to cover herself with the tattered remnants of her blouse. Her head swam, and she was having trouble piecing together just what had happened. Jack's body lay motionless, just a few feet from her. She desperately wanted to move away from him, but she was too weak. Miss W. stood between them, the point of the sword in the ground, resting on it as if it were a cane. The ancient gold tassel hanging from the sword's handle was bloody. The scream of the sirens grew unbearably loud and then expired into a moan. Christine dimly saw the Ware County Sheriff's car pull up into the yard in a whirl of dust, followed by an Emergency Medical Vehicle, just before she passed out.

She came to in Miss W's elegant parlor, lying on a red velvet sofa. An ice pack was on her cheek, and a crocheted afghan was covering her torn blouse. A tall, portly man with thinning gray hair was talking earnestly, respectfully to Miss W. He was wearing sharply creased brown pants and a beige shirt, and he turned a brown law-enforcement officer's hat self-consciously in his hands. Handcuffs hung from one side of his belt, and a gun in a brown leather holster from the other. He was saying, "Yes, Ma'am, Miss Eufalia. That was a mighty brave thing you done. I'm right proud of you. I'm sure you won't even have to come down to the station or nothing, but I gotta ask you please not to leave town or nothing for a little while."

"Well, my goodness, Buster Swain, you silly thing!" Miss W answered. "You know I never go *anywhere* anymore. I'm certainly not planning to change my habits now, not for any reason. And allow me to thank you for your prompt response to my call. I'd say that Ware County was very fortunate to have such an efficient sheriff's department."

"Thank you, Miss Eufalia. That's mighty fine praise, coming from you. I'll take care of the report—a clear case of self-defense. Yes, Ma'am. Now you just let me know if you have any more trouble at all. Don't you hesitate to call now, ya heah?"

"Of course, and thank you again, Sheriff Swain, for your excellent help."

"You're mighty welcome, Ma'am. And I sure think you're a brave lady. Yes Ma'am." Sheriff Swain backed out the door as if exiting from a royal assemblage.

Miss Worthington called out into the foyer, "Miss Tanner? You and Nurse Martin can come in now. My goodness, I believe Mrs. Radford is awake!" Then to Christine, "How are you feeling, my dear?"

Christine raised her head from the satin pillow and said, "I think I'm okay." Her throat was so sore that she could hardly swallow. It was painful to speak, her head was throbbing, and there was a sharp pain in her cheek. She gingerly felt the bandage on her cheek and realized that her hands were skinned up as well.

Bessie came bustling into the parlor. "Thank God, you're alive! You had us worried there for awhile. I'll swear if you ain't a mess!" She was followed by a substantial-looking woman in a starched and rustling white nurse's uniform and cap. "This is Mrs. Martin. She's gonna hang around till we're sure you're really okay." Bessie sat down beside her.

Christine nodded and attempted a smile in the nurse's direction and then whispered to Bessie, "What about Jack? Is he..."

"Naw, worse luck! He ain't dead. They took him to Blair Memorial. He's cut up pretty bad, but nothing permanent. He lost a lot of blood." She leaned close to Christine's ear and whispered, "Too bad our little Miss W. didn't cut off his balls, while she was at it!"

Christine laughed, in spite of her pain. "Stop it, Bessie. It really hurts when I laugh." Then, in a whisper, "Have you heard anything from Danny?"

"Not yet, but then nobody's been answering your phone, so..."

Christine sat up slowly, took a deep breath and steadied herself. "What time is it?"

"A little after 1:00."

"Can you help me upstairs? I want to be near the phone."

"Sure. Mrs. Martin? Think it's okay for us to go upstairs?" Bessie asked the nurse.

"Miss Worthington's making tea for us. Let's have a cup and then see how we feel." The nurse's smile was as starchy as her uniform.

A few minutes later, Miss W. came in with the tea service and a silver pedestal stacked with Bloomingdale petit-fours, and placed them on the coffee table. She began pouring tea into fragile pink-flowered china cups. "Well, Christine! It's good to see you looking so bright and cheerful again. I took the liberty of asking Mrs. Martin to stay with you today, until we can be sure that you don't have any serious consequences from our little excitement. Cream and sugar?"

"Yes, please. You're just wonderful, Miss W. I can't believe that you... I guess you know you saved my life today."

"Oh, dear! I hope that doesn't mean that now I'm responsible for you for the rest of your life," she said, with a giggle and a frivolous flutter of her eyelashes.

"I'll never be able to thank you enough. I wouldn't know where to begin."

"That's enough of that, now. Anyway, that's not the first time Grandpa's splendid old saber has had a little taste of Yankee blood."

Christine, Bessie and Mrs. Martin looked askance at each other. Nobody could think of anything to say for a moment, until Mrs. Martin put her cup down and stood up briskly. "Well! Let's see if you feel like walking now, Mrs. Radford," she said in her most professionally optimistic manner. She and Bessie helped Christine up and they walked carefully around the room.

"I think I'm all right. Let's try to make it upstairs." Christine turned to Miss W. with tears in her eyes and said once again, "You're really an amazing woman, Miss W. I owe you my life."

The three women made their way slowly up the stairs and into the apartment. Bessie lowered Christine gently onto the sofa near the telephone.

"Do I smell somethin' burnin'?" Bessie asked, sniffing the air with a mixture of worry and distaste on her face.

"Oh, Lord! It's the coffee-pot! I'd just turned it on when Jack... When all the excitement began."

"Don't worry. I'll get it," Mrs. Martin said and hurried toward the kitchen. "I'll freshen your ice-pack for you, too."

As soon as Mrs. Martin was out of earshot, Bessie put her hands on her hips and leaned over Christine. "Now what in the hell happened to you, girl? Where did that son-of-a-bitch husband of your come from?"

"Oh Lord, Bessie," Christine groaned, "he came down here to close on the house, and he got drunk and decided to... I don't know... *God*, he was *furious*! He found out somehow about Danny and me, and... Oh, Bessie! I thought he was going to kill me!"

"And he would've if it hadn't been for your little old landlady," Bessie said with a raucous laugh. "I didn't see him, but from what the police and the paramedics said, he got chopped up pretty good! Just what he needed, I'd say," she chuckled contentedly.

"Well, I hope it's over, now. How can everything go wrong at the same time? The terrible business with Madge. You talking about moving to Atlanta! As if I didn't already have enough to worry about…" She moaned and turned her bruised face toward the back of the sofa.

## Chapter 44

Danny leaned forward in the uncomfortable plastic chair, his forearms on his knees, and stared at the shiny terrazzo waiting-room floor of the intensive care unit. He could see his dad's worn, mud-splattered shoes and frayed work pants passing back and forth in front of him. Danny's mind had sunk into a numbed feeling of guilty helplessness. He had stopped trying to figure out why his mother had gone into the swamp, and what had happened to her there. The main thing was, he just knew it was his fault. She was dying, and it was his fault. He had lied to her—told her he was going fishing so he could be with Christine.

Christine! It was the middle of the afternoon, and he hadn't called Christine! She'd be worried to death! He stood up and started toward the pay-phone the sheriff's deputy had been using earlier.

"Dad, I ... uh ... I've got to make a telephone call."

Harland raised his eyes, blank with exhaustion and worry and nodded without comment.

*He knows who I'm going to call. Why didn't I just say it?*

As he dialed Christine's number, tears began to fill his eyes, and he was overwhelmed with a stinging need for the comfort of her arms.

The numb feeling that had been protecting him was washed away, and the whole spectrum of pain returned.

A strange female voice answered the phone. "Christine Radford's residence. Mrs. Martin speaking."

"Uh… Can I speak to Mrs. Radford, please?"

"She's sleeping right now. May I take a message?"

Sleeping? Christine sleeping in the middle of the afternoon? "Well…uh… Tell her that Danny called and that—"

"Hello, this is Bessie Tanner. Who's calling please?"

"Oh, Miss Tanner. This is Danny. I wanted to tell—"

"Danny! She's been waiting for you to call."

"Is everything all right?"

"Yeah, she's okay. She just had a little accident this morning, and—"

"An accident?! What happened? Is she all right?" Danny leaned his arm against the wall and pressed his head against it. He felt dizzy, disoriented.

"She's fine. Hold on a minute and I'll wake her up. I know she wants to talk to you."

After a minute he heard Christine's voice, soft with love and concern. "Hello, Honey."

"Christine! You had an accident?! What hap—"

"Don't worry. I'm all right. Where are you? Did you find—"

"I'm at the hospital. We found Mama. She got shot in the leg! She's alive, but she's pretty bad off. She's still unconscious. What happened to you?"

"Madge was *shot*? Oh, my God! Who—"

"We don't know yet. The police are all over! But what about *you*?"

"Don't worry about me. I'm fine. I'll tell you all about it when I see you. How's Harland taking it?"

"He's real worried. But Christine, he was so brave, and so smart, and ... Oh, I don't know ... He's a real hero!"

"I'm not surprised. He's a good man, Danny."

"I was so proud of him... The way he handled everybody—stayed so calm and everything."

"Sounds like the way I remember my father."

"But Mama... I really think she might be off her rocker, Christine." Danny's voice broke as he began to cry softly. "She went out there all by herself, way out in the swamp. Business-like, the Texaco station man said. And she had a rifle! I think she might have been lookin' for me," he sobbed, "but what was she gonna do with a *rifle*?"

"Danny, Honey, this thing isn't your fault! Whatever she had in her mind, she probably took the gun to protect—"

"Oh, I gotta go. The doctor just came out and he's talkin' to Dad. I'll call you back later."

"Bye-bye, Honey. Hang in there."

Danny hurried over to Harland and took his arm in both hands. The doctor was speaking to Harland in low, reassuring tones.

"... and I see no reason for less than a complete physical recovery. She was unconscious for some time, however. She's awake now, but still incoherent. We have a psychiatrist coming in to evaluate her later this evening. I'd rather wait until we hear from him before we predict just what her mental state may be."

"What about her leg? Will she—"

"We removed the bullet without any problem. She has a superficial wound which should heal okay. I don't anticipate any long-term effects from that. She's lost a lot of blood though, and she's going to need a transfusion. Are either of you type B-positive?"

"I am," Harland answered quickly. "I'll give blood. Be glad to." Harland's voice was calm and strong, but Danny could feel his arm trembling as he asked the doctor, "Can we see her now?"

"Sure, but don't stay in there too long. I'll tell the desk you've volunteered to give blood, and they'll set it up." The doctor shook Harland's hand and gave Danny a pat on the shoulder. "You guys did a good job, finding her out there and getting her here as soon as you did. You should be proud of yourselves." Then to Danny, "You'd better look out for your father. After he gives blood, he may feel a little weak. You need to get him home, get cleaned up and get something to eat, and then you can come back. She's all right for now. We're moving her to a room soon, and you can stay with her all you want to." He patted Danny's shoulder again. "You should be proud of yourselves."

The doctor's words stung Danny to the core. *Proud?* He looked down at the floor quickly, so neither of the men could see his eyes filling again with tears. *Proud?* It was *shame* that he felt now. He told himself that all of this was his fault—lying to his poor mama like he had. She had been out there looking for him! He just *knew* it! Hadn't he left her that awful note, saying he was going fishing with Mark and Jimmy? She must've gotten some crazy idea that he was in some kind of danger.

As he followed Harland meekly toward the ICU room, he vowed to himself to make it up to his mother, to be a better son, make up for all his lies. An orderly passed them, pushing a gurney with a heavily bandaged man who seemed somehow familiar to Danny. The injured man looked dazed, drugged, but tried to focus his eyes on Danny as he was rolled past. It made Danny feel strangely uncomfortable, but he quickly forgot it when he and Harland entered the ICU room.

Madge was strapped to the bed. Tubes were taped to her arms. Her face had been washed clear of the mud splatters, but it was red, scratched and swollen. There was a bandage across one of her temples, and oxygen nasal prongs in her nose. Her eyes were darting wildly from one side of the room to another, and she was straining against the straps holding her arms. She was babbling an incoherent stream of excited chatter, interspersed from time to time with what sounded like "Jesus" and "Whore of Babylon". Danny wanted to turn and run out of the room—wipe this hideous picture from his mind, but Harland walked calmly to the bedside and patted one of the heaving shoulders.

"Now, now, Madge. Don't you trouble yourself so. You're gonna be just fine. Danny and I are here. We're gonna stay close by and take good care of you. The doctor says you're gonna be just fine.

Just fine. You just relax now and don't worry about nothin', you hear?"

Madge showed no sign that she was aware of their presence, but continued to thrash her head back and forth, rolling her unseeing eyes and mumbling gibberish.

A nurse came in the room and touched Harland on the shoulder. "Mr. Wilkins, we're ready for you now—for you to give blood."

"Oh, yes ma'am." Harland responded quickly and turned to follow the nurse. At the door, he turned to Danny. "You watch out for your mama, Son, while I'm gone. Soon as I get back, we can go get somethin' to eat."

Danny stood frozen, terrified for a moment, staring at the almost unbearable sight of the agitated creature that used to be his mother. Then, overwhelmed with pity and guilt, he stumbled over to the bed and knelt beside it. "Mama, Mama, please be all right. I love you, Mama." He reached up and caressed her arm, next to the cruel straps holding her down. "Please, God, help us. Make her mind nice and peaceful. Make her well. Please, God." Sinking to the floor, he pressed his head against the bed and abandoned himself to tears.

He was still there on his knees when Harland came back into the room a little over a half hour later. Harland came over to the bed and took Danny's hand, coaxing him to his feet. "Any change?" he asked Danny.

"No. She just keeps thrashing around! It's awful!"

Harland took a tissue from the dispenser on the little table next to the bed and handed it to Danny. "Here, Son. Blow your nose and try to get a-hold of yourself. She's gonna be all right. It just might take a little time." He leaned over Madge and said softly, "Madge, Danny and me's gonna go get some supper, and get cleaned up. You'd sure be embarrassed for us right now, the way we look. We'll be back in an hour or so."

In the diner on the corner next to the hospital, Danny and Harland sat in silence on their stools, leaned their arms on the counter, and munched on their hamburgers. Without looking at Harland, Danny cleared his throat and said, "Uh ... Dad, I uh ... I guess there's some things I need to tell you."

"Okay, Son, I'm listenin'." Harland turned an impassive face to Danny.

"Well, I guess you know I've been ... I've been spending a lot of time with Christine ... Mrs. Radford. I guess I've ... well, I guess I've fallen in love with her."

"In *love*? Oh, Danny, Danny! You don't know what you're sayin'" Harland shook his head and looked down at the counter-top. "It's worse than I thought!"

Danny turned to Harland and pleaded earnestly, "I didn't mean to! I'll swear, I never meant for this to happen, it just did. It's like I couldn't help myself, Dad. She's so, so *sweet*, and so *beautiful*, and—"

"How long has this been goin' on?"

"I guess it's been more than a year, now."

"Lord, Danny! I wish you'd of told me before now."

"I wanted to. A couple of times when we were workin' on the car, I almost ... I just didn't know how to tell you. I know it seems weird, but—"

"But Danny, she's a married woman, besides being older—"

"I know all that Dad, but it's just ... It seems so natural. Like we were, well ... like we were made for each other. I know that sounds corny, but it's the *truth*!"

"Danny, you're a good person. I don't think you'd ever hurt anybody if you could help it. But this thing is ... It'll hurt a lot of people. You oughta ... It could mess you up bad." Harland looked away. "Well, it's somethin' you're gonna have to make up your own mind about. It's your life, but ..." With his elbows on the counter, Harland leaned his head in his hands and sighed deeply.

It sickened Danny to realize how he had hurt his parents, all because of such a *good* thing, the love and happiness he had with Christine.

*Christine! He hadn't called her back. He didn't know what kind of accident she'd had or how she was!*

"Dad, we'd better go get my bike and get on home. I need to—"

"Yeah, you're right. Let's get outa here." Harland picked up the check and went to the cashier's counter.

Danny left the diner with his brain raging with conflicting anxieties. Right now the top priority had become getting his bike and finding out what happened to Christine—seeing her, holding her, telling her about Madge. He was about to lie to his father again. Right after his attempt at being honest. But what else could he do?

He felt as if he would explode!

They left the diner and headed for the Texaco station with Danny driving. The nurse had insisted that Danny drive, since Harland had just given blood and might start to feel dizzy. Harland maintained that he was perfectly fine, and didn't need any help, but Danny was pleased to have a little bit of responsibility. He had so much to make up for! He wanted to reach over and pat Harland on the knee, or tell him how much he loved him or something.

"So Dad, you sure you feel like driving back home so I can drive my bike back?"

"Danny, I told you I'm okay. It's no problem."

As they started to leave the Texaco station, Danny pulled his motorcycle up beside Harland, glad for the protective anonymity of the helmet and for the high-pitched buzz of the little engine which effectively drained conversation of all emotion. "I've got something to do and then I'll be right on home."

Harland leveled an intent look at Danny and said, "Okay Son, do what you have to do, but don't be too long about it."

"Don't worry, Dad. Hey, are you sure you're okay with driving? You think I ought to follow you home in case you get dizzy or something?"

Harland's voice was cold. "I'm perfectly all right, Danny. See you back at the house."

Danny headed for the treehouse. He would only stay a minute. He had to see her—see what the "accident" was. The stranger, Mrs. Martin—see who she was. But most of all he had to—*had to*—have

Christine's arms around him as he told her about his mother. His poor, *crazy* mother.

Only Christine's loving arms could comfort him. Only she could understand. Only her goodness and purity could grant him forgiveness.

Behind the fierce-looking shield of his black, warrior helmet, his eyes were blurred again with the sting of tears.

## Chapter 45

By late afternoon, Christine was feeling almost like her old self again. She had taken a shower, dismissed Mrs. Martin and called the hospital to find out Jack's condition. She was told that he was going to survive Miss W's attack and be dismissed in a day or two. In the meantime, he would be under guard in the hospital, charged with aggravated assault. Christine still had trouble believing that the violent and bloody events of the morning had really transpired.

"So, whaddya think's gonna happen to Miss W?" Bessie asked.

"The way Sheriff Swain was talking, I don't think that anything'll happen to her, except maybe she'll get a medal of honor or something."

Bessie laughed heartily at this idea and said, "Yeah, I heard him tell her, 'That was a mighty brave thing you done, Miss Eufalia.' What a hoot!"

As peace and quiet returned to the apartment, Christine relaxed and hugged Bessie. "Thank you, thank you for coming over and taking care of me. My best friend. Boy, I sure needed your cool head and sense of humor today! Come on, let's see what's in the fridge for a late lunch, and you can tell me why you're leaving Waycross … why you're gonna leave *me*!"

They put together a hodge-podge lunch of leftovers, and settled down at the table. Christine felt the horror and confusion of the morning drifting away on the comfortable stream of their friendship.

"Okay, Bessie, start at the beginning and tell me why you're doing this."

"I guess it all started with the Billy Joe thing. You know he's out of the hospital and supposed to be seeing a psychiatrist. I don't know. Maybe he is, but I'm still getting' a bunch of heavy breathing calls, and I'll swear he's—well, *somebody's* stalking me. I'll swear, I'm a nervous wreck."

"*Stalking you*? How awful! Have you actually *seen* him?"

"Not exactly, but twice lately, I've thought I saw a man hiding in the oleander bushes in front of the apartment. I could see his legs and feet." Bessie shuddered. "And I just *feel* somebody looking at me when I'm at the grocery store or the drug store, and when I turn around to look, I think I see somebody—a man—disappearing behind the shelves. Billy Joe's stopped coming to the office to see Laura Mae, and… I don't know, maybe I'm just—"

"Have you tried to talk to him, or thought about calling the police?"

"Lord, no! What would I say? To him or the police?" Bessie shook her head in hopeless resignation. "I'd just make things worse. Men! Look what happened to *you*! They're crazy!" She jumped up and walked around the room. She was getting really wound-up. "Your crazy husband tried to *kill you!*"

Christine tried to keep her voice calm. "So you're just leaving? Leaving your two jobs, your friends?"

"I'm stuck where I am in both my jobs. I'll never get anywhere here. People think I'm—I don't know, goofy or something. And let's face it, you're really my only friend here. What little family I got left all live in Valdosta, anyway. I'm ready for something new."

"You already have a job?"

"Pretty sure. I sent out a few resumes—"

"Hey! We know how good you are at *that*!"

"—and one of the places is real interested. I've got an interview with them next week. It's a lawyer's office, a block from Five Points! I'd be right in the heart of Atlanta."

"But I'll miss you so much!"

"Hey! Come go with me. You wouldn't have any trouble finding yourself a job up there. What about that guy in your IBM class? Didn't he try to get you to come to work for him?"

"I'm still trying to get my life together here. Besides, I owe so much to Stan and to Miss W. Oh, Bessie. The truth is I couldn't stand to be away from Danny."

Bessie shrugged her shoulders. "Whatever ... Well *me*, I'm planning to get into Georgia State and get my bachelor's degree. If I get the job in that lawyer's office, it's three or four blocks from Georgia State. Perfect, huh? Then I'm either gonna get some paralegal training or, who knows, maybe even go on to graduate school and get a law degree. Hell—get polished up, lose some weight, get me some classy-looking clothes, get me a boy-friend that looks like Paul Newman. The sky's the limit!"

"It sounds wonderful! And you know what, Bessie? You can do *all* of that if you really want to. You're so smart! It'll really be hard for me to get along without you, but you're right! You owe it to yourself to get out there and see what you can do. And Atlanta isn't all that far away. We can visit each other … Oh, Bessie!"

"Yeah, you'll have to come up to see me, for sure. I'm getting a studio apartment in The Darlington: parking right there in the building, elevator up to my floor, no oleander bushes! I'm talking first-class all the way!"

Suddenly, Christine jerked to full attention, color rushing to her cheeks, eyes wide and hopeful. She jumped up from the table with a surge of joy as she heard the sweet, celestial sputtering of the Honda 350 coming up the drive.

\* \* \*

Bessie was stunned by the intensity with which Red clutched Danny to her. He had run up the stairs as Red ran out onto the porch. When he saw her bandaged cheek and the darkening bruised skin around her eye, he had cried out, "Oh, my baby, my sweetheart!", and picked her up with incredible tenderness. He cradled her in his arms and carried her back into the apartment, murmuring, "What happened, sweetheart? Are you all right?"

Bessie had accepted her friend's irrational infatuation with this kid—this boy, but she had never thought of their relationship as anything beyond healthy lust. She accepted it on the grounds of Red's passionate nature, her loving spirit, her loneliness, the humiliation of her husband's coarse mistreatment, her unconventional adventurousness. But now she saw through the crust of their physical attraction into a terrifying depth of feeling. She recoiled in fear and confusion. This was nothing like poor Billy Joe's crush on *her*. Not in the same universe!

"Uh ... Red? I'm gonna run now. Call me the minute you need anything, you hear? *Anything*. Good to see ya, Danny."

The screen door slammed shut behind her as she heard Christine calling, "Oh wait, Bessie! Thank you for coming over. I'll ... I'll call you later."

Bessie drove away with a heavy and disoriented feeling. She fervently wished that she had been spared the look into that abyss of ardor and devotion. It frightened her. Who in the world would choose to be swallowed up in that kind of passionate commitment? She was sure it would never happen to *her!*

So why this void in the pit of her stomach, this keen sense of loss? Of *yearning*?

\* \* \*

Danny carried Christine into the bedroom and laid her gently on the bed. He touched his lips lovingly to her forehead. "So, what happened?"

She laughed and pulled his face to hers and *really* kissed him. "Hmmm... I ran into the door. Boy, are you a mess!"

"I haven't had a chance to clean up since Dad and I were out in the swamp, looking for Mama. But, come on. What happened to *you*?"

"What happened to *Madge*? Is she okay?"

"The doctor says she'll be fine—physically. She's got a flesh wound in her leg, but they don't think it's gonna have any long-term consequences. We don't know for sure what happened out there in the swamp. She had a gun with her, Dad's .22 rifle, but we don't know where it went to. Looks like she was shot by somebody else—couldn't have accidentally shot herself—the angle and no powder burns and all that."

"Thank God she's gonna be okay."

"But, I don't know, she's out of her head. It's real bad. She's just jabberin' all this crazy stuff—doesn't know anybody—won't even look at you." He fell down on the bed beside her and they held each other in silence for a minute. "Now tell me. What happened to you? What was your 'accident'?"

"Promise you won't get all excited?"

"Whaddya mean?"

"It was Jack. Jack came over here this morning—"

"Jack? I thought he was in Pennsylvania."

"He came down here to close on the house, and he came by—"

"He came by *here*?"

"He came by here to ... He'd been drinking. He lost his temper and—"

"He hit you? Did he hit you?" Danny sat up, his jaw working, veins enlarging in his neck.

"He was furious. He tried to ... He chased me out into the yard and—"

"Oh, Christine!" Danny was up and pacing now.

"—he grabbed me and I tried to fight him off but—"

"He hit you, didn't he? I'll *kill him*!"

"Honey, please! Come here. This is what I was afraid of. I didn't want you to get all excited."

Danny pumped his fist into his open hand. "The creep!" He stopped and stared at her. "How did you—"

"Danny!" She got up and put her arms around him. "I'm perfectly all right. Really just a little embarrassed, that's all." She led him toward the kitchen. "Let me fix you a glass of iced tea."

"How did you get away from him?"

"Oh my God! You wouldn't believe it! Miss W. attacked him—went after him with that old sword of her grandfather's."

"Miss Worthington? That little bitty lady? I can't believe it!"

"From what they tell me, she cut him up pretty bad. The sheriff came and they took him off in an ambulance." Christine laughed in spite of herself. "Can you believe it? Can you imagine what a surprise it must have been for Jack?"

Danny didn't think it was funny. He pulled her to him protectively. "My poor baby. I should have been here—"

She shook her head and pushed him away. "Oh, don't be silly. You didn't have any way to know I was in danger. I had no idea—"

"What did the creep want with you, anyway?" He followed her into the kitchen and sat down in the chair she offered him.

"He's been really unhappy for a long time—angry ever since he got back from that oil rig job. I guess I was pretty cold to him—well, I know I was." She shuddered. "I couldn't stand to be in the same room with him, much less—"

"Did he know about *us*?"

"Well, he does now!"

"Oh, Christine! It's all my fault!" He jumped up from the chair and leaned over the sink. "You tried to keep me away from you, but I wouldn't listen. I couldn't! I tried, but—"

She moved close behind him, wrapped her arms around him and pressed her forehead against his back. "No, no, Honey! It's just as much my fault as—"

"I never thought it would hurt anybody. I never thought…" He buried his face in his hands. "I never really *thought* about anybody else."

"Neither did I, Honey. I guess we're both guilty of that. Me more than you. After all, I'm the one who was married."

He turned to face her, a ray of hope lighting his face. "But you're getting a divorce now. We can just be honest about it—quit having to lie and hide and—"

"Danny, we can't expect anybody to understand what this is between us. I don't understand it myself! Your friends, your family, this small town—nobody's going to accept us as a *couple*. It's not really their fault. It's not anybody's fault" She began to cry. "We just can't expect—"

"Then what are we gonna do?"

"I guess we'll have to ... We've got to stop..."

"Stop? Stop seeing each other? We can't ... I can't ... I *can't*! I can't live without you!" He pulled her to him and clung to her in desperation. "You know that. What are you tryin' to say? Christine, please!"

She eased away gently. "Just look what happened with Mark and Jimmy and your other friends. You can't give up—"

"They don't mean anything to me ... not like you do!"

"Danny, don't say that!" She was getting agitated now. "Your friends don't mean anything to you? Friends are for life. You can't let anything come in between you and them. I couldn't stand thinking I'd come between you and your friends." She covered her face with her hands and shook her head. "I couldn't, I couldn't!"

"Sweetheart..."

"And your mother! I feel like I drove her to—"

"No, no! Mama's not your problem. She's mine!" Danny took both her hands gently into his and kissed each palm. He led her out onto the screened back porch, sat in a big, old rocker and pulled her onto his lap. She rested her head on his chest and they let the comfort of the soft light of dusk and the cricket and tree-frog chorus envelop them. For a few healing minutes, they thought of nothing but the physical bliss of being together. But the reality of their plight soon took over again.

"So what are you going to do now, honey?" she asked him. "Tonight?"

Danny groaned, "I've got to get home in a few minutes. Dad and I have to go back to the hospital. But what about you? Are you gonna be safe from that… that creep?"

"He's in the hospital. In pretty bad shape, from what I hear. He's under arrest for aggravated assault, and they've got a deputy guarding him."

"Look, I'll try to come back and stay here with you tonight. If—"

"No, you can't do that. Your dad needs you worse that I do right now."

"But I don't want you to be alone."

She stood up and forced a confident tone of voice. "I'll call Bessie. I'm sure she'll come back over and stay with me tonight."

"Well, if—"

"And you'd better go now. Call me and let me know how Madge is doing. And don't forget for a minute that I love you."

"Oh, Christine! If only we could—"

She led him down the back steps, shuddering at the still intense memory of the terror of the morning, her legs twitching with the urge to run for her life again.

"Are you sure you're gonna be safe from that…"

"Of course, Honey. I'm going down to see Miss W. for a minute and then I'll lock up and go right to bed. Don't worry about me." She hoped he didn't notice the nasty little shudder that gripped her. "You've got enough to worry about with your poor mother. And I'll call Bessie and see if she'll come over."

"Okay. I guess I really have to go. I'll call you. Tell Miss W. that I think she's a champion!"

"Okay. Good-night, honey. And *don't worry!*"

## Chapter 46

Jack drifted in and out of consciousness. Where was he? He couldn't even lift his head off the bed. Images of rectangular lights in a perforated ceiling moved up from his feet through his aching head. Even worse, he kept seeing the face of the little piss-ant from next door. Had they really pushed him past the kid that was fucking his wife? Had he really passed him in the hallway? He forced himself into consciousness to clear his head of that hateful image.

God dammit, he was hurting something awful! He was in a hospital bed, needles and tubes connected to both his arms. Shit! Blood was dripping from a bag into one arm and some clear liquid into the other. Most of his upper body and arms were covered with thick bandages.

He could hear some crazy woman down the hall moaning and screaming out religious shit like "Jesus," "Blessed be the name of the Lord," and "Deliver me from evil."

Suddenly, the terrible memory of a witch-like figure loomed over him again. What the fuck had happened to him? Out of nowhere, this *weird* old woman had attacked him—blow after blow crashing onto him, slashing at his arms and shoulders. Surely, it had been a nightmare! But here he was, in the hospital, all bandaged up. Was he going to die?

"Nurse, nurse!" He couldn't believe the hoarse, gargling sound of terror in his voice. "*Nurse!*"

A hefty male figure appeared in the doorway. Like a figure from some out-of-date "B" movie, a pudgy-faced young man with blond hair cut in a flat-top looked in at him. A real cracker! He was wearing a tan uniform, and his hand fluttered nervously near a gun fastened onto his belt.

*What the hell is going on here?*

A nurse bustled past the fidgeting figure as if he weren't there. "It's okay, Deputy Wilson. I'll handle this."

*"Deputy?"*

The uniformed chunk turned away with a sigh of relief. "I'll be right here if you need me," he said and stepped out into the hallway. His reassurance would have been more effective if his voice hadn't quavered so much.

"Yes, Mr. Radford? You called for a nurse?" Her face and voice were stern and offered him no sympathy whatsoever.

"Where am I, and how did I get here?" Why was the bitch glaring at him like that?

"You're in Blair Memorial Hospital—"

"Am I gonna die?" He fought back tears.

"—and you're not going to die." She sniffed. "You'll have to ask Dr. Steinberg about your condition. In the meantime, just relax and try to get some rest." She turned to leave the room.

"But who was that ... that policeman in here a minute ago?"

"It seems that you're under arrest, Mr. Radford. Sheriff Swain will be in to talk to you soon."

"Under *arrest*?! For *what*? Hell, it looks like somebody tried to kill *me*! What the—"

"Sheriff Swain will explain the charges when he talks to you." She sniffed again, even more emphatically, and left the room.

He called after her, "But ... but what happened to me? Shit! What's goin' on here?" There was no answer.

Jack stared at the ceiling. Fuck! He was really in some kind of mess, now! What was it? The last thing he remembered was going by Red's apartment to give the fucking bitch a piece of his mind. Then he had this fuzzy picture in his head of some old witch whacking at him with a sword or something. Shit! He should never have even gone over to Red's, anyway.

*Fuckin' stuck-up bitch!*

He'd never been so miserable in his life! He checked out the tubes going into his arms. He'd just rip the goddamn things out and get out of here. First, he'd have to get out of this shitty little hospital gown and get his clothes on, though. Where were his clothes? He tried to sit up and check out the room, but couldn't even raise his head from the pillow. *Shit*! He closed his eyes and tried to think what to do. Dammit, they needed to shut that crazy woman up—the one down the hall moaning and shouting all that "Jesus" stuff! He couldn't think with all that noise going on. Why didn't they just stuff something in the crazy bitch's mouth?

A wave of sugary perfume almost took his breath away. "Weh-ull, my goodness! Mr. Radfud! Bless your little ole heart? Whut in the world's happened to you? I went by the hotel to pick you up for the closin' and I just couldn't believe it when the desk clerk told me that he thought you were in the *hospital*! Lawd have mercy! He said the poh-lice had been by there and went through your room, and everything! I'll swear—"

*Oh, God! Not this silly broad! What next?*

He rallied enough strength to interrupt her. "Whaddya mean—the *police* searching my room?"

"Goodness gracious, I don't know. I'm jes tellin' you whut the desk clerk said. And Deputy Wilson sittin' out there by the doah! I hope they're not gonna try to blame you for all this, uh ... trouble!" She came closer, smothering him with her perfume, and patted him on his knee. "Listen, I jes want you to know that I'll do anything for you that I possibly kin. I mean that! Anything! I jes think you are the finest man I nearly 'bout ever saw, and—"

"The closin', Miz Townsend! How's that goin'?" He kept his eyes closed. He couldn't stand to see that bobbing fuzzy head, those glasses with all those little colored jewels, that bright red lipstick smeared on her teeth! His knee twitched beneath her chubby grasp.

"Oh, the closin'! Weh-ull it's all set for 2:00 this afternoon. It sure don't look like you'll be able to git there—"

"Can we have it here?"

"Oh goodness, I don't know about thet, but you know whut? You could give *me* power of attorney, and I could take care of the whole thing for you. Bless yer heart!" She patted his captive knee.

Jack moaned and tried to turn away from the irritating voice and the fat little hand. "Oh, I don't know…"

She leaned dangerously close to his face and whispered, "Mr. Radfud, dear Mr. Radfud! Kin I call you 'Jack'? Don't you know that I'd do *anything* for you? *Anything*!"

He gasped in helpless revulsion, but was too weak to turn away or scream for help. He was trapped!

Mercifully, he was spared from having to answer, as the nurse and a doctor bustled into the room. The doctor beamed at him. "Mr. Radford! I'm Dr. Steinberg. And how are we feeling this morning?" Dr. Steinberg smiled down at him from the benign majesty of the medical profession. Jack felt like a wad of bubble-gum on a patent-leather shoe.

"Terrible!" Jack snarled at the immaculate pair. Their beatific smiles were impregnable.

Ellie Townsend backed out of the room with a flutter of her fingers. Her eyebrows danced up and down provocatively. "I'll be right outside, Jaaack," she sang in her syrupy drawl.

"So! We're not feeling all that great! You're lucky to be alive, Mr. Radford. You lost a lot of blood, you know," Dr. Steinberg said, sounding downright happy about it. He pulled back the sheet and examined the bandages. "Looks like the bleeding has stopped, though."

"Am I gonna be all right?" Jack was ashamed that his voice sounded so weak and whiney. "Are my arms gonna be okay?"

"I believe so. You have some physical therapy ahead of you, but most likely you'll get back the normal use of both your arms. You're a lucky man."

Doctor and nurse both smiled and nodded as the doctor repeated, "A lucky man!"

"When can I get outta here?" Jack asked. His eyes pleaded with the doctor for mercy.

"Oh, within the week, I'd say. Depends on how fast you heal."

*No mercy.*

Jack moaned as the doctor pulled the sheet back over his shoulders and started out of the room. "You look like a pretty healthy chap. Don't worry, we'll get you out as soon as we can." They were gone.

Ellie Townsend bobbed excitedly back into the room. "So, Jack *dear*," she tilted her head and smiled lovingly at him. "You want me to get a notary in here so you can go ahead and grant me your power of attorney? I mean, it sounds like you gonna be here for a *coon's age!*"

Jack groaned and turned his eyes back to the ceiling. "Yeah, I guess I'll have to." He cringed as she came close and patted his leg.

"Now don't you worry 'bout a single little thing! I'll be right back. I'm gonna take *real* good care of you!" Eyelashes and fingers fluttered again as she backed out of the room.

He had to get away from here—away from everything! As soon as he got his check from the closing, he was gone! Outta here! But what had the nurse meant earlier about being "under arrest"? And why had that fat cracker stuck his head in the door? Had that nurse really said he was under arrest? In trouble with the cracker backwoods *fuzz*?

"Nurse! Nurse! I need something for this pain!" he called out as loud as he could. The attempt to shout racked his chest with even more pain. To his chagrin, he felt tears welling up in his eyes—tears of rage, pain and frustration. He could just barely lift his hand to his face to wipe away the humiliating tears. He kept his eyes shut and his jaw clenched when the nurse finally came in an gave him a shot. He hated them all!

After a short time, he drifted off into a drugged sleep, which was soon interrupted by a deep voice calling his name. "John Alton Radford? Otherwise known as 'Jack Radford'? I'm Sheriff Buster Swain. I'm here to tell you that you're under arrest for the attempted murder of your wife, Christine Kennedy Radford. You have the right to remain silent. You should know that anything you say may be held against you. You have a right to be represented by an attorney. If you can't afford one, Ware County will provide one for you." Jack struggled to focus his eyes on the uniformed hulk standing over him. The hulk continued, "Do you understand what I'm sayin' to you? When you're well enough to be moved, you'll be taken to the infirmary at the Ware County Jail and charged with aggravated assault and attempted murder."

Jack moaned. His brain swam with questions, but he was too sedated to talk. All he could manage was a weak, "No, no, please! I didn't—"

"I'll be back to take your statement later, when you're more awake. Meanwhile, don't git no idears about goin' nowhere. We got a 24-hour guard posted at your door."

Then it was quiet. Jack tried to stay awake, to think. He had to figure out what to do. He couldn't let himself get fucked over by this bunch of country hicks! He had to get out of here. That was it! Get his money for the house and get back to Pennsylvania where he belonged. He drifted off.

"Weh-ull Mr. Radfud! Are you awake? My goodness, I do believe I've woke you up! I'm sorry, but I got Miss Frannie Emerson here with me now. She's a notary public." She leaned over him in a nauseating cloud of perfume. He moaned and opened his eyes to a narrow, cautious slit. "See, you *are* awake! Bless your heart! Kin you sign some papers for me? It won't take too long." He frowned, closed his eyes and nodded ever so slightly. She rushed on, "Oh, my goodness! I know you must be feelin' just terrible? I'm so sorry I have to bother you, but if you want me to git on with the closin' this afternoon, I just got to have your little ole signature."

Jack could barely hold the pen, and every slight movement of his arm caused him pain as he scrawled his name on the documents she held in front of him. There were so many pages to sign! He couldn't focus his eyes to read them, but blindly wrote his name beside each red "X" she had marked. She passed the papers that needed to be notarized on to Miss Emerson. She was making simple explanations of each document as he signed, but he wasn't absorbing anything she was saying. He didn't care! Much as he detested her, she was the only friend he had here—the only person who could help him get out of this mess!

Finally, it was over. Miss Emerson cleared her throat and ventured, "I sure hope you get to feelin' better soon, Mr. Radford," and left the room. He was left alone again with the dangerously enamored Ellie Townsend! She leaned over him, her big, soft breasts pressing on his bandaged arm, her perfume overwhelming him. "Oh, please!" he whimpered in protest. But it got worse! She actually *kissed him on the cheek* and murmured seductively, "Jack, dear," into his ear! He shuddered and turned his face away. She pulled back slightly and continued, "Now don't you worry. If everything goes okay at the closin', I should be back here early this evenin' with a nice cashier's check for you. Now you just git some rest, ya heah?" The perfume ebbed slightly as her high heels clicked away. Jack faded back into a fitful sleep.

He began to feel a little better by late afternoon. They were still pumping blood and some kind of clear liquid into him, and an ugly, fat nurse had fed him some chicken soup. God, he hated being so helpless! He'd like to tell them all how stupid they were, but he controlled himself. Main thing was, he had to get stronger, and fast!

By the time Ellie returned, flushed with victory and dreams of passion, he was sitting up and feeling strong enough to at least talk.

She had his check, and she wriggled it temptingly under his nose. "Guess whut we got here, big guy?"

After he had endorsed the check for deposit into his Pennsylvania bank and sent Ellie out to post it by certified mail, he relaxed a little. He had actually made a small profit on the sale, and now his return to his old life on the road in his own rig was assured. If he could just get back home, that is.

Damn that red-headed bitch! It was her fault that he'd landed in this hell-hole, anyway. He'd taken that construction job and moved down here because he thought he wanted to be with her more of the time—not out on the road so much. He was going to be Mr. Good Husband! Shit! Biggest mistake of his life! So how does she show her thanks? Takes up with a horny little teen-age cracker! Well, to hell with her! He was going to forget he ever knew her! Wipe her out of his head! He had plenty of broads waiting for him back home—just itching for him to give them a little roll in the hay.

He was able to eat some dinner, and felt much better. He got the nurse in for another shot of pain-killer and told her that he didn't want any more company that evening, especially Miss Townsend, his real-estate agent. He slept well most of the night.

Next morning, they had removed the I.V.s from both arms, and he was sitting up eating breakfast when he had his first visitor, Sheriff Buster Swain. Jack shuddered. The sheriff looked even bigger and dumber than Jack remembered from yesterday. The hick was munching on cheese puffs from an open family-sized bag in his huge hand.

"Good mornin', Mr. Radford. You look like you feel a lot better today. Zat right?"

"Uh… yes Sir." Then meekly, "Thanks."

"Well, that's good, 'cause I got a deal for you, but you better listen real good and pay close attention to every word I got to say, understand?"

"Y-yes Sir, I understand."

"First off, there's a few things that you, being a Yankee and all, probly need to know 'bout how things work down here in the South. Hmmm…" he popped another cheese puff into his mouth and paused to savor it. "We got some kinda strict rules 'bout how we treat our women down here. 'Specially fine old southern ladies like Miss Eufalia Worthington and her friends."

Jack face was blank. Who was he talking about? He had a fuzzy memory of chasing Red out into the yard, and of the old witch standing over him with a sword. That couldn't be the "fine old southern lady" that the sheriff was talking about, could it?

Sheriff Swain stuffed a handful of puffs into his mouth and ruminated a minute before continuing. His jaw worked from side to side. He gazed reflectively out the window. "Yessir, men have been known to disappear into the swamp for doing stuff like you tried to do to that little wife of yours, 'specially if they're niggers or Yankees." He chuckled and looked back at Jack. His mouth was smiling, but his eyes were steely hard. "We even have a few accidental castrations from time to time." He popped another handful of cheese puffs into his mouth. "But you're a lucky man!" He looked back out the window.

Jack's heart was pounding and cold sweat glistened on his brow. "L-lucky?" he stammered.

"Yep! You're a lucky man. You know why?"

Jack couldn't speak, but shook his head. His eyes betrayed his terror.

"I've decided to save all of us a lot of trouble, and save the taxpayers of Ware County a lot of money." His face hardened and his nostrils flared with hatred as he pinned Jack with an icy stare. "If you'll get your Yankee butt back up North where it belongs and never let your sorry ass cross back over the Mason-Dixon, I'm gonna just hold an open warrant for your arrest for aggravated assault and attempted murder. If you ever set foot in Ware County agin, *ever*, you're fried! Do you understand me? *Fried*!"

"Y-yes Sir! Thank you, Sir. I promise—"

"As soon as Dr. Steinberg says you can travel, you'll get a free ride to the airport, courtesy of the Ware County Sheriff's Department. We'll even have a friendly deputy accompany you to Allentown. Yeah, you're a lucky man, ain't ya?" He used his index finger to pick some cheese-puff residue from his teeth.

"Y-yes Sir! Thank you, Sir," Jack's voice quivered.

Next day, he was dismissed from the hospital and escorted to the airport.

Later that afternoon, Miss Ellie Townsend began contacting real estate offices in Allentown for possible job opportunities.

## Chapter 47

It was later than Danny thought when he finally got back home. How could he have stayed so long over at Christine's? It sure hadn't seemed that long while he was there. Damn!

By the time Danny came running up to the door, Harland had showered, shaved, put on clean clothes and was heading out.

"Dad! I'm sorry I took so long. I didn't mean—"

"Look, I'm on my way back to the hospital. Git yourself cleaned up and just come on soon as you can. See you there." He left before Danny had a chance to make any excuses. Harland hadn't said "Hello" to Danny, or even looked at him, for that matter.

Danny felt sick. He ran upstairs, showered and changed as fast as he could.

When he got to the hospital, he saw Harland standing outside the door to Madge's room, talking earnestly with a doctor. As he drew nearer, he could sense his father's agitation.

"—But she's never been away from home by herself, not without me—not since we've been married. Can't she stay here, or isn't there some place closer than Milledgeville?"

"I'm sorry, Mr. Wilkins. We don't have the facilities or the expertise to take care of her here. I can arrange for you to see her every day after the first couple of weeks of her incarcer... her treatment. There's a good, inexpensive boarding house a block from the main building where you might get a room. I'll have my office call you with the information, if you're interested in trying that."

"Oh, I don't know. I just don't know what to do." Harland's face was flushed and he was trembling. "Yes, I ... I guess I'd like for you to git me that number ... the boarding house number ... uh, please."

Danny patted him on the back and asked, "Dad, what's the matter? What's going on?" He wanted to take his father in his arms and hold him to stop the trembling.

"Danny! They've got to move your mama to a psychiatric hospital. She's gonna need some treatment that they can't do here!" Harland began to cry. "She's gonna be scared to death, Danny! She's never been away anywhere by herself! I don't know what to do!"

Danny held his dad close and rocked him gently. The warm physical affection he had yearned for in the past overwhelmed him. This gift of love and trust that his dad was giving him now, was incalculable. He wanted so much to have something to give him in return. If he could just comfort him, take this burden off his dad's shoulders—but he had nothing to give! He pressed his cheek against his dad's, wet with tears. "Daddy, Daddy! They'll take good care of her. They know what to do. We can't look after her the way she is now. I know it's awful, but—"

"I wish they could just give her some pills or something."

The doctor interrupted. "Mr. Wilkins, it's not going to be as bad as you think. I know it's hard to accept, but your wife has suffered a severe emotional shock. We're not equipped to even evaluate her properly here. Let's just see what's the best thing for her. Right now, she's a danger to herself and possibly to others. She'll be much better off somewhere that she can get the proper care."

"Oh God help her! My poor Madge!" Harland collapsed onto Danny.

Danny held him and spoke in a soft, reassuring tone. "Daddy, she doesn't even *know* us! We can't do anything for her right now. We just have to trust that they'll help her. Look, I'll do anything you want me to do for her—*anything*. I just think the best thing is for her to get some good, professional treatment, don't you?"

"Yeah, I guess. I hate it, but we don't have no choice, not the way she's carryin' on." Harland turned to the doctor. "When you think you'll move her up there ... up there to Milledgeville?"

"I'd say tomorrow or the next day. We have to make sure they've got room for her. Now, Mr. Wilkins, I have to warn you. They won't let you see her for a while. That's their policy for all their patients. She'll be getting some intensive evaluation and care. You should be able to see her after about two weeks, though."

"T-two weeks?" Harland looked stricken.

Danny shook the doctor's hand. "Thank you. Please have somebody call us when there's any change." He led Harland toward Madge's room. "Come on, Daddy. Let's go talk to her for a minute. She don't act like it, but I think maybe she knows when we're there."

Madge showed no sign that she knew they were there. She continued to thrash her head back and forth, her eyes wild and unfocused, but she was sounding a little bit better—saying words at least, even though she didn't make much sense.

"Jesus, Jesus, help me. God be with me. I am your avenging angel."

Danny patted her arm and murmured, "There, there Mama. There, there. I'm so sorry…"

Harland tried to explain to her that she was being moved to another hospital, and that he wouldn't be able to see her for a couple of weeks. He promised that he'd be there with her just as soon as they'd let him. He didn't mention the dreadful word, "Milledgeville."

Danny had to coax Harland out of the hospital. It broke his heart to see his dad so defenseless. This was the man who only yesterday had conquered the swamp and the swampers; had handled the sheriff's department with such dignity and diplomacy; had made the right decisions so easily; had acted with such courage, intelligence and sensitivity. Now here he was—broken! It was his love for Madge that had defeated him. No, not defeated! Danny had never been so proud of him before—had never loved him so much.

By the time that they met back at the house, Harland had regained his composure and had a plan. He had accumulated enough vacation and sick leave to take off work for more than a month. The two weeks that he wouldn't be allowed to visit Madge would give him time to arrange for some extended leave. He would get the boarding house number from the doctor's office and reserve a room. He certainly wasn't going to leave Madge all alone, scared to death in a strange place with people she didn't know.

Harland looked at Danny. All traces of the coolness which had followed Danny's confession were gone. "You can go to Baton Rouge and stay with your Aunt Stella while I'm gone."

"Baton Rouge? That's too far. How would I get to Milledgeville to see Mama? Anyway, I hardly know Aunt Stella."

"Well, maybe you could stay with Mark or Jimmy."

"I'll be perfectly fine here at the house, Daddy. I can take care of myself. Besides, I don't want to miss work."

*I can stay with Christine!*

"I guess you're right, Danny. I gotta get used to the idea that you ain't a little kid anymore." Harland smiled a little and shook his head. "Things are sure changin' around here."

"You know, I might... uh..." Danny couldn't go on. He was going to tell Harland that he might stay with Christine, but just couldn't chance upsetting his dad again. Right now, Harland was looking at him with an expectant air. Danny didn't want to see that open look change to aversion. "Uh... I might ride the bike up to see Mama and stay with you a few days."

"Of course. That is, if she's gotten to where she knows people."

Danny went into the kitchen, went directly to the refrigerator as he always did, and stood peering in. With keen disappointment he saw empty space where he had expected the usual casseroles and Tupperware containers of tempting victuals. What was wrong?

"Hey, Daddy! It looks like we're out of milk. And bread, too! And everything! There's nothin' to eat in here!"

"I guess your mother didn't get her Saturday shoppin' done. We'll have to go to the store ourselves."

"Well, I'm hungry right now! Let's go get ourselves a chili-cheese dog, whaddya say?"

"Sounds good to me!"

They headed out to the Tasty Burger with a new camaraderie—with the bond of war-buddies.

Later, as they ate their chili-dogs, Danny felt the tension ease away with every bite of the spicy, fatty food. He was relieved that Madge was getting some professional help. He had been worried about her for a long time and hadn't known what to do about it. Now it was out of his hands—and his dad's, too. He looked across the table at Harland. His dad was dabbing at his chin with his napkin, smiling and shaking his head at the mess they were making. Bits of melted cheese and greasy chili were dropping with satisfying plops with every bite they took. As Harland wiped his chin, Danny realized that he hadn't seen his dad wiping away the brown ooze of chewing tobacco from the corners of his mouth for a long time.

"Dad, what happened to that old Brown's Mule Plug tobacco you used to chew all the time? Have you stopped?"

"Yeah, I gave it up. It got to be more trouble than it was worth. Besides, the dentist told me I was gonna lose what teeth I've got left if I didn't stop. Madge never could stand it, anyway."

"Wow! That's great! Now you look more... well, uh, nicer... that is, you don't—"

"It's okay, Danny. I know you used to be ashamed of me, chewin' and spittin' and all. Now you don't have to..." Harland picked up the check and studied it for a minute. "C'mon, let's git outta here."

On the way home, Danny talked excitedly about his plans to enter South Georgia College. His grades had not been good enough to get into Georgia Tech, and at Miss W's suggestion, he had applied to the junior college to establish a better academic record, and eventually transfer to Tech. He would also be closer to home, which might be important now that Madge's illness had disrupted their normal family life.

*And closer to Christine...*

Harland shook his head in wonder. "You know, Danny, I've been amazed that Miss Worthington has gotten so friendly with you. I've always thought those Worthingtons were so rich and powerful and all, that they were kinda... well, stuck-up. And here she is, offerin' to send you to college. I can't understand it. How'd you get so friendly with her?"

"Oh, Dad! She's not stuck-up at all. She's a really sweet old lady. Smart and funny, too. I think she's kinda lonesome, all her family being dead and gone. She sort of thinks of me as her son. I think she's super!"

"Well, you're sure the lucky one. Me too, I reckon. I oughta get to know her, to thank her. I oughta do somethin' to thank her, I reckon."

"You know what, Dad? She really needs some help over there in that old house. It's kinda fallin' apart, it's so old. Some of the shutters are hangin' off. Maybe we could help her. The place needs painting, inside and out, and—"

"I thought you just painted the inside."

Danny looked down at the floor, shame-faced. "Oh, Dad! I… uh, well, I guess I lied to you about that. I was painting the upstairs apartment—the one where… where Christine lives. I'm sorry—"

Harland's face hardened, and he looked intently at the road ahead of them. "I reckon you've got a whole lot of lyin' to straighten out."

Danny's guilt beamed red off his face. He looked away. "Yeah, I guess so."

After an uncomfortable silence that seemed it would drag on forever, Harland took a deep breath and turned briefly to Danny. "You know what, Son? I'm not worried. You gonna get this all straightened out. I'm sure of it." He reached over and patted Danny on his knee.

Danny answered with conviction, "I will, Dad, don't worry."

But how could he straighten all this out? Why couldn't everybody just accept it that he loved Christine? *Really* loved her? That he was so happy when he was with her? That he couldn't live without her anymore? Maybe in time…

\*     \*     \*

Christine had called Bessie after Danny left, just as she had promised. And, of course, Bessie had been glad to come over and spend the night. Christine felt a little silly. Jack was in the hospital and certainly wasn't any threat to her now. But this gave them a chance to talk at length about Bessie's plans to leave Waycross. Christine began to share Bessie's excitement.

Bessie got a sly look on her face. "I don't want to beat a dead horse or nothing, but you really ought to think about coming with me. You could do real good up there."

"Hey, I'm not dismissing the idea altogether. I'm just not ready right now. I know you think I'm crazy, but I can't imagine being away from Danny. Besides, Stan still needs me. But Edda-Lou's learning fast. She'll finish her Cobol classes next spring, and maybe then..."

"Well, just don't forget. You've got a standing invite to come stay with me if you want to get going in the big city."

Next morning, Christine made breakfast and chuckled to herself as Bessie wolfed it down. She really loved Bessie, and she hated the thought that she would be leaving in just a few days. How lucky she was to have such a devoted friend! Being in Atlanta with her could be great fun, she had to admit.

*But Danny!*

Just the brief thought of leaving him made the sinking nausea of terror grip her stomach. How could she even think of being separated from him? She shook the treacherous thought out of her mind, put on some lipstick and went to the office.

Waycross was where she belonged.

*   *   *

Everything had changed for Danny. Strange, unwanted companions had moved into his carefree life; followed him everywhere, weighed him down. One was nagging, sniping, nasty—guilt. The other was reasonable, undeniable, gently insistent—responsibility. As hard as he tried, he couldn't shake them off.

His mind struggled with them all the time, and now, as he headed for the tree-house, the thoughts took on the erratic rhythm of the sputtering Honda 350. He saw Christine now in stolen, brief moments. His need for her was even more encompassing, her touch more precious, her comfort more essential than ever. When he remembered her suggestion that they might have to stop seeing each other, he had flashes of panic. His natural optimism and resiliency had always kicked in for him in the past, when he faced any kind of trouble. This was different. He found himself trapped between two conflicting but absolute necessities. The conflict was eating him alive.

He worried too, about taking his dad to meet Miss W. What if there was a confrontation between Christine and his dad? It wouldn't be natural to just go to see Miss W and not even go up to say "Hello" to Christine. Maybe he could find a time when he knew Christine wouldn't be there. But she was usually there in the evenings and on the weekends, when his dad would be off work and able to go over there. He'd have to talk to Christine about it. The sad thing was that he knew his dad would really like Christine a lot, if it weren't for *their* relationship. He wished he could show her off to his dad. Well, to everybody, for that matter.

How had he gotten into this mess? He hadn't meant to get in this deep. She was just so beautiful—so sexy! It wasn't just *him*. All his friends had thought the same thing. They had all wanted her. It wasn't his fault. He just hadn't been able to stay away, with her right there next door and all. If only he had just...

No way! He was glad it had all happened! He wouldn't trade one minute of being in love with Christine for all the happy times he had ever had—all put together. It would work out someway. It had to.

He pulled up under the big old magnolias, cut the engine and ran up the stairs.

\*     \*     \*

Christine had to laugh at herself. The mundane little putt-putt of the Honda had become the most beautiful music in the world for her! She ran out onto the porch as she heard it approach. She loved to see him stopping in the little cloud of dust, swinging his long, muscular leg back over the seat and pulling off his helmet. She knew he would look up at the porch for her, and she knew how her heart would leap at the beauty and joy of his smile when he saw her.

"Hello, Good-looking," she purred in response to the smile.

But the smile was short-lived. It was replaced with a look of worry; or was it yearning? And as soon as he had her in his arms, he whispered, "Oh, Christine, I don't know what to do. Everything's such a mess!"

"Oh, I know, I know," she said as she patted him gently on the back. "Come on in. I'll fix you a glass of iced tea. We'll work it all out."

She led him into the kitchen and pulled a chair out at the table for him. He slumped into it and stared at the floor. When she set the tea in front of him, he slipped his hands automatically around her lush little bottom and pulled her to him. She straddled his legs, sat in his lap and pulled him close to her. He pressed his face between her breasts and began to cry softly. They sat there for a while, as she absent-mindedly ran her fingers through his hair and cooed, "There, there, now. It'll be all right." As she rocked gently against him, she felt him swelling between her legs, and he began to work his lips down her neck in little kisses toward her breasts. She unfastened her blouse. She was not wearing a bra, and his mouth moved easily, naturally to an erect, pink nipple. He pulled her even closer and the soft sound of his crying changed to a faint moaning. He stood up, holding her against him and carried her into the bedroom.

Later, as they sat in the big rocker on the back porch listening to the woods music, the dark mantle of gloom began to settle around them again.

"I just don't know what to do," he whispered into the sweet-smelling warmth of her neck. "I wish we could just go away somewhere—where nobody knows us."

"Honey, that wouldn't really help. We'd never find a place where people would accept us as a couple, and—"

"—and I can't leave Daddy right now, what with Mama being so bad off. He's all upset about it. I've never seen him so, so—"

"—and you have your whole life ahead of you. You need to be in school, building a career. You need a girlfriend your own age..." She began to cry softly. The idea of his arms around some other girl tore her apart. She nuzzled against him even tighter, whispering, "Oh, Danny, Danny, Danny..."

"Listen, they're sending Mama up to Milledgeville in a day or two. In a week or so, Daddy's gonna move up there for a while, to be near her. How about I stay with *you* while he's gone. How's that sound?"

"Wonderful, wonderful!" She breathed in his scent, snuggling closer, relaxing against him. "Wonderful." She pushed the problems out of her mind.

They saw each other for the next two weeks in intense, hurried moments. Danny stopped by on his way home from work or they met for lunch at Josie's. She did her grocery shopping at Piggly Wiggly, where he had been promoted from bag-boy to cashier. She always got into his line so their fingers could touch as she pushed her groceries toward him. Keeping his face blank, he would murmur small intimacies to her, like "Hey, pretty lady, wanna fuck?" which would set off bursts of laughter from her, which he would counter with a puzzled look. She couldn't wait for the nights he would soon be spending with her.

\*   \*   \*

Harland counted the days before he could go to Milledgeville and see Madge. He worked extra hard at the shop, making sure everything was ready to turn over to his temporary replacement. He got Danny to introduce him to the elusive Miss Worthington, and offered to repair her broken shutters and refinish the big Brumby rockers on her porch. Miss W was so gracious and accepted his offer with such charm and gratitude, that he felt elevated into a higher society.

Of course, as much as he dreaded it, it was inevitable that he should see Christine Radford. He was up on the ladder, re-attaching a sagging shutter when their first encounter occurred. She had driven up in her rattley little VW and started to unload groceries. Harland tried not to look at her, but she called up to him in her lilting voice with its slight Northern accent, "Hello, Mr. Wilkins. This is such a nice thing you're doing. You just don't know how happy you're making Miss W."

He had to look down at her. "Oh, it ain't no big deal." He felt dizzy. She was standing below him, her arms loaded with groceries, looking up at him with her startling, clear green eyes. She seemed shy, hesitant. Was this really the woman his son, his *boy* was in love with? And she with him? It was impossible! He held tighter to the ladder and turned back to the shutter. "I'm glad to help out, seein' she's doin' so much for Danny, and all." He wished he hadn't mentioned Danny's name.

He concentrated on the shutter as she said, "Well, listen, if you need anything, I'll be glad to get it for you. I'll be glad to help. I'll be upstairs if ..." Her voice trailed away.

He didn't look at her as he said, "Thanks, but I don't need nothin'." Was that his voice, sounding so gruff?

As soon as he felt sure that she was upstairs and safely out of his sight, he came down from the ladder carefully, got into his car and drove to the nearest Seven-Eleven. He had to have a Coke.

If only he could turn the clock back a year or two! Maybe he could have seen all this coming: Danny's infatuation with his beautiful next-door-neighbor, Madge's slow descent into madness. Maybe he could have done something. If only ...

## Chapter 48

The Friday that Harland was to leave for Milledgeville, Christine had a terrible time concentrating on her work. Her mind was racing, and the clock was dragging forward with maddening sluggishness. She had already made one of Danny's favorite dinners: barbecued chicken, potato salad, green beans and apple pie. It was all waiting for them in her refrigerator. She only had to heat things up and make the biscuits. She was in a high state of sexual excitement as well; imagining his strong, sun-tanned hands on her body and his sweet-tasting mouth on hers.

At 4:30 she couldn't wait any longer and she dashed out, jumped into the VW and raced home, singing:

"I can bring home the bacon, fry it up in the pan,

And I'll never, never, never let you forget that you're a man.

'Cause I'm a woman ... a W-O-M-A-N (I'll say it again.)

Yes, I'm a woman ... a W-O-M-A-N!"

The biscuits were in the oven and she was setting the table on the back porch when she heard the Honda. She rushed into the bathroom and ran a comb through her hair and hurriedly brushed her teeth. The screen door slammed shut as she finished.

"Honey, I'm home!" he called. Her heart soared. He was so funny! And he felt just like she did. They were playing house.

She ran to meet him in the living room, jumped into his arms and wrapped her legs around him. He dropped the Piggly Wiggly bag he was carrying and whirled around with her until she was dizzy. She was squealing with laughter as they fell onto the sofa.

He growled seductively into her ear, "What's for supper, lady? Something sure smells good in here."

In her best Mae West imitation, she drawled, "Gimme a kiss, Big Boy, and I'll show you." After a prolonged kiss, she rolled her eyes. "Mmmm... Is that a flashlight in your pocket, or are you just glad to see me?"

"You'll find out soon enough."

"Oooo, I can't wait. But tell me, what's that in the sack? Somethin' for me?"

"Oh, yeah! I've got somethin' for you, all right."

She led him into the kitchen and opened the oven, to release a medley of intoxicating aromas from the chicken, pie and biscuits inside.

"Mmmm, wonderful!" he said. "Do you know how long it's been since I've had a home-cooked meal?" He handed her the Piggly Wiggly sack "Here, you'd better do something with this."

He had brought vanilla ice-cream and flowers. The flowers had not fared well during the motorcycle ride. She put the ice-cream into the freezer and put the beat-up flowers into a vase. They both laughed at the results.

After dinner, they made long, slow, exploratory love and followed it with a candlelight bath together. She rubbed her soapy breasts against his broad-shouldered back and she felt beautiful, supple, weightless. They rinsed and dried each other with sensuous languor, made love again and fell asleep in each others' arms.

That night there were times during his sleep when she could sense a ripple of awareness pass through his body; awareness that he was with her, and he would snuggle up to her, nuzzle his face deeper into her neck and breathe in her scent, pull her closer into his arms and sigh a little grunt of satisfaction like a contented, sleeping puppy.

Next day, when he got home from work, they took a picnic down Alligator Creek and returned at sunset, to the sleepy sounds of swamp life settling into night, and the magical pink glow of the parting sun reflecting up from the smooth, silent water.

Christine had never experienced such contentment and joy as she now did when she was with Danny. In stark contrast, when she was away from him, the doubts and the guilt crept back in. She couldn't get Harland's face out of her mind; the stricken look he gave her when he looked down from the ladder. She couldn't forget the tragic Madge, captured by madness, prisoner in the dreaded Milledgeville asylum. She couldn't dismiss the thoughts of Danny's fight with Mark, and his estrangement from his other friends.

Her break with her mother now seemed to be complete. She had gotten a jumbled, angry letter from her. Jack had told her mother and the Rev awful things about her, she was sure. She didn't care. Her mother had never really *known* her anyway, never supported her, never taken pride in her. She pushed it out of her mind.

Her world was now centered on Danny, and that was enough for her.

Bessie called her with progress reports every few days. In no time, she was installed in the job she had wanted and had applied for admission to Georgia State. Bessie begged Christine to come up for a visit, the sooner the better. Her excitement was contagious, and she got Christine's promise to come up for a two-day vacation. Christine planned the visit for the week-end that Harland was expected to be back from Milledgeville. Best to have some distraction scheduled for when her idyll with Danny would be interrupted.

\* \* \*

Danny found an excuse to stay in Waycross each time Harland asked him to come up to see his mother: he had to fill in for a friend at the Piggly Wiggly, Miss W was working with him on his application for Georgia Southern, he had a summer cold and just didn't feel like it. Each refusal gave him another two or three nights of bliss in Christine's arms, and added an equal measure of guilt to his already heavy load. In spite of the growing guilt, he still couldn't spare a single treasured day of what he felt was a dwindling measure of time in the tree-house. Although they didn't discuss it, Christine and Danny both knew that their days in paradise were limited—an awareness that lent intensity to each moment they shared.

Miss W was helping him in every way possible to secure his admission to Georgia Southern. Her complete faith in him, that he belonged in college and that he would be successful in school, made any reluctance on his part seem frivolous and unacceptable. They filled out his application forms together, and she guided him through the dark maze of writing his entrance essay. With new-found pride, he dropped the completed admissions packet into the mailbox.

He wished he could talk to Mark and Jimmy about his college plans, but he hadn't heard from them since the disastrous birthday party fight. He knew they would be curious about what had happened to his mother, but he didn't know how he would explain it without admitting to an onerous responsibility on his own part, so he didn't call them. It felt so strange and lonely not to have them by his side—on his side. It added an element of desperation to his growing dependence on Christine.

And so they held a sea of reality at bay in the comfort and shaky security of each other's arms.

\* \* \*

Christine packed an overnight bag and left for Atlanta on the Sunday that Harland came home from Milledgeville. On the drive to Atlanta, her head was filled with the minutiae of Danny's time with her: the simple little domestic things they did together, the way his jaw moved when he ate, the sound of his singing in the shower, the muscles in his back when he first got out of bed and stretched, the careful way he dried the dishes and put them away.

She arrived in Atlanta Sunday evening, and drove to the Darlington Apartments. Bessie was overflowing with good news and pleasure at Christine's visit. Bessie had opened and made up the hide-a-bed, cleared a shelf in the medicine cabinet, and made space in the closet for Christine's things.

They walked right up Peachtree for dinner—to an exotic Polynesian restaurant with Tiki torches, indoor ponds and fountains, and lush cuisine, most of which seemed to contain pineapple—fresh pineapple. Christine was enchanted.

"Ain't this something?" Bessie rolled her eyes with pride. "And you know what? They got a restaurant downtown where you sit on the floor and eat with your hands!"

"Sounds really elegant."

"Naw, I'm not kidding. It's Moroccan or something. I may not ever eat another chili cheese steak sandwich again!"

Christine reached across the table and took her friend's hands in hers. "Oh, Bessie! You're really happy, aren't you? I'm so glad for you."

"Yeah, I reckon I've finally found where I belong."

As Bessie described her job, her new friends, the variety of courses she wanted to take at Georgia State and her new life-style, her enthusiasm grew. "I walk around Five Points at lunch every day—the heart of the South! I'll swear, I can feel it beating!"

When they got back to Bessie's apartment, Christine fell exhausted onto the sofa bed, and slept like a baby All night, she dreamed success-dreams, where she was getting things accomplished and people were admiring her. She woke up invigorated, to the smell of coffee and frying bacon. Bessie made her promise to call Tim that morning, and when she did, she was surprised to realize how excited she felt talking to him again.

*This is not at all bad!*

Tim was delighted to hear from her, and he repeated his job offer. "We're growing like crazy here, and we're going to a wide-area network to connect all our branch offices. You'd love it, Christine! Learning something new every day."

"You know what, Tim? It really sounds good. Let me think about it a few weeks, okay? I'd have to make sure my assistant can take over for me. Stan's been so good to me—really saved my life. I couldn't—"

"Look, I know you could handle the job, and you'd fit right in. Trouble is, I've got to fill two positions right away—like *yesterday*. Can you get back to me in a week?"

"Sure, I can do that. I really do appreciate your confidence in me, and—".

"Wanna have lunch today?"

"Oh gosh, I can't. I'm meeting Bessie and—".

"How about dinner?"

"Sorry, Tim. It sounds great, but I really… I promise I'll call you by the end of the week, okay? And thanks. I mean it!"

Tuesday morning she left Bessie's, feeling strangely that she was leaving *home*. As much as she was looking forward to seeing Danny, her mind kept weighing the possibilities that seemed to be waiting for her in Atlanta. Maybe she was ready for a change—a step up. It wouldn't be like she didn't know anybody there, like it had been when she moved to Waycross.

And now, her situation in Waycross left her tired: frayed, worn out from all the guilt of her relationship with Danny. But God bless him! She did love him so much, but now she had to accept the heartbreaking truth that if she *really* loved him; if it was *love* she felt and not just *lust*; if she really wanted him to have a good future and a happy life, then she *had to give him up*. Tears filled her eyes. What a bitter pill to have to swallow! How unfair it was! She began to sob and had to pull off the road. There it was! The truth that had been gnawing at her just outside her consciousness. She couldn't deny it. God help her, she couldn't deny it!

*The test of my love is to relinquish it!*

She felt a chasm open before her—a chasm of distance and time. He would be in a new place, separated from her; in a new life, making new friends. Time would widen the chasm and the burning passion they shared would slowly cool.

Oh, Danny, Danny! How can I let go? How can I make it without you?

*It's just not fair! It's just not fair!*

## Chapter 49

Tuesday night Christine waited for Danny on the front porch. It was drizzling rain. The big old oaks were dripping, their festoons of moss hanging despondently. The magnolia leaves, shiny from the rainwater, reflected a pale, gray sky. Reflected her mood.

She was listening for the approach of the Honda without being conscious of it. Danny was such a integral part of her now that her body moved to his rhythms, her senses throbbed to his aura, even though her mind was somewhere else. He was like breathing to her—she didn't think about it, but she would die without it. Right now, she was thinking of all the reasons she should move to Atlanta. It would be the best thing for everyone: for her, for Danny, for Harland, for Madge, and even for Edda-Lou.

When he got there and took her in his arms, it was with a subdued affection, lacking in his usual exuberance.

"I missed you so much," he said, with a little catch of breath.

"I missed you, too—even though it was only two days."

"It was the two nights I missed so much," he sighed, "and I can't stay tonight. Daddy needs me at home. I guess the place was in a big mess when he got back, and he needs—"

"Honey, it's okay. I know you can't stay over—not the way things are right now." She looked away. "Danny, sweetheart, I … I'm thinking about … How's your mother?"

"She's a little better, Dad says." He turned and leaned on the porch railing, looking out into the sodden trees. "She still acts like she doesn't know him, but she's not so wild, so agitated. All the drugs they're giving her are helping, I guess." He turned to face her. "But that's not what you were thinkin' about, was it?"

"No, it's that I'm … I'm thinking about moving up to Atlanta."

"I knew it, I knew it." He took her shoulders and peered earnestly into her face. "But Christine! What are you saying? You can't! You can't do that! What are you trying to do? You can't leave me! Don't you … Has something happened?"

"Danny, you know I love you. I always will. You can count on that—always. *Always.* But it just seems like… It seems like our relationship, good as it is … *beautiful* as it is for us, is causing too many people to be unhappy."

"That's their problem, not ours."

"No, it's ours. We're the only ones who can do anything about it."

"Are you telling me it's over? You can't be! It can't be over!"

"We've always known this couldn't go on forever."

"No, no, no! *You've* said it couldn't last! *I've* always thought it could. I know it could. It can! I'll follow you wherever you go, Christine. I want to live with you. I want to *marry* you, for God's sake!"

She pulled him close and began to stroke his hair. "Danny, honey, be reasonable. You've got your whole life ahead of you. You need to be with girls your own age—with your friends. Look what's happened there already—the fight you had with Mark. You need to get a good education. You have a wonderful opportunity now with Miss W. on your side. If you go to college, you'll want to party with your buddies there. You can't drag around an older woman to your fraternity parties—".

"What are you talking about? I don't want to go to *fraternity parties*. Gimme a break! That's not my bag. I want to be with *you*. Anyway, you could go with me if—"

"I couldn't stand being around a bunch of college students. Danny, I'm too old for that! I'm too old to relate to any of your normal things. You've given up a lot of your life to be with me." She began to cry. "I can't bear to think that I've—"

"You haven't done anything except to make me the happiest man in the world. Hush now." He kissed her eyelids, picked her up and carried her to the bed. "Hush, baby. I don't want to talk about this now. I've got to leave in a few minutes. Let's make the most of them."

"Oh, I love you so much." She took his hands in hers and kissed each palm, then the little dip in the center of his throat, then his mouth. "I really do love you. That's why I can't—"

He covered her mouth with his mouth, and her objections with his desire. They made love tenderly, with a searing appreciation of the magnitude and the transience of this gift they had been granted. This gift that was costing so much to so many.

When he cranked up the Honda and waved goodbye, she called out to him, "But I'm moving to Atlanta, anyway."

He looked up at her. "What? I can't hear you."

"I'm leaving. I'm moving to Atlanta."

He waved goodbye. "Can't hear you. Bye-bye. See you tomorrow."

*Yes, tomorrow. We'll talk about it tomorrow.*

\* \* \*

Next day, in her office, Christine stared at the phone. She had Tim's card on her desk, and she picked up the phone several times and started to key in his number. Each time she tried, her hand would start shaking and tears would well up in her eyes. Each time, she hung up before completing the call. Finally, during lunch, she made the call, hoping he would not be at his desk. He was, though. She told him she would take the job.

"Thank goodness!" he said. "I thought you were never going to come to your senses. When can you start?"

"When do you want me?"

"How about tomorrow?"

She forced a laughed and told him she had a few things to take care of first, and of course she needed to give Stan notice that she was leaving, so it would probably be two or three weeks.

"Well, as soon as you can. But, Christine, you don't sound too happy about this. Is this what you want to do? You'll be working long, hard hours."

"Oh, Tim, I never have minded working hard. In fact it'll be good for me. I'll stay with a friend when I first get there, and I'll give you a call as soon as I arrive—let's say two weeks from next Monday, okay?"

"Perfect! And Christine, I'm really looking forward to working with you. You've got a great future in Atlanta, believe me."

After she hung up the phone, she ran to the bathroom and shut herself in a booth. She braced herself by pressing her hands on each side of the booth and leaned over the toilet bowl, fighting the nausea that almost overwhelmed her. After a few deep breaths, she overcame the dizziness and nausea, walked carefully back to her desk and tried to think positively about what she was doing. Okay. It was the *right* thing to do. No doubt about it. She should feel good about making such a difficult decision. She gave herself a mental pat on the back.

*Good Girl!*

She waited for some small measure of pride or sense of accomplishment to ease her pain. It didn't come. Instead, another wave of dizziness and nausea washed over her. She leaned over and pressed her head on her desk.

She felt a gentle pat on her shoulder.

"Christine? Are you all right?"

It was Stan. She looked up at him, and to her chagrin, her eyes filled with tears. She shook her head and forced a smile. "Yes, I'm... I'm okay. I just..."

"Look. I'm on my way to lunch. Why don't you come along and tell me what's the matter?"

"Thanks, but I've got to—"

"Come on. I won't take 'no' for an answer."

She felt herself on the edge of an embarrassing, hysterical outburst of tears. "Okay, I ..." She fumbled in her purse for a tissue, pulled one out and blew her nose. "I must be coming down with a cold."

"Well, come on, then. I know just the thing for that."

Christine got control of herself and followed Stan out to his car. On the way to the restaurant she talked about how well Edda-Lou was working out. But when Stan drove into the parking lot of Josie's Kitchen, she gave way to the flood of tears she had been holding back so valiantly.

Stan was at a complete loss. "Christine, what in the world's the matter? Are you sick or something? Is this about the divorce? Please, what's the matter?" He patted her back with a hesitant hand.

"Stan, I've ... I've got to resign. I hate to..."

"There, there. What ever made you think you have to do that? Do you need more money? I could—"

"No, it's not the money. It's ... It's personal." She took a deep breath. "I'm moving to Atlanta. I've already taken a job there."

"Whoa! Slow down here. Why are you doing that if it makes you feel like this?"

"I can't really talk about it. I—"

"Is it about that ex-husband of yours? Is he threatening you or something?" Stan's face turned red and his jaw muscles tightened. "If it is, I—"

"No, no, Stan. Please. It's not that. I'm sorry I broke down like this. It's so embarrassing. I'm really all right. You've been so good to me, and I like my job and all. It's just that ..." She sobbed helplessly into her tissue. "I can't talk about it. I'm so sorry."

Stan recovered his composure. "Look, Christine. Whatever it is, it can't be *that* bad. Wipe off your face and let's go in and get us some of Josie's potato logs. They're good for anything that ails you. Whatever the problem is, I'm on your side, and I'll help you anyway I can. Come on, now. Let's see that smile!"

Christine took a deep breath and looked up at Stan's rough old face. His dismissal of her trauma was so well-intentioned and so devoid of understanding, she just had to laugh. "Okay, Stan. Let's go eat some of those legendary potato logs. Just what the psychiatrist ordered!"

Inside, she tidied up her tear-stained face in the ladies' room. Back at the table, they began to discuss turning over her responsibilities to Edda-Lou. Stan agreed that Edda-Lou could probably handle the job, if he couldn't talk Christine out of leaving. They agreed on two weeks notice, starting the next week. A feeling of numbness began to take over Christine's mind and body.

She left the office a little early that afternoon and dropped by to see Miss W. When she told her she was leaving, she was distressed to see tears in the tiny old warrior's eyes. As soon as she got into her apartment, she called Bessie with her decision and got an enthusiastic response, to say the least. Bessie asked her again to stay with her at the Darlington until she could find her own apartment.

Throughout the day, she had watched herself perform. She was in a bad dream: her limbs numb and heavy, her heart a cold lump in her chest, her ears clogged with a dull ringing. Now she steeled herself for the *really* hard part—the impossible part, as she waited on the porch for Danny.

He came up the drive slowly, cut the engine and stood looking up at her. He didn't wave at her as he usually did. His footsteps seemed heavy on the stairs, and he looked at the floor as he approached her.

"Honey, what is it? Is Madge worse?"

"I've been thinking all day about what you said last night—about moving away. I think it's a terrible idea. I'm not ... I don't think I'm ready ... I can't make it without you. I thought you felt the same way."

She held him close. "I do, I do, but there's just no way around it. We're creating more unhappiness than we can ... can justify. It's not good for you. I'm ... I'm interfering with your life. It's not normal. It's not healthy for you to be so involved with someone who can never be ... can never fit into your life. I'm doing this because ... Danny, it's because I love you so much."

"You want to get away from me!" Tears filled his eyes. "I never thought—"

"Danny, you know that's not true! You must know how hard this is for me. Listen, it's not goodbye forever! You can come to see me in Atlanta sometimes. You'll be going off to Georgia Southern soon, anyway. We've both got to get on track with our lives, you especially. Please don't make this any harder than it already is."

He was really crying now, as she led him gently inside. "When are you leaving?" he managed to whisper.

"I've already gotten a job. They want me there in two weeks, so I guess—"

"*Two weeks*? Christine, don't do this. Don't do this to me—to us!"

"I'm going. It's all arranged. It won't be so bad." Now she too was crying. "We'll always have the time we've spent together—the swamp, the way we feel about each other."

They cried it out together and made their plans. Danny would help her pack, and would come up to see her as soon as she got her own place. For the first time since they had made love, he left without taking her. She collapsed on the sofa; torn, incomplete.

*What am I doing? I can't do this. What am I going to do? God help me!*

\*   \*   \*

Danny rode home in a daze. She couldn't be doing this! Had she stopped loving him? No, it couldn't be that! He would make her stay. He would think of something. Maybe he hadn't been romantic enough. Women liked that stuff a lot. He'd take her some flowers. They'd go out into the swamp. She really loved Alligator Creek. He'd take her out there and hold her hostage until she changed her mind about this. He'd hold her ...

Damn her! How could she think of doing this to him? Especially now, with his mother so sick, and his dad having such a hard time. He hadn't wanted to fall in love with her in the first place. Now she had him where he couldn't live without her. He wouldn't let her abandon him like this. He'd think of something.

His tears blurred the road in front of him.

*Oh, Christine! You warm, sweet, sexy, beautiful thing! What am I going to do?*

\* \* \*

Christine functioned from within her waking nightmare for the next two weeks. Danny stopped by every night to help her pack. He brought her a dozen roses. They made love with an ever increasing tenderness. She felt each moment pass by with a desperate sense of loss, as if she should grab onto it, slow it down, hold on.

They made one last trip down Alligator Creek, where she told Olin and Harry goodbye, and hugged each of the children. She had bought little gifts for each of them to remember her by. They stayed later than they ever had, and lay in each others arms while the sky turned peach and lavender in the west, and a pregnant blood-red full moon rose luxuriant through the cypress trees in the east. The black water glowed with rich, living tones of pink, red, orange. When they moved, they could feel the earth tremble beneath them. They paddled back slowly to the easy rhythm of the evening swamp sounds.

As the days passed, too swiftly, she sank deeper into her pain. She could feel Danny beginning to accept their separation, and although this was what she wanted, it broke her heart.

Finally the day came. She had shipped her few possessions to an Atlanta storage rental facility, and loaded what she would need at Bessie's into the small trunk of the VW. As she drove for the last time down the beautiful, oak-canopied drive beneath the sad, gray Spanish moss, she looked into her rear-view mirror. There he stood by the little Honda, watching her, his shoulders drooping, a hollow look of disbelief on his face. Miss W. stood a few steps behind him, with tears streaming down her face. He waved his arm at her and took a few running steps down the drive toward her.

Dear God, she couldn't leave them like this! She slowed down. They needed her. No, she needed them. In her whole life she had never had this kind of warmth, comfort, safety. She forced her foot back down on the accelerator. And she was driving away from it, from their love and their strength. It took everything she had to keep going down that drive, but she did it.

From this day forward, this pain would forever be a part of each separation for her: each job resignation, each move from a comfortable residence, each airport good-bye, each death.

She clenched her jaw and headed north.

*If she really loved Danny, she could do it!*

                                    \*   \*   The End   \*   \*

## *About the Author*

June McNaughton has lived in Atlanta, Georgia for most of her life and has five children, eleven grandchildren, and two great grandchildren. She is a retired computer consultant and technical writer, a prize-winning poet, a freelance writer and is Vice Chairman and on the board of the Village Writers Group in Atlanta, where she leads their novel critique group. This is her first novel, though she is currently working on two more.

Printed in the United States
1024500001B/91-186